SF SCARB
Scarborough, Elizabeth Ann
Cleopatra 7.2 /
R0021052088

D0046747

APR - 2005

CLEOPATRA 7.2

Ace Books by Elizabeth Ann Scarborough

THE GODMOTHER
THE GODMOTHER'S WEB
CAROL FOR ANOTHER'S CHRISTMAS
THE GODMOTHER'S APPRENTICE
THE LADY IN THE LOCH
CHANNELING CLEOPATRA
CLEOPATRA 7.2

CLEOPATRA 7.2

ELIZABETH ANN SCARBOROUGH

ACE BOOKS, NEW YORK

THE BERKLEY PUBLISHING GROUP
Published by the Penguin Group
Penguin Group (USA) Inc.
375 Hudson Street, New York, New York 10014, USA
Penguin Group (Canada), 10 Alcorn Avenue, Toronto, Ontario M4V 3B2, Canada
(a division of Pearson Penguin Canada Inc.)
Penguin Books Ltd., 80 Strand, London WC2R 0RL, England
Penguin Group Ireland, 25 St. Stephen's Green, Dublin 2, Ireland (a division of Penguin Books Ltd.)
Penguin Group (Australia), 250 Camberwell Road, Camberwell, Victoria 3124, Australia
(a division of Pearson Australia Group Pty. Ltd.)
Penguin Books India Pvt. Ltd., 11 Community Centre, Panchsheel Park, New Delhi—110 017, India
Penguin Group (NZ), Cnr. Airborne and Rosedale Roads, Albany, Auckland 1310, New Zealand
(a division of Pearson New Zealand Ltd.)
Penguin Books (South Africa) (Pty.) Ltd., 24 Sturdee Avenue, Rosebank, Johannesburg 2196,
South Africa

Penguin Books Ltd., Registered Offices: 80 Strand, London WC2R 0RL, England

This book is an original publication of The Berkley Publishing Group.

This is a work of fiction. Names, characters, places, and incidents either are the product of the author's imagination or are used fictitiously, and any resemblance to actual persons, living or dead, business establishments, events, or locales is entirely coincidental.

CLEOPATRA 7.2

Copyright © 2004 by Elizabeth Ann Scarborough.
Text design by Kristin del Rosario.

All rights reserved.
No part of this book may be reproduced, scanned, or distributed in any printed or electronic form without permission. Please do not participate in or encourage electronic piracy of copyrighted materials in violation of the author's rights. Purchase only authorized editions.
ACE is an imprint of The Berkley Publishing Group.
ACE and the "A" design are trademarks belonging to Penguin Group (USA) Inc.

First edition: December 2004

ISBN: 0-441-01206-X

This title has been registered with the Library of Congress.

PRINTED IN THE UNITED STATES OF AMERICA

10 9 8 7 6 5 4 3 2 1

For my mother,
Betty Scarborough,
with love and thanks

R0021052088

ACKNOWLEDGMENTS

I would like to thank Lea Day for inspiration and the use of books from the huge Egyptian section of her personal library, as well as for scouring Powell's City of Books for me for specific references. I would also like to thank Dusti Day for excavating her guest room so that I had a place to stay when I visited Portland on research trips. To Rick Reaser and Andy Taylor, as usual, I owe many thanks for the food for thought and the food on their table and for suggestions and advice on the story. Robert and Sheryl Bronsink and Beverly Berggren have my undying gratitude for coming to my house one day when I had been stuck for a month or two and sitting in my living room and letting me read more than two hundred pages aloud to them with only pizza and pop to sustain us. Dr. Susan Wilson, as she was during the writing of *Channeling Cleopatra,* was tremendously helpful with practical details about Egypt and Egyptians. Eileen Claire was again generous with her personal recollections of Alexandria and her many photographs and maps. And I would very much like to thank my agent, Merrilee Heifetz, and my editor, Ginjer Buchanan, for their support. Most especially I would like to thank the copyeditors, Bob and Sara Schwager, for their considerable contribution to the process of making the manuscript into a book.

CLEOPATRA 7.2

PROLOGUE

⟨𓂀⟩

The Book of Cleopatra's Reawakening

Herein do I, Cleopatra Philopater, Queen of Upper and Lower Egypt, the seventh Cleopatra of the ruling house of Ptolemy, set down the circumstances pertaining to the discovery of my tomb. This I do at the behest of my soul's companion in this life, Leda Hubbard, who asks it so that a play may be made of it and the story told to all the world thereby. For this we are to be endowed with, if not a queen's ransom, at least the price of a modest palace.

To begin with, I was awakened from the dead.

This was done by means of a magic uncommonly known even in these years of miraculous happenings. Quite simply, a portion of my body still connected to my *ba,* or body spirit, was used to connect my *ba* to another body, that of Leda Hubbard, a woman of low birth but high intellect. This magic is called a blending. Leda and I first blended as we dreamed. I learned that she, like myself, grieved for her father and had suffered betrayal. I knew of her love of books and words, her search for knowledge. But I also knew, even as she slept, that we were in immediate mortal danger. We awakened to our peril aboard a ship owned by our enemy.

With the aid of Leda's allies and our combined strengths, we prevailed and vanquished our enemy.

When we were safely ashore in what had once been my beloved Alexandria, I began to understand that, although I once more breathed and tasted, saw and smelled, was able to touch and to feel touch, the life I had ended with the cobra would in no way continue. No longer would I be concerned with the fate of the Egypt I knew, for it was either gone or buried beneath many generations of sand and captivity.

Octavian, who continued his dominion of both my lands and his as Augustus Caesar, this viper who murdered Caesar's own son, my Caesarian, is dead. That Marc Antony is lost I knew before my own death. His son, my Alexander Helios, was murdered like his half brother by Octavian. My other children, Selene and Ptolemy Philadelphus, were banished from Egypt and died in foreign lands without the benefit of an Egyptian burial. Thus I had no hope that they might enter into this afterlife as I have with the aid of that odd little magician, Chimera.

Alas, Leda's body is not capable of childbearing so there will be no more children for me, even if there are in this new age men worthy of fathering them. All that I loved, all that I lived for, is gone. Thus is my life ended, and so it begins again, without husband or children, title or lands or wealth of any consequence, great beauty or great power.

Still, Leda's loyalties are as strong as my own, and I find some comfort that the people whose fates concern her do seem to be worthwhile.

However, she has not been a queen and was not reared believing she was born to greatness. Her goals are as modest as her means, and this I must change.

We made a beginning by changing history as Leda's contemporaries have known it. We had no tension within us at this time, for our thoughts and longings were in unison. Both of us wished to revisit my tomb and learn what remained.

I imagined I would be able to go straight to it. During my lifetime, I had visited it clandestinely for years, secreting the most precious of the scrolls I saved from the burning of the great library. Later, when Antony gifted me with scrolls looted from the library in Pergamum, I had them copied and personally deposited the originals in the vaults within my second tomb.

Why a *second* tomb? Leda asked. But she answered her own question almost immediately. Grave robbers, of course, were the first reason I chose to have a secret place of interment as well as my public mausoleum. Anyone who has strolled through the marketplace has beheld the property that was supposed to be taken into the afterlife with long-dead pharaohs and other people of substance. Their tombs were built more for grandeur than for security. Looters broke in and stole their funeral goods and dismembered the mummies so carefully and expensively laid to "eternal" rest. I value my privacy and my dignity far too much to allow that to happen to me.

So, though no one knew but myself and one old childhood friend who became my most trusted priest, there was concealed within my mausoleum an underground passageway.

I have now watched many films and read many books and articles that claim to be about my life. Some of them say that I am a traitorous and disloyal person. They base their evaluation on the evidence that I had my brothers and sisters killed, disregarding the fact that my beloved sibs would have done the same for me had I not, as Leda says, "beat them to it." The truth is that I have always been a very loyal person and a true friend to those who do not try to murder me or betray me.

And Anoubus was always, if unobtrusively, loyal to me. He understood my true nature. I wonder what became of him under Octavian?

Ah well. Anoubus and I discovered the passageway and

the tomb when we were children of perhaps eight and six years. It was within the palace quarter, naturally, or I would not have been allowed there. We found it while playing in a disused part of the harem. Father did not keep as many concubines and wives as his forebears, perhaps because he loved wine and song far better than he loved women, with the possible exception of me.

The passageway was exciting for us, a secret to be shared, but even more exciting was the tomb at the end of it. I knew in my heart it had been one of the early tombs of my own ancestor, Alexander. Of course, it was empty then, but by the light of our lamps the marble walls still gleamed, and the spaciousness of the rooms rivaled that of my father's own private chambers. We scuffed away the sand to reveal a fine mosaic on the floor, the colors of its tiles bright even by our flickering lights.

Throughout my childhood, I escaped there often from my older sister, who hated me because Father preferred me, and my brothers. When I thought of it, I held my breath, fearing that some new building project would clear the entrance to my private haven, but this did not happen. When I assumed the throne, I myself cleared the area and had my mausoleum built over it, under the supervision of my friend.

As intimately as I had known it, when Leda and I tried to find it again, I doubted we ever would. My beautiful white-columned city, with its wide streets and its great monuments, might never have been. Now it lies buried beneath tall and ugly buildings, short and ugly buildings, and the streets are filled with noisy machinery, tearing along at speed far greater than that of any chariot or natural animal I have ever seen in all the life I knew before I awakened with Leda.

I knew approximately where the palace quarter had been only from the shoreline of the Eastern Harbor, and even this was much altered. Leda and I pored over maps from many time periods. None was more than someone's guess at the layout of the city of my birth, my youth, my reign, the city I gave to Caesar and to Antony, the city whose people, treasures, institutions, customs, and monuments I protected with every skill and wit I possess.

Leda showed me the artifacts retrieved from the harbor when it had been drained for excavation. Soon the sponsors of this excavation and the current government will attempt to reconstruct the shoreline as I knew it, to rebuild some semblance of my palace and the monuments of the time. This will be done not to house a new pharaoh or even a president, but for foreign visitors called tourists. It is a worthy project and I approve of it and mean to have Leda and myself consulting so that we may instruct the builders on the correct installation of each feature and structure.

But I digress. We examined these artifacts, most of which were large chunks of stone that were mere suggestions of the intricately carved and colored statuary and columns, building blocks and fountains that had once adorned my home. These items, more than any other thing, including the monstrous modern city, made clear to me how much time has passed since last I walked these streets. Not that I can walk them now without risk of being crushed by one of the speeding conveyances.

I saw a blunted and waterworn statue of myself I had commissioned as a gift for what we hoped would be Caesar's coronation. The cheeks were pitted, the tip of the nose and part of the chin chipped off. The details of hair and crown, clothing and jewels were mostly lost, however. It looked, it was, thousands of years old. Many pieces of the colossal statues of my Ptolemy ancestors whose images had lined the harbor and stood sentinel beside the great Pharos Lighthouse hulked among the cases and explanatory plaques. The bones of my past.

They saddened me, caused me to shudder. Though I had coolly faced the enemies who were my kin and the enemy who was the death of my family, as well as the cobra who was my ultimate deliverer, I was shaken with disorientation, with vertigo. How strange it was to be there viewing the scene of my former life as if from the wrong end of a telescope that saw through the distance of time rather than space.

Even so, another part of me, the part my father had trained in the ways of all of the pharaohs and satraps before us, was reading the plaques. I mentally restored and replaced the objects to their original installations. Seeing where they had been found from the maps and plaques, I calculated how far they might have tumbled during the mighty earthquakes that were my city's ultimate conquerors.

Leda showed me where she found one of my canopic jars. It had arisen from the seabed like Aphrodite from the sea following an earthquake. The simile is not inapt, as the discovery of this jar was responsible for my rebirth.

We spent many days and nights, accompanied by Gabriella, Dr. Gabriella Faruk, a close friend of Leda's and the director of Antiquities for the Biblioteca Alexandrina, poring over old books and records stored in the new library. At last I identified the area where I had once lived and approximated the place where I caused my mausoleum to be built. Using miraculous tools available to us through Leda's employers at Nucor, we located the site on a block of land containing a European-style hotel. Wolfe, who is to Nucor what we would have called a king, quietly purchased the building. We did not tear it down, but excavated the basement from within its walls.

Although Nucor (now calling themselves Helix) brought in their own teams to dig under our direction with the borrowed authority of Gabriella's position, it took every ounce of royal command I could pour through Leda to make those people disregard possible damage to the extant walls and floor of my mausoleum. I insisted they use whatever was necessary to remove the floor of the basement. "Jackhammers," Leda said. "Use jackhammers."

By the artificial floodlights and the muted roar of the generator, I goaded these on with a promise of the real treasures beyond. It went against all of their training, this I knew from Leda's inner wincing, but I was as relentless in this as I once had been in gaining Caesar's attention and regaining my throne. The building's walls in this section retained the heat, and it was close, the air stagnant and still.

Perspiration poured from us all. Leda's heavy hair was soaked through, and salty sweat poured into her eyes and dripped from her chin. Everyone stank like rutting goats. I thought of bringing incense to the site, but Leda tells me we are allergic to perfume.

When the jackhammers started, we were all forced to wear masks or choke on the dust.

All the time we worked, I feared we would never find it, that the passageway might have totally collapsed, the entrance lost for all time. I feared that all of my treasures, despite the careful preparations surrounding their storage, had been damaged by earthquake or water.

I prowled the mosaic floor of my death house like a caged leopard, although we were tortured by the pain in Leda's arthritic knees and back. Truth be told, Leda was not always there in spirit. Other bodily ailments also infringed upon her *ba*, and it had to absent itself for periods of rest before forced by the intensity of her curiosity to return. That was when I first realized that at times I might be alone in the body and in sole charge thereof.

Some of the excavators feared me, thought me mad. But I will tell you, of the ones who heard the rumors that it was Cleopatra Philopater's spirit seeking her last resting place, none who saw or heard me then doubted it. And at last, because it was there, where it had always been, once a broken column or two had been removed, I found it. The section of floor counterweighted to slide down into the passage when a certain sequence of tiles was pressed had not moved of its own accord.

Leda's *ba* was back within us when I touched the first of the tiles. Our finger could not seem to hold true to its target, so hard were we trembling with anticipation. "Let's get a grip here," Leda said. "This may not even work after all these centuries. There will probably be a lot more digging to do, because the passage is bound to be blocked, right?"

At first I feared that was the case, for though I pushed the correct sequence, I am sure, for I could never forget it, at first the floor lay static and motionless as it had since my burial. Twice more I pressed it, feeling the restlessness of the workers behind me. I felt like cursing them all for witnessing my helplessness.

"Sorry," Leda told me. *"But no, we cannot have their tongues and hands cut off. They are all under nondisclosure contracts, however, on penalty of forfeiture of vast sums of cash, and Wolfie . . ."*

"There!" I said, feeling the merest hint of a drop beneath my finger as I punched the last tile. "There."

"I think we may just need some WD-40," Leda said, and, turning to the nearest gawking digger, requested that some of the aforementioned, which seemed to be a magical potion, be obtained and brought to us. It was nothing but common oil. Olive oil would have worked as well. We squirted it from a metal can into the spaces around the tiles concerned. They drank it into them. I pressed the sequence again and nearly fell into the hole that gaped below my outstretched torso where a moment before the tiles had been.

"No actual cave-in," Leda said, after we examined the hole with an ingenious cold torch called a flashlight. Like many modern things, it is dependent upon captive lightning for its function. "At least not here."

The descent was not as gradual as it had been the last time I was aware of entering the passage. The earthquakes, no doubt, had shifted the passageway from the entrance so that we had to drop down into the earthen gap before we entered the part I remembered. It was a tunnel carved from the living stone of the earth. Many times we had to stop to dig away sand and earth to make room for us to continue. It took us two nights to clear the passage, though I had been able to traverse the passage in minutes and seek the solace of the deserted tomb, before I became its occupant.

At last we set foot on the first stair down into the antechamber. It was made of slabs of alabaster from Upper Egypt, stone much employed in my palace. Having been made for my illustrious ancestor, this portion of the tomb was Grecian in nature. As we entered the inner chambers, the flashlights illuminated the wall paintings illustrating my accomplishments and interests, my cartouche, my marriages, my children. We had to break into the next chamber, for it was sealed to protect its contents. Now two sets of two lights, each seeming brighter than Ra himself, were brought forth from above.

"No evidence of grave robbers, at least," Leda noted as we examined the seal.

I felt satisfied. My friend had chosen his confidants carefully, and apparently none had betrayed me.

The rest of the team was horrified that we would use pickaxes to break the wall, but I was not afraid of losing valuable evidence. I knew what lay beyond that wall and what was of value there.

As we finished widening the hole enough to permit us to insert a flashlight to see the interior, I gasped with dismay. The light reflected against the gleam of water on the floor. The sarcophagus appeared unaffected, but amphorae and caskets had been swept from their intended positions and settled into the shallow water covering the floor. Casting the beam so that it lit each section of the tomb, we saw that the wall paintings had been much damaged, and the ceiling bore a long, jagged gap that narrowed at the top. My canopic jars had been stored, at my direction, upon a shelf close to the ceiling. None now remained.

"The earthquakes," Leda said. "The pressure must have extruded the jar I found through all of the layers of earth. The water would have come from when the dam broke. But it looks as if the chamber resealed itself enough that the water that did get through seeped away."

"Yes, yes," I said. "But we must break into the adjoining chambers and see what damage is done there."

"Why?" Gabriella asked. "Your sarcophagus is here. Surely the mummy of Cleopatra is the most momentous item in her tomb."

"No," I told her. "There is the treasure."

"But your jewels were taken by Octavian before your death, according to historians," Gabriella said.

"Yes, that is quite true. The greedy pig would have left me naked had he not realized it would cause him more problems. The Romans did not love me, but my own people benefited by my rule. Octavian would have had difficulty controlling them had he publicly humiliated me in Egypt as he planned to do in Rome." Since I am part of a more literal "we" within the same body, I seldom use the royal "we" when speaking of myself in this incarnation. "However, jewelry was never my most valuable treasure."

Leda knew, of course. She was as excited as I was and as alarmed to see the water in my tomb. We struck the first blow to the sealed door between my body and the treasure I had caused to be collected and interred with it.

I believe some members of the archaeological team actually wept, though I could not distinguish tears from the sweat that covered us all as we broke into the chamber. To our great relief, the room did not appear to be touched by water. The vaults lining the walls were dry, and their contents appeared to be intact.

"Jars?" Pete, Leda's former lover, who was the engineer for our project, asked. "Your treasure is vaults and vaults full of jars?"

"They're really big jars," Leda said, teasing, as is her custom. "And jars hold stuff."

Pete continued to look puzzled until I reached into one of the vaults and with some effort, since the urn I chose had settled well and truly into the soft stone floor of the vault, removed it.

"*Please* don't break it open here," Gabriella moaned. "We have really done so much damage already."

"I just want to make sure the documents survived," I told her.

"*She's right,*" Leda said to me privately. "*With all due respect, Cleo, being as how this is your property and everything, since your death we've learned a few things about caring for these ancient things and preserving them. Wait until we can get them into a temperature-and-humidity-controlled room, and the scrolls will have a much better chance of being removed intact.*"

This vexed me, but since I could see that the urns remained sealed against the elements and that they appeared to be unbroken, I conceded.

Instead, I returned to the main room to inspect my sarcophagus. There, too, the seals appeared unbroken. "*I suppose you'll insist that I refrain from opening my own coffin as well?*" I asked Leda.

"*Absolutely,*" she said. "*Besides, I'm not sure you're going to want to see yourself in this state anyway. You won't be looking your best, you know.*"

I decided her argument had merit. If beholding the ruins of statues I had known in their full glory upset me, how much more would viewing the ruins of the face I had last seen in my own mirror? I was fifteen years younger than Leda when I died, and though grief and anxiety had taken its toll, I was still an attractive woman. Then. No, Leda was correct. I did not especially wish to see my mummy. At least, not yet.

So it came to pass that my unopened sarcophagus was removed to the Museon, along with the scrolls, my great treasure, preserved from the Alexandria Library and including the originals of the most important works from the library of Babylon, a gift from Antony.

All that I speak of did not occur in one night only, but events did unfold much more quickly than would have been the case had I permitted the team to dawdle and exercise the "proper fieldwork technique," they continually mourned.

Really, you would have thought it was their profession that lay dead in my tomb instead of me!

I did supervise the removal of my scrolls and the few other treasures I possessed, including my mortal shell. Working with Gabriella Faruk, I learned that it was she who had intended to house my *ba* before Leda took it into herself. Although Leda did not truly regret her choice to host me, she began regretting denying the benefit of my wisdom and knowledge to her friend. *"If it wasn't for that little misunderstanding over her being responsible for my dad's death, I would never have blended with you to keep her from it,"* Leda told me. *"Now it looks like we will be stuck in the basement of the museum translating your scrolls for the rest of our life because nobody else is qualified."* I reminded her that my mummy had been recovered and that it would contain the necessary cellular material. Thus it came to pass that a second part of me was blended with a second woman of this time. Gabriella and my second *ba* within her can do the menial tasks, since Gabriella is employed to do them anyway. We will, of course, assist from time to time when it pleases us to do so.

But Egypt has grown poor. It has been conquered and ravished many times since Octavian ended my reign. The world beyond seems to have become very large. Much of it is rich beyond anything I have ever known. A poor woman past her first youth has no chance to gain ascendancy in this time.

So if we are ever to regain power in this barbaric world where royal blood has little meaning and thrones of a sort are to be had only in deference to wealth, it behooves us to acquire some. Leda has no opposition to wealth. On the contrary, she loves acquiring objects and bestowing largesse upon her friends and family members. However, she does not use riches to gain more riches. She humorously calls herself a "power weasel," but the sort of power she refers to is the power of a courtier currying favor. She has very little experience at being the person whose favor is sought.

She will learn. Fortunately, we share a sense of drama, and I can work with that. My little scenarios, as Leda calls them, won me the hearts of both Caesar and Antony and kept me on the throne of Egypt. I daresay such episodes can be useful in other areas as well.

CHAPTER 1

Cleopatra awakened to her third incarnation. Since she had been in her mausoleum when she died, she was not surprised to be there still when she revived. For the most part, it appeared as it had when last she looked upon it. The leopard skins softened the marble floors. The frescoes on the walls depicted, Egyptian style, her accomplishments and favorite occupations. The high, deep windows allowed the light to flood the floor of the anteroom. Through one of these apertures she and her handmaidens had hoisted her poor wounded Antony so she might embrace him once more before he died. And yes, there was the overturned urn that had once held the cobra that killed her. All of these items were as she recalled them.

What she did find surprising was that she now had company. Instead of the single couch upon which her lookalike handmaiden Charmion had lain, clad in Cleopatra's regal robes to deceive Octavian into burning the wrong body, there were two gold-inlaid ebony couches draped in silks and furs. Each of these contained a woman. Neither of them was Iras or Charmion, and neither was herself. This gave her pause. She viewed the scene from a detached perspective, seeming to look down, which made her think that she was her own *ba,* the spirit that stayed close to the body after death. However, though the setting was the same, the players were totally unfamiliar. Besides the two sleeping women, there was a small, dark-haired, black-clad person with features of an Asian cast. This person had a priestly air and tended a vertical object that appeared to be a scrying glass of a type unknown to Cleopatra.

And then came the voice, her voice and yet a voice apart, emanating both from inside her and beside her.

"Greetings, Cleopatra Philopater, Queen of Upper and Lower Egypt. Welcome to your new life."

"Who are you?" she asked.

"You know the answer to that. I am also Cleopatra Philopater, Queen of Upper and Lower Egypt," her own voice answered. "Think on it! There is one of us for Upper and one for Lower Egypt. Unfortunately, we are no longer in power."

"Ahh," Cleopatra VII, the third incarnation, said. "I was afraid of that. It was no mere nightmare, then, the death of Antony and the triumph of Octavian? I most distinctly recall the cobra's bite. Even with the ill turn our luck had taken, surely we could not have chosen for the instrument of our death the only impotent cobra in all of Egypt."

"No, the cobra bestowed its fatal blessing upon us. We died, and our subsequent burial in our secret tomb was carried out by our loyal priests as planned."

"And now we awaken? And why is it, if we are the same person, that the part of me that is you knows all of this, and the part represented by me must be enlightened?"

"I preceded you. My hostess, Leda, refers to me as Cleo 7.1 and to you as Cleo 7.2."

"She sounds impertinent. Hospitality aside, you really should have her strangled."

"That would be inconvenient since I live within her body."

"You speak in riddles. I fear that having just awakened from death, I am not as witty as usual. Could you be a bit clearer, do you suppose?"

"I will try, though once you bond with your own hostess, you will learn much more of these matters from her, as I had to learn of them from Leda. In rather a hurry, I might add.

"You may be reassured to learn that the ancient priests were partially correct. It was indeed necessary to keep our bodies at least somewhat intact, so that there would be what is now known as cellular material remaining. Although our original flesh is dead, this cellular material from the remnants of our body has made a home for our *ba* lo these many centuries."

"Centuries?" Cleopatra 7.2 inquired.

"We have been—hmmm, how shall I put it?—dormant for several hundreds of years. Presently it is a time of much change, many miraculous events and objects of great curiosity. Wizards, scholars, and scientists have devised the means of reviving our *ba* and embodying it in the flesh of our hostesses."

"If they can do all that you say, why have they split us in two?"

"Because each of us could be revived from a few of our former body's surviving cells. Since that body contained many more cells than necessary for one revival, and since there is another hostess who urgently wishes our guidance and counsel, I determined that we—you, that is—should be joined with her, and thus quickened to life. So each of us is a complete Cleopatra but within a separate hostess. Mine is called Leda Hubbard, who is not Egyptian, is not royal, is no longer young, and suffers from several complaints of the body."

"And mine?"

"Yours is young and strong, her lineage Grecian, as was ours, but also Egyptian. Though she is not descended from Alexander, royal blood of a sort flows in her veins. However, she is no queen or princess. Her royal antecedents have been deposed."

"And yet she lives? Sloppy of the usurpers."

"Indeed. Very careless. For though she has no political power, still she seeks to help some of her people. She has been trying to improve the lot of women."

"Ah, yes, the gift and curse of leadership is not easily ignored, even when it would be safer to do so. We trust she will benefit from our example and experience. It may be useful to such a person."

"Our thought exactly. You are fortunate that we have preceded you into this day to which you are awakening. We have done what we can to ease your way. At our direction, this replica of our mausoleum was prepared for your blending. Also, at my suggestion, both Leda and Gabriella accepted the necessity for sleeping draughts so that you and I might converse freely before the blending sleep begins for you."

"Most considerate of you, sister," Cleopatra 7.2 said graciously, though she wondered precisely what the blending sleep might be.

"An interesting choice of address, since we are not sisters but one and the same. Were that not so, we would not be silently conversing with our two selves as we are now. It would allow the company's priest to know that an error had been made, and the blending would not continue. However, I see that all is well, that you and I are as two aspects of the moon.

"Therefore, sleep, my other self. Dream deeply of Gabriella, and she shall dream deeply of you. Leda and I within her body await your waking."

"Who *is* the funny little priest?"

"That is Chimera, one Leda says is a great scientist, and who I will tell you is the wizard who has made our new lives possible. Now you must join Gabriella, and I rejoin Leda. Sleep well, twin of my spirit."

Within moments after the pharaonic welcome wagon business was completed, Leda Hubbard's sleeping draught wore off. Her inner queen tucked safely back in the royal quarters of their now mutual brain, Leda arose languorously from the faux leopard skin draped across her equally faux ebony couch. She stretched and looked around her. Gabriella was still zonked out in the blending sleep. Chimera had disappeared, but a lab tech, or at least an earnest-looking young woman in a white coat, stood vigil over the blending device.

"You going to be here for a while?" Leda asked the tech.

"Until Dr. Chimera returns."

"Okay then. Tell Chimera I'll be back but I have to go see a payroll clerk about a check."

Exiting the darkened chamber, she stepped into the simulated daylight of the corridor outside, took the lift up four floors to the old crusader castle that housed the ground-level offices, and strode toward Wolfe's office.

If he wasn't otherwise engaged, it would save time to ask him to correct the mistake that had delayed her money a good week past when it was due. Why talk to a minion when the CEO of the corporation was an old school chum? Of course, she could have e-mailed or phoned about the check before but she'd been busy. It wasn't easy being two people at once, each with a separate agenda. There was all that constant inner negotiating interfering every time she started to do something. And then she had spent several days at Gabriella's villa while trying to prepare her friend for the second blending of Cleopatra. Besides, she had known she was coming to Kefalos with Gabriella for the blending and thought it would be easier just to pick up the check in person. She hadn't spent a lot of her own money since coming to Egypt so she'd had enough to get by, but there was supposed to be a lot more than she had gotten in the most recent pay packet.

Wolfe had a new receptionist, a guy who looked up from his computer screen impatiently, as though he was the head of the company, not Wolfe.

"Can I help you?"

"Is Mr. Wolfe in?"

"He is not," he said in crisp BBC English. "You have an appointment?"

"What does it matter if he's not in?" she asked, not liking the guy's tone. "If he *is* in, please tell him Leda Hubbard would like a brief word with him. I think he'll see me."

"He is not," the fellow repeated. "But possibly Dr. Calliostro can make time for you." He buzzed. "Leda Hubbard popped in, wanting to speak to Mr. Wolfe." A pause, then, "Very well. Dr. Calliostro will see you."

She started to say she didn't want to see Dr. Calliostro—whoever the hell that was—she wanted to see Wolfe. But she did need to clear up the pay packet thing, and, besides, she was curious. Who was Calliostro anyway? She didn't believe she'd heard that name on previous visits.

The second question that occurred to her, as Mr. BBC opened the door to Wolfe's office and motioned her in, was what was Calliostro doing in Wolfe's office?

A petite redhead with a pert nose and a dress that probably cost more than Leda was expecting in her extra-large pay packet rose and came around the desk, extending her hand.

"Ah, Dr. Hubbard! The discoverer of Cleopatra's tomb!

I am pleased to meet you at last. I was hoping you would be here for Dr. Faruk's blending, as we have a few matters to clear up."

"Her smile reminds me of my sister's," Cleopatra told Leda without an ounce of sentimentality. *"You would be safer shaking hands with a crocodile."*

"Oh, then you know that I haven't been paid my finder's fees yet for discovering the tomb and the DNA? Not to mention my regular check."

"Yes, of course."

"I'm relieved," Leda said. She wasn't. She could tell from the woman's tone that there was nothing to be relieved about, but she was fishing for information before she did or said anything drastic. "I should have known Wolfe—Mr. Wolfe would be thoughtful enough to let you know what to do about it in his absence."

"Not exactly," the woman said. "You see, Mr. Wolfe will not be returning to this facility. I have replaced him as director of this project while a new CEO for the parent organization is being elected by the board."

Leda strove to keep her voice level. "When did this all happen? I heard nothing about it."

"We don't normally send memos to former employees, Dr. Hubbard."

"Former?"

"Well, yes. Your employment was temporary and rather irregular at that. And while admittedly you did find the original DNA sample as you were requested to do by Dr. Chimera, you did not, in fact, deliver that DNA to us. In fact, you administered the blend to yourself, which is entirely against the stated policy of the project. Although your later contributions were certainly noteworthy, and we do appreciate the new specimen from the royal mummy, well, I'm sure you can understand our position."

"Not at all," Leda said. "Please do explain it to me."

"Why, it's simply that in blending yourself with Cleopatra's DNA, you availed yourself of a priceless company commodity that more than cancels out any wages or bonuses owed to you."

"If you'll read my report, you'll learn that I did it under extraordinary circumstances, to keep the material from falling into the wrong hands."

"You mean the late Mr. Rasmussen? I did read the reports—yours and others submitted to my office—and I'm afraid I can't see your objection to acquiescing to Mr. Rasmussen's request. Both you and Dr. Chimera seem to have become extremely possessive of what is essentially corporate property. As a board member and major shareholder, Mr. Rasmussen had rather more right to the specimen than you did."

"Stop referring to me as a specimen, woman," Cleopatra said from behind Leda's clenched teeth.

"Mr. Rasmussen had kidnapped Dr. Chimera, Dr. Faruk, Mrs. Wolfe, and several other people, Miss—what was your name again?"

"Doctor. It's Doctor Calliostro. Mr. Rasmussen was far too ill to have done any such thing and died during your so-called rescue. He can hardly defend himself, can he?"

"So that's what all this business about you replacing Wolfe relates to," Leda said. "Friends of Rasmussen's wanted him out as some kind of revenge."

"Oh, really, Dr. Hubbard. It doesn't take some conspiracy of Mr. Rasmussen's allies to see that this project needs new management. It is one of the most costly of our operations, but even with what we are charging for each blend, the process has not proved to be cost-effective. Therefore, deadwood is being removed so that we can move forward."

"Deadwood meaning Wolfe and me?" Leda asked.

"No need to take it so personally. You are welcome to

remain until tomorrow's flight for the mainland. Your return ticket is paid for after all. I don't believe we have further need of you at the moment, so feel free to seek other employment."

"*Banished?*" Cleopatra asked. "*We are being banished?*"

Leda smiled her father's vulpine smile, the one he'd used just before he cuffed a criminal. "Don't worry about us," she said, half to Calliostro and half to reassure Cleo. "After all, I'm a forensic scientist, and there's always a demand for someone who knows where the bodies are buried."

Cleopatra's third incarnation settled into the body awaiting her. The sleep was deep, though not so deep as death. Images and memories alien to her paraded through her being, and she answered each with images and memories of her own. The memories began with the most recent, the happy discovery of Cleopatra's tomb and Gabriella's part in it, Cleopatra's death by cobra, followed by Gabriella's first rescue of a woman being stoned for the crime of having been raped, countered by Cleopatra's allegiance with and love for Antony. Deeper and deeper into the past they journeyed. None of Gabriella's illegal, if noble, activities bothered Cleopatra's conscience even slightly, and to the queen's satisfaction, Gabriella understood perfectly why Cleopatra had needed to have her siblings slain. Thus it seemed that the most traumatic parts of the past had been broached without difficulty.

And then came the part where they began to awake, and the sensations of Gabriella's body flooded Cleopatra's awareness. She was young, strong, with all of her teeth and good hair, but something else, something very important to any woman, let alone one of Cleopatra's lusty inclinations, was missing. "By the gods," she groaned. "We're gelded."

All hell had broken loose by the time Leda returned to the blending chamber.

Chimera hovered near Gabriella, who moaned, whimpered, twitched, and cried to the gods in Greek, French, and an old Egyptian dialect that Cleo 7.1 refused to translate.

"What is wrong with them?" Chimera asked. He told her about the sudden change in Gabriella's demeanor and her crying out about being gelded.

"Oh, God," Leda said. Her own problems suddenly seemed a bit trivial. Not that they were. But they seemed that way compared with what her friend had lived with most of her life. "I—uh—it never occurred to me to mention to my Cleo about Gabriella's so-called circumcision. Her aunt told me about it. It's one of the kind that cuts away darn near everything that makes you enjoy being a girl, shall we say. I guess the blending triggered a flashback."

Chimera nodded, weary sadness washing over his-her-their—androgynous features.

The most extreme Egyptian "circumcisions" involved subjecting young girls to genital mutilations it usually took a seasoned sadistic serial killer to invent.

"*Why?*" Cleopatra within Leda demanded. "*Gabriella Faruk is a wealthy young woman of royal lineage, a scientist and scholar. Why was such a thing done to her? What crime did she commit? Was she a prostitute? Did she steal the husband of some powerful woman?*"

"*No, no. Nothing like that. Her stepfather had it done to her when she was a little girl.*"

"*A punishment? An extreme and cruel one not even my own family ever devised.*"

"*No, it's not supposed to be a punishment. It's a custom some of the people here still follow. It's supposed to be a precaution.*"

"*Precaution? Against what? Having children? Do they not wish their daughters to be mothers?*"

"*Oh, they can still do that. They just won't enjoy any part of it until at least after the baby is born. I think the theory is that if the girl doesn't have what it takes to have fun in bed, if sex hurts her in fact, then she won't go doing the nasty behind the backs of the menfolk. After she's married, it's supposed to keep her from straying, I guess because putting up with one guy is tough enough, why take on extra hardship? That's how it's supposed to work anyway."*

"But then she is never a willing consort, never enjoys . . ."

"Exactly. Only the guys get to enjoy it. And some of them prob- *ably get off on hurting the girls as much as they do making babies. But that's not what they say, of course. They say that the—er— operation—protects family honor. Whatever that means.*"

"And you did not think to mention this atrocity to me?"

"Well, we've had a few impending atrocities of our own to deal with, and frankly," Leda added with a shudder, "it hurts to even think about it and it makes me mad and we get all red in the face and our blood pressure rises, which is not good for us, so I just tried to repress it."

Gabriella's agitation dissolved into occasional sobs.

"Should we wake them?" Chimera asked.

Answering, Leda's voice took on the more formal tones of her inner Cleopatra. The queen habitually used Leda's husky lower register tuned to a melodious alto when she spoke. "No. It is very sad, but we should allow them privacy to mourn the loss. Gabriella perhaps has grown accustomed to her misfortune, even as a eunuch might, but the fresh aware- ness inflicted by my twin's reaction is surely painful to her. And as you heard, my other self is dismayed, to put it mildly. In our time, Rome considered us a great whore who gained power over Caesar and Antony with our wanton lustfulness. It seems none of them ever stopped to wonder if my hus- bands gained power over me by similar means . . ."

Her voice grew thick, and Leda felt her receding, retreat- ing into her own memories.

"*Ahem?*" Leda said.

"Oh? Excuse me," Cleo said to Chimera, continuing. "I meant to observe only that because of Gabriella's injury, such avenues of influence will be less open, if not closed altogether, to her and to my other self." She gestured gracefully toward the adjoining couch, sighed, then added wryly, "However, we Ptolemys are not unused to having horrors visited upon us by relatives. I—she—the *ba*—will adapt."

Chimera was called away from the chamber and seemed relieved to go. "We are still supervising the new practitioners of the process," the scientist explained apologetically. The small body drooped slightly, frailer, thinner, and wearier than Leda ever remembered seeing it. *Frazzled* was the term her grandma Hubbard might have used. Losing control of the blending process was bound to be hard on Chimera. And Leda knew her friend was wondering if blending Gabriella and the second Cleopatra had been a mistake.

But before she awoke, Gabriella first settled down, then seemed to be absolutely enjoying herself. She was still moaning but in a good way.

When she opened her eyes, the younger woman wore a bemused expression, full of wonder. And some embarrassment.

Leda felt a smile playing on her own face, compliments of Cleopatra 7.1. *"Aha! I believe my alter-ba has already done her hostess some good."*

"Gabriella does look a little like the cat who swallowed the canary. What's that all about anyway?"

"Can you not guess?" Cleopatra asked. Suddenly Leda was swamped with an entire Louisiana bayou of emotions and sensory impressions that were almost but not *quite* unlike anything she'd ever experienced before.

She was delightfully tangled in an embrace in which strong arms held her tight against the muscular torso of a man who was very obviously glad to see her. She looked up into a deeply tanned, ruggedly handsome face topped by curly brown hair. Her nose was so close to his that his eyes looked crossed, but they were very pretty chocolate-drop eyes with long, curling lashes and little crinkles at the corners. She and the hunk were sharing a bawdy chuckle, never mind about what, maybe just high spirits at being together for their mutual pleasure again. Also, they were a little drunk both with wine and with each other. She was happy, happy, happy. Which was odd enough. But even odder was that she knew for certain that he loved her—cared for her in a way that was completely different from anything she'd felt before. The way he was looking at her, however blurrily, the way he held her both as if he was afraid he'd break her and as if he was afraid she'd leave told her more than words or other quite compelling physical evidence impressively pressing against her groin. He loved her. He made her feel young and free, and he saw who she really was beneath her title and her beauty, and most certainly her clothing. The thought made her all juicy and flushed, and she clung to him.

Oh my. Somewhere along the way he'd lost his armor and that cute little skirt that showed off his very nice legs. The rest of him wasn't bad either, and at least one part was truly excellent. He used his teeth to pull the pin that held her garment together. They proceeded to blend as closely as they could without the benefit of DNA technology, demonstrating their mutual passion repeatedly in a variety of highly entertaining and satisfying ways. It was so great that she was sorry she had given up smoking because she couldn't roll over and light a cigarette between rounds. She was sorrier still that cigarettes hadn't been invented yet.

Then somewhere in the midst of all the sweet sweatiness of it, the memory changed, and the sweat became blood. He was in her arms still, but dying there from the wound he'd dealt himself, like Romeo, thinking she was dead.

Leda came back to the present, bummed to be left with nothing but the ashes of a few one-night stands and the affair she thought was true love until he cheated on her. It didn't matter. She knew now what it was supposed to be like.

Gabriella's sly smile said that she did, too.

"Oh. My. God," she thought. *"She's vicariously lost her cherry! All the gravy and none of the grief. That was really sweet of—er—both of you, Cleo."*

"Antony and I had a very special love. Private. Personal. Except of course from Iras and Charmion, my handmaidens, and I expect the closer friends among Antony's officers. Such passion is too overwhelming to keep entirely to oneself. We were mad for each other."

"I can well imagine," Leda said. *"You'd have been mad not to be."*

"I gather that your historians now choose to see me as a good but tragic queen, but I was really extremely fortunate that political necessity led me to bed the two men who became my great loves. Caesar was my mentor, my first love, my husband, my teacher. But Antony was—well."

"He certainly was," Leda agreed.

"But there was no reason until now to share such memories. You have your own to keep you company I know, though you have never confided in me."

"They're not much by comparison. Girl A meets boy. They get together. Boy meets Girl B, and they get together before he breaks up with Girl A. Girl A throws his faithless ass out. In other words, the sorry son of a bitch cheated on me."

"Antony cheated on me, too. He married the sister of the man who ultimately killed us."

"I guess I knew that. But you forgave him?"

"I extracted a price for the very public humiliation of his betrayal, but yes, I did. After all, the marriage was politically expedient for him, and I understood that all too well. It was easier for me to take him back because politics forced us together again. But it was the passion that kept us together until the end."

Leda sighed.

Gabriella, her smile gone, got to her feet. When she spoke it was in a voice calculated to carry through the vastness of a palace's throne room as the pharaoh delivered a proclamation, though her words sounded a little more like a formal prayer. "We give thanks for this blending that has revived our *ba* and renewed our life."

"Hi," Leda said. "I'm Leda. You would be the queen. I believe you've already met my uh—my queen."

Gabriella grinned a charmingly impish grin that was almost the same one Leda had seen her wear before. This one had just a touch more calculation to it and a little less mischievousness. "Ah yes! Our own special tomb robber."

Chimera reentered the room and seemed pleased to see Gabriella on her feet again.

"This is Dr. Chimera," Leda said. "But I guess you knew that."

Cleo 7.2 nodded Gabriella's head graciously. "You are a very great magician from what Gabriella tells me. Despite some discourse with the part of me that dwells in Leda Hubbard, I am at something of a loss to know why you chose to revive me in this fashion. Perhaps you were not aware of it, Doctor, but a great harm has been done to our physical vessel. Gabriella acquainted me with the circumstances of her maiming and feels that with my assistance, we may prevent future atrocities and avenge other women of our realm who have been so defiled."

Chimera murmured something noncommittal. The blend had been requested by all parties concerned, including the DNA's donor, which was highly unusual. The scientist for once had not been particularly concerned with why a second sample of Cleopatra's DNA was being blended.

Cleopatra continued, using Gabriella's lower register, charmingly accented. Gabriella's own accent was rather different. "But in the meantime, there is another boon we would ask of you, Dr. Chimera."

"Yes?" Chimera said.

"We wish you to bring back Marc Antony." This request ended with a rather girlish gusto that was all Gabriella.

Leda's heart went out to her. It was sort of an occupational hazard for archaeologists, falling for people who had been dead several thousand years. Cleo's memories were not going to do anything to help.

CHAPTER 2

Chimera's head shook regretfully. "We have no sample of Marc Antony's DNA. Nor has anyone requested him for a blend."

"Perhaps Pete . . ." Cleo suggested.

Leda quickly vetoed the nomination of her old boyfriend for Antony's new incarnation. "Not on our life. Besides, Pete's gone now. He's down near Aswan, consulting on the flood release project."

Cleo said, "Ah well, you know better than I if he would be a worthy vessel. Not every man would. Marc Antony was a lion among men and of great prowess and size."

"Besides," Leda said cautiously, feeling as if she were about to tiptoe into an emotional minefield, "the memories—the idea of the original may be a lot better than a blend. Especially because of your—uh—you know," she said to Gabriella, who had begun glaring at her.

Leda met her glare with a hopeless shrug, spreading her hands to say "hey, it's not my fault." Gabriella's shoulders slumped and she looked far less aggressive and much more doubtful than she had moments before.

"You queens may have created a monster," Leda told Cleo 7.1. *"Even if there was a host who could live up to your Antony, Cleo 7.2 couldn't do much about it in Gabriella's body. At least, I don't think they could experience what was just advertised. And frankly, I'm not sure we're a whole lot better. I know this body couldn't get into some of those positions anymore."*

Rather to her surprise, Cleo 7.1 agreed. Aloud she said, "Great passion of the sort Antony and I shared is perhaps easier to remember than to continue or to duplicate. We, Leda and I, look forward to future pleasures as yet unknown. To try to repeat past ones may ruin them."

"Is that the real reason, or do you fear that one Antony and two Cleopatras might present a dilemma?" challenged Gabriella's new guest.

Chimera had been looking from one to the other as if watching a tennis match. Now the scientist interjected, "This may not work, the blending of the same DNA with two different hosts, for a number of reasons. We consider it an experiment, and a timely one at that. Helix wishes to perform future blends more—indiscriminately—and will be anxious to learn the effects on all parties of having two hosts blend with the same entity. Other notable historical figures will have many who desire to blend with them. But we urge you to avoid rivalry over any of the past—assets—of your donor." The small Tibetan sighed. "The process is supposed to provide insight into the past and other people, not create discord."

Chimera might as well have been silent.

Gabriella's hand suddenly flew to her throat, her fingers patting the skin as if feeling for a piece of jewelry she'd lost. "Where is it? Do you have it?"

"What's that?" Leda asked.

"Our amulet containing a lock of Antony's hair and a scrap of cloth soaked in his blood from his mortal wound. We gave our priests specific instructions that the amulet must be interred with us."

"Well, that would be on your mummy, I imagine," Leda said reasonably. "Gabriella, don't you recall seeing something like that in the casket? We were lucky to be allowed to take the sampling of DNA out of the country. The other artifacts belong to the Egyptian government. They'd be with the mummy and the scrolls back at the museum in Alex."

"We must have it back so that Antony may be revived to rule at our side when we take our rightful throne once more," Gabriella's Cleo declared.

"We wish you luck, then," Leda said. "We've got a one-way ticket back to the States and no severance pay. Our services are no longer needed."

But Gabriella didn't seem to hear, or if she did, to care. She had turned her attention inward and was presumably engaged in an internal dialogue.

Leda addressed her own inner queen. *"Who is this blended entity anyway? Your evil twin? I thought you'd clued her in about your—our—all of our—role, or lack thereof, in your country's political structure? Any attempts on our part to take over the government of Egypt would be very much frowned upon."*

"You think it was not before, when our siblings waged war against us for the crown? Mere frowns are of no consequence to us, Leda Hubbard."

"Maybe not. But you had a right to the throne then that I think would be a little hard to enforce now. Besides, I don't want to be stuck in a throne room all the time. I'm allergic to all that perfume you used to splash around. I kind of thought what with your linguistic ability and all the books that had been written since you di—since your last life—you and I could haunt the libraries of the world when you're not helping locate other sites where promising DNA samples might be obtained, such as Alexander's tomb. Speaking of which, why didn't you mention your mummy was sporting DNA-enhanced jewelry? We could have pinched it before the

government got into the act, at least long enough to liberate Marc Antony's relics."

"I forgot to mention it in all the excitement. If you will recall, our joining was completed under circumstances more distracting than these idyllic ones our other self enjoys. Our urgent concern upon awakening with you was with maintaining your status as a living host for my ba."

"I see your point," Leda agreed, recalling the life-and-death struggle for Cleopatra's DNA that had resulted in her blending with the queen herself. *"You do seem to have different priorities than Cleo 7.2, though, you have to admit. She seems determined to make up for lost time."*

Leda was surprised to see dawn breaking over the Mediterranean when she, Chimera, and Gabriella emerged from the underground labs into the courtyard of the old Crusader castle. The castle crowned a volcanic crater at the center of the corporately owned Greek island of Kefalos.

Graceful white houses with blue-painted window frames and red-tiled roofs cascaded down the sides of the cinder cone to the intense blue-green horseshoe-shaped bay. Small sailing craft, several yachts, and a couple of company freighters dotted the harbor. One stretch of the white beach was paved with white-painted concrete that served as a landing strip, chopper pad, and motor pool for the Helix compound.

The air was still slightly cool with early breezes, and gulls coasted on the currents overhead.

Leda gave the vista from the citadel a last regretful look. Chimera motioned the women to board the company golf cart and drove them down to the landing strip. The place was even more of a hive of activity than it had been on Leda's previous visits. The changing of the regime was evident in the number of items being loaded onto and off of small aircraft.

When Gabriella climbed out of the golf cart, Leda followed and started to give her friend a farewell hug.

"Bye, Gabriella. Stay in touch."

"Of course," the Egyptian girl said.

"We will always be a part of each other," her voice added in huskier tones.

Leda felt an answering *"yes"* from within her.

With a playful bilateral air kiss Gabriella skipped away to board the chopper that would take her back to Alexandria.

Wordlessly, Chimera climbed back into the cart.

Leda cast a last look at the gangly, dark-haired figure climbing aboard the helicopter.

"I wish we were going to be around to keep an eye on those two," she told Chimera, turning away from the field and continuing toward the villa. "I'm a little worried about them."

The state of Chimera's villa announced his departure. Formerly, the rooms had been uncluttered but comfortable, elegant in a minimalist less-is-more way. Now, except for packing boxes, the whole place was virtually bare.

"I hope you didn't pack my beer yet," she said.

"No need," the scientist said. "We will not be taking the fridge." She grabbed one of the beers as Chimera opened a large white cardboard box and pulled out a tall glass. This was filled with iced tea from the pitcher that was the only companion of Leda's imported beers.

They dragged boxes out onto the piazza to sit on and another for a table. Sipping their beverages and perched on boxes, each gazed at the sea.

"So where are you going then?" Leda asked, after the beer was a third of the way gone and the nice chilly sweat on the bottle had long ago run down her arm and evaporated, so the glass was warm in her hand.

Chimera looked directly at her for the first time since they'd left the blending chamber. "We are taking a sabbatical, then returning to the lab in Norwich to do further research."

Leda said. "So how's that going to work? Calliostro told me Wolfe is gone—I gathered from the entire company and not just the project. You and he have always done the screenings and follow-up interviews when necessary, not to mention the blendings."

"We have been told that we have been too restrictive in our choices, too discouraging of potential hosts and too discriminating when deciding which donor DNA to seek." Chimera gave a little wave of the hand. "And so we have trained new assistants. A team of psychologists, led by Dr. Calliostro, will be screening the clients. All of this causes us much concern, Leda."

"I can well imagine," she said. "My mind fairly reels with scenarios in which a badly handled blend could ruin the world or at least the life of the client and maybe all of their friends and relatives, too.

"We begin to fear that our happiness was bought at a very high cost to others, Leda," Chimera continued. "That is why we decided to accept the invitation of the Padma Lama and seek enlightenment in the mountains for a time."

"The Himalayas?" Leda asked.

"Oh, no. The Rockies. The Padma Lama established a monastery in Vail, Colorado, after he fled Tibet. The Himalayas are much too risky, with the Chinese government constantly harassing anyone coming into them on the Indian side."

"Well, it's good you'll have a vacation, then. I'm glad you were here for Gabriella's at least. Now she can decipher the scrolls while we go see the rest of the world. I do wonder about something though, Chimera. I only bring it up because if you're going to do more research, you may want to look into it. It seems to me that Cleo and I are more mixed than blended."

"So we've observed. Although it does seem to us that your accent and hers are sometimes mingling in each other's speech. Also, the timbre of your voices is more alike than it once was. And perhaps it is simply a sign of her growing familiarity with our times, but Her Majesty seems occasionally to employ some of the slang and occupational jargon unknown to her original time."

"Really?" Leda and her inner queen asked in the same voice but with two attitudes. Cleopatra was somewhat pleased at how quickly she was learning, though chagrined to think she might be lowering herself somewhat by adapting to Leda's distinctly plebeian ways. Leda wondered how differently others might see her and treat her if she was more queenly. It could be a good thing, provided it didn't go too far.

Chimera continued. "Some blends are completed almost at once, and with others, truthfully, we do not know if completion is even possible. It seems to depend on many variable attributes in the host as well as the traits encoded from the donor DNA. Gabriella's version of the donor noticeably varies from your own."

"She takes after the Ptolemy side of the family more than we do," Cleopatra said. "The part of us that desires power and conquest and to carry on the dynasty. It's very stimulating and exciting, you know. However, it can be tiring and leave little time for reading and recreation." She yawned, and Leda realized they were both very tired.

"We'd better turn in. Got to get up at o-dark-thirty to catch our chopper for the mainland in time to meet the flight back to Portland. It's only been a year since Daddy was killed, but the law enforcement community, after much political back and forthing, according to my brother, Rudy, who is also a cop, are finally holding a memorial service for him. Dad and Gretchen are coming of course. Daddy isn't about to miss his own funeral."

Chimera sighed. "Soon we will all be out of Dr. Calliostro's path so that she may implement the board's plans. She says she is sure that no matter what reservations Helix may have, the blendings have great value."

Chimera actually made a face.

"Ewww," Leda said. "So she's going to be the one to make something of it, is she? Now that you've made the little contribution of inventing the whole process. With you and Wolfe out of the way for a while, she can probably convince everybody it was all her idea. Of course, she'll welcome you back in time to share the blame when someone hosts Hitler or Charles Manson so the company can make a profit."

"True. That is why we will be doing more extensive research on how the process can be reversed reliably at any time. We also wish to learn if we may tailor the donor DNA to blend only those parts unlikely to cause harm to the host."

Cleopatra nodded Leda's head wisely. "That must suffice, I suppose, since it seems the hosts will bear even less scrutiny than they have heretofore. I ask only that if you learn someone is blending with Octavian, you give us enough warning that we can either have the samples destroyed or strangle the host during the blending sleep."

Chimera's personal belongings were few. Some books, a week's worth of clothing, an album of wedding pictures, and a laptop computer no larger or heavier than a standard-sized notebook. The information that was too complex to store in the scientist's head, field notes, plans for the design and construction of both stationary and portable blending devices, and other data, was on computer disks stored in miniature on X-ray-proof microchips that slipped easily into a small, beaded amulet bag Chimera always wore as a pendant, concealed beneath a shirt. Since the information technically belonged to Helix, they had custody of the original hard disks and hard copy, but Chimera carried the data as well for security's sake.

The boxes sitting around the villa were Helix property, so all Chimera needed to board the copter to Athens was a single checkable bag plus a briefcase containing the computer, now loaded with games, a change of clothing, the wedding album, and a used novel to read aboard the aircraft.

The copter landed in Athens, and Chimera walked to the main terminal. The walk was invigorating. After so much time shut up in an underground lab, or with one's nose to the microscope, a cornflower blue sky padded with puffs of white cloud, fresh, if somewhat jet-fuel-scented, air, and a long, flat place to stretch the legs felt wonderful.

By the time Chimera entered the terminal, a fine sweat beaded the scientist's skin. The sensation of the air-conditioning gently evaporating the sweat to a new coolness on every exposed pore was a pleasant sensation.

The lines at the ticket counters were so long, they merged into a combed crowd of people, all shuffling and twitching and trying to sit on their luggage. Chimera thought gratefully how convenient it was that the company helicopter crew could transfer the single suitcase needed for the trip.

Oddly, it was the suitcase the scientist first spotted through the crowd instead of the people pulling it. The reason it was odd was that Chimera's suitcase was rather ordinary except for the Helix company logo stamped on both black cloth sides in scarlet-and-gold letters. If one was accustomed to looking for the logo, it was quite noticeable. But not as noticeable as the two shaven-headed maroon-clad Tibetan Buddhist monks towing it behind them, looking through the crowd until one of them met Chimera's inquiring gaze.

"Yo, Doc!" one of them called, before bowing over his steepled hands.

"Yes?" Chimera said, but was drowned out by the crowd. The monks made a beeline for the scientist, however.

"Greetings," said the monk who had not already spoken, bowing over *his* steepled hands. This monk spoke with a Tibetan accent much like the one Tsering and Chime had had when they came to Europe. "You are Dr. Chimera, are you not?"

"I am," Chimera said, barely remembering to use the singular among those not initiated into the secrets of the blending process. "And I must say that you are the most unusual baggage handlers I have ever encountered."

"We're not—" began the first monk, a handsome young black man. "Oh, I get it. That was a joke, huh, Doc? We're not baggage handlers. We're here on behalf of our Dorje Rimpoche, the Padma Lama."

"I am of course delighted to see you, though I had not thought to do so until I got *off* the airplane in Colorado."

"We're here to head you off at the pass, Doc," the African-American Tibetan monk said. "Dorje Rimpoche really wants to connect with you, but the thing is, he's not in Colorado anymore."

"No?"

"No. There was an avalanche, see, and the monastery was at the bottom of it. Three of our brothers are progressing toward their next lives as a result, but Dorje Rimpoche has settled for a more earthly journey to Dharmsala. He asked that we reroute you to join him there. He believes he can arrange for an audience with the Dalai Lama. Cool, huh?"

"I am distressed to hear of your disaster," Chimera said, also bowing over steepled hands, "but am grateful that Dorje Rimpoche survived and took such pains to see that I do not miss my chance to consult with him." Then the scientist's security-ridden recent past on Kefalos revealed itself. "I hope you won't mind showing me some identification?"

"Oh, yeah, sure," the American said, flipping out a passport with his picture in his robes, proclaiming him to be Meshaq Karim Shakabpa Jones of the Padma Monastery in Vail, Colorado.

The Tibetan monk also displayed an American passport. He was Lhamo-Dhondrub also of the Padma Monastery in Vail, Colorado.

Chimera smiled and bowed again. "Thank you for saving me a long journey in the wrong direction, brothers. I place myself in your hands." But as the scientist said this, a voice inside belonging to neither Chime nor Tsering warned that this was not a good idea. Not a good idea at all.

CHAPTER 3

Leda tried to sleep on the way home, but it was her first transatlantic flight since her blending. Cleopatra, who was well versed in mathematics and other sciences, asked a great many intelligent and difficult questions about the plane, the sky through which it traveled, and the lands and waters beneath its wings. Leda answered as best she could for the twenty hours it took to fly from Athens to Portland, counting a lengthy delay in Frankfurt because of mechanical problems. Cleopatra very badly wanted to leave the airport in Athens to explore the city. Though she, like all the Ptolemys, was Macedonian Greek by birth, she had never visited the capital of the country from which her family originated. She pressed Leda's nose to the windows leading to the parking lot as if she were a kid in a candy store, and her pleading was downright pitiful.

"*Look, we have a few things to sort out, then we'll come back and take a grand tour, I promise,*" Leda told her.

"*How can we?*" Cleopatra lamented, her tones inside Leda's head throbbing with the tragedy of the lost opportunity. "*We *are penniless, the powerful people we know have been deposed, and we have been banished."*

"Not exactly banished, just temporarily minus the funds to return on our own," Leda said. *"And things can change. They can always change."*

"Yes, I know!" Cleo wailed from within her. *"Queen one moment, captive the next."*

"They can change for the better, too," Leda said. *"For instance, you were dead for a while, and now you're alive again, sorta."*

Cleo was not convinced but contented herself with asking many questions, most of which Leda responded to with, *"I don't know right offhand. We'll look it up when we get home."*

In Frankfurt, Cleo once more bombarded Leda with questions that required her to review mentally what she knew of the First and Second World Wars and the German economic recovery since then. She'd read a lot of military history and the subjects had been of great interest to Duke, so she'd always felt she was pretty well prepared. It was embarrassing how much she didn't know. And you couldn't bullshit someone who lived inside your own head.

She finally was able to stop the geography and history quiz long enough to place a call to her sister Rusti to tell her about the delay. "Oh, great! Your cats are driving me crazy, you have a stack of mail three miles high, and a ton of phone calls from all sorts of people. Lots of them are complaining that you haven't answered their e-mails, and some woman from an outfit in L.A. has been calling every other day wanting to know if I know when she can get ahold of you. You want her number?"

"No, I'll catch up when I get there," Leda said, feeling tired already with the catching-up she'd have to do. "Oh—there, our flight's being called. We should be there in another twelve or thirteen hours or so. And we'll have to go through customs, of course."

"Don't worry," Rusti said.

She spent the rest of the flight writing down Cleo's questions as fast as she could. She dearly missed the laptop computer the company had issued her when her lab computer was lost in the recent earthquake. She had filled up her notebook, the unused pages of her address book, and the margins of every magazine on board by the time they reached Portland. Plus her hand throbbed like a sore tooth from writer's cramp.

Rusti was not at the waiting area outside the security barrier in Portland, nor was she at baggage claim. Finally, as Leda was looking for a phone (her cell phone, also company property, was history), Rusti sauntered through a distant door, her ear glued to her own cell phone.

"At least she's easy to spot," Leda said. *"I just look for someone who looks like me."*

"She does indeed bear a strong family resemblance to you," Cleopatra said. *"The same heavy dark hair, the same nose, a body of much the same shape. Can we trust her?"*

"If it doesn't involve being on time for something, yes," Leda told her other self. *"And no, we will not have her assassinated. She—uh—amuses us."*

"Oh, hi, Leda, there you are!" Rusti cried, finally sticking the phone in her purse and enveloping Leda in a hug. "Good flight?"

"Not especially. Great to see you, though. How are the cats?"

Cleopatra said, *"I see nothing amusing about her so far, but she seems pleasant enough. Are you quite sure she isn't plotting to kill you?"*

"You're confusing her with Mother. She'll be at the funeral. But we can't kill her either. Too many cops around, including my brother. He might understand, but he wouldn't cover for us."

Rusti said, "Sorry it took me so long, but I got another call from someone with a German accent named Gretchen. She sort of acted like she knew me, but she said to tell you she'd arrived and would meet us at the church tomorrow. Who is she? Maybe another stepmother nobody knows about?"

Cleopatra 7.2 was thrilled by the short flight home from
Kefalos to Alexandria. The pilot handed Gabriella a headset when they boarded, and she sat in the copilot seat.

They flew into Alex over the huge cofferdam, repaired following the earthquake eight months before, once more holding back the eastern harbor. Below them anthropologists crawled around the sea bottom seeking the ruins of Cleopatra's palace and other royal structures that had crumbled into the waves during the ancient earthquake that destroyed the Pharos Lighthouse.

The absence of the lighthouse was the first thing Cleopatra noticed. "I thought that would stand forever. It seemed immortal as the gods."

Gabriella explained about the earthquake and pointed out the changes in the coastline from Cleopatra's day.

"*Astounding. The lighthouse, the royal compound, the statues—all gone. Even the water in the bay.*"

"*That's only temporary. They'll let it refill when they've reconstructed the coastline as it was in your time.*" Gabriella was glad she could promise that something would be what the queen considered normal again someday. Cleopatra's chagrin and disorientation were painful.

"*The last time I saw this bay it teemed with Roman ships and the crippled remnants of my navy.*"

"*Perhaps we will find the wreckage as we excavate the ocean floor,*" Gabriella said.

Cleopatra granted her the image of a slightly pained smile, "*Somehow I do not find that comforting.*"

"*I'm sorry,*" Gabriella said. "*It's hard for me to realize that events that are ancient history to me must seem to you to have happened only yesterday.*"

"*Hard indeed. We have much more to impart to each other if we are not to go mad,*" Cleopatra said, and thereafter confined her questions to the operations of the cell phone and the aircraft until they landed. She had already explored the wonders of golf carts before they left Helix's Greek island base.

Mo's taxi, a minivan, stood baking on the airstrip beside the Quonset hut occupied by Helix's combination air traffic controller and customs officer. An entity that invested as much in other lands as Helix did enjoyed the status of a sovereign nation within the host country's borders, and as such was responsible for its employees' international travel.

Mo opened the door of the taxi and slid into the driver's seat.

"*I am still not clear on how these conveyances move without the benefit of horses or servants . . . or birds, in the case of the last one,*" the queen said, casting an awed look back at the helicopter, which was lifting off again.

"*They have combustion engines. Actually, automobiles were invented while people still rode in carriages pulled by horses so the engines that power the cars are said to have 'horsepower.'*"

"*Ahh,*" Cleopatra said, considering. Then, "*I do not understand.*"

"*Yes, well, I have arranged to take leave from my regular work to conduct research for another week. During that time we will read a great deal and watch a lot of television. I hope that will help me explain a great deal more to you.*"

"*Very well. And then we must find Antony's hair and take out the cellular material so that we may lodge him inside a worthy recipient. Then I can help as you explain this life to him.*"

The cab turned south. "*Are we not going into the city?*" Cleopatra wanted to know.

"*No, first we will go to my home. I have some responsibilities to take care of there.*"

"*Ah, you have a villa on the lake? I see we are heading in that general direction.*"

* * *

But when they came to Gabriella's family compound, which sat along the portion of the mudflats and marshes still unoccupied by industrial factories, Cleopatra exclaimed. *"But where is Lake Mariut?"*

"That's it," Gabriella told her. *"That's how it's been for many years."*

"But this is a swamp! Where are the lake's harbors? They are as important to us as the maritime harbors for bringing goods into the city from the rest of the country, and taking goods into the country from the city and from Greece and Rome. Mariut and its mate Edku all but make an island of Alexandria, surrounding it on the south, whereas the sea encompasses the northern shore, and the Canopic Channel of the Nile is to the east."

Gabriella saw the images Cleopatra was remembering. They were far more awesome than any artist's sketch, taking in clear green waters, sparkling blue skies, flocks of seabirds, and men pulling shining fish from the waters. A few large homes of white marble guarded the shore well away from the busy docks. The visual picture was wonderful as was the smell of the air, the feeling of the breeze that cooled Alexandria like no other place in Egypt. But most surprising to Gabriella was that except for the voices of people raised in speech or song, the sound of hammers and chisels ringing against stone at some remote building site, the thump of cargo nets hitting the docks as ships were unloaded, everything was remarkably quiet. No motors of any kind, no planes overhead, no cars on the road, no radios, televisions, cell phones, air conditioners, or appliances. Primitive, perhaps, and inconvenient. But quiet.

"Not any longer," Gabriella told her gently.

"What happened?" Cleopatra wondered. *"Was this also the work of earthquakes, that the water was swallowed by the desert?"*

"We're not sure, but the Canopic Channel apparently changed

courses or dried up at some point. Without the Nile to feed it, the lake has dwindled to what you see before you."

It was easy enough for her to try to imagine the past from accounts in historical documents or computer simulations. But in Cleopatra's day, Gabriella's time was unimaginable. The Queen of the Upper and Lower Nile had probably never given much thought to what her home would be like over two millennia in the future. Even if she had, she would have had no basis for visualizing planes, trains, crowded motorways and high-rise apartment buildings, and roads that would have thrilled the Romans. And quite appalling ugliness.

"I do not understand. How can people live here without water? How are the cisterns filled if the Nile no longer flows here? Are you able to drink seawater in this age?"

"More motors," Gabriella told her. *"They power huge hydraulic pumps that bring the water in through pipes—like the aqueducts."* She tried to visualize the city's water supply but found it difficult. She didn't actually know all that much about the modern conveniences most of the city enjoyed. And she found what she did know conflicting with the images Cleopatra held of the deep, vaulted cisterns underpinning the entire city since it was first built by her ancestors from the plans of Alexander the Great. *"Your cisterns serve no more purpose than to attract a few scientists and some visitors who marvel at them. My colleagues have mapped only a few, though tales are told of many more. During the wars, when bombs were dropping"*—she visualized planes dropping bombs and felt less incredulity than she would have thought from the queen who had known Greek fire—*"they were reinforced, and people went below to shelter in them. They are mostly empty now— you can stand in the water if you want to risk schistosomiasis or worse. They've been filled with silt in some places and collapsed in others, but they're still like magnificent underground cathedrals,*

vaulted temples that never see the sun and no longer touch the Nile."

"Yes," Cleopatra said. *"Very much like temples. Not Egyptian temples in design, perhaps, but I have always felt that the scale on which they were built owed something to symbolism as well as practicality. Our people were very much intrigued by the underworld. Alexander planned one for them in the very design of the city. But I am surprised that you say you have mapped only 'a few.' The cisterns contain many cells, but these are built along grids, and the grids intersect. I have signed orders and approved plans for their repair and improvement, and it is essential that they be accessible to one another. How else would our city's workmen maintain them? How else would the water settle evenly throughout?"*

"Yes," Gabriella said. *"Privately, some of us have discovered that. But there is no funding for the officially sanctioned exploration needed, so my allies and I have found different uses. I think you'll approve."*

"I'm intrigued. I also wonder—before you found the cisterns, did you find my Alexandria? Even from here I can see there's very little of it left."

"As you saw, the royal quarter was totally destroyed, and whatever remains still lies in the bed of the bay. That is why it's empty now. We are hoping to resurrect your city as it was and make an exhibit for visitors from all over the world to see. Your help with that will be invaluable."

"I look forward to it already," Cleopatra said as politely as if they were meeting at a dinner party instead of inside the same skull.

"Much of the rest of the old city has been subsumed in the building of the new. In the late twentieth and early years of the twenty-first century, my predecessors in this area concentrated on what they called 'rescue archaeology.' When a new road or large structure was constructed, or old structures were torn down, if the contractors ran into anything indicating an ancient site, they were required to allow us to excavate the site first. There was little time to do it and less money, but much of what we know about the ancient city now

was either discovered or verified at that time. I can show you much of what they found when we go to the Biblioteca next week."

"And my tomb?"

"Leda and your counterpart made rather a mess of that site, so some of my colleagues are now gathering more information from it. The bulk of the work, examining your mummy and the papyri we found with it, are ours to investigate at least initially."

"That is fitting."

Gabriella's home was humble and, though the queen did not express it that way, funky, compared to the palace, but it had effortless comforts the Lady of the Upper and Lower Nile had not enjoyed, at least, not without employing a lot of servant power, like hot and cold running water and lights in every room, not to mention the water closet. Cleopatra liked that very much. They had had toilets of a sort in her day but not like the ones invented by Thomas Crapper.

Gabriella made a point of visiting with each of her resident "relatives" and mentally introduced the queen to them. *"This is the current Auntie Jasmin. She is supposed to be mute because actually she's Syrian."*

"How is it that your aunt is Syrian? And why is she current?"

"My aunts are well-known to be very traditional Muslim ladies who wear heavy face veils in public. Therefore, I have an extra aunt or two who can change depending on who is staying with us at the moment. No one is the wiser since no one besides us ever sees this aunt unveiled."

"Ah."

The food was simple, but it did not give heartburn, and the bed was luxurious indeed. They fell asleep, thinking to dream of Antony, but actually they dreamed about Portland, Oregon.

For the first day or two, Gabriella toured the city, particularly the dig sites showing remnants of Cleopatra's day. She slipped in with a group of tourists to see the virtual-reality re-creation of the temple of Heliopolis that had been discovered at Abu Qir. They stood on a platform and looked out into an empty room that turned into a great temple, the white pylons carved and painted with hieroglyphics and pictures of the gods.

Cleopatra was astounded. *"What magic is this? May we enter now?"*

"No, because it isn't really there. It's not magic, though. If we tried to step off this platform, we'd find that the first step could be our last."

"Ah, the temple is a mirage, then? I thought so."

"Yes, but it's a man-made one. A computer simulation projected holographically onto the space in front of us."

"But it is not magic?"

"No. Although I admit it seems like it. I can do some of this sort of thing myself, though on a much smaller scale."

"Show me!"

"It is rather tedious, actually. Let's wait until we return to work. So, tell me about Heliopolis. The people who discovered the underwater ruin think it disappeared around the same time that your reign ended. Is that true? Did you worship there?"

"More properly you should ask was I worshiped there. And no, I was not. I know that it once was there, but not during my life nor, I believe, during my father's."

Their touring was cut short by a message from Gabriella's contacts, informing her that she was needed to travel to Port Said to rendezvous with a certain lady from the Saudi royal family. The lady wished to escape her illustrious family and seek asylum in the West. Once Gabriella met her, the lady would be disguised in a full burkha as Gabriella's maidservant while the two of them traveled to the isle of Delos. A large part of the island was owned by Gabriella's aunt and coconspirator, Contessa Virginie Athene Dumont. Virginie, Ginia to Gabriella, would arrange the Saudi lady's passage to Western Europe or America. All of this Gabriella imparted to Cleopatra as they traveled.

"*It is good that you are being introduced to my other work at such an early stage in our relationship,*" Gabriella told her. "*I wanted to blend with you as much for this, for your strength and ingenuity, as I did for your knowledge of the scrolls.*"

"*I also think it is good,*" Cleopatra agreed. "*This aunt of yours, you trust her? In my experience, sharing a blood relationship constitutes no high recommendation.*"

Gabriella bit her lip, considering. "*The truth is that she did betray me. But she was blended then, and it seems that the aberration was caused by her blended entity. She had the process reversed. Never, before or since, has she shown any other sign of untrustworthiness. She has always been as passionately devoted to this cause as I. And so, so—I choose to trust her. I place my life and those of the women we serve in her hands. Besides, she is well placed to transfer the women, and we have a good cover. I cannot do this alone, or even with you. It takes many bodies in many places to snatch these women from the claws of an unjust system. We do not all know each other, but it is necessary, here, that Ginia and I work as a team. So, yes, I trust her. I more or less have to.*"

On the trip to the port, Cleopatra exhibited considerable curiosity. "*You say the woman is royal. What harm would befall her if she is unaided? Is she competing with her siblings for the throne? I can well sympathize with that!*"

"*No. In our time, in these lands, women don't have thrones, though sometimes they have titles. This lady is a princess, actually, but she is still pretty much a prisoner most of the time in her own home.*"

Cleopatra lost interest at that point, her voice no more than a quiet musing that to be royal was to *be* a prisoner.

Driving along the coast, however, Gabriella saw mirages at sea. If she forgot to blink, barges and battleships, yachts and cruise ships were replaced in her vision by primitive sailing ships with banks of oars on either side. That would have been interesting if she could have stopped to enjoy the historical vision she was being treated to, except that the road also disappeared if she did not maintain strict conscious control over what she saw. As they neared the ferry to Port Said, the traffic became thicker, and Cleopatra became rather agitated. *"What is that body of water?"* she asked, looking south toward the Suez Canal. *"When did this city come to be?"*

But at last they reached the rendezvous point, and Gabriella gave the Saudi lady the new papers that had been prepared for her. The lady almost blew it at the duty-free shop, forgetting for a moment that she was supposed to be a servant and therefore not able to buy every luxury that caught her fancy. To make things more difficult, Cleopatra was curious about each thing the woman eyed and demanded interior explanations before causing Gabriella to laugh uproariously or admire extravagantly, drawing unwanted attention to herself and her "servant."

The customs inspection was more rigorous than usual. Though the agents expressed little interest in Gabriella and the Saudi lady once they reached the checkpoint, it took them over two hours standing in line to pass through the gates and meet Ginia's yacht.

"What's the holdup?" she heard a tourist ask another one.

"There's been some trouble with some characters trying to blow up the canal," replied a red-faced man. "Seems they found the explosives before any damage was done but didn't catch the terrorists."

Gabriella was more annoyed than alarmed. Someone was usually trying to blow up the canal, it seemed. They boarded the yacht without incident, and the lady was duly deposited on Delos. It was quite late when they arrived, so they spent the night. Cleopatra was curious about the island. She was of Greek heritage, but although she had spent time in Rome, she had spent almost none in the land of her ancestors.

Ginia said, "Perhaps you—two—would like to come

with me when I feed the cat colony, Gabriella. That would allow you some new perspective on the island. Afterward, I can have the copter return you to Alex."

"When did you start feeding cats?" Gabriella asked.

"Around the new year. I had one neighbor who used to do it, but she died over the holidays. One can't just let them starve. Come, you'll enjoy it. They're wild, but they became quite used to her and are coming to know me as well."

Gabriella and Cleopatra were both charmed when Ginia led her niece to the ruins of an ancient temple. They were suddenly surrounded by cats of all sizes and descriptions. Though some of the cats had tattered ears and battered coats, most appeared sleek and well fed. Both Ginia and Gabriella had carried sacks of food up the hill to the ruins, and now Ginia gestured Gabriella to go away from her. "Feed the smaller ones and the kittens while I distract the big handsome brutes," she said.

The cats purred ingratiatingly and regarded their server with large round amber eyes. Cleopatra purred within Gabriella. *"It is fitting to be welcomed back to the world of the living by the acolytes of Bast,"* she said, stroking cat heads with her knuckles while her palms dispensed largesse. *"One can learn much from cats. Grace, dignity, playfulness, independence of thought and action while appearing to acquiesce to those stronger. Unfortunately, most of my illustrious royal ancestors never got past the stage where they ate their young."*

Later that morning, as Ginia's private helicopter lifted up over the island, Gabriella looked down to see a single black cat sitting atop a column, as if awaiting worship. Its fellow cat colonists might never have existed.

By the time they landed, Mo, who was actually named Mohammed, had returned to Alexandria with the taxi and picked them up at the airport, then returned them to the villa in time for the afternoon meal.

Gabriella said to those around her, "And now, I must

return to work. The queen awaits my personal attentions."
It was a little joke on more than one level, and Gabriella's
Egyptian aunties smiled and nodded and urged her not to
tire herself, she'd get wrinkles.

Mo again drove her in his taxi. She told Cleopatra that
her cousin always stopped work to eat with the family and
returned to the main part of the city afterward. Since he
owned his own cab, he set his own schedule. Cleopatra approved of the private driver, even though he was a relative.

As prearranged, a message was left at a certain souvenir stand in the souk, inside a particularly cheap and
gaudy vase. When the customer for the vase bought it, he
passed it on, and the person to whom he passed it also
passed it on until finally it was read. "It is done. She is two.
They are four in three."

CHAPTER 4

It was a stirring service. The remnant of Duke Hubbard blended with Gretchen Wolfe didn't know whether to be embarrassed or pleased that Gretchen kept bawling every time someone eulogized him.

She wasn't alone. Four of his ex-wives showed up, as well as all of his kids and his grandkids. The street outside the church looked like a parking lot for cop cars, and a mounted unit directed traffic in the church's lot. Representatives from every law enforcement agency in the state were there, most of them guys he'd worked with in some capacity or another. Even the sun darted out briefly from behind the clouds in honor of the occasion.

The sheriff told a funny story about watching him subdue a prisoner. The minister delicately skirted the issue of how many wives Duke had had and anything about which children he had by them, and concentrated on his widow and grandkids.

"*Hey,* Frau Doktor, *dry up. You're drowning out the preacher,*" he finally said to Gretchen. "*Look there, that's Cherie, my widow. Cute, huh?*"

"She dresses as if she is going to a party, not your funeral," Gretchen sniffed.

"Well, it's not a funeral, remember? Just a memorial service. And she knows how much I liked seeing her in blue . . ."

Rusti and Leda sat with the family in the pew in front of Gretchen's.

When Gretchen began crying again, Rusti blew her nose and whispered to Leda, "So you never told me who Gretchen *is* anyway. Another of Daddy's conquests?"

"Oh no, she's happily married to Wilhelm Wolfe, my—used-to-be—boss. She and Daddy are—were—very close, though—I mean, before he died. Not like the rest of his women. Gretchen's a real soul mate." Leda caught the look Duke/Gretchen cast at them and winked. Tearfully, but it was a wink.

Then a friend of Duke's got up and started telling everyone about the Officer Hubbard coloring book he had written and illustrated in Duke's honor. He talked about the times Duke rescued pussycats from burning buildings and all the kids he'd befriended, even after he busted them.

Gretchen howled.

"What's the matter?" Duke asked her. *"They haven't told any of the embarrassing stuff yet."*

"Nein, nein, it is how they love you, how they respect you. To think I almost refused to help you, and you are such a good man—were such a good man."

"Yes, well, now I'm part of a good woman and a fine physician. It could be worse."

Afterward there was a ten-mile motorcade to the veterans' cemetery, with highway patrol blocking the entrances to the freeway between the church and the VA hospital at the extreme diagonal end of Portland. No one was letting a little thing like the lack of a corpse deter them from giving him all the pomp and ceremony of an officer-killed-in-line-of-duty funeral, even if it was a memorial service. They were

going to plant a headstone so everyone could come and visit. That was nice. There was some advantage to having your services take place eight months after you died. People had time to prepare to do things right.

Even Duke choked up a little—or choked Gretchen up—when the police pipe band played "Amazing Grace."

By then the rain was splatting down by the teacupful upon the roof of the little stone grotto where Leda joined the family to stand in line to receive condolences. Cleopatra, shivering as the goose bumps rose on Leda's skin, complained, *"Your father could have died a second time by drowning had he been here. We should have worn a cloak."*

Leda said, *"Nah, he was an Oregon native. He knew how to swim and walk at the same time. A cloak would have looked suspicious. People are gobsmacked enough to see me in a dress."* Rusti had bought a purple-sprigged white number for her especially for the service.

As folks filed away and before Gretchen could open her/their mouth, Duke latched on to Leda and Rusti. "Let's go get something to eat at the Peking Palace. I'm starving," he said.

"And you, *liebchen,*" Gretchen added to Leda, "You look as though you need feeding. You look so cold, and you have lost weight. You are getting enough sleep, *ja?*"

"I try," Leda said. "But my body can hardly keep up with all the activity in my head, and when I do sleep I wake up, well, let's say less than rested. But do you really think I've lost weight?"

"*Ja,* yes, I think so, yes."

Rusti said, "That's real nice of you to invite me, too, ma'am, but if it's all the same to you and Leda, I'll pass. I'm on nights, so I need to grab a quick nap then get to work."

"You can't pass," Leda told her. "I'm riding with you, remember?"

"No problemo, kid," Duke said, then corrected in

Gretchen's voice, "*Liebchen*. We are having here an international driver's license, *ja?*"

"Portland can be tricky," Rusti said, sounding concerned and guilty.

"We can manage—with Leda's help."

Rusti seemed a little freaked out and almost burst into tears again when Gretchen threw her arms around her in a hearty bear hug. "You know, for a little bit of a blond thing, you hug a lot like my daddy," Rusti told her.

Gretchen smiled Duke's smile as Rusti dashed up the hill, carrying her purse over her head to keep the rain off, and scrambled into her car. She caught Gretchen's fatherly smile as she adjusted her mirror. Her eyes widened, then she shook her head and returned the smile with a weak and watery one of her own, waggling her fingers in farewell.

Once in the car, Leda said. "I feel shitty for not telling her. But I don't think she'd understand anyway."

"Besides," Cleopatra added aloud, "she might betray us. You never know with family."

"What a thing to say," Gretchen clucked.

"Yeah," Leda said. "Cleo's family's even crazier than ours. Although *they* believed in giving each other quick, comparatively painless deaths instead of lifelong torture like we do. But the last thing she remembers, she lost a war, had her husband die in her arms, and committed suicide. Then when she joined me she found out her kids had been killed. It's enough to upset anybody. On top of which, we're now broke."

"*Ja,* I know. It is a terrible thing, what the board of directors has done. Wilhelm is beside himself with worry and anger. To be treated so, a man of his experience and contribution to the company! They are mad, the board, to do this to him and to Chimera."

"They sure are. What will he do now?" Leda asked. She hadn't really thought twice about Wolfe.

"Oh, they have sent him to a seminar—remedial management or some such nonsense. It is humiliating for him, but he agrees to it so that he maybe can help you or some of the other blended people if they need him. So foolish are the people in charge now that they may expose blends sometime in the future."

"Surely not? After all they've done to keep it a secret?" Leda asked, but not incredulously. Helix was starting to make the U.S. Navy, from which she was retired, look sane and logical by comparison.

"First we eat. Then I will show you already what is happening. Is there somewhere we can go that is secure?"

"Yeah. Rusti's deck. It's got a roof over it, so we'll be fairly dry. If the rain isn't enough to drown out any bugs, there's the dog next door. He never stops barking as long as someone is out there. Although why anyone would want to bug me when I was just fired, I don't know."

"Even if *Fraulein Doktor* Calliostro doesn't realize your importance, there are those who will," Gretchen told her. The voice was Gretchen's, but the concerns and priorities sounded like Duke's. "So, we will go to Rusti's deck where the dog will bark and we may pet your *Katzen*. Your papa, he misses his Boris."

"I hope Cherie is taking good care of the old rascal," Duke's voice said, just before they got out of the car. He'd have to keep quiet while they were in the restaurant and remember to let Gretchen speak for them both. His voice coming out of a petite blonde was bizarre enough to attract unwanted attention.

"Rusti says Boris sleeps in your chair and smacks anyone else who tries to. Cherie has not let him ride your bikes however."

"He's a safe enough rider, but his claws are hard on the upholstery," Duke said.

"How many *Katzen* do you have, Leda?" Gretchen asked.

"Two who feel like forty," she replied.

"I actually had forty living in the palace," Cleopatra said. "More or less, depending on the crop of royal kittens and the number who left us to bless other homes. They were closely associated with Ra, as you know, Leda, and kept down the vermin, though alas, only the varieties with four or more legs."

Michael Brody Angeles did not find the sniper who ended his boss's hegemony over a portion of the Mexican drug trade, nor did he stick around long after the murder to ferret out the shooter. Leave that to the police and the *federales*. Hell, it could have been the *federales* who offed Espinosa. The job was not one Angeles planned to put on his résumé anyway. It was a stopgap between the revolutions, juntas, and other paramilitary operations that he joined to make use of what he considered to be the only real skills he had.

It was not a way of life guaranteed to make you a real happy, trusting sort of person, but he chose Egypt for a new base on the strength of a newscast and a long-ago unconsummated love affair. He was old enough and experienced enough to know that it was a flimsy thread on which to hang his future, but he had a sentimental streak that would probably be the death of him.

He needed to get the hell off the American continent altogether. It wouldn't take Espinosa's old friends long to gather intel on him and his past connections to U.S. law enforcement, nor would his fellow bodyguards fail to remember that he had been very unhappy about the way the last operation went down. He was going to take the blame, like it or not. He had to get away fast if he was going to survive. Espinosa's business had long tentacles.

Back to the States was not far enough. Besides, he had to

work. Being the bodyguard of a drug lord in Mexico was one thing. Working for organized crime in the States in any capacity was not something he cared to risk.

All of this had gone through his head in about two seconds as he stood at the airport counter while everyone else was busy looting *Jefe* Espinosa's body outside. That's when he recalled seeing Leda on a TV newscast. She was a big shot archaeologist now, actually the one who had discovered Cleopatra's tomb. A lot of time had passed since they'd been on shipboard together, but she might be able to help him for old time's sake. If not, the Middle East was certainly a market for mercenaries. And from what he'd heard, so far Egypt wasn't anywhere near as bad as Iraq, Iran, or Syria.

So he bought the ticket for Cairo and caught a train to Alexandria, hoping she'd remember her old shipboard almost lover.

Almost because the Navy frowned on that kind of thing, not that it had mattered much to him. But while Leda was funny and offbeat, she was disciplined about all the little rules he liked to test. Especially when he drank. So after several memorable evenings together, they went their separate ways. He was dropped into the South China Sea on a mission. She wasn't. It was that simple.

They didn't meet up again. And after he spent seventeen years in the Navy, won three silver stars and a Purple Heart as a SEAL in 'Nam, he was dishonorably discharged as a liberty risk because he drank. The little prick who brought the charges against him that ended his naval career was too young to have been in a real war. Hell, he hadn't even been to Saudi freaking Arabia.

Once he got to Alex, he asked around, but the word was that Leda had already gone back home.

So there he was in a country he'd visited only briefly in

the past, with no connections and a limited visa. What he really wanted was a drink. He'd slept on the plane, and that had kept the urge under control.

He'd stopped drinking and gone to his first meeting the day he left the Navy—or it left him. Just on principle. They said he didn't seem to be able to stop, and he had to prove to himself that he could. Now, wanting a drink, he set about finding a meeting.

Used to be he had to go into a bar to get the right contacts for a new job, but nowadays, with everybody so health-conscious, even guys who faced lead poisoning or worse on a regular basis, a twelve-step meeting worked just as well. The same people you used to meet in bars were at the meetings. What was left of the same people. The ones who hadn't stopped drinking were mostly dead.

He stopped at the American Express office and used the courtesy computer to find the time and location of the next meeting near his hotel—10:00 P.M. at the Palais Ptolemie conference room. If he hustled, he could still make it.

The tough part was crossing the street. Alexandria traffic was almost as good as a junta for getting the old adrenaline pumping. He'd been here once before on another mission, several years ago. Now he took a deep breath, squared his shoulders, and stode across the street as if he owned it. Nobody braked for him, but the cars somehow dodged around him, and the donkey carts slowed until he passed. By the time he stepped into the door of the Palais Ptolemie he was sweating despite the comparative cool of the evening.

The chairs set up in the conference room were about half-full, which wasn't bad. Not entirely to his surprise, most of the members were male, his age or younger. Most were foreigners like himself. He guessed that quite a few of them were armed. He was not. He'd had to leave in too much of a hurry to pack. His favorite sidearm was in an airport trash can in Mexico City. He probably could have taken it past the security guards but it wasn't worth attracting attention to himself. He did not wish to be detained in Mexico.

He took a seat next to a suit, a guy maybe in his late twenties, early thirties, good-looking, good manicure, swarthy, dark aggressively curly hair that hadn't seen a barber lately. Mike remembered when he had looked kind of like that, young and hot instead of just burned-out. During the formal part of the meeting, which was conducted in English, the guy introduced himself as Galen. He had a little tic at the corner of his left eye.

Mike didn't see any of the mercs he remembered from his previous gig in Alex, though he did notice one Arabic-looking guy who didn't introduce himself. Nor did the leader of the meeting ask him to. Which was real strange.

Mike filed it, but he was there to make contacts, so during the social part of the proceedings, he asked, "So, Galen, you from Alex?"

"Me, no! I am from Athens. My boss died unexpectedly while we were conducting business on his yacht in the western harbor. He died before—you would say payday?"

"Bummer, man. I'm out of work, too. My boss is also recently and suddenly deceased."

"A wonderful thing, these meetings," Galen said. "We all have so much in common. My boss, though, it wasn't sudden. He was old and had been sick a long time. It was a near thing for me really, that he died when he did. It wouldn't have been worth having all his money to have that old crocodile inside me."

"That kind of business, was it?" Mike said, backing off slightly. "I'm straight myself, but hey . . ."

"I do not mean he wanted a homosexual relationship with me," Galen said stiffly. To Mike's amusement he even seemed a little shocked. "No, it was something else. Very strange. You probably would not believe me if I told you, but actually, I can still go to a certain place and request that some famous dead person's spirit be implanted in my body along with mine."

"Do tell?" Maybe Galen wasn't gay, but what he was saying didn't make a lot of sense. Not that it was unusual for Mike to meet people who said odd things that didn't seem to make sense.

"You don't believe me." Galen sighed and shrugged.

"Not at the moment, but I'm willing to be convinced," Mike told him. "How about a cup of coffee after the meeting, and you tell me all about it?"

"You are buying?"

"Oh yeah. My boss was more considerate than yours. He didn't get killed until after payday. So tell me, any leads on a new job?"

"Maybe one. Let me speak to someone, and perhaps he will meet us later."

That was how it usually worked with the small jobs. With the big ones they just came in wherever you were working and recruited you on the spot. So this was probably some two-bit deal, but Mike couldn't afford to be choosy. A new job would do more than provide him with income. He ought to be able to score a firearm and a new cover out of it as well. He would feel better when he had both, even this far from Mexico.

CHAPTER 5

The Chinese restaurant was as gilded and dragon-ridden as Leda remembered. They sat down in a booth still wet from the clothes of the previous occupants. Genuine carved wind dragons presided over the red vinyl cushions. The authentic speckled Formica table was streaked from where it had been hastily wiped, and smelled faintly of disinfectant. Some people liked greasy spoons. Duke's style had always been greasy chopsticks.

Gretchen ordered Duke's and Leda's favorites for them all and when the mounds of food arrived, dug into it with relish. After six or seven mouthfuls though, she laid the sticks across her plate, looking very sad.

"What's the matter?" Leda asked between bites of kung pao chicken and pork fried rice.

"It does not taste good with Gretch—*mein* mouth. She—I—have never cared for Chinese food. It tastes bitter to me. This is apparently a matter of the body chemistry instead of simply preference."

"Poor thing," Leda said. She finished quickly, and they drove toward Rusti's.

"I am still hungry," Gretchen declared. "We will stop at the market for some snacks, *ja?*"

Leda wasn't hungry but she was always interested in snacks, so she splashed into the store, too, and waited at the checkout stand while Gretchen gathered her goodies.

She almost wept at being in an American grocery store. It was so full of all kinds of stuff to eat, most of it bad for you, but also, there at the checkout stand was a rack full of magazines including her four favorite tabloids.

With fond anticipation, she read their idiotic headlines. MARILYN REBORN AS 450-POUND SUMO WRESTLER. Hmmm, they were reaching for it even more than usual these days. FINALLY I HAVE ELVIS INSIDE ME! CRIES FAN. IF JFK RUNS FOR PRESIDENT AGAIN, WILL HE WIN EVEN THOUGH HE'S NOW A CHINESE-AMERICAN DRAG QUEEN AND A REPUBLICAN?

Not as enjoyable as usual, these headlines. She bought all of the magazines, sagged against the wall opposite the checkout counters, and read the last paragraph of each story. Yep. Just as she thought. They were all about supposed blends who wanted to exploit the past fame of the blended guest. They didn't go into detail about the process or where it came from, but they were describing blends, although sometimes in hokey magical terms. Yuck. She hoped Chimera didn't read tabloids, because these would not make the scientist happy.

Once they were in the car again, she told Gretchen about the articles. Frau Wolfe shrugged. "*Ja*. We know. Wait."

They pulled into the driveway at Rusti's during a lull in the monsoon. Her cats, Newt and Zul, started yowling before Leda could unlock the door. "They're starving," Leda said, opening the door and turning on the light. Two cats, one black and sleek and one fluffy orange tabby, both well fed to the point of pudginess, sat calmly blinking up at her. "Hi, guys, miss me?" she asked.

Gretchen bent and scratched the orange one behind the ears.

"Don't make a pest of yourself, Zuley," Leda said. As she bent to pet Newt, she accidentally brushed the mountain of mail Rusti had stacked by size on her desk. Leda had been too tired even to look at it the night before and didn't even want to think about the phone messages filling an inch-thick pile of Post-its. Her past correspondence sins of omission had caught up with her. Starting with the graduation invitations and ending with the junk-mail catalogs, the envelopes avalanched to the floor. The cats were delighted and began pouncing at the cascading paper, catching credit card solicitations in their paws and playing them like mice, shredding catalogs, and generally making a mess of Rusti's entryway. Leda bent and picked up as much as she could carry, ripping her *Archaeology Today* from Newt's claws.

She carried the armload of mail to the glass wall with the French doors leading to Rusti's deck. More of the missives showered the cats as she tried to open the locked doors without using her full hands. Gretchen finally got the hint and came to her rescue. The two of them slipped through the doors and out onto the deck without any cats escaping, mainly because the cats jumped in the air and ran down the hall when they heard the dog next door begin his alarm. The deck's roof dripped beads of rain in a steady curtain, too thin and not noisy enough for privacy.

Leda's dress was soaked and the afternoon chilly. She stepped back inside and grabbed the horse-patterned woven tapestry from one of Rusti's easy chairs.

Gretchen didn't seem to mind the weather. She sat down on the step leading to the covered hot tub and opened the lid of her laptop computer, which Leda hadn't actually noticed her carrying before.

"You're going to check your e-mail?" Leda asked. "For that we need to listen to Fang next door?"

Gretchen grabbed the hem of Leda's dress and pulled her down onto the step, then pointed at the screen. One by one she clicked on the messages, which looked to Leda like spam.

"Young and Gorgeous" the subject line read. "But nobody took me seriously until I got an amazing personality transplant. Instantly I became more intelligent and interesting, and a better conversationalist . . ."

"Increase Your Charisma! You too can be fascinating simply by hosting one of hundreds of exciting historical celebrities!"

"Important People Want to Get to Know YOU!"

"THIS is how they're advertising a process that cost me every cent I made in Egypt?" Leda asked.

Gretchen shook her head. "These messages do not come from Helix. We were able to trace the messages to contract employees for several other major international corporations, however, some of them owned by Helix board members."

"Hmmm," Leda said. "Sounds like the board members took the process out of Wolfe's hands so they could pirate it."

Gretchen's word choices, if not her actual voice, were Duke's when she replied. "Yes, it does. But so far as our sources can tell, no one else is actually performing the blends. They're sure advertising them though. And what's even weirder is that *these* messages are coming from some of the same sources."

"Protect Your Individuality! Don't allow others to steal your precious DNA codes. Following these simple procedures and using our patented device, you can ensure that your hair and nail clippings, bodily fluids, and other code-bearing personal discards are destroyed immediately . . ."

"Need More Money? Part-time work as a motel maid at select locations can earn you Big Buck$$ for simply using our kit to collect trash your guests dispose of!"

"What?" Leda said. "No advertisements for grave robbers and body snatchers?"

Gretchen dismissed this by snapping the computer lid shut. "Already Helix has done this since the process was developed. It is nothing new. However, what is new is that some of the people who have been blended have disappeared."

"How can that happen? The people who get the blend are mostly pretty high-profile, just because they have to be rich enough to afford the process," Leda said. "Why hasn't there been more in the media about it?"

"A good question. Each of them is supposed to be away on a holiday, or a business trip, but when the place is contacted, they are not there. Their cell phones, faxes, and e-mails go unattended. And yet, no one seems concerned. Decisions are made by underlings or 'instructions' are supposedly sent from the missing person, but no one actually sees this person, not even paparazzi."

"If the paparazzi can't find them, then they're *really* missing," Leda agreed. "Maybe you ought to go keep Wolfie—Wilhelm—company at that business seminar he's taking."

"So we have already decided," Gretchen agreed. "Although Wilhelm is not blended, he is a logical target. Fortunately, our blend was never official, so no one in the company now knows of it. Not even Wilhelm. So! We have arranged for people we trust to track our movements. But also we wanted you to know of this. You have all of our numbers. If you cannot reach us by any of them on any given day, contact this number. And be very careful yourself. We have no clear idea what is happening or why."

"You got it," Leda said. "And on a less dramatic and more practical note, I have to ask for a small loan. Calliostro left me high and dry."

"That is definitely my kid talking," Duke's unaccented voice said. He laughed. "We were prepared though. We'll just dig into Gretchen's magic pocketbook here."

"That's definitely my *dad* talking," Leda said, nostalgia roughening her voice. His women's purses had always been a source of extra funds for Duke, whether to treat the children and later grandchildren or to buy a new motorcycle.

"A thousand dollars U.S., this is enough, *ja?*" Gretchen's voice asked.

"It will help. I guess I'd better start looking for a new job."

Gretchen departed, and Leda looked after her feeling troubled and sad. Sure, Daddy was blended with Gretchen, but it wasn't entirely the same. And despite the occasional flash of clear communication from her dad, Duke and Gretchen increasingly seemed to her to be truly blending as Chimera intended people to do rather than staying distinct personalities, as they had at first. Oh well, Daddy had always got himself all wrapped up whenever he had a new wife—even though in this case it was someone else's wife—so it wasn't as if it was anything new.

She sighed and was trying once more to wrest her mail away from the cats when Rusti's phone rang.

"Hello, this is Iris Morgan from the Osiris Agency again. Has Dr. Hubbard returned as yet? I need to speak to her very urgently, as I've mentioned."

"This is Leda Hubbard. How can I help you?"

The woman on the other end said, "I am so happy finally to speak to you. As to how you can help us, I am calling on behalf of the producer of a new series for Edge TV. You've heard of Edge?"

"No, I've been out of the country," Leda said. Jet lag was making her stupid now. Some of what the woman said didn't register. "Is this Edge a new cable channel? If so, you're wasting your time. It's no good talking about signing me up for any new cable service now. I haven't found a place to live yet . . ."

Iris Morgan laughed a laugh that reminded Leda of Billie Burke's as Glinda the Good in the old *Wizard of Oz* movie. "Dr. Hubbard, I assure you I am not a telephone solicitor. Edge is already available on most standard cable and satellite hookups both in the States and in the British Isles. But I'm not calling to sell you anything. I'm trying to arrange a meeting between you and Roland Bernard, the Emmy-award-winning producer of the upcoming series he wishes to discuss with you."

Leda gulped and told herself to be cool. "I suppose this relates to the discovery of Cleopatra's tomb?"

"Yes, indeed. Mr. Bernard is in Kennewick, Washington, at the moment, meeting with one of our consultants. He would like me to arrange a dinner meeting with you as soon as possible. Is tomorrow out of the question for you?"

"I had a hot date with my sister at Burgerville, but I'll see if I can get out of it."

The Billie Burke laugh again. "I'd say to bring your sister, but she'd probably be bored with the business end of it."

"She's working evenings this week anyway," Leda said, not that the woman was interested or really needed to know. "Where does he want to meet?"

"We'll send a car to pick you up about seven. Is that okay?"

"Sure."

"I'm so glad to finally get to speak to you, Dr. Hubbard. I look forward to learning more about your work. Good evening."

"You, too," Leda mumbled, distracted by Cleopatra in the background moaning, *"What will we wear? You have no gowns, no jewels, not even cosmetics!"*

"I've got this dress," Leda said, looking down at the purple-sprigged number which by now looked as if she had worn it on a campout instead of to a funeral. Cleopatra's silence said as much. *"It'll wash!"* Leda told her. *"And I have lots of jewels. They're out in Rusti's garage somewhere. Packed. Besides, it's not a date, it's business."*

"So was meeting Caesar. So was meeting Antony. Business, both meetings. I did not dress to please myself. I dressed to impress upon those I was meeting that I was a wealthy and formidable queen whom they would do well to impress. Has Rusti any milk?"

"Why? Got cookies?"

She opened the refrigerator door, revealing rows of bottled water and beer.

"How about beer?"

"To bathe in?"

"Oh, puh-leeze! Forget it! We're lactose intolerant! We'd probably get hives or something. And Cleo, about the wardrobe, getting ourselves rolled up in a rug is out of the question, just so you understand."

CHAPTER 6

Mike and Galen easily found a beachfront coffee shop with a view of the excavation in the eastern harbor. The excavation somewhat marred the ocean view farther out because it was lit with floodlights. These were not only to keep looters at bay but also illuminated the area for the evening crew of archaeologists who prowled the scaffolding on the ocean floor like a particularly sophisticated ant colony.

Mike admired the pragmatism of the folks in hot climates who were neither mad dogs nor Englishmen. They sensibly retired indoors during the hottest part of the day and to compensate extended both work and social activity late into the evening.

A waiter arrived carrying a water pipe. Galen looked inquiringly at Mike.

"Never touch the stuff," Mike said. "My late boss—well, to tell you the truth, Galen, I was scraping the bottom of the barrel there. Working for the boss of a drug syndicate is just not *me,* though no offense if that's what you were doing."

"My boss took many drugs. He was a very old, very sick man," Galen said. "I would not say he was above trafficking in them, but that was not his business when I worked for him." He pulled out a pack of cigarettes and extended it to Mike, who waved both palms in a negative gesture.

"No thanks, I don't do that anymore either. I may have failed to die young, but I figure if I keep off the booze and smokes, I might still stand a chance at making a good-looking corpse someday."

"If you disapprove of drugs, what did you do for this boss of yours?" Galen asked casually, though Mike knew he was deliberately probing with something in mind. The kind of mercs who attended the meeting where Galen was were not casual people.

"Oh, bodyguard stuff. Not my kind of thing. Usually dull, and you have too high a profile walking beside the big man all the time. The cops take an interest that reflects badly on your character if you know what I mean. Also, if your boss takes the bullet, and you don't, there's always some ally or enemy ready to correct the shooter's mistake. Which is my present problem. The law is actually the least of my worries right now. I was hoping to find something that would get me out of sight, let the regime change without me around to, uh—influence the investigation into the gentleman's death."

"Ah, I understand. My boss's business is now being fought over by my former associates. Me, like I said, I wanted no part of the old man's proposal."

"You've got me all curious about that, buddy, I have to tell you. What is this about the boss wanting to get into you in other than a uh—loving—way?"

Galen tapped his cigarette lighter on the table, corner after corner, rotating it in his fingers and sucking on the cigarette as he considered the question. "My boss was like many rich old men—he had everything except his youth and health. He thought he had found a way to attain those and live on in one of us. There were three others and me he had handpicked. I do not believe he picked us because he thought we were the most worthy to succeed him, as he said. He picked us more on the basis of our youth and looks and—endowments, if you will pardon my immodesty."

Mike raised both eyebrows. "More power to you, man."

"We attended a very strange meeting with him at a company called Nucor. He was on the board of directors. Even so, this company had very strict rules, so he spent a great deal of money to be sure that we could be present at the meeting. He had to buy us each what they call a 'blending.' What he wanted was for them to take his DNA and blend it with one of us, whichever of us decided we would accept both his presence and his empire—"

"Whoa, whoa, back up there, Galen. How does this thing work, this blending? How would the guy's DNA get into you anyway?"

"They have a machine that makes it so that the DNA can enter your brain through your eyes. It implants the memories and personality characteristics of the person whose DNA you get on your own—consciousness, I suppose you would say."

Mike gave a low whistle. "Very sci-fi."

"Yes, but it's true. I know he was interested in Cleopatra but not for himself. No, he admired no one enough to take them into him. He wanted to join one of us. Creepy, is that the term?"

"Very creepy indeed. Cleopatra huh?" Under his breath he muttered, "Goodness gracious shit oh dear, it certainly is a small world."

"Yes, he even kidnapped a couple of women and the head scientist at that company. And some old fellow, a security guard, the father of one of the women, ended up dead. I think that was an accident, but it was a big mistake.

The daughter unplugged my boss's life-support machines. That woman brought the world down on the old man's schemes with everything from the police to the curse of the pharaohs."

"What did she look like, this woman?"

"Nothing special. She had hair like a Grecian or an Irish girl—very thick and dark, but she was American. The other woman was Egyptian. The doctor was from Tibet, I think. Why?"

"If she brought down your boss, I want to make sure and avoid her." Changing the subject, he said. "So, are you going to go have yourself—what is it?—blended?"

"Absolutely not, though I could. I have their card. I can think of no one I wish to inhabit my body with me. Can you?"

"Not offhand. Seems a shame though. You could maybe get the DNA of one of the old pharaohs, find out all the secrets, where treasure is buried, that kind of thing. You'd never have to work again."

"Maybe not. But I like to work."

"Yeah, me, too. So, how about it? You got something going?"

"Hmmm, yes, maybe. A Muslim group, not all of them Egyptian but all Middle Eastern. Unlike a lot of the organizations, they don't seem to have any problem hiring Europeans. I can put in a word for you, tell them you're interested. My contact is bringing more details of the first assignment to the meeting next week."

"Yeah, that'd be great. You're a pal."

"Where are you staying?"

Mike told him, and Galen shook his head. "Pricey. Your money will not last long there. I know a place that has room and is cheap, with a maid, too."

"Cool. Lead on, brother."

Everything was great till they crossed the street. This time of night, around eleven, traffic was not as thick, but because there was more room to move, the vehicles went a lot faster. The coffee shop, being on the beachfront, was on the water side of the Corniche, the main drag running east to west, separating the water from most of the city. Galen moved into the street with assurance, obviously used to it. Mike was taking a deep breath, getting ready to brave it, when the lorry came barreling around a corner. Galen was on the other side of it, and Mike didn't see his prostrate body getting further mashed into the pavement by other oncoming vehicles, so he figured his new buddy had made it.

Then he saw him leaning with his head against a streetlamp, his arms hanging at his side in apparent limp relief.

Mike seized an opening in traffic and sprinted over to him. "Hey, man, that was a close one! You okay, Galen? Galen?"

Galen had nothing to say for himself. Mike touched him, and Galen fell forward, which was when, by the silvery glow of the streetlight, Mike saw the big dent in Galen's forehead and the weird angle at which his once-sculpted nose listed. His eyes were wide-open and already starting to glaze over.

"Damn, buddy, you didn't have to take it so hard," Mike said, and pulled Galen's arm around his own shoulders, dragging him into an alley as if he were passed out drunk. He checked to make sure they were unobserved. A lorry that looked very much like the one that Galen hadn't dodged drove by the alley's entrance. It was going fairly slowly compared to the rest of the traffic. Mike ducked back behind a pile of rubble and other stuff he didn't even want to think about. All he could see, between the darkness of the evening and the shadows in the lorry's cab, was a reflection off a pair of eyes watching the side of the street instead of the road and the glow of a cigarette tip. Then it was past.

Mike dragged Galen back a little farther to make sure they were well concealed, and rapidly searched through his clothes. He had to hope that his radar was off and the lorry driver hadn't just done a hit on Galen. If Galen was on someone's s/hit list, then his death would have been in vain, at least as far as Mike was concerned. But the man was between jobs, for one thing, though past grievances weren't out of the question. However, the lorry hadn't exactly plowed over him and backed up. It just knocked him headfirst into a pole. Nobody was *that* good at making something look like an accident. Of course, that could be why the driver came back, if it was the same one.

Mike considered the risk for a moment, then shrugged and continued collecting Galen's effects. What the poor guy no longer needed, Mike sort of did. Like a wallet containing a passport, international driver's license, a small amount of Egyptian currency, Mike wasn't sure how much, just offhand, three business cards and oh, joy! A sidearm and shoulder holster. A nice little Beretta Model .380 caliber fully loaded with fourteen rounds of Glazer ammo. A bit on the antique side but plenty of stopping power. The blue-tipped Glazer rounds, hollow points filled with lead BBs, could do as much damage as a .357 Magnum. He put on the shoulder holster and Galen's suit jacket to cover it, though it was hotter than hell even in the cool of the evening. Stuffing the other items into his own pockets, Mike propped the body up until he located the nearest manhole, which was, fortunately, almost at the entrance to the alley. Then he dragged Galen to it and shoved him in.

He went back to his own hotel and studied the documents. With a few items easily found at a copy shop, he could doctor the ID to be his very own. He and Galen were similar in height, weight, and coloring. He would have to cover up his own white hairs and act more—boyish?—to make up for the age discrepancy, but otherwise he could use it all. He turned his attention to the business cards. Abdul Mohammed, Antiquities Consultant, Abdul Mohammed, Antiquities Consultant. Two of them. This was no doubt the dude with the job. The third said simply, Chimera, Nucor, and an address on a corporate Greek island. He started to toss it, then stuck it back in the wallet. He'd hang on to it, just for grins. You never knew what might come in useful.

He found the address of Galen's lodgings stuck inside the passport and moved his stuff over there after seeing that nobody was going to question him. The Egyptian bohab, sort of a combination security guard and caretaker at the apartment building's gate, seemed to just assume a new European was moving in and he had somehow missed the going of the last one.

Mike altered Galen's papers while waiting for the meeting. When the time came, he returned to the Palais Ptolemie conference room and looked around. The guy who hadn't introduced himself was there again and again there wasn't a peep out of him while everybody else stood up and said, "Hello, I'm so-and-so, and I'm an alcoholic." Sometimes friends came along, too, but they usually identified themselves as such. This guy just pretended to be invisible. After the meeting was over, the fellow was still hanging around, looking a little puzzled.

Mike walked up to him and said, "I'm taking a wild guess here, but are you Abdul Mohammed?"

His eyes narrowed at Mike. "I am. And you are Mike, I heard you say. However, I was expecting that Galen would be here again."

"That's why I wanted to meet you. It was Galen who

suggested I contact you about the job. I'm afraid he had to go underground for a while—quite a long while."

Cleopatra's narrative:

Rather than spending the day in preparation for our momentous meeting, as I counseled, Leda declared that we were out of some medicine she required and must "take the bus to the VA."

It would have taken less time to cross the desert on a camel! The bus—a large rectangular vehicle holding far more people than any conveyance I had previously encountered, save only the airplane—was not entirely to blame for the length of our journey. We arose early and walked to the clear wall of glass, parting it to step out into the new morning. The rains of the previous day had been replaced by sun and only a little wind to chill our Egypt-warmed blood. Having ascertained that we would not be rained upon, we instead drenched ourselves with water in what Leda refers to as a "shower," washed and dried our hair, dressed in one of the dowdy ensembles she has worn since first I joined her, and walked briskly to the place the bus was known to frequent.

When it arrived, we stepped into it and put money into a container. We did not even get to sit down but, because of the crowd, stood all the way, clinging to seat backs and hand straps when the bus's passage was less than smooth. It stopped many times during our journey, to dispense and admit various people. We crossed a broad river on a ribbon of gray stone containing many many other conveyances, all wheeled and all roaring.

This bridge of stone was one of a family of such bridges lacing the river like a Roman sandal. Looking down the river, one could see them all clearly arching across, the traffic parading now steadily, now erratically, back and forth across the waters.

At long last the bus climbed a steep hillock atop which sat
two palaces larger than any I had ever occupied. These were
also joined by a bridge. This city is very fond of bridges, it
seems, even to span dry ground.

We entered one of these buildings. Leda said this is
where military people go when they are no longer serving
but require the attentions of doctors. For soldiers who needed
doctors, these people appeared to be remarkably healthy and
whole to me! Most had the majority of their limbs still firmly
attached. Many were quite old, a condition seldom seen in
soldiers of any nation in my experience. They sat around the
corridors like so many courtiers awaiting the pleasure of
their pharaoh. We made our way to a line of people, and
stood behind the last of these. Moving gradually forward, at
last we came to an opening in a wall where two people stood
receiving the people in the line. Leda submitted her request
for the medicine she desired. Instead of handing it to her,
the people merely acknowledged that she had spoken. She
accepted this and walked into what appeared to be a banquet hall. We sat at a table and read from a book she brought
along for that purpose. It contained a fantastic tale of a land
preserved by dragons from periodic rains of what seemed to
me to be Greek fire. The dragons communicated with each
other and their riders in somewhat the same way that Leda
and I communicate, except, of course, that a dragon and its
rider did not share a body. I thought this might be an entertaining place to visit and wondered if this land was far and
whether or not it had a library where we might study.

Every once in a while, as we read, Leda would look up at
a screen set high above our heads over the doorways. The
names of people appeared there. When one's name appeared,
one's medicine had been prepared, and one might return to
the window and accept it.

By the time we received the containers of medicine, the

dragons had flown to the star dispensing the Greek's fire, we had imbibed two cans of a sweet "soda," devoured a bag of salty vegetable chips and two bars of chocolate. We had also made three trips to the lavatory. But at last we had the precious pills and returned to the street to once more "catch the bus," though no catching was required as it stopped at its accustomed resting place.

This bus traveled past many shops with colorful garments in the windows. Had I had my way, we would have disembarked and used some of Gretchen's money to purchase a suitable raiment for the evening. However, Leda would not move from her seat.

We returned to Rusti's by five in the evening, to a house silent except for the mews of greeting from the cats and the barking of the dog from the adjoining house.

The purple-sprigged gown was in Rusti's washing machine. Its background had been white. However, before her departure, Rusti apparently decided to toss in some new facecloths she had recently purchased. They were of a special manufacture, imported from China, and yet they bled their colors onto our one good dress.

"That settles it," I said. *"Rusti must die."*

"I tend to agree," Leda said. *"But we should wait until she pays the rent this month, so we will have a place to stay a while longer."*

"You are very devious," I congratulated her.

"I have another idea you're going to like," she said. *"As you have gathered, I am not much for buying clothing unless it is purple or has a cartoon logo across the front of it. My sister, on the other hand, is a clotheshorse. We are approximately the same size, give or take a diet here and there. I'm sure that in exchange for her life, and because of the contrition she will no doubt feel when she learns she ruined our one good dress that's not in storage, she won't mind if we raid her closets."* Following this pronouncement, an evil

cackle escaped our lips as we hastened to pillage the closest wardrobe.

Garment upon colorful garment was pulled from its hanger and held before us. All of the colors in the fanned tail of the peacock were represented. A blue of marvelous brightness, a green heavily spiced with yellow, a deep turquoise and a lovely rust orange. Other garments were the pink of flamingos and an even stronger purple pink that could rarely be glimpsed on the horizon as Ra arose and retired. Ra's own brilliant yellow color was also represented, and scarlet and, of course, purple. After much discussion, during which I refused to allow us to don several far-too-casual and concealing garments of lowly cloth that Leda favored because of their purple color, we settled on a scoop-necked sleeveless bodice of the peacock blue that flowed loosely over matching trousers. Our body's legs are long and the hips small, so trousers are quite becoming. Leda would have been quite content with this, but I found another treasure—a flowing knee-length robe that draped from the shoulders with delicious suppleness and cupped our forearms in bands of iridescent blue much the same hue as our trousers. The robe was figured with swirls of design in the same blue, and turquoise, and, to mollify Leda, purple. The background of the material was sheer as my finest linen gown, but a soft fur of velvet comprised the multicolored designs. Once we had selected these clothes, we shed them again and padded barefoot to the garage, where, after much cursing and more death threats against Rusti, Leda located her cache of jewelry.

Never had I suspected that she would own such splendor! With her modesty in matters of clothing, I expected she might wear a small chain or two, perhaps an extra pair of earrings, but in this I was mistaken. True, there was little gold or fine metalwork among her treasures, though what there was often was silver, far more precious in my country than gold, which was plentiful and common. But what she did possess was to my eyes even finer. Pectorals made entirely of interwoven beads of glass in even more delicious colors than Rusti's wardrobe, earrings of the same manufacture and brilliance, with long tubular beads that swung to our shoulders. She had many many examples of each and, best of all, most of them bore the sacred symbols of my kingdom. "Compliments of my friend the beader," she said.

"We should commission more bracelets and perhaps a circlet for our hair," I suggested, gleefully adorning us with a pectoral bearing kneeling and winged Isis flanking, to my pleased surprise, my own cartouche. Leda wore only a plain wrist chronometer she called a watch (I suppose because it watches the passage of the sun and moon to interpret the time of day for the wearer) and an even plainer band of some silvery metal with a man's name engraved upon it.

"*My watch and my POW bracelet will do nicely, thanks,*" she said with all of the agreeableness of a bad-tempered camel.

"*We need not remove them,*" I assured her. "*We could simply overlay them with finer jewels.*"

"*I guess you haven't been here long enough to hear that less is more,*" Leda said with a superior air.

I had no answer for such a ridiculous statement. It had the strange effect of plunging me into gloom. This new life was so odd, so very different from all that I had known. Spending the day in Leda's pastimes and personal concerns, exploring her everyday life insofar as she had one at this time, had been soothing. I had not thought of my lost family and kingdom, at least, not often. This life is so different it is like a dreamworld, where I need not concern myself with memory or responsibility. I had, of course, exercised my vast knowledge of the more superficial womanly arts to prepare us for the evening to come. But not once had either of us broached the subject of the evening's serious business. For the most part, I would need to disguise my presence and allow Leda to conduct our end of the conversation. I would help her with negotiating the final agreement, of course. I have learned from her memories of her past dealings that she is often too modest or too solicitous of the welfare of others to obtain the most favorable conditions. This particular pact dealt with my life, my tomb, and my reign, however, and I therefore felt entitled to negotiate my own terms. I only hoped she would agree.

"Okay, what's the matter?" Leda asked. I found myself staring out of our eyes straight back into them again. *"See? Mascara! Eyeshadow. Lipstick. I've been using cosmetics for the last five minutes without a peep from you."*

"Perhaps shock will explain my silence?" I suggested facetiously. I did not attempt to obtain her cooperation beforehand, for I knew that whether or not she gave it, she would do as she felt best unless I could override her objections when we both understood the situation.

"Very funny. I think we look fiiine," she said, twirling.

At that moment, a chime announced the arrival of our transport.

Have I yet mentioned the speed at which these vehicles travel and the vast distances they cover in little more than a few heartbeats? The distance from Rusti's house to the city is almost as far as from Alexandria to what is now called Cairo, and within that distance there is also a mighty river with which to reckon. And yet, this is done effortlessly, casually, almost thoughtlessly.

Before our trousers had a chance to crease, we were handed out of the long black vehicle Leda calls a limo and into the care of a uniformed guard in front of yet another palacelike structure. A hotel, Leda said. This one was much more like an actual palace than the VA hospital. Here was luxury in rich woods and deep, patterned carpets over marble floors. Clever candles kindled by the scientific magic of electricity sparkled from a thousand tears of crystal illuminating our path from above.

As we entered, a woman dressed in a long scarlet gown split to the hip turned, smiled, and waved to us. At her neck and fingers jewels shot back the light from the chandeliers, matching the crystal teardrops in their brilliance. Her hair was black and fell in curls from a jeweled hair ornament. Her body was slender, and the gown well became it, but her movements were more purposeful than graceful. Glancing at her feet and noticing the severe elevation of her sandaled heels, I was somewhat surprised that she could walk at all.

"Dr. Hubbard, there you are!" she said when she drew nearer. She held out her hand. "I'm Iris Morgan."

Leda extended our own hand to shake hers and said her name in exchange for Iris Morgan's.

"Mr. Bernard is having a short business meeting with our financier, so it fell to me to come to meet you. I am, of course, delighted." She sounded ever so faintly annoyed to have been excluded from the business meeting, however.

She led us around to some carved wooden doors and pressed a button with the finger of a hand bearing long nails that matched her gown. From behind the doors issued a groan and a few clicks, then invisible servants opened them and we entered a box whose other side was glass. This box ascended upward and ever upward, climbing what seemed a mountainous height while we looked down upon balcony after balcony of rooms, and farther down into a banquet hall filled with people. At last, when I thought we were going to meet Ra himself, the box stopped, the invisible servants once more opened the doors, and we stepped out into an impressive hallway in which a single door faced our glass box.

"Oh ho, the penthouse no less!" Leda exclaimed, and gave a low and quite common whistle of appreciation. From this I gathered that in her culture chambers that are high in elevation are also elevated in status and, as we were soon to see for ourselves, luxuriousness.

CHAPTER 7

Gabriella was accustomed to doing her most serious work, the nonadministrative part, after everyone else had gone home. After her leave of absence, she had been kept so busy with meetings, trips to the field, fund-raising, and other tasks that she could only give Cleopatra a brief introduction to the museum. Even so, the former queen was verbally and visually impressed with the newest version of the library that had once been her pride and joy. *"How beautiful! This building is not like ours, of course, but it has lovely lines—a lovely skeleton, you might say. And oh, look at that! How ingenious! The scrolls are cut into small pieces and set between boards so you need not unroll them. Very clever."*

All week long as they worked in the crowded offices, schmoozed with patrons, discussed acquisitions, Gabriella had chortled gleefully to her secret friend. *"They would be thunderstruck to know you are here. I wish we could tell them."*

"The time will come," Cleopatra said.

But after ten days, the novelty of Gabriella's more public duties had worn off. Just before closing time, she arrived at the Biblioteca dressed in her real work clothes—a pair of grubby trousers she wore on digs and her Marvin the Martian T-shirt. The contents of tombs tended to be extremely dusty, muddy, or otherwise untidy, at the very least. Some of the items she'd examined from the discoveries uncovered when the sewer pipes had been moved were far worse.

"Where are my scrolls?" Cleopatra asked as soon as they entered the library that evening. Gabriella had promised they would spend the night in study, as indeed she needed to do. The scrolls held priceless knowledge, and the longer they were left unattended, the more chance there was that they would be damaged and some portion of them lost forever.

"They're in the basement, waiting for us to translate them and prepare them for display," Gabriella told her. *"We should get to it while we have the chance."*

"My—body—is there as well?"

"I believe so. Unless someone has moved it in my absence. It was supposed to be kept below until we could study the mummy's wrappings and the charms and amulets that might have been wrapped with them. You did cause charms and amulets to be wrapped up with you, didn't you?"

"Oh yes, certainly, and I would very much like to find the amulet with Antony's hair so we could remake him again."

"Let's wait until the place empties out a bit. I don't want us to be interrupted when you first behold yourself again. In the meantime, we can translate."

Gabriella turned to a side door and a flight of steps leading downward. The building was new, paid for in part by generous contributions from foreign investors such as Nucor. One of the chief glories of it was lost to the patrons above. Instead of a drafty subbasement, this new museum boasted climate-controlled workrooms with lighting that was adequate for reading ancient script but sufficiently diffuse to avoid harming brittle old manuscripts and artifacts.

Gabriella's workstation was crowded with urns from Cleopatra's tomb. *"Where shall we begin?"* she asked, surveying the veritable Dead Sea of scroll-filled urns.

Cleopatra studied the wax seals of the urns, then brought one of the vessels over to the table. *"This one is from the library at Pergamum. After Caesar accidentally set fire to part of our collection, the Pergamum one claimed to be greater. Antony brought it back as a gift for me from Asia Minor. I never really got the chance to examine the volumes yet, however. That's why I had them in my tomb. Something new to read in the afterlife! Let's see what they have to say."*

Slipping on a pair of white gloves and placing a respirator over her mouth and nose as she opened the urn, Gabriella set to work. Soon both she and Cleopatra were so absorbed in the translation that they didn't notice the time or that the creaking and groaning of footsteps, and even the roar of the vacuum cleaner in the hallways, had ceased.

However, when the scuffling and whispering began upstairs, she looked up from her translations.

"Something is wrong?"

"Yes. No one should be here but us."

She picked up the receiver of the telephone on her desk to call the police, but the line was dead.

Reaching into the desk, she drew forth a little revolver and started for the door.

"There are many whispers. How can we face them all with that small weapon?"

"We probably can't. I just want to get a better idea of what's going on."

But suddenly there were footsteps on the stairs and half-shouted commands. To her horror, the men behind the footsteps and voices seemed to be heading for her office. But one room short of it, they stopped.

"The mummy!" Gabriella and Cleo thought simultaneously.

"There it is. The infidel bitch's mummy. Grab her and let's go."

"*We must stop them,*" Cleopatra said.

"*Yes, but how? Whoever they are, they will be armed and there are several of them and we have only one body. When they leave, we'll get to a phone and notify the authorities.*"

"*How I long for the days when* my *authority was all that was needed. But I understand. They must not know we are present. I have only begun this life with you. I do not wish to end it quite yet.*"

"*We are in perfect agreement on that issue.*"

The men's steps seemed lumbering and clumsy as they passed the office door. She heard the rattle of falling objects and tried to imagine what they might be.

From upstairs there was more scurrying, more whispers, and then quiet. As soon as the men in the corridor outside her office left, she would try to escape through the main building. Their footsteps began climbing stairs, the grunting more pronounced.

"*Hmph,*" Cleopatra said, "*I was not that heavy fully fleshed. They make a great deal of fuss over hauling a mummy that must be as light as dried leaves.*"

A door opened and closed, and for a moment there was silence. Gabriella rose and crept to the door, listening.

Which was fortunate because she heard more footsteps from overhead, voices, more footsteps and then, after a moment, a brief scuffle.

Merde alors! *The bastards are working in shifts!* Gabriella thought.

With the help of Duke's contacts in Helix security and Gretchen's deep purse, they had no trouble learning where Wolfe supposedly had gone to attend his seminars. The only problem was, he wasn't there.

Not that the receptionist and later the seminar leader were much help. "Very sorry, *Frau Doktor* Wolfe, but *Herr* Wolfe has not attended our sessions for several days."

"He is ill? Where is he?"

"I cannot say exactly, *Frau Doktor.* He was not ill when last I saw him. I saw him argu—having a discussion with—Dr. Bartoth, one of the board members, and I do not recall seeing him after that."

"This Dr. Bartoth, he can be found where?" Gretchen asked with a raised eyebrow.

"I'm not privy to that information, *Frau Doktor.* Excuse me, but I have a session to lead just now." He turned on his heel and left.

Gretchen started after him, but Duke said, *"Whoa, there, partner. I don't think he knows any more than he's telling. Let's see what we can find out about this Bartoth and have a chat with him, shall we?"*

"It is wrong, Duke. I am thinking maybe he has been made to vanish like those other people. We are too late."

"Don't get too hasty. My wives had to hunt way harder than we've had to when I wanted to get lost."

"But my Wilhelm does not wish to be lost! He would call me."

"He lost his job. Maybe he's at loose ends just now. But you're right in thinking it's a little fishy."

"It is whole oceans full of fishy, my friend."

"Something we can do real easy is check your joint bank account. See if he's made any withdrawals. Of course, if he's on company business still, they'd pick up the tab, but if he just decided to get lost . . ."

"This he would not do. But yes, we will check."

But Wilhelm Wolfe had not touched his and Gretchen's joint account in several weeks.

Gretchen was not the sort of female who cried at the drop of a hat, but she was seriously raising their body's blood pressure with her anxiety.

"Look here, hon, getting all uptight is the last thing you should

do right now. You're a doctor, a scientist. You do investigations of your own to find out what your patients have. We use the same kind of attitude when doing a police investigation . . ."

"Missing persons, you are saying?"

"Any kind. *We've already started following the first rule, which is not, you'll be glad to know,* cherchez la femme (Duke was pleased that his association with Gretchen had given him a pretty creditable accent when he used a French phrase these days. Had he still been alive and in his own body, that could come in useful when *he* wanted to cherchez some femmes, but these days, he didn't have to cherchez very far, being something of a femme himself, at least superficially). *It's follow the money. The next thing we should do is talk to some more of our well-bought friends at Helix and see if we can access his company credit card records."*

"You are not thinking he is buying things for another woman?" she asked, the insecurity that had led to her blending with Duke surfacing again.

"After all the little things we've taught him recently? I don't think so. If ever a guy looked like he could have his cake and— uh—eat it too, it was Willie. I mean, of course, from what I could tell after everything was over and you were both dressed again and had the lights back on."

"You peeked!"

"Would I do that?" he asked innocently, but she could tell of course that he was lying. He even meant for her to know that. Ah well, she was a doctor after all, and they did use all the same organs for everything else now. Why not?

"Why, *Frau Doktor!* We're blushing!"

Ja, it was so, but she didn't mind too much. It made her feel rather deliciously naughty—kinky, as they said. Good! She saw Wilhelm so seldom that it should be memorable when they did get together. It was for her, certainly, and Duke, who was in an excellent, uh, position, to know such things, felt that it was for Wilhelm as well.

"No, *the point is that if he's spent money on his company card, we'll know it's probably business but also it will tell us where he's been, if not where he is right now.*"

But several hours later and many dollars poorer, they learned only that Wolfe's company credit card had not been used since before he left Kefalos.

"*I'd almost rather we hadn't found that out after all,*" Duke said grimly.

CHAPTER 8

By the time he was hired, and Abdul Mohammed and his buddies explained the mission to him, Mike was sorry he had ever followed up on the lead, sorry he had ever heard of Abdul Mohammed, sorry he had ever met Galen, and sorry that he'd come to Alexandria.

He didn't like the sound of this operation at all. These guys were going to make their points by blowing up ancient Egyptian national treasures. The political and military targets were too well guarded, and lately even the tourists had the special tourist police force shepherding them around like border collies. The group had tried to blow up the Suez Canal, but all that had accomplished was losing several of their younger and more foolhardy "patriots" to martyrdom aka suicide. Not that anyone actually explained all this to him, but he could tell from the pointing at the maps and floor plans, the body language, and the Turkish Arabic from his boyhood as a Navy brat. The others all seemed to assume that he didn't speak Egyptian, which was true enough. But he could make out some of what they were saying nonetheless.

The target of this mission was the newly expanded and remodeled Biblioteca Alexandrina library/museum complex in the heart—or maybe more accurately the brains—of the city. The library and its satellite museums had been built in the late twentieth century by UNESCO. In the meantime the older museums, the Graeco-Roman among them, had fallen into disrepair, their buildings plagued with leaking roofs and damp basements. The recent earthquake had been the kiss of death. Now their collections were to be housed in the Biblioteca as soon as the construction was complete. So much of Egypt's most recent history as well as the more distant past, was stored here, along with the manuscript collection.

Despite the fact that a lot of the manuscripts were sacred Islamic ones, the terrorists considered the library a juicy target. Abdul Mohammed explained to Mike that because of the holy texts the destruction would be selective and limited. "Charges will be set here," he said, indicating a map, "and here and here. But under no circumstances will they be set here. Therefore, we will exit under the wing of Allah." He smiled at his little wordplay.

Once the mission was under way, however, Mike knew that something was rotten in Alex. His suspicions were amply confirmed when he smelled the BO of his attacker as the dude tried to slip a garrote around his neck. Swearing mentally since it was hard to do so physically with his wind cut off, Mike stepped back into his attacker close enough to feel if the guy really loved his work, stomped hard on the man's instep, used the slack his backward move had created to twist, grab, and throw his attacker.

Much as Mike would have liked to inquire how he could possibly have offended his bosses so deeply as to be on their hit list this early in the operation, he couldn't risk letting the guy answer. The answer would be to yell at his buddies and bring their multiple wrath upon Mike's head, and that would not do. So he recycled the garrote, a piece of piano wire, in an environmentally sensitive if violent manner, and dragged the corpse to the nearest mummy case. The mummy didn't take up much room anymore and didn't make any complaint about a bunk buddy that Mike heard, so he hauled his would-be assassin up and tipped him in on top of the older resident.

What a revolting development. But Mike couldn't say he was exactly amazed or astounded that one of his supposed criminally bent copatriots of the revolution would try to do him in. Nor did he think for a moment it was something he'd said or a simple personality conflict.

He had no doubt that old Stinky there was following a set of orders completely different from his own. In fact, he suspected the whole mission had lost something in the translation. What he was told probably bore little resemblance to what was actually going down.

What this was supposed to be about was a little looting to fund The Cause with negotiable collectibles and a couple of small strategic explosions so the organization could claim credit for the coup. Terrorist groups liked doing that so the government would know exactly who was harassing them. He thought he'd understood someone to say they were going to swipe Cleopatra's newly discovered mummy and hold the old girl for ransom. Given what Galen had told him, it would be interesting to see who paid up.

He didn't like to think that Galen had set him up—probably Galen was the original candidate for Dead Employee of the Month. Hmmm. He needed to reassess the goals of the organization he thought he'd just joined. They would not be taking credit for this operation after all. They wanted *him* to take the credit. Which probably meant that his body would have been unrecognizable as that of a murder victim while at least providing some clue as to his identity as a Westerner. If Galen was to have filled the role originally, probably any non-Muslim fundamentalist more-or-less-Western guy would do. An infidel barbarian running dog capitalist lickspittle lackey American boy such as himself must have been a real bonus. No wonder these people had seemed so damn friendly when he was briefed on the mission.

He'd thought it odd at the time. Friendliness was not actually one of the characteristics he expected from terrorist employers; but then, it had been so long since he had been in the company of anything remotely resembling genuine friends that he was willing to settle for "not openly hostile." You just checked the hand patting your back for cutlery first and smiled back. It was still war after all. The only thing about this kind of war was that it was far less clear where one side began and another ended. He should have realized something was wrong when it was just the driver, himself, and the "security specialist" in the minivan earlier on. When he asked where the others were, he was told that they were already getting into position at the site, but there hadn't been enough room in the van, so it had come back for the two of them. He hadn't actually ever seen the other conspirators yet. He'd just assumed they were around. Everyone was to meet back at the souk two streets over, where the minivan would be waiting to whisk them away, out of sight of police cars and fire wagons.

His particular assignment had been to stand watch while the security specialist, the same guy who tried to kill him, disabled the alarms at the Museon. Afterward, his understanding was that the remaining terrorists were supposed to flit about like so many bad fairies swiping stuff, setting explosive charges, and committing acts of seemingly senseless destruction. He was sweating from more than the heat as he reasoned that what was left of his own personal person, had the strangler had his evil way with him, would no doubt be discovered in the destruction caused by a far larger explosive charge than he had been led to expect.

Mercy. His trusting nature had betrayed him again. He, or rather, his mangled American remains, was supposed to take the blame for destroying these priceless artifacts—part of an American plot to—what? Mistreat and burgle the downtrodden Egyptian government again or some such happy horseshit as that.

It really didn't have to make sense when you were dealing with people who were inclined to hate you at the drop of a hat anyway.

He kept his—Galen's—sidearm handy and skulked around among the mummy cases and other exhibits. He had the odd feeling that he was quite alone, however. The others were supposed to have waited until the alarms were dismantled to come in, but that had apparently been a lie. Maybe the alarms had been dealt with earlier. No one had come past him, but there were many entrances and exits within the Biblioteca complex. But if anyone else was there, they were better at covert ops than he was because he didn't see a soul. He did, however, become aware of a faint ticking. Feeling a bit like Captain Hook when the croc came to call, he tracked the noise to the first of the explosive devices. Hmmm. These people had gone to a lot of trouble on his behalf. They'd apparently not only dismantled the security system but also preset the charges so everything would be ready to go as soon as he was dispatched and his corpse left to take the blame.

The bomb was a primitive satchel charge, a pound of Semtex wired to an alarm clock timer all in a handy carrying case; but its crudity wouldn't have kept it from making ancient hash of the contents of the building. He found it behind another mummy case and disarmed it. The case was an old metal lunch box, which would have made great shrapnel. Picking it up by the handle, he carried it with him. Should he and the library survive the night, he didn't want some unsuspecting kid picking the thing up tomorrow.

He himself was perfectly comfortable carrying the bomb along with him, swinging it a little as he walked. Demolitions was a specialty of his. Modesty prevented him from putting it on his résumé—that and caution. But like most boys, he liked explosions. As long as he was not the one exploding. Maybe one of these days he'd retire and return to 'Nam and disarm land mines so schoolkids could plant trees there. That idea was as close as he got to the white picket fence, wife, and kids. He'd tried the wife and kids part, and it hadn't worked very well. She didn't appreciate explosions. Especially his explosive temper. Not that he laid a hand on her, but he yelled a lot and stomped around and she got scared and took his little girl and disappeared. He hoped wherever they were they were going to Al Anon.

Bomb number one had had five whole minutes remaining. That was probably enough time for a prudent man to break a couple of display cases, grab some of the gaudier loot, and escape with his epidermis intact. Normally, Mike considered himself a reasonably prudent man. He liked breathing well enough. But the truth was, he knew he should have been dead many years ago and many times since. It didn't especially bother him. What did bother him was being set up, betrayed, discriminated against, dammit, because of his race, nationality, and, well, lack of religious affiliation.

He knew it was juvenile to decide to show them what they got for messing with him, but there were certain kinds of impulses he didn't even try to control. The best payback here and now was the complete failure of their mission. It was a gamble. If they won, he didn't find all the bombs in time and one of them blew him up. If he won, none of the bombs went off, and nobody found anybody's body except maybe the guy in the mummy case after he got even stinkier. The whole carefully orchestrated mission would be a non-event, and he was just the guy to make it all *not* happen.

First he had to find the other charges. If he were a bomb, where would he hide in this building? Ah yes, the little red circles Abdul Mohammed had pointed out on the floor plan as being the sites for the explosives. From what he could recall, and he did pride himself on a photographic memory where such things were concerned, the first charge had been in one of the specified locations. So he set out for the other sites, stalking the building as silently and swiftly as a very hungry leopard who really didn't want to screw up catching dinner.

He kept moving and kept listening hard, hoping the other bombs had clocks, too—and that they weren't digital.

It didn't matter in the end because they were more or less where they were supposed to be, at the strategic points that would cause the most damage to the most area. He located three more devices, all larger than the first one he'd found. The last one he disarmed with half a second to spare. He cringed when the time expired and had his fingers halfway to his ears, but there were no explosions. With a deep sigh, he stood and began looking for an exit. Which was when he spotted the open door under the EXIT sign. Hmm. Here he was with a fistful of satchel charges and no place to dispose of them. The basement might be a good place. There could be another sewer or maybe an incinerator—that wouldn't set off the Semtex. Nothing would except an electrical charge. As he approached the doorway, however, he saw that there was a light on down below. Surely his former colleagues were not still hanging around? If they were, what joy would be his!

At first the hallway appeared to be deserted, though he spotted an open door. Then another one opened and a slender dark-haired woman in khaki slacks and a Marvin the

Martian long-sleeved crew-necked T-shirt stepped into the hall. She looked as surprised to see him as he was to see her, and a little squeal of despair escaped her. Cute. But she wasn't supposed to be here. Nobody was supposed to be here. She pulled a gun on him.

"I have a pistol," she said redundantly.

"I see your pistol and raise you four pounds of Semtex," he said, brandishing his bombs. "Who the hell are you anyway?"

"I am Cle—I am Dr. Gabriella Faruk, and I work here. Who are you? is more the point."

"Never mind that right now. You didn't happen to see a bunch of terrorists go by recently, did you?"

"I didn't see them. I heard them, though. My mummy!" she suddenly seemed to recall a previous problem and darted into another room with an open door. He followed her. An empty sarcophagus with a splintered lid and some flakes of dried bandage were at the center of the room.

"Looks like it walked away," he said.

"We must have it back. It is my—the mummy of Cleopatra VII, Queen of Upper and Lower Egypt . . ."

She sounded as if she were about to list the queen's other titles, but he grabbed her arm in the hand that wasn't holding the Semtex, and said, "No use crying over spilt mummies, Doctor baby. We need to vacate the premises before someone decides to come back and make sure we join her majesty in the Land of the Dead."

"There is a way out into the courtyard back there," she said. "The ones who stole the mummy took it that way. Alas, we will not be in time to see where they go."

She hurried on ahead. He spotted something gleaming in the light still glowing from the open office doors. He stooped to pick it up. A little golden winged scarab set inside an ankh. There was a bail attached, as if it might have been a pendant of some sort at one time. It looked old and valuable, and he had gone to a great deal of trouble with no other tangible reward, so he tucked it in his pocket and followed the doctor's shapely butt up the stairs.

Once she reached the courtyard level, she turned toward the street, but he caught her arm and pulled her back.

"But we need to call the police."

"*You* need to call the police. I need to avoid them, and I have a couple of other things to do. And you'll want to be alive when you call them, so I suggest you follow me so we can avoid being intercepted by the guys who set these." He jiggled the satchel charges. "I expect at least some of them may be waiting over there, across from the entrance, wondering about now why the library has failed to go boom. They could decide to come investigate."

"You know an awful lot about these people for someone who wants to avoid them," she said sourly.

But she followed without further comment as he led her to the street behind the Biblioteca, then circled around the entire complex via side streets until they reached the souk. His leadership and mastery of the situation was marred only because he had to ask her which streets would take them back where he wanted to go.

When they reached the souk, he looked around until he spotted the minivan parked in a deserted alley a block or so away from the main body of the marketplace. This was where he had been told it would be. He supposed they saw no reason to lie to him since he was supposed to be in several inanimate pieces by now. "You go ahead and make your phone call, Doctor. I have a little chore to do."

She gave him a short, quizzical glance, then walked away into the marketplace in search of a phone or maybe a police station. He turned to his own task at hand.

He had the wires from the Semtex in his pockets. Selecting one of the charges and one set of wires, he rigged it to the ignition of the minivan. "Go with Allah, you mothers, if he'll have anything to do with you," he muttered with a final twist of wires.

Then he walked into the souk and found a booth carrying suitcases, one of which he purchased and into which he popped the Semtex packages. It also carried veils that hung from a rod and concealed him while he watched the van. Before too long, his supposed coconspirators, with the notable exception of Abdul Mohammed, returned to the van. Mike supposed that since they didn't bring the mummy with them, the boss must be disposing of it in some other fashion. The men were arguing among themselves in fierce low voices and climbed into the van with much gesticulation and probably a little name-calling, from the look of it.

He felt the heat of the blast through the veils and pretended to go lookyloo with the rest of the crowd, which was the least conspicuous thing to do.

Gabriella Faruk also came running. He caught her before she reached a policeman. "I don't think you're gonna need them right now, Doc. I just took care of most of your problem."

"But my mummy!" she said.

"I have a good idea who has it and how to find him."

He thought she'd be full of questions, but instead she grabbed his arm and dragged him toward a taxi that was pulling up as close to the souk as it could get. "In that case, you must come home with me. We have much to discuss."

Leda let Cleopatra take the helm as they entered the penthouse suite. The queen had been doing that sort of thing her whole life, after all, and had restored some of the grace Leda had lost during years of study and occasional illness, the stiff knees and stiff back from leaning over books and corpses.

Two men sat in leather chairs flanking a fireplace lit by

a bonfire's worth of white candles ensconced upon a leafy wrought-iron screen. One of the men sprawled sideways in his chair with his right leg hooked up over the arm. He was wearing khaki Bermuda shorts and in case she was in any doubt about his identity, a white T-shirt with PRODUCER ON THE EDGE written across the front.

The other man she also recognized, though she hadn't seen him on any *Time* or *Fortune* covers lately. Andrew McCallum was the same freckled, jug-eared, red-haired boy wonder he had been then. Now, however, silver threads gleamed among the copper, and his face had a maturity more evident in his expression than complexion, lines, or lack thereof. She had never seen him in person before, but her first thought was that the pictures didn't really do him justice. He was a lot more attractive than depicted, and it wasn't just because of his billions. He was dressed a bit more formally than Bernard, in nice trousers and a jacket that was Harris tweed, unless she missed her guess. The effect was spoiled slightly by the waffle stompers on his feet, but she'd heard somewhere he lived in Scotland most of the year now, so maybe he was what they called a hill walker. He rose when she and Iris Morgan entered the room. Seeing the men's attire, Leda was glad she wasn't quite as overdressed as Iris.

"Dr. Hubbard, we're so delighted you could make it," McCallum said, sounding rather formal but still quite a lot warmer than Bernard, who waved and pointed to his cell phone, which was jabbering away at his right ear.

"It's nice to meet you, Mr. McCallum. I didn't realize you would be here."

"Oh yes, Edge TV is one of my projects. A market for my screenplays if nothing else. I've been branching out into more creative pursuits since—well, we'll discuss that later. Drink? We have wine, bourbon, Scotch, of course, or sherry if you prefer?"

"I like a nice ale?" she said hopefully. This time it was Leda of course, not Cleopatra.

"I believe we can have some sent up. Excuse me just a moment." He picked up the house phone, and said, "Is Heifeweizen to your taste?"

"I love it!" she said.

He put in the order and almost before he hung up the phone room service knocked on the door and brought in a silver tray with a chilled crystal mug and three bottles of her favorite Portland brew. She was glad they brought the bottles. It was part of the fun of specialty ales, in her opinion.

"We'll be having dinner soon. Was your trip from Egypt pleasant?"

They exchanged a few more remarks of equally deep relevance before Bernard disengaged himself from his phone.

"So, Leda," he said. "I hope you don't mind if I call you Leda? Call me Ro. Everybody does." She was glad he said that. She would have a hard time calling him Mr. Bernard, since he appeared to be about twelve years old. "Iris told you about the project. We know you've just returned from Egypt but are assuming you won't have any problems going back with our tech crews and experts to plot out the development of the program?"

Cleopatra said, wreathing Leda's face in her most roguish smile, "If I find your offer sufficiently attractive, certainly."

The three of them, with Iris Morgan chiming in now and then, discussed details for a short time before dinner was served. It consisted of a salad and an excellent seafood pasta that Leda managed, with some difficulty, to keep out of her beadwork.

They discussed the project further over cappuccino.

"Your voice is lovely," McCallum said. "How do you think you might bear up to narrating the program as well as appearing in it as yourself?"

"Normally you would pay two people for these jobs,

yes?" Cleopatra, who was learning fast how to be working-class, inquired sweetly.

"Of course," McCallum said.

"If Andy doesn't have a problem with that, neither do I," Ro said, slinging himself to his feet. "Okay, kids, that's it for Iris and me tonight. We need to check out a couple of other locations," he said, winking at Iris.

"Oh, oh yes," she said.

"I promised to take her dancing," he whispered. Leda thought they'd make a funny couple, him in his Bermudas and Iris in her slinky dress, not to mention the discrepancy in their ages. Iris looked to be about Leda's own age. Not that boy toys were unusual anymore, but it was a little unusual when the man had the money and power. Ro took care of one discrepancy by disappearing into one of the bedrooms and reemerging in a tux.

"Rude of him to wait until now to don his finest garments," Cleopatra said.

"I imagine he thinks of it more as a costume," Leda replied, with an image of herself shrugging.

When they had gone, Leda smiled at Sir Andrew, who was looking after the couple with a bemused expression. "I didn't realize they were an item," Leda said. "Iris introduced herself on the phone as his agent."

He smiled. "She is. She's also his grandmother."

Not knowing what else to say to *that,* Leda changed the subject. "I know of course that you're famous as a businessman. You wouldn't be the same Sir Andrew McCallum whose name appears on the copyright page of the Scottish murder mysteries by Andrew Walters, would you?"

He beamed. "I am. How did you figure that out? I didn't think anyone knew who either of my—personas were."

"I always look on the copyright page when I'm reading a new author who writes like an experienced author, to see if I recognize their other name. I read everything, so a lot of times if, say, a romance writer turns to mysteries, I know them. If I'd known you were going to be here and had my books unpacked, I'd have brought some for you to sign. I loved *Death of a Border Riever* and went out and bought all the others."

"I'll have signed copies of them sent to you when I return home," he said. "But though I was accused of romanticizing Scotland once upon a time, I don't think anything I've written could be classified as a—what are they called?—bodice ripper."

"No, though frankly, if you want to increase your sales, you could use a few more racy bits. But don't get me wrong. I love the books the way they are. Who you remind me of is a sort of modern Sir Walter Scott," she said. "Not quite so many detailed descriptions, but beautifully done descriptions where you need them, and such good insights into people. Then, too, there's that kindly feeling you get from his work even when horrible things are happening to the characters."

"Thank you," he said, looking a tiny bit uncomfortable. "Actually, I'm glad you brought that up because I wasn't sure how to approach you about this. I write like Sir Walter Scott because it's actually he who does the writing, with my help on updating his style. I'm a blend, you see. I am also one of the original large investors in the Chimera Process and happen to know that you, too, are blended."

"I thought that was a secret," she said.

"There are few secrets from those holding the purse strings," he said, more grimly than primly, Leda thought. "I was on a screening committee for deciding whose DNA should be cultivated for blendings. When your rather unusual situation transpired, naturally the committee was consulted."

Leda nodded, hoping that Gretchen's blend with her dad

hadn't gone past the committee, because Wolfe was probably on it. Thus far Gretchen hadn't seen fit to tell Wolfie about the other man more intimately involved in her life than her husband.

"The board recently voted to re-form the committee with broader parameters as to who was an appropriate donor."

"So I was told," she said.

"Yes, well, I don't approve of what is happening. I know that Chimera's successor on Kefalos rather abruptly dismissed you, and I wish to apologize for that. I am hoping that what we're proposing to do here will in some measure counteract what I fear is a grave mistake on the part of Helix."

"How far has the cat been let out of the bag?" Leda asked. "I've seen stuff in tabloids and on the Internet but haven't noticed anything in the less-jaundiced branches of the press thus far."

"It's being leaked slowly. Some of the stories and Internet solicitations are plants by Helix, deliberately appearing to be unreliable. Much as they would like to increase their presence in the market, there is still some fear of political and legal repercussions, depending on the governments of the countries where they operate. What we actually want to do with the Cleopatra program is to have you present the finding of the tomb and the events leading up to and away from the queen's death in her own words, from her own viewpoint. We will allude to but not focus on the process that allows you access to the queen's thoughts and memories."

"And I to Leda's," Cleopatra interjected.

"Yes, exactly. What do you think? It is an historic opportunity, but it would also expose you to a great deal of publicity and negative attention from everyone from the Egyptian government to casual crackpots the world over."

"I think I may regret our ability to speak or understand thirty languages," Leda said. "And I will have to make it clear to Cleo that no matter how annoying these people are, we're not allowed to have them killed. I also think that we will be needing combat pay for this program in addition to what the usual fee is."

"Let me put it this way," Andrew said slowly. "If you actually follow through with this, I will personally guarantee to make you wealthy enough that you can afford to hide out for the duration of your life in fine style if you so desire."

"Please accept, Leda," Cleo said. *"From what I have learned from you and our mutual research, my reign has been trivialized throughout a history largely written by my enemies. We could set the record straight."*

"What we will probably do is make me look like a nutcase," Leda told her. *"And what about Gabriella and Cleo 7.2? Will we expose them when we come out of the closet—or I guess you might say tomb? We don't really have a right to do that."*

"Then we will not if they do not wish it. We must contact them and discuss that aspect of the matter."

To Sir Andrew, Leda said, "Cleo is all for it, but I really feel like I need to think it over a little."

"Take all the time you want. But I hope, knowing what we have in common, that you will at least tell *me* the story of how you were blended with the queen, how her canopic jar came to be where it was, how you found the tomb, all of it."

"Are you asking this as Andrew McCallum, Helix board member, or as Sir Andrew Walters, author relentlessly searching for fresh grist for his mill?"

"Both, but more the latter perhaps."

"Okay, but only if you'll tell me what it's like to host Sir Walter Scott and how you guys have managed. You seem a little better integrated than we are. I'd like to hear more about it."

"I believe we may be in need of a few more pints and

drams in that case," he said, picking up the phone to ring room service.

They sipped their drinks slowly, but their talk soon picked up a quicker pace, their words tumbling over each other as they compared experiences and insights and realized how much they had all—Leda, Andy, Cleopatra, and Sir Walter, needed to talk, tell their stories, share their complaints and revelations.

When they grew stiff from sitting so long, since even the plush armchairs of the penthouse became uncomfortable when pressing on the same body parts for too long, they stepped out to the balcony and watched the sun rise over the river, while Sir Walter talked about sunrises he had seen from the hills of the Border and from Edinburgh Castle. Cleopatra spoke of dawns along the Nile and over the Mediterranean Sea. Leda chimed in with dawns from the deck of a battleship and having no dawns aboard a submarine, while Andy also spoke of being dawn-deprived while working with his computers and accounts till all hours, when mornings only meant the opening numbers from the stock exchange.

Cleopatra admitted that she often missed the sunrise while making plans for buildings or battles, excursions or dramatic displays to parade her country's wealth and power in hopes of staving off conquest for another few months. And Sir Walter said that he often missed sunrise when his writing carried him into breakfast.

Speaking of breakfast, was she feeling at all hungry? Because he definitely was. He was told this particular hotel fixed a smashing bowl of oatmeal. Leda wondered if they did eggs Benedict properly. But when Andy said they made the best cinnamon-roll French toast in the country, everyone decided that was what their two mouths should eat.

After Andy ordered, Cleopatra paced Leda back and forth

for a bit, then lifted the mug with the dregs of her ale. "To sunrises one cannot see from the tomb!"

"Sunrises!" Walter and Andy agreed, downing the last of the dram in Andy's fist.

By the time their plates bore nothing but the syrupy tracks of vanished toast, the sun was well up.

"I understand there is an exceptionally fine bookstore here in Portland," Andy said in Sir Walter's voice. "I would very much like to see it."

"That can be arranged," Leda said.

"We would not be conspicuous wearing evening attire and arriving in a limousine?"

"Anything goes at Powell's," she assured him. Then Cleopatra piped up, flickering her lashes flirtatiously at Andy, "Though perhaps it would be good to return to Rusti's house first. As we have talked the night away, she will assume we have done more than talk."

By the time the limo pulled up in front of Powell's City of Books, the store that occupied an entire city block of new and used books and associated wares, it was nearly 11 A.M. Rusti had been sleeping and hadn't even noticed when Leda came in, changed from the evening outfit to one of Rusti's more fetching aubergine scoop-necked knit tops and pants, and returned to the car where Andy waited.

As they stepped into the bookstore, Leda suddenly swayed on her feet and reached out for something to grab hold of.

"Leda? Are you all right?" Andy asked, taking her elbow.

But she was neither Leda at that moment nor all right. She was Cleopatra and in desperate trouble.

She saw herself as she had once been in time-frayed royal robes, her fragile body being almost pulled apart by the rough handling of several men. Initially, the scene before her seemed to be a memory, except that she could recall no such incident ever occurring within her lifetime. All the while they were tearing off bits of her, another part of her listened helplessly, detached from her plight so that she seemed to be able only to hear the argumentative voices of her tormentors. They seemed more clumsy and impatient than purposely cruel, not because they were not cruel men—she felt that they were—but because she was only an object, and one could not be cruel to an object.

The impression was so strong that when the vision faded, she expected to find cuts and bruises on her body at the very least. But she saw only Andy's freckled brow creased with concern. Leda once more regained awareness of her surroundings.

Man, I had the weirdest nightmare, she thought, shaking her head and thumping her forehead with the heel of her hand, as if to clear it.

"Leda?" Andy asked, "What is it? What's the matter? Did you faint?"

Her first instinct was to deny the vision that had overcome them as a nightmare while they were still awake. But then she remembered with relief that Andy understood. If the episode had anything to do with the blend, Andy and Walter might well have had a similar experience that would shed light on her own.

Shakily, she led him over to the little coffee and tea shop within the store, and over a pot of tea, in low tones, Cleopatra told the others what she had seen and felt.

"I dreamed it, too," Leda said. "But not as vividly as that. Have you—two—experienced anything similar?"

Andy shook his head. "No. Never. I dream Walter's story ideas, of course, and he dreams spreadsheets at times, which he finds disturbing, since he was never much good with money. But the only violence has been in our blended imagination. Mostly sword fights. A few hangings. But that's all."

Leda sipped her tea for a moment and mused to Cleopatra, *"Maybe because you are the less corporeal of us, when you saw my nightmare it was more on your plane or something, which is why it seemed more real to you."*

"It was real. It was happening to me. Perhaps the feeling of detachment I experienced was actually you having the nightmare."

"Whatever," Leda replied. She was still baffled.

Chimera followed the monks—and the suitcase—through the terminal until they reached the Indian Airlines counter. The monks presented three tickets, and Chimera presented a passport for identity confirmation.

Aboard the plane, after a lengthy delay in takeoff, during which the monks meditated and Chimera attempted to follow suit, the flight attendants served beverages. Chimera had the window seat, with the monks occupying the other two.

Sipping fruit juice, Chimera noticed that it had an odd taste and looked a bit cloudy. Before the scientist could mention this, however, sleep overcame all other functions.

It was a long and deep sleep, and by the time Chimera awakened, the plane was landing in Delhi.

Two things, other than the odd drink and deep sleep that followed, puzzled Chimera. The middle and aisle seats of the row were vacant and the scientist found that the inside of his cheek was a bit sore and raw. The other passengers crowded the aisle.

Chimera blinked and found it hard to focus, but finally rose and followed the others to the front end of the aircraft. "Did you happen to see when the Buddhist monks who were with me left?"

"Yes, of course, sir," the male flight attendant said. "They departed when the aircraft landed in Dubai, sir. You were sleeping very soundly. I remember."

What were two Buddhist monks going to do in Dubai in the Arab Emirates, Chimera wondered. Oh well, they had not mentioned that they were leaving, but then, perhaps they had not wanted to disturb their sleeping companion. Chimera hoped that was the explanation, but was afraid that it was not. Perhaps another team of monks was meeting the plane to shepherd the scientist on to Dharmsala.

But of course, they weren't.

CHAPTER 9

The driver of the taxi, who evidently knew Gabriella Faruk, drove them to a compound in what had once been a fairly ritzy section of Alexandria.

"You must tell me what you know," Gabriella said. "It is urgent that we get the mummy back again."

"It wouldn't do you any good if I told you," Mike replied. "They're rough characters. Besides, they plan to hold the old girl for ransom, so you'll have a chance to get her back if your museum can pay enough."

"Unacceptable," Gabriella told him. "We must get the mummy back. Cleopatra's DNA is worth a fortune, and there were other things as well, the amulets and charms wrapped inside her bandages. Some of them were priceless."

"I thought she hadn't been unwrapped yet. How do you know?"

"You wouldn't believe me if I told you." She stopped speaking suddenly, and called out, "Gihen, please find Mohammed for me. I must return to the library at once."

A fully veiled woman in a bright blue dress appeared.

"Yes, Gabriella. I will radio him at once. But you look weary, my friend. Is there something he could bring you from the library so that you need not return?"

"If only there was! But no, it's something I must find for myself."

Mike wondered if maybe his new trinket was worth more to her than it would be to any other potential buyer. "Something like this maybe?" he asked, withdrawing the scarab from his pocket and holding it out of her reach for her to see.

"That's mine! Give it to me at once!" she commanded. *Very bossy, even for an academic female,* he thought.

"Unh-uh, finders keepers," he told her, closing his fist over it. "Unless you give me a good enough reason—or enough good reasons, that is." He rubbed his thumb and first two fingers together meaningfully. "This has been a pretty unprofitable night so far. I'm willing to negotiate if it's all that important to you."

Her reaction was startling. She seemed to be having a desperate internal struggle to control herself. "Please excuse me," she said. "But don't go anywhere, and don't let go of that amulet."

Then she got up and paced the courtyard back and forth three times. At last, as if she'd been having a seizure, the tension that drove her relaxed. Her walk slowed and changed, acquiring a sinuous roll of the hips, somewhat lost in the baggy cargo pants, but a spectacular movement nonetheless. When she turned back to him, she was smiling as if they shared something. Good Lord, she was coming on to him! This happened to the heroes in men's adventure novels and even best-sellers whenever the guys in the books met beautiful, brainy women. The girls instantly turned into steamy temptresses who turned all of their brains, talents, and skills into erotic manuvers to get him into bed. Well, adrenaline rushes such as the one they had—face it—shared did have an erotic component, which was one of the reasons he kept going for them, he knew. But usually there were no temptresses around—not living ones anyway.

"Lady, I don't know what you had in mind to exchange for this trinket, but I'm thinking cash myself. I ain't sayin' you ain't pretty, but I need something a little more bankable. On the other hand, if you have the cash *and* you really sorta like my manly rugged good looks, we might work something out."

She laughed. It was a throaty chuckle that went straight to his groin. "My dear new friend, you are getting, one might say, your cart ahead of your ass. While I do indeed like your looks, as what woman would not, I was simply trying to decide what to tell you about the amulet. You may find what I have to say difficult to believe. But if you snap the right wing of the scarab back, you will find that the center opens." She sat down beside him at the little table where they'd been having coffee. She scooted her chair close to his and rested her elbows on the table, moving her fingers in an elegant and graceful way to indicate how he should move his, though she did not seem to be trying to get closer to the locket. He did what she said.

"Inside you will find a lock of hair. It was cut from the head of Marc Antony as he lay dying in the arms of Cleopatra. It contains his DNA."

"So?" Mike thought immediately of what Galen had told him but kept his horse-trading face on. He could have sworn that Gabriella had not been wearing perfume when they were in the cab, but now she exuded a subtle scent that he found distractingly stirring.

"So a person such as yourself, open to unusual financial opportunities, shall we say, must be aware that there is a very lucrative market in DNA these days. It is a somewhat clandestine market, true, but there are those who would pay handsomely for a few cells from any reasonably notable individual. Can you imagine what a great price you might get for the key to the great Marcus Antonius himself?"

"Aha! I thought that might come up," Mike said, waggling a finger at her. "You're talking about those guys at that Nucor place, aren't you? The ones that—uh—blend, isn't it called? Blend old dead people with live ones?"

"Helix," she said.

"What?"

"The company changed its name. It's called Helix now. How did *you* find out about the blends? I hope it isn't common knowledge among people of your—er—calling?"

"No. I met this guy who used to work for a fellow who was very into it till he got snuffed. I think a mutual friend of ours might have had something to do with it. At least, they said on the news that you girls were the ones who found Cleopatra's tomb. You and Leda."

"You know Leda?"

"I know a lot of things," he said. "See, this guy who worked for the fellow whose name I can't recall . . ."

"Rasmussen?" she asked, learning forward a bit. "Could it have been Rasmussen?"

"That's the one," he said, though he wasn't sure. "This fellow, Galen, said his boss, this Rasmussen, had paid for one of these blends for him. Galen told me all about it. He wanted no part of it, he said. I guess he thought he had a life but then somebody, not me, honest, but somebody else, decided otherwise. I was with him when he died. Terrible thing. Tragic. So young. And generous. I was his sole heir, it seems. He left me all his stuff, including this." He flashed the card at her, holding it out of her reach.

She didn't look all that surprised and she didn't look all that unhappy. She sat back in her chair and crossed her legs in a way that would have been sexy except for the cargo pants. "Ah, well, then, you do know where to market my— the contents of the amulet then, don't you?"

"Indeed I do," he said, adding, "And you're not exactly giving me a good reason to give it back to you. Quite the contrary. In fact, if you were preparing to make me an offer, you're driving the price up. I can't help but wonder why that is. I know you aren't stupid."

She shrugged in a way that made Marvin the Martian positively leer from his vantage point atop her breasts, which rose and fell with a Jell-O-like quiver with her gesture. The courtyard had seemed quite cool when he arrived, but now it was getting very warm. "I am hoping my honesty if nothing else will disarm you. You see, I have spent many of the years of my career studying Antony in order to find what became of his treasure."

"What treasure?"

"The treasure he looted from Byzantium. Not just the library scrolls in Pergamum. We found those in the tomb. The precious jewels, spices, and metals he looted from the city have never been found. At first it was assumed that they flowed into the coffers of Rome, but there is no evidence to support that. And Cleopatra was not in possession of them. He gave her the scrolls from the library and a trinket or two, but the rest he must have hidden. And the secret of the hiding place died with him. If he confided in Cleopatra, she told no one. We now study the scrolls to see if some might be her own account of his death, and possibly his deathbed confidences."

"I still don't get why you're telling me this if you want me to give it back to you."

"Because you deserve to know. In reviewing what occurred tonight, I have come to the understanding that you saved my life, the Biblioteca, the priceless ancient scrolls that will be the object of my most passionately devoted study for the rest of my days.

"So you must understand that although you have all the information you need to sell the amulet for a lot of money,

I am the one who really knows how to use what it contains. Who knows what fascinating knowledge that treasure would reveal? And of course I would include you in any financial profit to be made from its secrets."

Of course, she wasn't mentioning that if *she* found this treasure she was talking about, the Egyptian government got the whole thing and he got nothing. Maybe she thought *he* was stupid.

"You are a real sweetheart," he said. "And that's a generous offer. What do you say we sleep on it, and I'll let you know in the morning?"

About that time Mohammed, the cousin and cabbie, showed up in the courtyard. "Sorry to have disturbed you, Mo," Gabriella said. "I won't need that ride after all, but maybe, since you're here, you'd show this gentleman to one of the men's guest rooms."

Mike blinked at her twice. She wasn't flirting anymore. Not, he thought, because he'd failed to take her bait, but because the woman who'd been flirting with him was no longer there. The scholarly Dr. Faruk in the funny T-shirt and baggy cargo pants was back, wild-haired and intense, but not in the same way as she had been a few moments ago.

"Aw, Doc, don't be such a bad sport," he said, low enough, he hoped, so that she heard and her male cousin didn't. "I thought we might work something out together tonight from the way you were—you know, coming on."

"I was not!" she whispered fiercely. "Or rather—never mind. Just follow Mo. We'll speak of this after we've—each—had some sleep."

He gave her a look, more in sorrow than in censure, and followed the cabbie. His door had no lock on the inside. He fell asleep with Galen's pistol under the pillow and the amulet clutched in his left hand. He told himself to wake up when someone came to try to take the amulet away from him or in two hours, whichever came first.

* * *

"You will understand I have no choice but to report my husband missing, *ja?*" Gretchen said to the Helix corporate headquarters when they failed to produce an accurate location for Wolfe.

But once she was alone again she asked her inner cop, *"But we are reporting this to which authority? We do not even know what country he is in."*

"True. And you can't just go to Interpol with a missing person report, even if he's an influential missing person. Not unless you think someone is trafficking in him, or he's trafficking in somebody else."

"This is Wilhelm we are discussing, Duke. You will take this seriously."

"I am, doll, I am. I'm just trying to tell you how it works. We need to report that he's missing to the nearest police and let them know that we don't know where he is, then they can go to Interpol on our behalf. Probably a liberal application of incentive would grease the wheels."

"Money. Ja."

Duke was a little surprised at just how readily they got action for a few lire and a little name-dropping. He thought at first that the Italian police were solicitous mostly because Gretchen was a cute blonde with deep pockets. But he was not entirely right.

"Signora," an officer said deferentially, "I can imagine how distressing this is for you. We will give this matter the most urgent priority."

"Danke," Gretchen said, then added, *"Grazie.* You understand that the company officials are denying that Wilhelm is missing, and yet, they do not tell me where he is, only where he is not."

"You've made that clear, and I quite understand your concern. You have my personal guarantee that we will leave no stone unturned to find him."

"Hmph," Gretchen said. "I am hoping he is under no stones at all. Here is my hotel. I will wait there, when I am waiting. When I am not hearing from you in three days, I am waiting no longer, you understand?"

"*Si,* yes, *ja, signora.* Perfectly."

Though the man's expression was sympathetic and his downright uncoply Latin effusiveness seemed sincere enough, Duke was still surprised when there was a knock on their hotel room door that night.

"*Signora* Wolfe?" said the eye on the other side of the peephole.

"*Ja?*"

"We have news of your husband. May we come in please?"

Duke eyed them warily. It still all seemed too easy.

"You do not look like the Italian police," Gretchen said.

"No, *signora,* we are with Interpol. When the Italian police contacted us about your husband's disappearance, we were able to locate him. But he isn't in Rome."

"He is not? Where is he?"

"If you'll let us in, *signora,* we will explain and take you to him."

Gabriella finally pulled off her dusty, sweaty T-shirt and pants and bathed, then defiantly pulled on another T-shirt to sleep in. Her alter ego had been strangely quiet throughout her bedtime preparations. *"Nothing to say? Good. And you needn't think we are going to slip into that man's room and try to take the amulet from him. He is a very dangerous person. I hope he can help us recover your mummy, but I'd really prefer he leaves."*

"Calmly, my dear. Calmly. I think slipping into his room would be rather fun actually but not to take the amulet from him. He's very handsome, isn't he?"

"If you like that sort of looks. And he's not to be trusted."

"He helped us tonight and with a little effort on your part, we could win him over."

"He seems willing enough to help us locate your mummy without additional incentive, and I think you've been quite winning enough for one night. As for the amulet, that sort is only interested in money. Perhaps we can buy it back."

"Do it my way, and he'll beg us to take it as a token of his devotion."

The telephone beside the bed rang. It was three o'clock in the morning. "Yes?" Gabriella said cautiously.

"It's Ginia. Listen. You must post a guard and not leave the compound. The Saudi princess had a change of heart and telephoned her mother. A strange helicopter landed on the pad and picked her up. The stupid woman led them straight to me, and I don't doubt she'll tell them about you, too. I dismissed my staff, locked up the house, and had my pilot pick me up and take me to Kefalos."

Gabriella sighed. "I have not had a very good day either, Ginia. But perhaps you're overreacting. She probably won't tell them anything about our operation. Why should she? She might change her mind again."

"I don't think so. A few minutes ago the shore patrol from Mykonos called to tell me that a yacht weighed anchor offshore from Delos. It dispatched two landing crafts full of people. The patrol promised to investigate for me. I pay them well enough. But I fear the woman may have been forced to tell about us, which means you, too, are in danger."

"She was never here," Gabriella said.

"No, but we didn't conceal your identity or mine. It wouldn't be hard for someone to find your residence. I wish that you would . . ."

The phone went dead in Gabriella's hand. "Damn," she said. As she stepped out of her room into the courtyard connecting her compound with that of Mohammed and his brothers and all of their family members, she reached for the switch to turn on the fairy lights along the path. Behind her, the glow of her bedside lamp died as the switch flipped uselessly between her fingers.

She quickly stepped into the deeper shadows, trying to blend with the darkness as noises and low whispers penetrated the courtyard. Keeping to the wall, she slunk around the perimeter, feeling the roughness of the exterior stucco under her fingers. Behind her she felt rather than saw her own door flung open. Two figures darted inside. They whispered curses on finding the room empty and crashed back out again, no longer stealthy. The noise of their movements reverberated in her ears like the explosion earlier in the evening. She recoiled from it, wishing she had had time to arm herself or at least get dressed. Then someone grabbed her, at the same time clamping a hand over her mouth.

"Shhh," a voice whispered into Gabriella's ear. Mike Angeles. Probably that was good. "We're being invaded."

He took his hand from her mouth. Her teeth had bitten into her lips in several places. "I did notice," she whispered back.

"Sorry to have got you into this," he said. "I should have known there'd be others and they'd come looking for me."

"Actually they didn't," she said. "These people are looking for me."

"You? Why?"

"Maybe this could wait until later? I need to warn my cousin and his family."

"Excuse me." Mike pushed her aside. Instead of satchel charges, he now brandished a small handgun with which he dropped the shadowy figure who suddenly loomed up in front of them. Before the gun stopped smoking, another figure dropped onto him from the courtyard's roof, and the men began struggling. Gabriella tried to pull the stranger off of her ally, but once more someone grabbed her.

Why did these things happen when she had nothing but her T-shirt between her and her attackers and that perhaps not for long?

He held her tightly around the throat and she felt the sharp edge of a knife tickle her jugular.

CHAPTER 10

Cleopatra's narrative:

We drank tea from amusing mugs while sitting on a small stool at a table almost as small. For a time, Andrew held our hand, purely out of concern for our health, of course, as Leda assured me. I knew better. I have seen that look in the eyes of other men. Mild and unprepossessing as Andrew McCallum appears, he must have drive, must have fire and ambition. Otherwise, how could he amass so much uninherited wealth? And in my experience, that sort of drive and fire often indicates fire in other regions, those useful to a woman who wishes to acquire favors.

Furthermore, from Leda's memories we know that Andrew's guest, Sir Walter Scott, was well-known as a romantic and a fantasizer, one who loved grand lives and sweeping tales—such as my own. Earlier, that part of him had expressed considerable interest in my saga, but now, when Sir Walter came forth, it was generally to answer one of Leda's rather breathless questions about one of his books.

Which shows that my hostess certainly knows her way around certain kinds of men as well. When we left the sanctuary of the tea shop to continue our exploration of Powell's, the first place we went was to what Leda referred to as an "antique" leather-bound collection of Sir Walter Scott's books, which Andrew presented to us, signed, along with the three volumes written under his pen name of Sir Andrew Walters. Scott, the grandson of thieving ruffians who were minor gentility in his native land, is inordinately proud of the "Sir." It indicates a special favor on the part of the monarch. At one time it was given to those who were half courtier, half soldier, particular friends or favored servants of the royal house. Nowadays it is granted, he says, to confer honor to his country's celebrities, be they writers, musicians, artists, soldiers, or other noteworthy persons, especially those of great wealth.

It seems a useful institution. I am slightly chastened that in all of our generations of Ptolemys since Alexander, not one of us thought of it.

Leda seems very impressed with some of the books that were once owned by others. Many of the books in our library were owned by others—until we considerately made copies for the original owners and acquired the books for the library, where more people could have the benefit of them.

After signing the books, Andrew telephoned his chauffeur and had him collect and pay for the books and take them to the car. Afterward, the servant reappeared with a capacious box that rolled on wheels, and trailed us at a discreet distance.

This truly was a magnificent place—and I am sorry to say it made my Great Library pale by comparison. Of course, in this age they have devices that copy manuscripts at amazing speed, and many of the books had duplicates sitting on the shelves next to them, but even so, it was miraculous to behold. Rooms and rooms of books, shelf upon shelf of colorful covers of papers whose textures were more varied than the fabrics available in my land. A feast of books, whole floors of them devoted to particular subjects—travel, with an entire bookcase devoted to Egyptian studies—folklore, philosophy, medicine, cosmetics, any and all possible subjects. I was awestricken, amazed, stupefied.

"Cool, huh?" Leda inquired smugly. *"Thought you'd like it."*

"It rivals the Pharos Lighthouse as one of the wonders of the world," I admitted.

"It's even better because it still exists, and the lighthouse doesn't," Leda replied. She does have a tendency at times to, as she would put it, rub it in.

We wandered the rooms for hours, now and again plucking up books to examine or buy. Andrew generously, and rather recklessly, offered to purchase whatever we wished. I could actually feel the acquisitive glint kindle in Leda's gaze. However, as we had no place of our own to live, she managed to control her powerful lust and confined us to a single carefully chosen rolling-cart load.

We spent glorious hours in there while, with Andrew, we examined many books, reading aloud from what Leda calls "dust jackets" and first pages to each other. Most of these books are so small that one can hold the entire text in one's hand without it rolling across the floor or flying off in a dozen different directions. If there is a fault in this place, I would say that it is that the vast majority of the work contained within its walls is in a single language and of comparatively recent vintage. There is no chance to read various translations and interpretations in order to gain a deeper understanding of the meanings held within each volume. On the other hand, some of the books do not seem to require actually being read in any language at all, as the illustrations on the cover tell much of the story. The man with the long hair and the bared chest, holding a similarly attired woman, for instance. Time and language have not changed the stories people tell very much after all, it seems.

Andrew paid for our loot, and we returned to the car to

return to the hotel to join Ro and Iris again to discuss further details of the production.

The chauffeur placed our books onto the wide, cushioned bench in the rear of the vehicle so that we might gloat over our acquisitions.

I was thoroughly enjoying this when the books vanished, Andrew vanished, the light of day vanished, and I was in darkness.

The cool of the rainy afternoon was replaced by the heat of my native land. A hot sand-bearing breeze rasped against the bare skin of my legs and arms. This was surprising since a portion of myself recalled that I still wore the trousers with which I had attired myself at Rusti's. Nevertheless, it seemed that I wore only a single thin short garment.

In the next moment something—a hand smelling of tobacco and—Leda's senses supplied the name—cordite—clamped onto my throat with bruising strength, lifting me from my bare feet and choking me with brutally strong hands. Something sharp pricked me just under my right ear, the blade biting into my skin. He was going to—Leda said—open our jugular—cut our throat.

Then, suddenly, both blade and hand released their pressure and we started to fall. Abruptly, new hands replaced those of the assassin's. "Leda, are you all right? Is it happening again?"

I nodded. "I believe I understand now. I have joined minds with my sister soul and felt what she felt. I must telephone Gabriella at once. It is very different in some ways from what I felt the first time, but I am positive now that this is what has happened. My twin and her hostess have been attacked twice within the last few hours."

Leda reached into her bag for her cell phone, but Andrew handed her the car phone recessed into the back of the driver's seat. "It's got a bit more juice than the average cell," he said.

Leda, heedless of the traffic whizzing past them on the bridge, dialed Gabriella's home phone number. A recorded voice in Arabic told her something she didn't entirely translate but picked up enough words to gather that the phone was out of order. Although it was probably too late for Gabriella to be at the Biblioteca, Leda knew her friend sometimes worked nights, so she dialed her office number there.

A man's voice answered.

"Who is this?" Leda asked.

"Who is *this?*" he asked.

"I am calling for Dr. Faruk. Is she working late by any chance?"

"Not any longer."

"Who *is* this?" she repeated.

"I am a police officer, madam. Please state your name and reason for calling."

"I'm Dr. Hubbard, Dr. Faruk's associate, and I'm calling from the United States. What has happened to Gabriella? Please put her on the line if she's able to come to the phone."

"Calm yourself, madam. No harm has come to Dr. Faruk. There has been an incident here, and she is returning to help us with our inquiries."

"Thank you. Please tell her I called and to call me as soon as possible."

But the policeman had hung up.

Gabriella had learned a few self-defense moves, though she was by no means a martial arts expert. Her dangerous activities required the use of brains and contacts to maneuver herself and the women she was protecting from peril to safety. She could butt her assailant in the chin with her own head, but he could sever her vein before she had a prayer of disarming him.

Suddenly there was a loud crack. Had he shot her? It seemed like overkill when he was ready to slit her throat. Then something sharp fell onto her nose followed by a rain of other objects and a shower of something coarse and powdery.

His knife hand relaxed, but before she could react, the arm restraining her also dropped, though he still almost pulled her down with him as he crumpled to the mud-brick pavement of the courtyard. Her aunt Fatima stood over him, brandishing the base of a large ceramic planter with the remains of her favorite jasmine bush and soil still dangling from it.

Mike Angeles doubled his opponent over with a jab to the midsection then drop-kicked him in the head, sending the man sprawling.

"You okay?" Mike asked Gabriella.

Behind them, Mo and his brothers and their older male children, armed to the teeth, poured out into the courtyard.

The attackers didn't even try to take them on. Someone yelled a command, and the man Mike had felled scrabbled away like a crab until he could gain his feet and run.

"You're not having a real good day, are you, lady?" Mike asked her.

"I've had better."

"Good thing your relatives are well armed. Unusually well armed." He looked around as Gabriella's kinsmen and women lowered all manner of automatic rifles, assault rifles, and other implements of selective destruction. "What is this? You guys rob caravans for fun and profit or what? If so, need any help?"

"Nothing like that," Gabriella said. "And there's no profit in what we do. I doubt it would interest you. I spend a great deal of my own money on it, and sometimes, like tonight, you find your efforts have gone unappreciated."

"Speaking of which, you could either say thank you or

slip me a little tip. I seem to have saved your life."

"Perhaps," she said, cautious again. *"What is the matter with you?"* Cleopatra asked. *"He did. This very attractive man just saved our life. He should be rewarded."*

"Maybe, but what if he is only trying to gain our trust for some purposes of his own? He seems to turn up at strangely opportune moments. He was working for the people who stole your mummy. I'm sure of it."

"Clearly he changed his allegiance. Men do that if sufficiently motivated."

"Yes, but we know nothing about *his motivation. It can hardly have been our charms, since he had already removed the bombs before he knew we were there. So, unless he had some as-yet-undisclosed reason for turning on the others, he may have been told to win our confidence and infiltrate our organization. I find it very strange that this compound has been invaded so soon after the attack on the museum and that he is here for the second event as well."*

"Luckily for us. He did *save our life.*"

Mo called out to her. "Gabriella, Hamid was stabbed. He has lost a great deal of blood."

Hamid was the bohab, gate guard and groundskeeper, for both compounds. A distant relative, he had served in that capacity faithfully for many years.

Gabriella sprinted off to tend to her wounded kinsman.

She didn't see where Mike Angeles went, and with no guard at the compound's gate, neither did anyone else.

Mike slipped out of Gabriella's compound while she was commiserating with her relatives, who had congregated beside her and the wounded man at the front gate.

Mike left the way the terrorists had come in, over the rooftops.

When he reached the opposite side from the courtyard, he didn't drop immediately into the street. Instead, he crawled around to the front of the house, where the entrance gate was tightly closed. Below he heard the voices of Gabriella and her family.

Dawn was just breaking, making the light a little tricky, but directly across from him, on a rooftop on the opposite side of the street, he saw movement, two black-clad figures, one stooping, another lying down. The rising sun caught like a drop of blood on what Mike figured was a sniperscope.

He'd been expecting something like that. Since the direct assault had failed, picking off the inhabitants of the compound as they left it wasn't a bad alternative.

He scooted back around the way he'd come, silently lowered himself to the ground, and approached the other house from the side. It wasn't that hard to get up. They'd left a knotted rope. Mike pulled himself up with ease and swung his body up onto the tiles.

His boot caught on a loose one and it clattered to the street.

He waited, expecting someone to run across to his position and put him out of his misery. Rather to his surprise, nobody did. Maybe they had heard, though, and were waiting to ambush him when he reached their position. He only saw one now, the horizontal one, about fifty feet away. Maybe the other guy had gone for coffee? He'd be quick and not give the other one a chance to return and discover him.

His target lay facing Gabriella's compound, his rifle rather carelessly pointing at the entrance. What was this, amateur hour? The guy didn't seem to know how to hold his weapon. Something was wrong here.

Mike was not surprised when his flying sprint closed the distance between himself and his target before the other man made it all the way to his feet. He was surprised that the man didn't move from his position, even when Mike was on top of him.

Then Mike saw what the man's black mask and the

dawn's ruddy light hadn't let him see before—or what had happened while he was crossing the street and climbing up to the roof. The guy had his head on backward. It had been twisted till his neck broke.

Mike sat back on his heels and considered for a moment. So—there were *two* groups of black-clad people—no, make that three, counting the gang at the museum—skulking around the general vicinity tonight? Maybe the body in front of him was the work of one of Gabriella's relatives, but you'd have thought someone would have mentioned it. Oh well. Crisis over. Problem solved without any work on his part. He'd been going to leave this guy as a sort of hostess gift for Gabriella, to thank her for the hospitality, but now he'd just have to send her some scented soap or something.

CHAPTER 11

While Gabriella was examining Hamid, the police arrived. "Dr. Faruk, we would like a word with you," the officer in charge said.

Gabriella blinked stupidly and almost asked them where they were when they were needed. It took her a moment to think why they were there at all.

The policeman saw her confusion. "The break-in at the Biblioteca, Doctor. You called to report it. We naturally assumed you would be there to meet our officers and point out the damage and what articles were stolen. It's taken us some time to examine the scene and even longer to contact someone who could tell us where you lived. Why did you not remain behind?"

Gabriella blinked again. "Shock, I suppose," she said finally, returning her attention to Hamid's wound.

"What happened to this fellow?" the officer asked.

She thought fast. If the police knew why the Saudi lady's relatives had attacked the compound, they were likely to side with the Saudis. And they might look into things at the compound she preferred to keep quiet. "Oh, he is my uncle. He was coming to collect me at work and surprised the intruders. As you see, they wounded him. Partly it was to look after him that I left the Biblioteca."

"And yet you are only now treating his wound?"

"We were detained," she said, deliberating about whether or not to betray Mike Angeles to them to throw them off her own scent. It seemed the only viable distraction. "One of the conspirators apparently had a change of heart. He removed the explosive devices but insisted that I leave with him. My uncle was collected by my cousin Mohammed and brought back here. I finally convinced the man to come back here with me, too. His friends stole Cleopatra's mummy, the one I recently helped locate. This man said he had some idea where they might be keeping the mummy. Of course, its value is inestimable, and I had to humor him in hope that he might be telling the truth. I'm glad *you're* here to interrogate him now. You'll find him over there." She nodded toward the section of courtyard where she had left Mike Angeles.

A moment later the officer sent to look for him returned. "The man was there, according to other witnesses, sir, but left just prior to our arrival."

Gabriella shrugged. "He is obviously a very experienced criminal. I'm sorry, but I can hardly be expected to anticipate his actions."

"Naturally, Doctor. We are not suggesting that you should. But we would like your assistance at the Biblioteca nonetheless."

"Can it not wait until morning, Captain? I am very weary from the shock and stress of this day."

"I can appreciate that, madame. However, the staff will begin arriving soon, and while my officers can prevent them from entering, we wish to have your corroboration of the damage to your area with minimal interruption to the normal operation of the library. I'm sure you are the first to appreciate that."

"Yes. Yes, of course," she said. She became aware of the other officers goggling at her bare arms and legs. "If I can get dressed first?"

The captain nodded stiffly.

As she turned, she saw her aunt Yasmin standing warily just beyond the circle of the police. She gave her a wink and a slight nod in the direction of her own room.

Yasmin, clad in her black robes, melted easily into the shadows and was inside Gabriella's room when the younger woman arrived.

"Two attacks in one day?" Yasmin's whispered question was somewhat admiring. "Who have you offended now, child?"

"I tell you honestly I have no idea why any of the usual suspects should choose this time to be more offended than others, to the extent that they attack us. But we are none of us safe here until we discover who is launching these assaults and cause them to stop. Therefore, it is time to use the plan we arranged before."

"As soon as you return," Yasmin agreed.

"I will not return here. Mo knows where I shall emerge if all goes well and in time will meet me with a few necessities, but for now he will help the rest of you pack and guide you to the beginning of your path. Your rubber boots are in readiness. Be sure to take them the rest of the way with you when you ascend into the city to make your way to those who will shelter and protect you. As soon as you are safe, leave your marks as we discussed, one for each, so that Mo may ascertain you found your way. Should trouble befall you, wait. Do not wander from your path, or you may become so lost we will not find you in time to prevent you from starving. Remember what happened to Sitt Miriam, the Afghan warlord's wife."

"*What happened to her?*" Cleopatra asked.

"*Drowned in a foot of water when she became lost and died from exhaustion. She wandered off when Fatima was guiding her in from the desert and stopped to kill a snake.*"

"*Where did this happen?*"

"*In the aqueducts Alexander caused to be built beneath the city. We have long used these to come and go secretly from the compound when conducting our friends to safety. After my colleagues have finished working for the day, the necropoli also make good hiding places for our friends. The tomb robbers over the centuries interconnected the passages so that the three major necropoli of the city have access to the aqueducts. That is the positive aspect. The negative is that it has allowed water to enter some of the tombs, making work difficult for those of us who would preserve . . .*"

"Enough! I understand," Cleopatra said. "*Did I myself not issue decrees to repair and extend the aqueducts?*"

"Do not forget our rubbers, stay where we are if we become lost, remember the fate of those who were disobedient!" Yasmin said. "You speak as if we were children."

"There are children among us," Gabriella replied, tugging on the rugged clothing she wore while digging, cargo pants that unzipped to make knee-length shorts, a T-shirt, an outer shirt, a scarf for her hair, and a voluminous skirt to cover the pants. She had plastic boots in her office, and a compass, and, most importantly, maps of the aqueducts and necropoli. She slipped her cell phone, now recharged, into her bag, but she knew it wouldn't help her when she went underground.

Her preparations complete, she returned to the gate, where Hamid was being removed by ambulance. His transfer to a safe house could be arranged later.

The police captain nodded with approval, relief, and

perhaps a bit of regret at her more decorous costume and, with a hand on top of her scarfed head, helped her into the backseat of the police car.

Dropping to the ground, Mike made his way to a busier street and caught a taxi to the Helix corporate airstrip.

There he presented Galen's credit card as well as the pass to the past his late friend's late boss had bought for him. He was proud of how effortless his forgery of Galen's signature looked.

Once they arrived at the Kefalos airstrip, the easy part was over. Mike went to find someone who could stir him together with Marc Antony's hair follicles at least long enough to find the treasure Gabriella mentioned.

That had been a weird incident. He began to wonder if maybe she was blended, too. She certainly sounded like two different people at times. In retrospect, he decided she probably was. It wasn't something he was used to factoring in, but it looked like that was going to have to change.

But people apparently didn't just walk into the facility and order a blend like they'd order a haircut.

He showed all and sundry Galen's doctored ID and the business card with the doctor's name on it, but the pilot had radioed ahead, so he was detained at the airstrip until a teenage Greek girl driving a golf cart showed up to claim him.

The golf cart took the mountain like a goat with a Harley engine. Once at the top, they entered a ruin.

"There must be some mistake," Mike said. "I'm not a tourist. I'm here for the—"

"Oh yes, do you think I don't know that?" the girl asked with an airy wave of one hand while she used the other to drive them straight into a wall, which turned out to be a holographic elevator. "This is where everybody comes."

The elevator purred down an indeterminate number of floors—there were no markings on it that said lingerie, hosiery, or housewares, much less something simple like numbers. When they reached their floor, the door opened, and the girl drove out and down the long corridor. While she drove, she spoke into a cell phone or walkie-talkie, and a door about a mile away opened. A woman in a lab coat stood there waiting. If she wasn't exactly smiling, she at least looked lukewarmly welcoming. "Hello, Mr. Kronos. We accessed your file when you presented your card in Alexandria. It is customary to make an appointment prior to undergoing the process, but I presume this is a preliminary visit to select your donor?"

"Actually, no. I—uh—brought my donor with me." He took the charm from his pocket. "By a hair. Marc Antony's hair, actually."

She held out her hand. He pulled his back.

"Sir, we'll have to test the specimen to ascertain that your information is correct. You wouldn't want to be stuck hosting a Roman tax collector for instance, would you?"

"I guess not. But let me take it out of the amulet first," Mike said. "It's gold."

"Yes, I see that. But of course, if the specimen is genuine, it will be worth considerably more. I'll personally return the amulet when the specimen has been successfully and safely extracted. As old as it is, it would disappear if you attempted to extract it now."

"We can't have that, can we?" Mike agreed. Grudgingly, he handed over the little hunk of treasure.

She left him standing there and disappeared behind the beakers and computers. Meanwhile a rather tasty young thing in a lab coat conducted him to a lounge.

The TV was tuned to CNN, and the magazines looked current. He noticed three laptop computers set up on a table and asked the girl what they were for.

"Research," she said. "If you would care to access our database, we've had our librarians compile files on the notable individuals whose DNA we've acquired or that is of interest to us. You can also access the Net from it if there's someone you want to know about who's not in our DB."

That sounded like a good, if slightly scary, idea. Mike tried the Helix DB but couldn't find a lot on Marc Antony, though there was a lot on Cleopatra and Julius Caesar. He did an on-line search and came up with a few disparaging bits by a contemporary of the general's, but apparently not a friend. No mention was made of Antony's conquests, other than sexual, or any possible misplaced treasure. His defeats were discussed at some length, however.

Mike sighed. The guy was described as a heavy drinker. This was not going to be easy.

By Galen's watch it was only about an hour and a half before the first woman reappeared, handing him the locket. "Your vessel, sir. It's quite possible from what we can tell that the sample is, as you believed, from Marc Antony. It's also quite possible that it's not. Can you give us any other information, or are you satisfied that your source is correct?"

"She seemed pretty sure—I mean, yes. I'm willing to take the chance. This thing is reversible, isn't it?"

"There's a high probability we can reverse the process within a limited time, though you may have residual effects. There are no money-back guarantees, however."

"No, no, that's not what I meant," he said. He was thinking about it. Gabriella knew her stuff when it came to mummies, he was pretty sure, and *she* had seemed pretty sure about the Marc Antony specimen. And the treasure.

What the good Dr. Faruk had said about Antony's treasure made sense. The guy needed to finance world conquest, according to the story Mike remembered from the History Channel. Why would he surrender all that loot to Rome when he supposedly was representing Rome in the field? Cleopatra was rich. She didn't need the negotiable assets. He'd given her the library to keep *her* sweet.

So it stood to reason that there was treasure, and if he, Mike, resurrected Antony, he'd know where to find it. Oh well, what the hell. He was due for another change anyway. He hadn't had one for at least fifteen minutes or so.

"I have it on excellent authority that the specimen is authentic," he said in his best imitation of a college professor.

That seemed to satisfy the woman. She led him to a large chamber that resembled a deluxe hotel suite. Except that the bed was only double size.

She waved him to the bed. "Please make yourself comfortable, sir."

Mike nodded and lay back on the bed. "Wouldn't a lab table be more atmospheric?" he asked, wanting to make a more suggestive joke but not wanting to give the woman any ideas. She was built like a refrigerator and had a mustache like Groucho Marx.

She ignored his question and said with the warmth of a prerecorded instruction manual, "After the blending, you will need to sleep thirty-six hours or more for the process to begin."

"Kind of a honeymoon, huh?"

"If you like to think of it that way," she said, and came at him with what looked like a couple of pairs of eyelash curlers minus the handle. "Please don't be alarmed, but we must ensure that you don't blink during the transfer. These retractors may be somewhat annoying at first, but they won't be in place long enough to cause you serious discomfort. The actual procedure is very quick."

Mike didn't like that part. It reminded him of interrogation rooms he had heard of but so far been fortunate enough to escape. "Why is that necessary?"

"The process uses encoded light to transfer the DNA in the sample to your retinas. The retinas must remain fully accessible during the transfer."

"Can't I just wear goggles or something?"

"You will. But the splinting of your lids is also necessary. Do you wish to continue?"

Mike thought about it, about what Gabriella had said, about treasure, about how his life hadn't amounted to much so far and seemed to be getting seedier all the time. Getting up close and personal with one of history's greatest lovers *and* fighters seemed like a sound entertainment investment if nothing else. In his line of work, getting a bigger television wasn't real practical. Maybe he'd attract a better class of employers—or victims, with a famous Roman general on board. With the treasure, he could finance a war of his own. Or not. Probably not. He could at least retire and do the land mines to landscaping project.

"Okay," he said finally.

"You're very lucky you decided to do this when you did. Up until recently, the inventor of the process, Dr. Chimera, handled everything personally. The doctor was somewhat overly cautious, even though he—they—had been through the process as well. We're under new management now, and so the long screening process that used to be required of both the DNA and the host has been much abbreviated. We do think our clients are wise enough to know if the procedure is for them or not, without us dictating to them when and with whom they may blend. I do need to ask once more, however, before we begin, although you signed the waiver of responsibility already—are you sure you wish to go through with this? Have you any further concerns you wish me to address?"

"Just about the reversal thing. How long have I got?"

"It varies, I would think, but up until a certain time, it seems to be possible."

"Seems to be? Haven't you tried it?"

"Most people do not wish to reverse the process. The few who did were able to reverse it fully, but each case will be different. Have you specific doubts?"

"No. No, go ahead."

Mike settled back against the comfy pillows and the woman—Dr. B. Amalfi from her name tag—applied the retractors, which were cold but only pinched a little, then fitted the lenseless goggles over them. They reminded him of nippleless bras or crotchless panties, an interesting analogy which kept his imagination busy while the process was completed. It took about the same amount of time it might take to have a photograph taken.

He wasn't even aware when she removed the hardware from his eyes. First, he had the odd sensation that someone was watching him, then all of a sudden he started remembering things he knew he couldn't possibly have done. Finally, he fell into a deep sleep full of confused dreams. He started to awaken sometime later with an urgent craving more compelling than it had been in many years, "By the huge hairy balls of the bull, I need wine, and I need it now!"

CHAPTER 12

"Damn, I can see you're going to be a lot of help," Mike said. "No wine. We've been sober for twenty years, man, and we're going to stay that way."

"I outrank you," Marc Antony told him. "I am a general, and you are nothing but a mercenary—like those Gauls. I will have wine, and I will have it now or I'll have you killed."

"That would be a big problem for you," Mike told him. "Where do you think you are exactly and how do you think you got here?"

He felt the confusion of the other man, the memory of loss, pain, the last touch of his lover's hand. The despair at the desertion of his god and at the knowledge that he himself was considered a deserter from his own country.

"Yeah, yeah," Mike said. "So you died, big deal. Tell me about that treasure."

"What treasure?" Antony asked, but Mike could feel him holding back.

"You know what treasure. Look, I think you'd better assess your situation here. Look down. Look at the body you're in. It's all me, *all the time. If you get drunk, I get drunk, and I'm not going to do that, so just forget it. Getting drunk in my line of work will get us killed."*

"In my *line of work, getting killed was what you expected. Getting drunk was a way to enjoy life while it lasted."*

"Yeah, well, I've found it lasts longer if you do it sober."

"Maybe it just seems longer?"

"You're in denial."

"I don't believe so, no. Unless this is a very large boat we're in here."

"Don't get cute. I have a T-shirt with that joke. I knew it was old, but I didn't know it was as old as you are. Anyway, what I'm trying to tell you is that anything I do, you do, and vice versa, so you may as well clue me in about the treasure, Cleopatra, and all that stuff. Like I said before, if you get rich, I get rich. If I get laid, you get laid. If I bleed, you . . ."

"Yes, no need to demonstrate," Marc Antony said much more drily than he liked. *"Is this sorcery?"*

"Not exactly," Mike said. As he struggled to explain it, the explanation, both the part Mike deliberately clarified and the rest of it, became clear to Marc Antony. All but the bits that were so modern he had no reference for them. Mike's memories tried to make up the deficit and nearly succeeded.

"So Cleopatra is dead, and you found my essence in a lock of hair she had saved?"

"Pretty much."

"You have doubts about my essence or doubts that Cleopatra is dead."

"Well, she was dead, and most of her is still dead, but I think maybe something happened to her like happened to you and me. The Egyptian librarian, Gabriella, seemed to know a lot more about you and Cleopatra than just book learning."

The entire internal dialogue took place in the first few

moments after Mike awakened with his new buddy on board.

Dr. B. Amalfi reentered the room and looked inquisitively at him. "We've been monitoring your external responses. How do you feel?"

"I, for one, think I need a meeting," Mike said. "I don't suppose there's a support group for blended people, is there?"

She said, "No, though our predecessor planned to start one."

"It'd be a good idea. Thing is, you need to build trust. These old-timers come aboard, they got a lot of issues. First, they're not who they used to be. Second, they didn't expect to be anybody, and third, they may not be who they were cracked up to be in the first place. I think this guy I have with me here has some *serious* trust problems."

Inside of him, Marc Antony barked a short laugh. Aloud he said, "We're both trained to kill people. My Caesar was murdered by most of the rest of my government. I believe we have good reason not to trust."

"Like I said," Mike told Amalfi, "issues."

She smiled, white teeth in a surprisingly friendly display that made her mustache seem insignificant beside the game host smile that rendered her actually somewhat attractive. What did the B stand for, he wondered? Betty? Becky? Babs? Bambi?

"If you are having doubts, Mr. Kronos, perhaps you would like to speak with one who has undergone the process and had it reversed? The lady is staying here with us now."

"Yeah. That might be a good idea."

"I'll find out if the contessa will see you."

The laws of hospitality could be extremely inconvenient at times, Abdul Mohammed reflected. He had henchmen and a minivan to replace, a mummy in the room once occupied by Selim, one of the men who had been killed in the explosion of the minivan. He also needed to launch the next mission and, neither last nor least, find that loose cannon of a mercenary. The man's body should have been found after the bombing of the library. Neither the bombing nor the body materialized. This was a matter of the utmost concern to Abdul Mohammed, who had standards to maintain and an example to set if he was to succeed in his goals.

However, at present he was forced to listen politely to someone else's setbacks.

Amir Marid ibn Yasin Abu Kadar was a good customer, a patron of Abdul Mohammed's cause, and an unhappy man.

He sat on the screened balcony of Abdul Mohammed's home in the heart of Alexandria. The balcony was quiet and relatively private. The house was on the water side of the Corniche, and the balcony faced away from the noise of the street and toward the sea. The refreshing salt breeze did little to cool the choler of the amir, who sat sipping a soft drink and complaining bitterly. "I come to you, my friend, as one head of a household to another. My father indulged my younger brother, sending him to the West for his education. It had disastrous results for our family. Hakim spoiled his wife and daughter. He sent the girl to France to study. Fortunately, she is a rather stupid girl and came home before long. But she learned bad habits while she was there. When my brother was killed in an auto accident, I became the guardian of my brother's wife and children. This girl has been constant trouble to me. I sought to marry her to the son of one of my wife's sisters, but she found excuses to delay the marriage. Then we learned she was carrying on a flirtation—possibly an affair—with our chauffeur. I spoke to her mother about the poor upbringing she had given this girl, but before I could deal with the girl, she disappeared. The mother warned her, for which, of course, she received the punishment due her for such behavior.

"I have been searching for my poor misguided niece for a week. Meanwhile, I have moved her mother from my brother's home into my own, where my wife and mother can keep an eye on her. They informed me at once when my slut of a niece called her mother. I have the caller ID and traced the number to the island villa of a rich Greek woman. I forced the girl's mother to tell Mariam she must return at once and sent a helicopter for her."

"It sounds as if it ended well, my friend," Abdul Mohammed said soothingly.

"I suppose so, but I could not understand how Mariam eluded me for so long. I finally was able to beat it out of her when she returned. It seems the Greek woman has a network of accomplices, including an Egyptian woman Mariam understood to be a relative. The Egyptian woman met Mariam and spirited her away to the island, where she would be taken to Europe for who knows what immoral purposes. I suspect that these women are brothel keepers and slave dealers. Naturally, I sought to avenge my honor upon them and their accomplices. Those who helped Mariam escape my home have been appropriately dealt with, and I sent back some of my security force to capture the Greek woman while I led a party here to find and punish the Egyptian."

"Commendable zeal on your part, illustrious friend," Abdul Mohammed told him.

"But the woman lives in a fortified house full of armed fighters. Your police seem to be in league with her because they arrived before we could subdue the resistance. My nephew stayed behind, thinking to pick the woman off as she left the compound. When he did not return after a day,

I sent someone to look for him. They found him dead, his neck broken."

"My deepest condolences," Abdul Mohammed said with a small bow. "May Allah receive him in paradise."

"Indeed. But meanwhile, the Egyptian woman remains at large, free to corrupt other sheltered girls and dishonor their families. I am a busy man, Abdul Mohammed. I have many matters to attend to at home and cannot stay here indefinitely to finish what I have begun. Therefore, I ask for your assistance in this matter of disposing of the Egyptian woman in a suitably exemplary fashion. My people in Greece have orders to do likewise with her confederate."

"I am always your humble servant, gracious friend, but alas, I find myself shorthanded at the moment." He explained about the aborted mission and the explosion, the treachery from within his own ranks.

The amir was unmoved. "As I explained, it is a matter of family honor."

"Of course, of course. I meant only that a direct assault on the woman's stronghold would be difficult in my present situation. However, an indirect approach . . ."

"I knew I could count on you," the amir said.

Cleopatra's narrative:

Soon after I experienced the strangulation of my newly embodied soul-twin, I also experienced a sense of relief and release. She was safe, though I did not know the particulars in the same way that I had known her danger. However, by the time I was certain that she was safe, Leda had telephoned Gabriella Faruk and received answers that deepened her worry for her friend.

Then she tried the private cell phone number of Gretchen Wolfe, whose messenger reported that the user was unavailable but invited us to leave a voice message. This Leda did, with a frown at the instrument in her hand.

She turned to Andrew. "Look, I realize we just met, and you don't know me well, but your station wants to produce this program and—well, I need to borrow some money. I have to get back to Egypt and see what's going on with Gabriella. Gretchen Wolfe might be able to help, if I can reach her, but so far I can't."

"I can do better than loan you the money," Andrew replied stoutly. "Let's return to the hotel and meet with Ro and Iris again. I think we can mount a preproduction expedition that will pay your way and provide you, and Dr. Faruk if need be, with a cover and the dubious protection of safety in numbers."

"Ah," I said with relief, *"we have another protector."*

"Riiiight," Leda replied. *"And who's going to protect him if whoever's been after Gabriella comes for us? Whole boatloads of tourists have been wiped out by terrorists along the Nile. There's always the tourist police, of course, but what if someone is paying them? Andy is a good target for ransom."*

"True," I admitted, but nonetheless, it felt good to be accompanied by a man who commanded wealth and influence, if not, alas, an army.

There followed two days of miracles, in which Andrew caused to appear a number of scrying glasses that greatly resembled the television set at Rusti's. However, unlike the television, which impersonally performed certain plays on certain stations without regard for the viewer, these marvelous items allowed Andrew and indeed, ourselves, to speak with various individuals whose faces appeared in the glass. Sometimes many appeared at once, sometimes fewer, sometimes only one. But the result was that within that two-day period, Andrew purchased a boat for our journey, assisted Ro in rounding up videographers, photographers, and experts of various sorts, as well as actresses and actors to portray Iras, Charmion, Antony, Octavian, my priests, and myself in a reenactment of my death. All of these people were to accompany us on our journey, although the main portion of the filming would not take place until later, Andrew said. All he spoke to seemed amazed and bewildered at his haste.

"I didn't think you could possibly get it together this fast," Leda said. "From what I've heard, TV productions, especially new ones, can be kind of glacial."

Andrew shrugged. "Most of the delays are about money, getting the money, keeping the money, paying the money. When it's the moneyman who wants things to happen, they can, as you see, happen pretty quickly."

Various assistants now crowded the hotel suite armed with their own telephones so that the chatter sounded like my palace at festival time. Food came and went, airplane reservations were made for people in all parts of the world, authorities were notified.

Leda was on the telephone to Rusti, whom she called as soon as we returned to the hotel and who, by the end of day two, had finally succeeded in repacking our bags and delivering them to the hotel. Leda also called her brother Rudy, who brought his wife Dana and their children to the suite to bid her farewell. She was not so successful at reaching Gretchen Wolfe, within whom resided her father's *ba*. Nor did she hear anything further from Gabriella. For my part, I watched and listened within myself for any indication from my soul-twin as to the whereabouts or state of well-being of her hostess and herself.

The Italian jail cell was a miserable hole in a rather grand historic building in the center of Palermo. The cots were cement, the toilet a hole in the floor, and two other inmates had been looking at Wilhelm as if they wanted to eat him until they saw Gretchen. She looked much tastier to them, or so they eloquently enthused in gutter Italian and, just so she didn't miss the point, with graphic hand gestures.

"*Basta!*" the constable said, running his nightstick against the bars.

"*Those guys are no class act,*" Duke said, "*but at least they look happy to see us. What's wrong with Wilhelm?*"

His inner question was outwardly expressed by Gretchen at the same moment. "What is wrong with him?" she demanded of the constable.

Wilhelm, clad in the filthy remnants of his silk shirt and the even filthier slacks to one of his designer suits, sat on a bunk with his elbows on his knees and his head in his hands. He looked up dully at the clamor of his cellmates, but his eyes weren't focused. Both Duke, from his police work, and Gretchen, from her medical practice, recognized that he was still suffering from the effects of some sort of drug. "Wilhelm, *liebchen,*" Gretchen said as softly as possible, considering the alarm building within her. "I am here, your Gretchen. Speak to me."

This set up an even ruder stream of verbal filth from the cellmates.

Gretchen turned to the constable. "Out. You will bring him *out* of there, now. The Interpol inspector did not say he was incarcerated, or that he has been drugged. But I am a doctor, and this, my husband, is an important man."

"*Si, signora, si,*" the constable said placatingly. Though she had not been using it much, Gretchen did speak passable Italian, and the constable explained that *Signor* Wolfe had been detained by a patrol officer for his own protection after being found staggering drunkenly down a street in a dangerous area of the city.

As he explained, he unlocked the cell and used his nightstick to restrain the other prisoners as Gretchen entered, knelt in front of Wilhelm, and spoke in her kind, firm doctor voice as she examined his pupillary response and reflexes.

"You can walk, *liebchen, ja?*"

He nodded, and she put one of his arms around her shoulder and slipped one of her arms around his waist while holding on to his limp hand with her own. She registered two things. His wedding ring was missing, and he smelled as if he had never washed in his life.

Once they were outside the cell and it had been locked behind them, the constable assisted. There was paperwork to do, but much as it pained Duke to see it, a healthy contribution to the constable's personal branch of the policeman's benevolent fund rendered the formalities unnecessary. The constable helped Gretchen load Wilhelm into the little sports car she had acquired for the trip, and when they reached their hotel, the doorman and bellman helped her get him to the room. She was very strong, but she wasn't very large, and her husband outweighed her by at least seventy-five pounds.

For a tip large enough to let him buy his own hotel, the bellman helped disrobe Wilhelm and sat him on a chair in the shower. Once the bellman left, Gretchen disrobed and stepped into the shower, too, turning on the water and washing both herself and her husband, rubbing up such a brisk froth of soap bubbles and scrubbing both of them so hard that Duke almost failed to find anything erotic about it. He very carefully did not share his thoughts with Gretchen at that time. It was literally as much as his soul was worth. Gretchen had come a long way, but for a doctor, she could still be a little prissy.

However, Duke was alarmed that Wilhelm, although he seemed to be coming to under the influence of the soap and hot water, followed by the cold rinse Gretchen drenched them with at the end—some masochistic remnant of the Norse side of her heritage, no doubt—registered almost no response to his naked and slippery wife. A damned shame in Duke's opinion. Gretchen was a good-looking woman with a beautiful body she had exerted an uncommon amount of time, energy, and money to acquire and maintain. She and Wilhelm didn't have all that many chances to shower together. What the hell was wrong with the man anyway?

She grabbed the towels and after hurriedly patting most of the damp off herself and wrapping the towel around her hair, rubbed Wilhelm down to the next layer of epidermis, so that his naturally fair skin, no longer artificially tanned as it had been the last time Duke saw him, glowed red under her ministrations. Her bare feet slapped against the cool floor, leaving dark steamy tracks as she padded to the door, grabbing the fluffy white terry robes from it. Slipping one around herself and knotting the tie firmly, she bundled Wilhelm into one, too. Fortunately, he was coming to a little by then and tried to help. Still, they slipped a couple of times, once getting him out of the shower and once on the floor as their wet feet hit the tiles, and Gretchen buckled under his weight.

Between her determination and Wilhelm's increasing cooperation, they made it to the bed, where they collapsed, still entwined. Whereupon Wilhelm fell back into a fairly natural sleep, and Gretchen allowed herself a few tears while she resolutely kept vigil.

"*I want to know something,*" Duke said, figuring the tricky potentially sexy bits were past enough that he could safely remind her of his presence again.

"*I want to know* many *things,*" Gretchen replied, still angry at finding her husband in such a state.

"*Yeah, well, me, too. But what I most want to know is how they knew at the station that Wilhelm was him. Right now he doesn't look much like the picture we gave the police, and he doesn't have his ring or his wallet, from what I could tell while we were lugging him around. With no ID, in the shape he was in, he could have rotted in there forever."*

"This is very easy," Gretchen said. Reaching into the trash, she extracted the filthy pair of slacks and turned the band up, running her clean finger lightly over a raised cloth tag clearly printed with the name Wilhelm Wolfe.

"You sew his name inside his clothes like he was going to camp or something?" Duke asked incredulously.

"I am doing this since first we are married, ja. My mama did this for my papa and my brother and me so I do the same for Wilhelm. No one provided such labels for your clothes when you were alive?"

"Not since my mom did it when I went to boot camp," Duke said. *"And none of my wives ever did it. I mean, why would they?"*

Gretchen tossed the pants back into the trash and nodded at her snoring husband. *"For this reason. Here,"* she said.

"Okay, point taken."

She picked up the phone and called Armani in Rome, telling them to send a courier with clothing in Wilhelm's measurements, which they had in their files. She realized when she finished that since the Interpol detective brought her to Palermo, she had neglected to charge her cell phone. This she did, and got dressed to await the arrival of the Armani courier.

At some point she fell asleep, and was awakened by the musical signal from her phone, which played "Edelweiss" instead of ringing. Instantly she was alert, and snatched it up. *"Ja?"* she said in German. "This is *Frau Doktor* Wolfe speaking. What is it?"

"Gretchen! It's Leda. I'm so glad to finally reach you. Where are you? Did you find Wolfie—I mean, Wilhelm?"

"He is here beside me, Leda!"

"That's great. Listen, I'm coming back over to Egypt with a TV crew. Andy—I mean, Sir Andrew McCallum, is a friend of Wilhelm's and on the Helix board. He'd like to consult with Wilhelm on this, too."

"You are arriving when?"

"We're flying nonstop to Alex, so we'll meet you there tomorrow at about two. Okay? Oops, 'scuse me. Gotta run. Love you, Dad, Gretchen."

"Bye, kid," Duke said to a dial tone.

CHAPTER 13

Having already landed in Delhi, Chimera considered traveling on to Dharmsala to meet the lama. But if the monks had not been entirely honest about their destination, the scientist wondered if they were telling the truth about other matters. While pondering whether to continue by ground transport to the Himalayan area that had become Tibet in exile or to board another plane headed back to Athens or to the United States, Chimera fingered the pendant worn ever since their blending. The back came away in the scientist's fingers. Worried lest the tiny storage unit with the information and blueprints fall out, Chimera examined the pendant, the clothing worn at the moment, and the surrounding area. The chip was gone, and with it all of the highly secret information it had contained.

No, Chimera decided, the monks decidedly were not what they seemed.

And, alas, the pleasurable part of the trip would need to be delayed now while Chimera reported the extent of the loss to Helix and retrieved the lost data from them. The scientist needed it as a basis for future work.

First, however, Wolfe should be told of the theft. Chimera understood Wolfe's attitude toward the project but could not say as much for the current administration. However, dialing Wolfe's number yielded a recording saying that it was out of order. So Chimera next tried Gretchen Wolfe's number.

Gretchen was very mysterious but said that she and Wilhelm would be on their way to Alexandria as soon as her husband was able to travel, probably the next day. She urged Chimera to join them.

Finally, Chimera found a phone and dialed the number of the Padma Lama's monastery. The monk who answered was very surprised to learn that the monastery in which he was standing had been destroyed by an avalanche.

Chimera caught the next plane to Athens and on to Alexandria.

"Come on, man, this is cool. Think of it like we're in the ultimate buddy movie together." Mike said this aloud to Marc Antony after the latter finished complaining about coming down in the world to a teetotaling, cross-worshiping soldier whose loyalty was sold to the highest bidder. Mike was trying to be conciliatory, a fairly unusual role for him.

Mike's image of a buddy movie confused Marc Antony further. The general failed to understand the full meaning of images involving two men on horses plunging over a cliff, two women in a car plunging over a cliff, a black man and a white man blowing things up and escaping explosions caused by others, an Asian man and a white man doing something similar, and other unconventional pairings engaging in other stimulating but seemingly meaningless activities. Possibly these were like the Centurion lovers who would fight to the death for each other, but somehow Marc didn't quite believe it.

"Okay, forget the buddy movie," Mike said, sensing his confusion.

By that time they were in the little courtyard at the villa where the Contessa Dumont was lodged. The contessa, a woman whose slender elegance was edged with fragility, waved at him to sit in the white iron chair opposite her own, across the green-striped-umbrella-shaded table.

She extended her hand. Mike would have reached for it but found himself giving her a short, almost Japanese bow instead. She smiled. "Ah yes, your new guest must not be in the habit of shaking ladies' hands. I am Virginie Dumont, but please call me Ginia. I feel we are destined to be friends."

"Are we?" Mike asked. He was a little puzzled. Maybe he had come up in the world already by blending with the Roman general. Contessas did not normally seek him out as a social equal.

"I believe so. You have already met my niece, Gabriella, before your blending. It was I who warned her of the attack on her villa. In fact, that is why I have come to stay on Kefalos for a time. My own home was besieged by black-masked men angry over my choice of houseguests. Gabriella spoke to me of you when she called me back after her own attackers had fled. She said you saved her life twice in one day. And this, I understand, was before your blending. I very much hope that we shall be friends, therefore. My niece is very precious to me. And yet"—she smiled and waved him to the other chair—"I betrayed her most cruelly during my own blending with Pandora Blades. Which brings us to your present state, does it not?"

Mike nodded. As a support group, this was a little too intimate for his taste. "Doc Amalfi says that you got yourself unblended. Was it because of what happened between you and your niece when you had whatsername on board?"

"That was part of it. I—we—behaved very badly and because of certain aspects of Pandora's personality were vulnerable to unscrupulous people I would normally have guarded against. In her own time, among her own associates, she was brilliant, tragic, passionately devoted to art and her love. But blended with me, shall we say, she lost the focus that made her great? Hers was an obsessive personality, and she fastened on another magnetic man to worship, one even less worthy than her original lover. I had hoped that by blending with her, I would acquire some of that fire and creative genius I have always longed for, and she might acquire some peace, a lesser pain than that she suffered during her brief life, and could use my wealth to fully realize her potential. Obviously, the combination didn't work that way. And so we parted."

"Did she mind? I mean, she'd be dead again, right?" Mike asked. Although the newly conscious part of him that belonged to Marc Antony stayed silent, it was alert and paying close attention.

"I'm not sure. I think perhaps she felt she would be in total control, and I would be the one banished, but it didn't work out that way. Her code was wiped from my brain, is how I think Chimera phrased it. I suppose someone else could blend with her if they wished, but I would personally advise them against it."

"*Hah! You see how it works, General, sir? I can get rid of you, but you can't do without me.*"

"*I did not ask to be here,*" Marc Antony reminded him. "*Death does not frighten me. I fell on my own sword as honor demanded when the time came.*"

"*Or when you thought it came. But you goofed. Don't write this life off too quickly until you see what it has to offer. Especially with the help of that treasure of yours—ours.*"

Ginia continued, "Would it be too intrusive of me to ask with whom you blended?"

"Would it be real rude of me to decline to answer right now, ma'am?" Mike asked. "I'd sort of like to get used to the whole thing and to this—uh—person—before I talk about it too much. I appreciate you sharing your experiences with me, though." On impulse he added, "You know, I got the impression that maybe your niece had been blended herself."

"I hope you won't think me rude if I decline to answer *that,* Mr. Kronos."

Mike blinked for a moment, then remembered he was known there by Galen's name.

"Such information should be disclosed only by the party involved," Ginia continued.

"That makes sense," he said. "I just wondered, since she seems to have some pretty powerful enemies for a librarian."

"Gabriella is far more than a librarian, Mr. Kronos. She is the head of the antiquities department for the Biblioteca Alexandrina and one of the discoverers of the tomb of the great Queen Cleopatra. At present, she is the highest-ranking woman archaeologist in Egypt."

"I'm impressed, but I can't see why someone would send a private army after her. Especially when the library had just been looted."

"We are involved in a—charity—shall we say, that, while it helps many deserving individuals, apparently angers others, those who have a vested interest in oppressing the—people—we assist. At times our work can be rather thankless. Recently we attempted to help someone who had a change of heart and returned to the situation from which we were trying to extract her."

"It was a woman? What do you do? Run some kind of international women's shelter?" He was being facetious and was a little surprised to see dismay wash over the contessa's face.

She quickly hid it with a smile and a brief nod. "How perceptive you are. It is something like that, yes. But we do not wish it to be generally known. I'm sure, having been at Gabriella's during the invasion of those who did not appreciate her intervention, you can understand why."

"Yeah, I can see where in this part of the world it wouldn't be a popular cause. But I say good for you, lady." He said this so heartily she again appeared startled. Well, he was glad his ex and daughter had had a shelter to go to when he went ballistic. He was glad now, anyway. "Speaking of invasions, excuse me, but I need to be getting back to Egypt and seeing a man about a mummy."

By the time the police had finished questioning Gabriella, she felt she would rather have continued dealing with the terrorists. The questions were relentless, interminable, and repetitive, the same ones asked over and over again as if to trip her up. They seemed to think, despite the courtesy they accorded her because of her high position (unnatural for a woman), that she had somehow had something to do with the vandalization of the library. They left and returned no fewer than four times during the day, apparently hoping to trap her into contradicting her own story. She was so weary that she feared she would do so through misspeaking rather than the lies they would assume she was telling. In between she had tried to work, tried to record the damage done, tried to translate a bit more of the manuscripts, but now it was once more long after midnight and into the morning of the following day, and still she had not been to bed. Nor, in fact, was she sure where she would be making her bed that night.

About the time the police finally left her alone, she received the first telephone call. One word: "Whore." In Arabic, but pronounced with malicious relish.

Others followed for the next three hours. Heavy breathing mostly, whispered threats and obscenities. She stopped answering the phone.

As the midday break came, she packed up her purse and pockets with the maps, a compass, a small hatchet and collapsible shovel, a headband with a miner's light attached to it as well as an extra handheld flashlight with extra batteries, candles, and a gas clicker to back those up, a bottle of water, and a Snickers. She also took a sweater and a fold-up rain slicker. And her expandable clear plastic galoshes.

"A clever enemy would kill us for the maps alone," Cleopatra observed. *"They would be invaluable in carrying out clandestine plots. Is your cousin meeting us outside?"*

"No, he's still helping the family evacuate the compound."

"Then what is to keep our enemies from abducting us as we leave the building?"

"They will not see us leave the building because we will leave from beneath it. This complex was built on the site of your great library—or at least one of the annexes. Naturally, an institution with the reverence for the past this one has did not destroy the site upon which it is built. The foundations were laid to surround it. It still lies below this level."

"I'm glad to hear that. Are people studying it?"

"No, that happened before this was built. But it's been preserved for future study. One of the less well known discoveries was the cistern that lay beneath it—access was discovered by some workmen, but since it was just another cistern, little attention was paid to it at the time. In the late twentieth and early part of this century, Isabelle Hairy made an exhaustive study of the cisterns either found or rumored to exist. After she departed, the maps she made were mislaid, and no one else took much interest. The emphasis has been on the exploration in the harbor. My family has had a long-standing interest in the city's underworld, however. Our home is on the site of an older compound with its own cistern."

Carrying on the internal dialogue, Gabriella checked the hallway, then opened a narrow door that seemed to lead to a broom closet. However, it contained a rather plain inner sarcophagus, which was locked. Gabriella unlocked it and opened it. Inside it was hollow and led to a flight of stairs. *"One of my predecessors had an overdeveloped sense of drama,"* she explained. *"He was also addicted to very bad movies from the 1940s."*

"Yes?" Cleopatra was puzzled.

"About mummies and the tombs on their curses and how they came back to life. They were very silly horror films."

"I see nothing horrible about having been a mummy, then coming back to life. It's what we were all promised would happen someday."

"Yes, well. When we have the time we will view some of them, and you'll understand why this doorway is a bit of a joke."

The staircase leading down was industrial metal formed into an elongated spiral. At one point it pierced a plywood ceiling and continued to the stone beneath. Gabriella kept her flashlight in motion, on the lookout for snakes or scorpions or even large stones that might trip her up. Once she stepped off the last stair, she made her way to a corner of the vast area that had once contained the wisdom of the known world. A slab of stone was set with a metal ring. Gabriella hauled on this until she managed to move the stone aside. Her flashlight beam caught the cheerful yellow of a painted metal ladder's top. The rest of the ladder was lost in darkness.

Fitting the band with the miner's light onto her head, she switched on the light, took a deep breath, turned sideways, and stepped cautiously down onto the top rung. It wobbled but held. Before each step she inclined her head to light the way.

"You are not afraid to do this alone?" Cleopatra asked.

"It's part of how I make my living, and, besides, I'm not alone. Now I have you. Actually, I've never minded tunnels and caves. Our cistern has a hole high in the upper part of the wall. It connects not to the next house, because in the old days there were no other houses beyond ours. Instead, it was apparently dug by grave robbers as a way to escape undetected from the necropolis. My cousins explored that and many of the other cisterns and necropoli beneath the

city when they were youngsters. Back when we had an ancestor who was a king—not a direct ancestor, mind you, but with the same family name—he was deposed by a revolutionary government. Our family hid in the cisterns and necropoli until they knew how they might fare under the new regime. Long before that, one of the early saints was said to have hidden out in them, also using the connections the thieves made among the systems. In places they're blocked, but my cousins and I have done some extracurricular exploration and excavations to make routes down here. Only I'm not very sure about this one. According to Hairy, it is part of the great grid that connected with the mideastern branch of the Canopic Channel."

"That is quite true. We should be able to follow the grid all the way to the southernmost wall of the city."

"The walls aren't there anymore, but neither, I suspect, is most of the grid. Parts of it were blocked off and reinforced to act as air-raid shelters, and parts of it were blocked with silt and debris from natural cave-ins. The original channels have been destroyed as the city was built. But some of this still connects to the storm drains we use during monsoon season."

"What of the floods?" Cleopatra asked. *"What time of the year is it? We might drown!"*

"Oh, we have to discuss that yet. The Nile no longer floods. A great dam has been built—more than one actually, far upstream, where it makes an enormous lake. Many of the ancient sacred temples you knew and most of Nubia now lie underwater."

"But—why?" Cleopatra asked, appalled.

"So there could be a stable population along the banks of the Nile, mostly, and the cities not be endangered by the floods."

"And for this they drowned half of Egypt?"

"It seemed like a good idea at the time. Now we're discovering that without the floods, there is no silt, and without the silt, the land and the river both are much poorer. People have to use fertilizers for the first time in our history."

"But that makes no sense!"

"It did for a while. But now that the negative effects of the dams

*have taken their toll, a project has been under way to reengineer the
dams to allow silt-rich waters to pass through, creating an artificial flood that will raise the river so it can flow into newly dug irrigation ditches as well as the old ones. It will not be as high or as
beneficial as the floods once were, but better than it is now."*

"I must see this."

Gabriella considered what she had just said and caught
her breath. *"I hope we don't see it from too close a perspective. The
first release is scheduled for this week. If we are still down here
when it happens—well, we won't be, surely."*

She changed the direction of her thoughts. *"There's to be
quite a celebration. Once we're above ground again, well away from
here, Mo will collect us, and we'll leave Alex for a while, maybe go
to Cairo so we can see some of the festivities while we get lost in the
crowds until these thugs find others to torment. Which won't take
long, they hate so many people."*

*"How will my beloved find us? Once the handsome mercenary
takes our bait and the amulet to be blended with him, that is?"*

"I don't know. Does he have our cell phone number?" Gabriella
asked. She was unaware that at that very moment her cell
phone was ringing except that it was muffled by the para-
phernalia in her bag.

CHAPTER 14

"Still no answer?" Andrew asked, as Leda hung up the phone once more.

"No. Not at the house and not at her office. I'm going to try her aunt. She might know what's going on."

But the phone at the contessa's villa switched at once to the voice mailbox. Leda left a message saying that she was concerned that she could not reach Gabriella.

"Try not to worry," Andrew told her. "We'll be in Alexandria by next Thursday anyway."

"We can find her there unless . . ." His voice faltered uncertainly and his eyes widened with question. "Unless you think she . . ."

Leda sat still for a moment, then said in her elegant, slightly accented voice, "Not dead. I'd know. But she is in trouble. I keep thinking of a place, dark, stone, cool . . ." She shrugged, the fabric covering her shoulder shimmering with the gesture.

"A tomb perhaps?" Andrew asked. His voice was hushed with the excitement the image gave him. He'd confided in Leda during their first long talk that as Andrew McCallum he'd cared only for modern, highly technical devices with practical applications. But once he blended with Sir Walter, the writer's love of antiquities, their mysteries and stories, became a consuming passion of his own. With Sir Walter's acquisitiveness and Andrew's money, the collections, though started late, had already grown to such proportions that he had added a museum wing to his home in the Scottish Borders.

"Perhaps," she said. "As you say, we soon will know."

Just then, the telephone rang. Andrew answered. "Yes, Contessa. She's right here. I'll put her on."

The Contessa Virginie Dumont sounded slightly out of breath. "Your message was forwarded to me and I tried to call you back when I got it, but it was blocked then, saying you were no longer available," she said. "I am on Kefalos. We were betrayed by one of the people we tried to help. Gabriella and her family were attacked, the police told me, although the idiots implied that perhaps they were not and Gabriella made up the story to cover for her supposed part in a robbery and attempted sabotage of the Biblioteca last night."

"Why in the hell would they think something like that?" Leda asked.

"Perhaps they were led to believe it by people who wished them not to look too closely into the matter."

"You think they were bribed?"

"Probably. They are certainly wrong. I spoke to her when I called to warn her, and she could have been killed but for this rather devastating man I met later, here on Kefalos."

"Wait. What man?"

Ginia explained. "His name is Galen Kronos and after meeting my niece he—well, I cannot discuss it on the telephone." There was a bit of a giggle in the contessa's voice. Leda was annoyed. Ginia shouldn't have mentioned the guy's name if there was something about him she wasn't going to discuss because it was too sensitive.

"Odd that he rescues Gabriella, then ends up on Kefalos at the same time as Ginia," Leda mused.

"Not all that odd," Cleopatra replied, amused. *"I have a feeling that my counterpart may have had a hand in that. If the man was as devastating as Ginia says, he may be a worthy vessel for Antony."*

"She must have found that doohickey then, the one with Antony's hair. I'm surprised she'd hand it over to a strange guy, tell him to go blend with Antony, and he'd trot right off to do that little thing. I've never known devastating guys to be so accommodating myself."

"I believe I may be able to help you change that, Leda dear," Cleo purred, smugly, Leda thought. *"Our Andrew, for instance, appears ready to accommodate you in most matters."*

"Yes, well, I feel sort of the same about him. What's not to like? He seems like a real grown-up person, not just another bad boy. He knows all about the blend, is blended with a great author, also a real grown-up person but with a lot of brilliant romantic notions. He thinks, reads, is age-appropriate, not bad-looking, thinks I'm not bad-looking, and I like him a lot. But Cleo?"

"Yes?"

"When it comes to being accommodating on our behalf, please remember that I'm somewhat older and a whole lot creakier than you were the last time you indulged in horizontal refreshment with Antony. I'm not sure what it was exactly you did in bed that rendered Romans so—accommodating—but I hope if it was really athletic, you'll respect your vessel and tone it down a bit, okay?"

"Was it bad news?" Andrew asked.

She told him.

"Poor lass, this is a great strain for you, isn't it? Have you been sleeping at all?"

She admitted she had not.

"You should lie down, get some rest. There are two extra rooms in this barn of a suite. I'll call you if anything comes up."

Gratefully, she agreed, though she doubted she'd be able to do more than a quick nap. However, as soon as she lay down, she was plunged into a deep, dreaming sleep.

The cisterns were three stone-vaulted stories deep, and although Gabriella's flashlight was not strong enough to make out many details, she knew that many of the repairs had been done with ancient columns from other structures, the capitals stuck on upside down on some. Still, it was an awesome feat of architecture. It was actually something for which Egypt was well-known.

They descended past the first arch and the second, but as they approached the ground, Gabriella's light picked up the black gleam of water quite high on the columns.

"*I was afraid of this,*" she moaned to herself.

"*If the floods no longer come, from where came these waters?*" Cleopatra asked.

"*It must be left over from the quake,*" Gabriella guessed. "*My guess is it's salt water, not fresh. Perhaps it filled these lower levels when the sea came flooding back into the harbor, but there is a blockage closer to the shore that prevented the waters from receding into the sea again. This is too high for us to wade. We'll have to take our chances on the street.*"

She began climbing back up the ladder but when she came to the opening through which she had descended into the cistern, she found it was no longer open. A stone slab sat directly overhead. She could not budge it with the single hand she could spare from the ladder, which trembled beneath her feet.

"*Trapped,*" she said. "*Probably unintentionally. Some enterprising security guard no doubt remembered the excavation and that it had an entrance to the cisterns.*"

"*An awkward time for your guards to become efficient,*" Cleopatra said. "*What is that smell?*"

"*Sewage probably. They rerouted the sewers when the cofferdam was built and may have punched through too far in places—or perhaps it's more earthquake damage. That's the least of our worries now. I truly don't want to swim in this, but if we can't go back, I don't know what else we can do.*"

Gabriella had been focusing on her dialogue with Cleopatra so totally that she was startled when the boat glided past two levels below her.

"What's a boat doing down here anyway?" she asked aloud.

The boatman looked up, seemingly as startled as she was, and waved. A gold tooth glinted in the beam of a lantern he held aloft.

"What is a lady doing down here anyway?" the boatman answered good-naturedly. "What did you do that brought you here?"

"I'm an archaeologist with the Biblioteca," she said, ignoring the odd way his question was phrased. He was a tall, imposing man with an aristocratic look about him, but she thought anyone who would choose the cisterns as a place for a boating holiday had to be a bit strange. "I was checking on the effects of the recent earthquake on these cisterns, but my colleagues seem to have forgotten I came down here and blocked off the door to the upper regions."

"Ah," he said as if that made perfect sense. "I am in charge of this place, checking the integrity of these cisterns and the water level. I have seen many snakes and rats down here, lady, and the water is almost eight feet deep. It will be deeper still when they free the river. You had better ride with me."

"Thanks. I guess I'd better," she agreed, and descended the ladder again to climb into the boat.

The boatman was a rather majestic-looking older man,

late fifties or early sixties perhaps, with a hook nose and a humorous mouth. He helped her settle into his boat before lifting his oar again. She shivered. It was chilly down there. She pulled the sweater from her pack.

"I have a thermos of hot coffee, lady. You would like some, yes?"

"That would be wonderful," she agreed. She realized suddenly she had had nothing to eat or drink since her dinner with Mike Angeles the previous night, which seemed as if it had happened years ago. The boatman wiped the edge of the plastic thermos cup, poured steaming and fragrant coffee into it, and offered it to her. She sipped it gratefully, warming her hands on the cup. It felt wonderful going down, though the taste was a bit strong and slightly more bitter than usual. The brand, no doubt.

She had hoped it would wake her up, but suddenly her weariness was too great for mere coffee to contain. Her hands trembling, weak with lack of sleep, she was able just barely to return the cup before she felt her eyelids getting heavy, right there, sitting up in the boat.

Somewhere a dog howled. *"What's a dog doing down here?"* she wondered and began to worry that it had been washed in with the earthquake and was starving and injured or more likely starving and drowning somewhere in the watery labyrinth of the cisterns.

"I've heard that howl before," Cleopatra said. *"Between the time the snake bit me and the time Octavian came into my mausoleum."*

"Oh, you think it's Anubis, then? I bow to your experience but really, doesn't one dog sound pretty much like another?" Just the same, chills unrelated to the temperature ran down her spine. Though how she could tell them from the chills that *were* related to the temperature she wasn't sure. There were quite a lot of those.

The slap of the boatman's oars and the warmth of the coffee soon changed that, however, and she felt herself nodding off. The lamp cast peculiar shadows on the arches. She was mildly surprised, in her drowsy state, to note that these shades were not long and even but short dapples of figured darkness, almost like hieroglyphics. In fact, she became sure that if the boat had not been traveling so quickly, she could have read them.

Shortly after serving the coffee and returning to his oars, the boatman had begun singing a little tune under his breath. His voice was magnified by the echoes in the cavernous chambers, and it seemed less a song and more a chant. It was soporific. The coffee had not done a thing to keep her awake. She dozed again, and as she did so, the chant grew louder and the shadow hieroglyphics moved and shifted, though how she could tell with her eyes closed, she didn't know. Perhaps this was all a dream?

"Dead? What? Again?"
"So it would appear. Are not the names of Osiris writ by magic upon the arched ceilings?"

"Ah, so they are."

"Sokar, Osiris, Wennefer." Yup, Leda decided, that would be Osiris, he who was blue of head and with turquoise on his arms. It was dim in the Field of Reeds, but you could still make out the colors a little—the rain hat the boatman wore was definitely blue, and his shirt did look turquoise.

"Field of Reeds? We did not come to the Field of Reeds. Only to the cisterns beneath the city."

"Oops, sorry, those things poking up out of the water look like reeds to me," Leda said.

"So they are. But how? These cisterns are entirely of stone."

"Cracks maybe from the quakes?" Leda surmised. A babble of interior voices discussed the idea.

Leda had, of course, seen herself in dreams before. But she'd never talked to herself in four-part harmony in previous dreams and anyway, she wasn't seeing herself, or even

Gabriella. She was seeing Cleopatra exactly as she appeared in the queen's own memory of her reflected image. Except, of course, that she was wearing baggy modern clothes and carrying a knapsack.

So, whose dream was this anyway? Hers? Cleo's? Gabriella's? Hard to tell. It seemed to belong to them all. Asleep, she and Cleo blended more completely than during waking hours. Now it seemed that perhaps they all drew closer in sleep.

"Is this the bit where our heart gets weighed?" she wondered to anyone who might pick up the thought. She received the image of Cleo shrugging, distracted by the scene opening before them as the little boat—a barge of sorts really, because those weren't actually oars the boatman used but more of a pole—plied the reed-choked underground waters.

"Don't give me that. You ought to know this stuff. You've done it before, after all. If we're going to have our heart weighed against a feather, I've got some serious explaining to do first."

Cleopatra's focus returned from the dimly lit progress of the boat. *"Why do you say such a thing? We have lived a blameless life this time."*

"Maybe since you've been on board, but you just ask Rudy if you think I have. Of course, I've never murdered anyone, and I haven't actually ever stolen anything, though I have borrowed Rusti's clothes on occasion and relocated other little articles, especially when I was in the Navy. I don't lie about things—I evade the questions. And watching Daddy cured me of getting into too much trouble with bad boys."

"That is a very good start," Cleopatra said, seeming relieved. *"But—ah—I do not think this is the part where our heart is weighed. See you? Osiris docks the little boat and our sister climbs from it to shore. How can it be that we have come so far, but look! She climbs and as she emerges from the underworld, she is just inside the city wall—"*

"There's not one anymore, you know."

"Yes, but I know well enough where it is, even without the proper landmarks. Formerly the Nile entered at this point and branched off into the channels my ancestors caused to be dug to supply us with water."

But climbing from the boat had stirred Gabriella's consciousness. She no longer dreamed, and the connection, if not broken, sagged like the string between two tin cans. Leda fell back to sleep dreaming of Andrew and his wonderful library.

CHAPTER 15

Gabriella emerged from the underworld into a breezy dawn breaking over Alexandria, most of which lay behind her. She pulled out her cell phone and to her dismay saw that she had forgotten to turn it off. The batteries were dead again.

She shoved the phone back into her bag and looked up the street that turned into Canopic Way leading to Rosetta or to Highway 1 to Cairo. A minivan taxicab slowed as it reached her. It was not a familiar one, but Mo leaned across the passenger seat. "Need a ride, lady? Climb in the back like a regular passenger," he told her.

She was so glad to see him she didn't even ask how he had known to be there at the precise time she needed him.

"Was there much difficulty?" he asked her once he'd rammed the minivan back into the torrent of traffic.

"No. For you and the others?"

"All are safe just as we planned. Twice I have traded cars with friends to keep our enemies from my own trail."

"You weren't followed?"

"I do not think so. You?"

"I wasn't followed but the cisterns were flooded. I caught a boat ride with a man who was apparently some sort of city maintenance person—no. Wait. How can that be?"

"How can what be, cousin?"

"The man brought me all the way from the cisterns beneath the Biblioteca to this place. But the parts known to us do not extend this far."

Mo shrugged. "Perhaps they've been enlarged recently, and you have been too—preoccupied—to notice. Certainly some things have changed if the city has assigned someone to look after them. Or perhaps the quake broke down some of the old barriers?"

"It seems unlikely," Gabriella said. Quake damage was seldom so convenient. The most recent one had already resulted in the discovery of Cleopatra's canopic jar and DNA and subsequently her tomb.

They fell silent, both considering the ramifications of her journey but neither wishing to discuss it further.

"So," Mo said, breaking the silence, "where do we go now?"

"Cairo. I think now is an excellent time to clear out of Alex for a while. There are to be a great many boats making the journey to Aswan for the release of the waters. Perhaps it is time for us to embark on that journey up the Nile I've had that nagging need to make. But—Mo?"

"Yes?"

"Let us cross back over the bridge and take the Desert Highway. We would see the pyramids and the sphinx once more."

"Very well," he agreed, hearing in the request from his cousin the politely phrased command of Cleopatra.

He concentrated on his driving until they were beyond the edges of Alexandrian traffic. Of course, the highway was still busy—both of them were—but it was a straighter shot with fewer vehicles turning onto and off the road.

She dozed for a while, despite the traffic noise. When she awoke, she found Mo was snatching glances back at her in the rearview mirror. She met his eyes and he put his arm up and waggled his fingers back at her in greeting, then stretched the arm across the back of the front passenger seat.

"You have bad dreams, little cousin. Other than the recent catastrophes, what is troubling you?"

She smiled slightly, "You mean other than almost being blown up, murdered, or possibly only my family murdered while I was kidnapped?"

"Yes, other than those little things," he said, answering her smile with the ghost of one that did not quite break through his worried frown. "I do not think matters are working as you hoped they would. All of us assumed that once you found Cleopatra's tomb, you would relax, enjoy your triumph. When you told me that in spite of our mistake before, you wished to blend with the queen and she had consented, I thought, ah, now she will be happy. She will learn the secrets of the ancients, which have always fascinated her. But no, you have become withdrawn and silent even to us who love you, you snap at times, and are always distracted. We who love you miss you. Come, tell your old Mo your problems as you did when we were kids."

Gabriella sighed deeply and leaned forward from the backseat of the cab to lay her head against the arm her cousin had stretched across the raggedly upholstered back of the passenger seat.

It was indeed wearing, this balancing of the skills, needs, and knowledge of two different personalities, particularly under the stressful circumstances of the last twenty-four hours. She had hoped for a longer and more peaceful settling-in period.

"You're right, Mo," she said. "I've been under a lot of strain, and I know it has been difficult for you, too. You have been with me through it all, everything that has happened here and much of what occurred on Delos. You know what we went through, even causing a death to achieve our goals. And yet, I fear, now that I have achieved it, instead of adding to the legitimacy of our cause, my blending with Cleopatra has put it in greater jeopardy."

"Is it not always so with a great risk that might bring great rewards? And even so, we have seen little evidence of the queen in your demeanor. And it was not your fault or hers that terrorists attacked the Biblioteca. Nor was the attack on our home the fault of your blend. It was, again, the result of the risks that we take to help the mistreated women, as we have done these many years."

Mo's eyes in the mirror were even darker than usual with concern and ever-ready sympathy.

"*If only my brothers had been like your cousin,*" Cleopatra observed wistfully, "*there would have been no need to kill them nor to ally with Rome. Why is it that you have not married him? I gather that cousins marry all the time these days.*"

"*I guess because neither of us wants to. Mo is like a brother to me.*"

"*As if that matters.*"

"*Perhaps not, but also I am like a brother to him sometimes as well. That sort of thing does matter. I gather you had no fraternal feelings for Antony?*"

"*None whatsoever. But what about the financial side of things?*"

"*My money comes through a trust administered by Ginia. She has been married several times and doesn't really approve of it. She knows what has been done to me also and would be very surprised if I decided to marry anyone, especially my Egyptian cousin. So you lied to our brave friend about that supposed treasure for nothing.*"

"*I did not lie to him! Antony ruled half the Roman Empire before Octavian made war upon us. You know of the gift he made us of the Pergamum Library, but what you don't know is that Alexandria never received all of those books. Somewhere along the way, some of them were lost, along with a great deal of other tribute Antony acquired for his war chest. He did not ever give me gold, as Egypt was richer in gold than any other land in the world, but he did not send it to Rome, either, as far as I know. I never asked what he did with it. We had so much else on our minds, then. Perhaps he will tell us when the American returns blended with him."*

"You seem very sure that will happen," Gabriella said.

"Aren't you? That sort of man risks his life for the love of riches. He would die for them. Taking on a second life in order to gain such a prize as I described to him should be no problem at all. Oh yes, he will blend with Antony and Antony will return to me— us—within him."

"I rather doubt it," Gabriella said glumly. "Once he finds out where the treasure is, nothing will cause that one to make even the slightest detour in his plans."

Cleopatra smiled within her. *"You are underestimating Antony."* Actium and her beloved's political marriage in Rome occurred to them both at the same time and Cleopatra shrugged. *"Or perhaps not. In that case we will have to seek him out, I suppose. Without being too obvious about it, of course."*

"I rather think the police will be seeking him for us. He said he has an idea where your mummy is, and I'm sure the authorities would like him to confide that information to them."

When she awoke, Leda told Andrew about the dream.

"It was the cisterns? You're sure? Might it not have been a flooded tomb complex?" Andrew asked. His voice was hushed with the excitement the image gave him.

Leda shook her head, smiling slightly. "No. This wasn't just impressions like the other times. This was very clear, perhaps because it was a dream and took place when I was asleep. I didn't have the rest of the world making psychic static between the Cleos, so we got better reception, I guess you could say. Anyway, she seems safe for now, and we'll be in Egypt soon."

It wasn't quite soon enough. Wednesday on her way back

to the hotel from Rusti's, Leda was once more snatched from her own time and place and felt herself, blinded, deaf, and unable to speak, suddenly, roughly, lifted. The movement tore at her so that she felt she might fall to pieces. Then, as with the other episodes she had experienced, she was back in the cab, which pulled up to the hotel.

Fortunately, she made it up to Andrew's suite before the second part of the incident occurred. It felt similar to the first one, except that when it stopped, when at last her bones settled back into their sockets and she could see and hear once more that she was safely back in Portland, she lay on the floor of the hotel room, left with the impression that the wind was blowing right through her.

"Are you all right?" Andrew asked, pressing a glass of water into her hand for want of anything better to do.

"You must think you've taken up with some kind of nut or something," Leda said.

"No, no," he said, and his voice carried a slight Scottish burr. "You're communicating with your other half. I'm sure you're right about that. It's not mental illness, it's a gift."

"Gee, I wish they'd just sent a card," Leda said, accepting the water and drinking it in a single swallow, as if it were a shot of something more substantial.

He laid his hand on her shoulder, and without thinking about it, she reached up and covered it with her own.

The following day Andrew's private jet left for Alexandria with an intermediate stop in Athens, where it picked up the Wolfes and Chimera, who had flown into the larger airport by helicopter from Kefalos.

By midnight that night, Portland time, they arrived in Alexandria, and the next day began their preproduction work on the program, which had by now been titled by someone who had read entirely too much H. Rider Haggard, *Finding the Femme Fatale Pharaoh.*

* * *

As soon as he arrived back in Alexandria, after a brief stop to collect his weapon from the place where he'd stashed it before leaving, Mike Angeles made his way to Gabriella Faruk's family compound. Since Gabriella/Cleopatra was able to convince him to take on Marc Antony, she was his best hope of getting Marc Antony to level with him about the treasure.

He took the bus, with much comment from Antony on damn near everything both on and off the vehicle. Mashed in with other hot, sticky, smelly people, he was sweating buckets when he left the bus about two blocks from his destination. A good stiff breeze dried him so quickly he was almost chilled before he'd taken two steps. A few more steps rectified that, however, and he was dripping again. His skin and clothes reeked with the food odors emitted by everyone else on the bus.

He took a deep breath as he approached the entry to the compound. It was open, and nobody seemed to be guarding the door. But then he remembered that the bohab had been injured, so that probably explained it. Though if he'd been running things, the guard would have been replaced immediately, especially considering how he got hurt.

"Will I know her?" Antony wondered. *"Will she know me? What will I say to her?"*

"How about 'hi, honey, I'm home,'" Mike suggested. He was still outside the compound, sniffing, listening. *"Not that I'm sure we're going to have to worry about it for a while. I have a feeling we may be the* only *ones home."*

"But she wanted me here. You said so. She would wait. I know she would." He seized control of Mike's feet and carried them through the entrance and the outer room, also wide-open, and into the courtyard. *"Cleopatra!"* he called. *"It is your Antony returned to you from death itself, my love!"*

"Will you keep it down, *dammit?"* Mike demanded. *"I thought you were a hotshot soldier. I should have known better. Officers!"*

"Is there a war I should know about?" Antony asked. *"I gathered that Octavian has been dead for some time."*

"Just trust me, pal, there is something wrong here."

"How can that be? The place looks empty to me."

"That's what's wrong. She's got a big family, and they all live here. Or did. I wonder if the bad guys came back after I left. If they did, I bet they brought a tank or something. These people were armed to the teeth. But there's nobody moving now, no lights, no sounds, no smell of food being cooked . . ."

"On the bright side," Antony said, *"there's no stench of death, so either they're all fine or were killed very recently."*

"Thanks for the input, General, sir," Mike said. His weapon was in his hand now, and he prowled around the courtyard. It was closing the barn door after the horses had been plundered to try escaping notice now that his Roman guest had just announced their presence to all of Egypt, but with Mike stealth was habit.

The courtyard was untidy. The dry fountain was broken, which as far as he remembered it hadn't been before. A scrap of something white blew across the tiled path several yards away. Several other scraps and tatters hung from the bushes and draped across upended ceramic planters.

The wind gusted with a sudden whoosh, and he did hear a sound after all—doors and the shutters of the courtyard windows knocking from frame to wall and back again, a scrabble of gravel rattling across the paving stones.

"The doors are open," Antony said, whispering even though he wasn't speaking aloud. *"I think we ought to look around. Perhaps they left some clue—food or drink maybe. We could taste it and see how fresh it is, and we would have some idea of how long they've been gone. I still have a powerful thirst."*

"And I may have been born much more recently than you, but it wasn't yesterday. Anyway, you're out of luck. I'm not sure what Gabriella is, but most of her family seems to be Muslim, and they don't drink."

"What are Muslims doing in Alexandria?" Antony asked, evidently having failed to notice the mosques they passed on the way, the veiled women on the bus, that sort of thing. Mike wasn't too surprised. He'd been there. The guy was still worried about his next drink. *"Hah! Don't tell me. Rome couldn't hold on to it without Cleopatra's help. Once we were gone, it fell to the sultans."*

"Yeah. It did. Later." The doors all opened outward, which was good because that way nobody could be hiding behind them. He simply had to look inside to see that the rooms he passed had been torn to pieces, everything broken, shredded, or pissed or crapped on. Still, there were no bodies, so maybe this was spite vandalism committed after the intended victims got away. Off to his right was the room he remembered as being Gabriella's. He didn't really expect it would be any different than the others, but it would be sloppy not to look.

"Shit!" he said when he looked in.

"It looks as if someone's here, at least," Antony said. *"There's a body on the bed. Now, that smells dead to me, but old dead, if you know what I mean."*

"Shut up and let me think!" Mike said, and added, also from habit, *"sir."*

For a change, however, Marc was on the money. The body on the bed *did* smell, though not strongly, of old death. She had been dead a very long time but when they drew close enough to see her it was Marc Antony rather than Mike who sank to his knees and began to cry.

"Oh, Cleopatra! Oh, my love!" He took the mummy's crumbling hand, still holding a flail, in both of his, and leaked tears all over it.

With great effort, Mike unclenched his fingers from the queen's dead body. He didn't want someone to come on them and find him bawling over this dried-up blackened bundle of bones with her glass eyes and her face frozen in rictus. And he was confused because superimposed on the mummy as she was now he saw the queen in the bloom of life, her skin flawless, her wide intelligent eyes closed in sleep, her hair without the wig short, lustrous, and soft as bird down. Still, he himself was not the kind of guy to cry over women. Even dead ones. But then, he wasn't Italian, so maybe that was the difference. Mexican men did cry over women but only on culturally approved occasions, like the death of a mother or a wife's dead body after you'd killed her and her lover. Guys who were sloppy with their crying tended to be sloppy in other emotional directions where he could not afford to go.

"*Sorry, buddy,*" he told Antony as he remembered that yeah, he had cried when his wife and little girl left him. Not in front of anybody, though. "*That lady is valuable archaeological remains and therefore property of the government of Egypt. You're gonna break her, and let's not go leaving my DNA all over her, shall we?*"

"*We can't leave her like this,*" Antony said.

"*No, I know. But don't try to pick her up. You'll break her to smithereens. Looks like a fair amount of that's been done already.*" One foot had fallen off and was at the end of the bed. "*It's got to be Abdul Mohammed's gang because they're the ones who stole the mummy. But what does he have against Gabriella anyway? He must have sent those goons here, too, but I never heard anything about it when I worked for him. And now, if we report having found the mummy, it's going to make her look guilty of stealing it. What to do. What to do.*"

CHAPTER 16

The production company spent its first full day in Alexandria being told they couldn't visit the tomb or the excavation in the harbor bed where Leda had first discovered Cleopatra's canopic jar without the permission of Dr. Faruk, who was out of town for an unspecified time. It was possible she could be contacted later at the Cairo Museum of Egyptian Antiquities, but she was expected to be in the field most of the time and unreachable.

Leda tried not to worry. She knew from the dream that Gabriella had made a clean, if somewhat damp, getaway, though she wasn't sure what the other, less clear and far scarier episode of—connection—she supposed you'd call it, was about. It was almost too vague to be psychic, and though she felt that Gabriella was associated with it, it wasn't precisely *about* her. It was far too confusing and disturbing, and she couldn't do anything about it, so she attempted to put it out of her mind.

Meanwhile she taped some preliminary background material overlooking the harbor, showing where her beluga laboratory had been before the earthquake. They wanted her to go into "the tragic death of her heroic father, Duke Hubbard," but she refused. That was private. Of course, Daddy would have loved the notoriety. She would have loved to suggest that they contact Gretchen Wolfe for further details about the accident but figured that would complicate matters unnecessarily. Gretchen, Wolfe, and Chimera kept a low profile. Wolfe was still a bit the worse for wear from his ordeal.

She took the crew on a quick tour of the various artifacts, exhibits, and landmarks that had helped her (with the as-yet-unmentioned assistance of the queen herself) locate the hotel beneath which the entrance to the tomb was buried.

But by then Ro had decided he wanted to film interviews and a reenactment of the theft of the mummy, though the theft was old news hardly worth one of those little ticker tape updates running underneath the general blather on CNN. However, the crime remained big news in Egypt and on the archaeological news lists on the Internet.

They spent all afternoon Friday setting up. Iris was kept busy with phone calls and meetings with various experts. Ro hired extra camera people from the Egyptian TV industry to shoot the coverage for this part of the program. Stela Beer even sent over a huge styrofoam cooler full of beer for all concerned and agreed to be one of the local sponsors. By evening, the beer was gone, the cooler emptied, and the Biblioteca Alexandrina bristled with more policemen and government officials than it had right after the theft.

Leda was such a vital part of the proceedings that of course she had to participate, even though they had nothing for her to do but stand around looking scholarly. The Edge TV folk talked among themselves about lighting and camera angles when they weren't grilling the police for the benefit of the cameras. Normally they wouldn't have started filming so early, but Ro said they could not pass up a chance to interview the investigators of this dastardly crime. The Egyptian authorities preened and pontificated for the cameras. The narrator chosen for the non-Leda-specific bits of the program, a prominent American Egyptologist most distinguished by the fact that she was also the only Navajo Egyptologist in the field, questioned them. Dr. Nizhoni was brilliant, but she was also slender and photogenic and possessed of a gorgeous, lilting alto voice only slightly spiced with the tribal accent.

She was also way more patient than Leda could have been. Over and over and over again she had to ask the same questions as the Edge crew shot different takes. They started and stopped countless times attempting to capture on the faces of the interviewed cops and authorities expressions correctly grave or shocked or whatever, trying to get the police to speculate about the things Ro thought they should and Leda knew they shouldn't.

This took place in the basement, next door to Gabriella's office, the crime scene where Cleopatra's inner coffin now lay empty.

Leda yawned. She had said her piece about fifty times already, and her back and legs were stiff and sore from standing. She thought she might see if there was an open office with maybe a chair. Chairs looked too relaxed for TV purposes, considering the enormity of the crime under discussion.

She stepped out into the hall. An office two doors down had no cops and no crew hanging around. It was unlocked so she turned the knob and opened it, reaching for the light as she stepped inside.

A voice from the darkness said, "Hey, lady, can I interest you in a used mummy?" and a hand reached out to keep hers from flipping the switch. "Close the door first, okay?"

"Eek," she said feebly. None of the self-defense moves she

knew were easy to pull off when you couldn't see the person you were defending yourself against.

The door shut without her cooperation, and the light came on. "Sorry, Leda, didn't mean to scare you, but I don't want to be spotted by the cops either."

"And why would that be?" she asked, surveying the dark and handsome stranger in front of her. He wasn't actually very tall—about the same height as her own five-eight. But he was compactly built, giving an impression of solidity without an extra ounce of anything but muscle. And come to think of it, he wasn't exactly a stranger, either. The silver-streaked black hair had not had the silver streaks before, but the twinkly bad-boy blue eyes, manly chin, and wry grin were memorable. "Mike, right? You nearly got my friend Edie kicked out of the Navy."

Surprisingly, he looked a little embarrassed. "Yeah, well, I was drinking heavily then. Got kicked out myself for it later. But right now I'm trying to keep a friend of yours *out* of trouble, and I need your help. Only I'm not sure how much the cops know about my—er—recent activities, and I have better things to do than to help them with their inquiries."

"I have a couple of inquiries of my own," Leda said in a fierce whisper. "What the hell are you talking about?"

"I found Cleopatra's mummy in Gabriella's bed."

"What were you doing in Gabriella's bed?"

"I wasn't in her bed. I was looking for her. The place is deserted, but somebody came in and trashed it and left the mummy as a calling card. I have an idea who it was, but I don't really know why, except that if the mummy's found there—"

"They'll think she stole it, though why anyone would be lamebrained enough to think something like that is beyond me."

Then suddenly, he drew her toward him and kissed her

fiercely and possessively and began disarranging her clothes. "Whoa there, big fella," she said, and started to push him away. Then from within her Cleo cried, "Antony! You have returned!"

"Cleopatra, my queen, when I beheld your lifeless and shriveled body I nearly died again but here you are, in the flesh, and I . . ."

"It's not just her flesh, buddy, it's mine, too. And while you kids may have a long history, Mike and I don't. There's a roomful of senior policemen just down the hall, and if you don't cease and desist pawing me at once, I'm going to yodel for them."

"*You wouldn't! Leda, this is my Antony.*"

"*Only partially. Besides, I thought you'd put him behind you. You want to dump Andy for this guy? Because I know the character he's inhabiting, and, trust me, it wouldn't be a good trade.*"

"*You are so cold-blooded. It must be growing up with all that rain.*"

"*That and a dear daddy who has been married five times,*" she said. "*Anyway, I think he's got the wrong Cleo. He has a previous acquaintance with Gabriella, and my guess is she's got dibs on this version of Antony.*"

"*Yes, but if I hadn't permitted it, Gabriella wouldn't—*"

"*Don't go there, okay? It's too complicated. Maybe this will cool you off. Mikey is a cute guy, but he's no Roman conqueror. He doesn't have an army or millions or probably a pot to piss in or a window to throw it out of. And as for the part of him that interests you, we ain't gonna pick it up because, girlfriend, we got no idea where it's been.*"

"*You are a cruel, cold woman, Leda Hubbard, but what you say does inspire caution at least.*"

"*We'll just take a few deep breaths and think of blizzards and Popsicles—no, scratch that—blizzards and driving on ice and . . .*"

Apparently, a similar exchange had been occurring

within Mike/Marc because he released her, took two steps back, and jammed his hands firmly into his pockets.

"So, as I was saying, we need to move the mummy, or Gabriella is going to be blamed. I came to find her in case she was still here."

"She's not," Leda assured him.

"But you'll do. I know you and she discovered the tomb together. I saw it on the news. Got any suggestions as to where we can move the body?"

"Sure. Let's bring it back here. That's the safest thing."

"How do we manage that without having a lot of explaining to do?"

"Elementary, my dear Michael. We just do a purloined letter number and stash her in the storeroom with the rest of the mummies until we can arrange for someone to 'find' her. I came to know this place pretty well when Gabriella and I were first uncovering the tomb."

"Sounds good. Can you tear yourself away from your photo ops and fans long enough to help?"

"No problem. Just keep Antony's hands to yourself, and we'll get along fine. I even know where I can find help we can trust. Chimera, Wolfe, Gretchen, and Andy would all help. We'd have to go back to the hotel for Chimera and the Wolfes, though."

"Whoever they are, we have no time to go looking for any of them. We don't know how much longer this place will be open, do we? I'm assuming we need to do a certain amount of sneaking."

"That's affirmative. Okay, let me get Andy, then. For one thing, if we get caught, his billions can smooth over a lot of problems, and, for another thing, he'd never forgive me if I left him out of something like this."

Mike's voice lowered and took on an Italian accent. "And it matters to you, this man's forgiveness?"

"Don't answer that," Leda warned her inner queen. Aloud she said, overruling the mutiny rising within her, "You betcha."

Leda found Andrew leaning on a pillar off to one side, while Ro explained his concept to the dignitaries and policemen, now gathered in the rotunda upstairs in the middle section of the library. "How long do you think we'll be?" she asked the financier.

"Ages yet, I expect. You could go back to the hotel if you want, though. I believe your part in this is finished."

"Actually, I was wondering if you could slip away with me for a bit without being noticed. Something's come up, and we need your help."

"Oh? How much do you need?" he asked.

"We don't need your checkbook, sweetie. We need your masculine upper-body strength. And the keys to the rental van. And a cover story."

He brightened considerably and looked almost completely awake once more. "Really? It sounds illegal."

"It is. Sort of. We're trying to undo a frameup so to speak. We'll explain in the van. Coming?"

"Yes. I think I have even arranged my excuse already. It was about time to see to it." He yawned, caught Iris's eye, pointed at his watch, and walked his first two fingers away from his body to indicate he was leaving. Iris smiled distractedly and nodded. Probably if he hadn't been the moneyman, she wouldn't have bothered to smile at all, Leda thought.

Twenty minutes later Mike, Leda, and Andrew loaded Cleopatra's mummy gently into the purloined Stela Beer cooler, now emptied and thoroughly dried. It was designed to look like a mummy case, once the decorative lid was in place.

Never was a mummy moved so tenderly, since for some reason Leda via Cleo felt each jolt the body received, each crack in its ancient fragile wrappings and epidermis. The mummy was wrapped in the blanket on which it lay—no doubt the same one in which it was transported to Gabriella's bed, since it seemed to be draped over her covers, still disheveled as she left them when the attack began.

Loading the cooler back into the van, the mummy snatchers took another twenty minutes, with one brief detour, to return to the Biblioteca, where Mike and Leda entered from the downstairs door, which they'd left unlocked. They had a rug draped over the cooler to disguise it.

"Hmm," Cleopatra said. *"This occasion is not at all like the other one in which I had myself disguised inside a carpet."*

"A good idea is worth repeating."

As if Mike were a workman helping her store some soon-to-be-neglected artifact, Leda led him into the complex of storerooms beneath the Biblioteca, rooms that were in their own right as labyrinthine and mysterious, and certainly as full of grave goods, as any pharaoh's tomb. Here was where items still to be conserved or cataloged waited their turn for the attention of the few human beings qualified to attend to them.

Once well inside the storerooms and out of range of the security cameras, Leda and Mike moved several crates and boxes and stowed the cooler behind them, then piled containers on top of it, restoring the stored articles as much as possible to their original places.

Standing back, Leda surveyed her handiwork and turned to ask Mike what he intended to do next, but he had vanished. She shrugged and joined Andrew upstairs, where he was enjoying coffee and the Krispy Kreme donuts he had earlier asked to be flown in from the franchise in Rome.

She snatched up the last donut and the dregs of the coffee. The donut compressed into cloudlike sweetness between her teeth. "Ummm," she said. "The perfect distraction."

"Mrs. Wolfe suggested it when she heard we would be interviewing policemen," he said. "It seems to have been the right thing to do."

"Yeah, well, Gretchen knows what cops like."

Soon afterward she and Andrew returned to the hotel. "That was fun," he said. "I'm glad you included me in your little conspiracy. Though I can't help wondering who that other guy was. I mean, who he *really* was."

"I don't exactly know that either," she said. "I met him in the Navy. He was a SEAL then but later got kicked out for being what they call a 'liberty risk.'" He had a drinking problem and a loud mouth when he drank. I gather he's cleaned up his act since then. Ginia Dumont said he helped Gabriella out of a couple of tight scrapes, though I have to wonder how he happened to be there when she needed him to be. And um—well—he's a blend, too, Andrew."

"*Is* he?" Andrew asked, though he didn't sound at all surprised. "Let me guess—judging from the looks he sneaked at you I'd say it had to be either Caesar or Marc Antony."

"Bingo," Leda said. "Antony. At the other Cleo's instigation, I gather. And I didn't even want to ask about the rest of *that* one."

"And how do you—does Cleopatra in you—feel about that?" he asked, too casually.

Leda shrugged. "I'm not sure, and she's not saying. I think she's a bit confused, to tell you the truth."

He smiled at her fondly. "That's one thing I adore about you, my dear. You always do seem to tell me the truth. Very few people do, you know. I find it quite refreshing. By the way, I have a little surprise for you."

"Yes?"

"We are leaving for Cairo tomorrow, then on to Luxor. Ro wants to set some of Cleopatra's story against what a lot of people are calling "the rebirth of the Nile." The boat we'll be using is—"

"Let me guess, an exact replica of Cleopatra's barge."

"Not quite that good, but certainly more convenient. It's a replica of the boat that was used in the filming of the 1979 movie *Death on the Nile*, and it looks very much like it on the passenger decks. But it's completely modernized and updated. It looks like any other luxury river yacht until we want to make time. Then we activate the air cushion and—well, needless to say, I've had the propulsion mechanisms and the entire engine room completely refurbished and overhauled."

"Your yacht is a *hovercraft?*" Leda asked.

He nodded as happily as any small boy with the shiniest fastest bike on the block. "Yes! It can do up to 150 miles per hour. I have a smaller one—a flarecraft, on the Tweed outside my New Abbotsford home." Despite the mention of his Scottish manor, à la Sir Walter Scott's beloved historic home in the care of the Scottish Trust, the boat owner was all Andrew McCallum, techno whiz kid.

"Cool!" Leda said. She was trying to imagine an art deco hovercraft, but meanwhile didn't want to sound unimpressed.

"I knew you'd be pleased. What with you having been in the Navy and Cleopatra having owned a navy."

As they fell asleep that morning Cleopatra mused, *"I wonder what he really wants."*

"Who?"

"Andy. He seems in no rush to bed us."

"Well, I think he'd like to, but he's just sensitive enough to know it's going to take me a while to get used to the idea again."

The inner queen gave an inner sniff of disdain for that idea. *"In spite of all your experience, my dear other self, and your much-avowed distrust of some men, you have learned little of the species as a whole."*

"Maybe I just never learned that much about politicians."

"Well, I have, and, like it or not, a man of Andy's wealth and

influence is a politician whether he holds a scepter or not. He is too understanding, too accommodating, too helpful, too forgiving, too good."

"Yes, but I've heard it's like that sometimes when you find the right guy. Happily married friends of mine have told me they couldn't believe how understanding, helpful, accommodating, and forgiving of their faults the right person was once they found him or her."

"Hmm, yes, but were their right people spending billions to impress them? Not that I think less of him for it, mind you, but I suspect our Andy's exemplary behavior is motivated by something other than our womanly charms, scholarly erudition, and delightful—if somewhat dramatic—company. Both my Caesar and Marc Antony loved me and usually did what they could to please me, but I never lost sight of the fact that had I not been Egypt, the richest country in the known world, my charms, if no less thrilling, would have been less amply rewarded."

"You sure know how to spoil a good time," Leda grumbled, punching her pillow. *"He's just a nice nerdy billionaire who acquired a romantic streak late in life and appreciates a girl with the same qualities. Now let's get some sleep."*

Abdul Mohammed's plan should have worked. It was simple, took care of two problems, would cause the person he wished to harm great damage that would ruin her career and possibly land her in prison, where she could no longer annoy his benefactors. In fact, while she was in prison if the benefactor wished to have her killed, he could then easily do so.

He had thought himself a model of flexibility to have conceived of the plan so brilliantly. He had sent back a team to finish the job started by Amir Marid ibn Yasin Abu Kadar, but his operatives found the compound deserted. Although the place had been watched, and no one had seen anyone coming or going, only the sand and the wind remained. At first he was angry and ordered the place looted (as if it were necessary to give such an order), but then he had an even better thought. He had on his hands a most inconvenient mummy, supposedly that of Queen Cleopatra. He'd ordered it stolen thinking to have a ransomable treasure, but so far such an item was much too hot to be marketed, and to publicly destroy it, which was the way for its destruction to make the most impact, could possibly have left a trail leading back to him. It was more amusing to use the mummy to destroy one of its discoverers, thus implicating her in the museum's attempted sabotage and robbery. He had friends among the police who had already suggested to their colleagues that it might be an inside job and that there was only one museum staff member in place the night of the attack.

So he planted the mummy and waited for the police to return to the compound to look for Faruk and question her again, whereupon they would find the archaeologist missing and the mummy in her bed. The illogic of an expert who had dedicated her life to preserving antiquities treating such a valuable one in such a careless manner did not trouble him. It would be suggested that perhaps the woman had a drug habit acquired on those trips she often took to her wealthy relative in Greece.

But for some reason, his informants and the police officials they were to notify were not available after he had the mummy planted. Finally, he managed to locate one of them at the museum, of all places, where they were ingesting donuts with an American television crew. His people seemed to have forgotten that they were not actually *good* policemen and had been enjoying regaling the foreigners with stories of their more colorful cases, including the invasion and robbery of the museum.

By the time these worthless devils convinced their friends of the need to search the Faruk compound again, it was well into the next day. While the police found the site of the looting, they found no mummy. In fact, his informants said, they felt that their original suspicions of Dr. Faruk had been mistaken. Clearly, from the damage to her home, she might have been a target of the attack on her workplace as well. They expressed concern about her, since she had disappeared from the museum without anyone seeing her leave. But then, later in the day, they got word from museum officials that Dr. Faruk was simply on a business trip to Cairo and various sites along the Nile.

This little favor for a friend was turning into a great inconvenience. Abdul Mohammed telephoned the amir and informed him that since he had lost so many men in the explosion following the aborted bombing of the museum, he simply did not have the manpower to follow Faruk up the Nile. He reported to his patron what had been done, and the amir agreed it had been a brilliant plan, had it not been a failure. But now, Abdul Mohammed said, his attempts to avenge the honor of his friend had cost him a valuable piece of property. No one had any idea what had become of the mummy. Once the compound was discovered to be empty and the mummy planted in the accursed woman's room, he had removed the watcher from the street.

The amir laughed lightly. Perhaps Cleopatra had simply arisen and walked away, he suggested. Perhaps Abdul Mohammed should lock his doors at night and beware of bandage-trailing shadows.

And Abdul Mohammed must not halt his important work of undermining the hold the ancient infidel religion still maintained on Islamic Egypt. The amir himself had a yen to see the Nile at this time of year. It was a good time for a family outing and an object lesson for the female members of his family. No matter how clever or how high a position she had artificially achieved, a woman was still a woman and could easily be put in her proper place. He would see to that and leave Abdul Mohammed to blow up whatever it was he wished to blow up next. Of course, if the amir needed a bit of assistance, he might call on his old friend. Surely blowing up a temple, a dam, or a tomb couldn't occupy all of his time and manpower?

CHAPTER 17

"Does your other voice speak so loudly and so long within you that you cannot find peace, cousin?" Mo asked.

Realizing that he had waited perhaps twenty minutes for an answer to his previous question while she waged an inner debate, she gave him a smile that was much thinner and fainter than he deserved. "You guessed it," she told him.

Mo shook his head sadly.

"Don't worry so much," she said, sitting up and giving him a consoling pat on the arm. "After all, you have helped me get this far."

"If you have the sort of problems Ginia did after her blend, I will not be proud that I have helped," he said, and heaved a dramatic sigh before starting the engine again.

"He takes a lot on himself, for a mere driver," Cleopatra said. *"I know he is your family, but you are clearly the ranking person, the one with education and erudition . . ."*

"There you are wrong," Gabriella told her. *"Mo drives a taxi by choice. He has degrees in history, philosophy, and psychology, which is what makes him such a very good cab driver."*

"Why does he not teach?"

"*He is a male of the royal line. At one time laws kept him from holding any job for which he was qualified. Now it is simply the custom to deny the good positions to the men in our family. My sex is an advantage in this instance because I have not been seen as a threat up until recently. Now that I have influence, and some money behind me, I could help Mo advance to a professional job, but he refuses. He says it would not leave him time to help with my real work with the women, and besides, he gets plenty of opportunity to use his education while driving people around. You would be surprised at some of the exalted personages who prefer riding with Mo to hiring a limo. My other cousins, his younger brothers, are not so well educated as he is, but all of them are intelligent and work quite hard. Except maybe for Salah. He's a bit slow.*"

Mo spoke again, more hesitantly. "I am only guessing this, but I think you have taken on a problem you do not know how to solve. You have wanted the political power to change the lives of women in our country and its neighbors, and you have wished for academic power and advancement in your career. But until now, you have not tasted real power. Such as being a queen. Now that you know—and now that the queen has returned, she must wish to be queen again. This is true?"

"*I see what you mean,*" Cleopatra said, smiling inside her, "*he is indeed a very perceptive man, your cousin.*" And this time she took it upon herself to answer, "Yes, Cousin, that is what I wish. Real power. Although Cleopatra Philopater has been credited with little to show for her reign but two love affairs and the loss of Egypt, she made some very beneficial changes in her country. She could implement beneficial changes in it again, if only she had the power."

When he looked back at her again, Cleopatra and Gabriella both saw that Mo knew he was speaking to the queen. "As always, we will do our best to get you where you wish to go, Lady, but it will not be an easy thing. Unlike matters in the days of Cleopatra, women have no power now. If a princess were to kill her brothers and sisters to gain power, she would be put to death, and no protector could save her. Still, Allah has a very good sense of humor and perhaps will provide a way."

As they continued up the Desert Highway, the heat increased, and the air quality disimproved as they drew nearer to Cairo in the late afternoon. The main bulk of the city sprawled across the Nile, a hive of noise and activity.

Mo had been lost in his own thoughts when Gabriella's voice spoke from the backseat. "Of course, I do not know exactly where we are, but are we not near the place where the great pyramids stand? Why can we not see them?"

Ah! The queen was awake even if his cousin still slept. Cleopatra seemed to be getting used to him and was becoming almost chatty. He looked in the rearview mirror. Gabriella sat as still as before but her eyes were open. It was as if she were sleepwalking. Mo found this rather creepy but he answered the queen deferentially as befitted their respective stations. At least as she would perceive them.

He gestured toward the souvenir shops cheek by jowl with mud huts, service stations, and fancy villas that had sprung up along the highway. A triangular crown seemed to top the second floor of a mud-brick home. "Great Queen, if you look closely you can see the top of the pyramid of Khafre—there! But as for the rest, from here they are obscured by these buildings."

"Ah, yes," she said. "I can see a little. But why are these structures in the way? There seem to be many people living here and yet, the West Bank is reserved for the dead, and no person prosperous enough to build these edifices would wish to live here."

"Perhaps not in your time, Great Queen, but these days, as it may have come to your attention, Egypt is populated largely by Muslims, who do not share the beliefs of the ancients regarding zoning restrictions. By situating their businesses and homes close to such a magnet for tourist wealth as the pyramids, families not formerly prosperous become so."

"What a pity. I have looked forward to seeing them."

"We will see a little more from this road as we draw closer. However, we would have to turn onto the pyramid road to see them closely. There are many tourists there now, jostling and being very rude. I fear you would find it most unlike a royal procession." He didn't mention that his cousin still seemed to be resting, if not sleeping, and that it was a rest he was loath to interrupt.

But Cleopatra said, "No, no. My poor Gabriella is too exhausted for such an excursion. A great pity, but perhaps another time."

Despite her casual words, Mo heard an undertone of loneliness and loss. The queen, though enfolded by the body and soul of his cousin, was cut off from those who would have known her home as she did. He felt for a moment the longing she must have for the sight of something familiar, if not exactly the same as it had been when last she saw it. It made him appreciate the value of those objects men held to be immortal. Anchors in time, they would be, for one out of her own time.

"There is another way, Great Queen, if you do not mind a slight detour."

Gabriella's lips curved in a mischievous and yet eerie smile, "A detour? Dear Mo, know you not that our journey has been more rapid than the flight of a gazelle compared with its duration when last I came to this place? By all means take this detour of which you speak."

He swung south onto the new Loop Road and east toward the Cairene suburb of Maadi, where many Americans lived. Maadi was situated on a hill south of the city. Then he drove west again until they were looking out across farmland.

In the distance the pyramids stood bathed in the glow of sunset.

"Ahhh," said Cleopatra. "When last I beheld them my love was with me, and my children."

As Mo drove closer, the pyramids swelled in size until it seemed that the car sat beside them in the desert, while the moon rose over their tips.

"They do not shine as they once did," Cleopatra said reflectively. "Once their sides reflected the very shape of the moon and stars."

Gabriella's own voice spoke then. "After your time, the people who settled here carried off some of the outer blocks and spoiled the surface. Then, too, there is a problem now with what is known as acid rain, which eats the stone."

Mo smiled into the mirror, "You have not been this way before, I think, cousin?"

"No, I haven't. I'm always in such a hurry when I come to Cairo, taking meetings and dashing out to digs." Her eyes were awake now, fully the eyes of a living person, and dancing with wonder. "This is beautiful. You remember my friend Susan Wilson, Mo?"

"The American woman who writes books and brokers deals between American businesses and Egyptian ones?"

"Yes. Susan says that because the pyramids are dwarfed by the expanse of the desert, one doesn't fully appreciate their enormity. She says it is like picking a Christmas tree in a lot, then bringing it into your house. It did not look as big in the lot as it turns out to be in a confined space."

"Oh," Mo said blankly.

"Yes, well, my experience of Christmas trees is limited also, but I believe I understand what she means tonight."

Later they reconnected with the Giza road and drove across the Tahrir bridge into Cairo. On the river below the bridge, large beautiful boats vied with the usual feluccas and short tour boats, seeking the deepest part of the channel.

Mo drove them straight to the Nile Hilton. The hotel had a room permanently reserved for visiting museum staffers, since the Museum of Egyptian Antiquities was right next door. The reservation of the room was particularly fortunate at this time. The desk clerk looked a bit crestfallen to see her and complained that she was not expected, but that, of course, since the doctor required it, the museum's room was in readiness.

Mo smiled as they walked to the elevator. "No doubt finding a room where there are none to be found is worth a sizable tip for an enterprising man."

"Not exactly opulent but a good arrangement," Cleopatra said, when they reached the room. Mo thought that she spoke aloud for his sake. He had felt intimidated by her presence in his cousin before and now found himself being pleased by her acceptance of him. It was disconcerting, but, still, he could understand why many great men of her time were so charmed by her.

"Not so good as it seems," Gabriella informed Cleopatra. "This hotel and the Sadat bus terminal, as well as the traffic on the highways and bridges, generate much pollution, which penetrates the museum and damages the exhibits. Now we must get more rest. I have a meeting in the morning with the director of antiquities at the museum to determine what if any part of your scrolls should be transferred here."

She promised to lock the door and admit no one, and he departed, returning again to drive her the block to the museum the next morning.

He refused to leave her side even after she was in the meeting room until he saw that everything was as it should be, and she received cordial treatment from her colleagues. Then he wandered around the museum until the meeting finished.

His behavior was not considered odd or overly protective

despite Gabriella's protective stature. He was, after all, her male next of kin. The highly conservative, even fanatical Muslim men—and she said there were more of them all the time, even in her professional circle—probably considered Mo's honor compromised because his kinswoman privately closeted herself, unveiled, with unrelated men.

His avid interest in certain exhibits excited no particular attention. The calls he placed on the cell phone he brought from the cab were ignored by those around him. He was waiting on a woman, of course. Naturally he was bored and calling a few friends to pass the time. He did what he could to reinforce this impression by rolling his eyes, tapping his toes, and lighting one cigarette after another.

But before Gabriella emerged from the meeting around noon, he had made considerable progress, contacting and making his reports to the required parties.

"I've been patient with you, son," Marc Antony told Mike in the fatherly voice Mike imagined he'd probably used to rally his troops back when they were losing battles. That had to be it because Mike was now about the same age as Marc Antony had been when he died. *"You have it all wrong about the treasure. When you lie expiring in the arms of your beloved, you realize that the real treasure isn't gold, it's your love, your life."*

"Yeah," Mike said, *"because when you're expiring in the arms of your sweetie, you know you aren't going to need any gold, but you would like a little more love and life to enjoy. You sort of conveniently forget that an enjoyable life and love, for that matter, don't come cheap. So now that you're on your feet again, fella—or should I say* my *feet, our life is going to require financing. Hence the treasure. Meanwhile, we need to save money, and you didn't much help by making us run off before we could hitch a ride with Leda's well-heeled friends up the Nile."*

"I couldn't help it. The woman contains the essence of my queen, and I could tell already that her heart belongs to that wealthy man."

"There's another woman who contains the essence of your queen, too, and her heart—do you always talk like a cheap romance novel about this stuff?"

"I'm Italian, so censure me in the Senate if you don't like how I express what is in my heart."

"Yeah, well, I'm Mexican, but I only talk that way in Spanish. Hmm. I guess they don't call them the romance languages for nothing. It's okay to talk to women like that because they like it, and it might get you somewhere, but between us men it sounds overly dramatic in English."

"English? You mean the tongue of the Britons, those hairy barbarians who paint themselves blue and go naked into battle? I do not even know that language, so how can I be conversing with you in it?"

"These days Britons usually shave, no longer paint themselves blue, and only go into battle naked if they're attacked while in the shower. I was born in the USA, so English is my official first language, even though I learned Spanish at home. Since I'm the guy whose body we're in, the blend's universal translator seems to be using my language. Sorry, buddy, but times have changed."

While he carried on what was intended to be a multilingual conversation and led two lives inside himself, the Egyptian countryside moseyed past outside the windows of the train. All along the Nile people worked clearing old irrigation ditches, putting the finishing touches on new ones, and repairing the stone walls on the river's bank.

The train was crowded but not as crowded as the waterways, and with a little baksheesh, he'd scored an air-conditioned second-class seat to Cairo's Ramses Station, with stops at every village and mud hut along the way.

He needed to find Gabriella, not just because of Cleopatra,

but to see if she could give him any more information—not to mention some kind of official sanction—that would let him search for the treasure. And he needed to hook up with Leda again in case her rich new boyfriend might want to bankroll the project. But for now what he needed most was to have a little time to hear himself—the new part anyway—think. No sense involving anybody else until he knew where the treasure was located.

"Time is not all that has changed. Frankly, I feel cheated out of my proper afterlife. I'm damned if I can remember anything about feasting with the gods. This world you claim used to be the one I knew is uglier than a battlefield on the day after, more crowded, and smells worse, too. My Cleopatra loves another. And despite all of this you begrudge me a glass of wine to smooth the edges?"

"Marcus, read my mind if you can, okay? Your edges were already way too wine-smoothed. The Cleopatra in Leda isn't our Cleopatra—not the one who got me to blend with you anyway. That's Gabriella, the contessa's niece. A very classy lady, and smart. She's younger than Leda, too, and cute in a sassy kind of way. And I think she already likes me since she told me about the treasure."

"No doubt that was Little Egypt's way of getting you to embody me."

"Little Egypt?"

"I call—called—call?—Cleopatra by that name since although she is Egypt—or was—she seems—seemed—too young, too fragile, and so very small for such a weight of responsibility."

"So anyway, I think that—er—Little Egypt is still waiting for you inside Gabriella, so you can't use losing your true love as an excuse to drown your sorrows. Face it, when you were alive you were a damn drunk. That last battle you fought was a textbook example when I was in the Navy of how not to fight a battle at sea. History remembers you as a loyal follower of Julius Caesar, a rival of that nephew of his, Cleopatra's boyfriend, and pretty much a screwup otherwise."

"You read Plutarch, didn't you? He didn't like me. He was a friend of Cicero's, and that old goat tormented me and plotted against me until the day I was able to have him killed. Plutarch never forgave me. And, of course, he didn't like Cleopatra. She was a woman, and he didn't think much of the sex. Of course, nobody knew her like I did."

"That's why you gave her a library but kept the rest of the loot for yourself?"

"It was gold. Egypt overflows with gold."

"Past tense, buddy. Up until now not even the river has been allowed to overflow."

"Of course it does, during the annual floods. Why else do you suppose they have the Nile-ometer?"

Mike formed an image of himself shaking his head. *"Nope. They built a dam or two that took care of that."*

"Who would do such a thing? Rome?"

"The Egyptian government and the Soviets from what I read."

"What are Soviets? Oh, I see. Gauls and huns mixed. Terrible combination, that. But why would they do such a thing? Even to Egyptians in our time, the Nile was as much a goddess as a river."

"Damming provides power and makes irrigation easier. That was the theory anyway. Turns out, the silt that's always made the valley so fertile gets dammed up, too, so now the Nile Valley farmers have to use fertilizers where they never did before. So in a couple of days they're letting the river out on a short leash—enough of it for long enough to silt things up, they're hoping."

Marcus wasn't really listening but seemed to be thinking fast, calculating, weighing possible good against possible bad. *"Where exactly are these dams anyway?"*

"The first one's at Aswan; the High Dam is farther upstream."

"This does not bode well. I thought perhaps if the floods no longer came, it might make what you seek easier to find. How much farther upstream is this second dam, and what effect does it have?"

"Let me put it this way, buddy. It's drowned several ancient temples and monuments."

He suddenly found himself chuckling, then guffawing, drawing a breath, sniffing, then giggling a little before it hit him again—the image of piles of bars of gold with the Nile waters rising high above them while crocodiles and hippos swam merrily around. At that point he burst into such gales of mirth that he thought he would choke on it.

Under all that he demanded, *"What's so damn funny?"*

"You are, son. You are. You went to all that trouble to steal my spirit so you could steal my treasure and never realized that, from what you tell me, it's been submerged beneath the great river for lo these many years."

"Let's be clear about this. I didn't steal anything, man. I'm giving you a chance to live again, in partnership with me. The gold would have made sure it was a comfortable *partnership, the kind I guess you would be used to when you weren't out in the field. Without it we will be back in the field pretty soon, getting our butts kicked, if your past experience is any indication of how you're going to affect my performance in battle. Where the hell is it anyway?"*

"I have no idea now. I stuck it in a cave under my fort near the Isle of Philae. When we abandoned the fort I forgot about it."

"Forgot about it?" Mike demanded. *"How the hell could you forget about all that gold?"*

"I was more concerned with saving our kingdom from my countrymen. Egypt is rich. I am rich. It wasn't all that important at the time."

"Man, you really were *drinking hard back then, weren't you?"*

"I'm a soldier," Antony said. *"Of course I drink hard. I would like to be drinking hard right now."*

"Sorry about that. I've been clean and sober for twenty years, and I'm not about to louse it up because of you. In fact, maybe you were supposed to be blended with me so you could see what you could accomplish if you weren't drunk all the time."

"What would you know about it? I was a soldier!"

"Me, too. I was a SEAL—that's an elite branch of the Navy. But I got kicked out for being a liberty risk—they didn't think

they could trust me when I'd had too much to drink. They gave me a couple of chances to shape up, but I didn't really take them seriously. Then they told me they figured I couldn't stop. I didn't want to think there was anything I couldn't do, so I stopped. It wasn't that easy, but I did it with the help of a bunch of other people with the same problem."

"That's just—strange," Antony said. *"Didn't you get thirsty? A man must drink something."*

"There's water. Coffee. Tea. Soda pop, There's even alcohol-free beer. None of it is the same of course."

"I don't know what any of those things are," Antony said. *"Well, water of course. But we didn't drink that. It was for bathing."*

Mike switched back to the topic that interested him. *"There has to be some way to get to that treasure. Unless someone else got to it first, and if they did, it would have had to be a long time ago. Something like that would have been in the news."*

"You don't make much sense sometimes, Michael."

"I mean there would have been a widespread message so that everyone knew about the treasure being found. It would be in history books probably, and I've never heard anything about it."

"I hid it well."

"You don't think you could find it again?"

"Not if it's underwater, no. In the old days, the cave would have been covered by the floods and the entrance difficult to reach most of the year. This new lake I see in your mind is a much greater obstacle."

"Yeah, but it has a low point, too. I remember reading about how they had to move some of the temples that were submerged after the second big dam went in. They were less submerged at some times than others. Maybe if you combine that with this controlled drain, we'd have a chance of finding the loot. When would the river ordinarily be at its lowest level?"

"In the summer, of course. Before the rains begin."

Mike's inner calendar and Antony's didn't jibe. Using his

CHAPTER 18

Before Gabriella had time to think, Cleopatra flung her into the arms of the man she knew as Mike Angeles. For an instant, he seemed startled, then his brown eyes kindled and his arms closed around her so that she had to elbow him in the ribs to get loose.

"What? Shit. Sorry, lady, I . . ."

"Darling, did she hurt you?" the woman *he* knew as Gabriella Faruk asked in low tones throbbing with emotion. To his surprise, Mike Angeles found that other parts of him were throbbing, too, not just his rib cage from the sharpness of her elbow but other more pleasurable throbbing as well.

"I'm sorry, too," Gabriella said. "I hope I did not puncture one of your lungs or something. She told me you would blend with Marc Antony, but I wasn't so sure."

"Say no more, *cara mia,*" he said, sweeping her back into his arms, and wrapping them around her so that he could gently but firmly cup her elbows in his hands. Then he kissed her—or rather, they kissed each other, fervently and for such a long time that when she opened her eyes again

Gabriella saw that they were drawing outraged looks and a few leers from several of the other people in the café.

"Ahh, at last I am alive again," Marc Antony said.

"Yes," Cleopatra breathed, leaning into him even more heavily than his grip strictly required. "These people thought they revived me before, but until this moment I might still have been entombed. Oh, my love, my husband, is it really you?"

"More or less," replied the man Marc Antony occupied.

"I am going to lose my job if we remain here like this," Gabriella said. "Public displays of affection between the sexes are highly frowned upon."

"We'd better get a room then before these kids have us going at it like a couple of bunnies," Mike told her. "I'm sorry, Doc, but I don't know what else to do."

"It is the most discreet thing," she agreed, though five minutes before she would have thought it scandalous. "I have read silly books where it is said that a lover's body seemed to have a mind of its own, but that was before blending! If only they knew!" Her chest felt so tight it was hard to breathe, much less speak, her skin was flushed, her heart was thudding, and every cell in her body yearned toward his.

"The Nile Hilton is just . . ."

"Not there!" she cried. "Anywhere else but not there. My colleagues all go there. We can try the Heliopolis Hilton," she said.

"Oh, okay. I guess we should get a cab then."

"It is a shame my cousin the taxi driver was called away to business in Alexandria," she said, then realized why she needed a taxi. "Or perhaps it was a very good thing. Mo is a very modern person, and he knows about Cleopatra, but I'm not sure the modernity entirely extends to me."

In the taxi, as a precaution against untimely passion, he sat in the front with the driver and she, her eyes never leaving him, sat in the seat behind, rubbing his neck with fingers that suddenly seemed longer and more shapely than Gabriella had ever noticed them appearing before.

When they reached the hotel, he said, "Damn, I haven't got any cash. Have you?"

She laughed giddily, "I'm surprised! I was beginning to believe you think of everything."

They hardly had time for those few words, since the original occupants of the two bodies could exchange only a few words between longing looks, prolonged embraces, and stolen kisses, as well as much touching. Gabriella thought self-consciously that she must look like a cat in heat; but inside of her, Cleopatra was suffering with the need to be physically reunited with her lover. And what, really, were she and Mike going to do about that? Ah! A cold shower perhaps. They would take cold showers, and that would cool the ardor of their respective blends until they could decide what to do. Not that she really knew what to do. She couldn't even run in the other direction. She knew without so much as an internal conversation that Cleopatra would not allow her feet to move. She might have a stroke, something like that, if she tried. This was a situation Chimera had not included in his cautions for the newly blended.

For Mike there was no longer any wondering about the treasure or anything else. How in the hell was he going to rein Antony in so he didn't rape this poor woman? It wasn't like she was some bimbo he picked up at a bar in the old days or one of the danger-addicted babes he sometimes hooked up with before, during, or after his various jobs. She was a respected, well-educated professional lady and—God, how could he ever have thought of her as merely cute? The arch of her brow, the curves of her neck and back, those slightly parted, moist pink lips, the enormous tip-tilted black eyes and that flood of curly dark hair he could imagine brushing his bare chest, thighs . . .

It was a good thing the hotel had a last-minute cancellation, or they might have embarrassed themselves in the lobby.

Mike could barely get the key card in the slot, and paying closer attention to the procedure evoked imagery that made it even harder—more difficult—for him to hit the target. Finally, she guided it in, twisted the knob, and they entered together.

Mike was able to free an arm long enough to pull the door to and lock it behind them.

Cleo and Antony reasserted themselves immediately, locking their bodies in another lengthy and stimulating embrace.

Behind Cleopatra's langorous and loving gaze, Mike saw Gabriella's fear and confusion. "I'm sorry about this," he said, though he didn't know why he should be apologizing since his blending with Antony was *her* idea. He just wasn't sure the "her" whose idea it had been was Gabriella.

"Yes, well, I should have seen this coming." She pulled away from him as if ripping off a Band-Aid and made for the modern bathroom that had been installed during the conversion of the old palace.

"Where are you *going?*" Marc Antony wailed.

"To take a cold shower, and I suggest you do the same." Grinning, he started after her. "When I have finished."

"I don't think that's such a good idea," Mike told her, as he tried to rein in Antony. "Not if you want to discourage them, I mean, though I'm not certain it's going to do any good. If I were you, I wouldn't get naked anywhere within a fifty-mile radius of him—us. Assuming, of course, that you don't want to just let them have their wicked way with us."

"And what would be so wicked about that?" Cleopatra purred as she began unbuttoning the sleeves of Gabriella's overblouse before starting on the buttons covering Marvin the Martian's image on the T-shirt beneath it. Still unbuttoning in a maddeningly sexy way, Cleopatra swayed back toward him. "We have waited millennia to be reunited. It is wicked to keep us from each other."

She reached out to unbutton something of his, which made Antony roar like a bull, but Mike caught her hand, though he stroked it as he held it. "I know you want to and he wants to and frankly, I wouldn't mind at all, in fact, I'm going to have to—uh—sublimate—pretty soon or . . ."

Cleopatra's other hand now strayed in a very frank and highly dangerous way. "Oh yes, I do see what you mean," she said, and giggled.

"Stop that!" he said insincerely.

To his surprise, before Marc Antony could reach his arms out for her again, she sighed and retreated to the edge of the bed.

"You modern people are such prudes!"

"I'm trying to be a gentleman," he growled. "And it doesn't come all that naturally, so watch it, lady."

"I know," she said. "And you are very sweet. But it is not what you think. She wants you, you know." As she said this, Gabriella's face flushed so he could see the change even in the darkened room.

"No kidding?"

"Oh yes."

He waited, and Gabriella looked up at him so he could see that it was so.

"That would make everything a lot easier," he said, but stayed where he was. Antony tried to protest, but something in Mike's attitude stopped him.

Gabriella laughed nervously. "You look at me as though I am—what is the term?—booby-trapped."

Then he laughed, too, much harder than the very slight pun warranted. Being weak from laughter gave him an excuse to sit down beside her.

"You tell me, Doc," he said, lifting her chin so she had to

look him in the eye. This was not a good way to conduct an interrogation, since Antony and Cleopatra climbed back into the psychic driver's seat—or was it the backseat?—and made the situation much more urgent with another embrace that, by the end of it, left him shirtless and Marvin the Martian leering up at them from the floor.

Gabriella still said nothing, then it dawned on him, what Cleopatra had said before. "Have you never made love before, like she said?" he asked. "*Pobrecita!* For your maiden voyage you seem to be drawing a kinky cross-time foursome. But corny as it sounds, Doc, I will be gentle."

Cleopatra spoke up. "You'd better be, or Antony or no Antony, I'll have you strangled."

"Fair enough," he said. If they waited any longer, he wouldn't have to worry about being gentle or not for a while anyway. A guy could only just get so tense before something had to give.

This time when Marc and Cleopatra went at it, Mike and Gabriella joined in, but when her skirt came off she stopped.

"Mike," she said. "It isn't that I am shy. I—I have these scars. Horrible ones."

He stroked her hair and kissed the bridge of her nose. "Is that all, *querida?* Maybe you haven't noticed, but I won't be posing for any body wash ads myself." He dropped his pants a little and twisted so she could see the scar running down his spine and cutting a wedge out of one hip. "That was a machete." He raised a trouser leg to show a calf missing another hunk. "A shark with poor aim. And this one"—he drew his finger down the muscular bulge of his left arm where a ridge of proud flesh puckered—"that was where a bullet passed before it killed my friend Clive."

Her hand rested on his arm for a moment. "These are battle scars. I got mine when I was a little girl and could not fight back. You've heard of what some families do to their girl children?"

"You mean that female circumcision thing?" he asked, wincing. "Ouch."

"It is a mutilation, Mike. Mine is the most severe kind. I cannot feel what women are supposed to feel when they make love."

"Really? How do you know if you've never tried?"

"Everything is gone . . . well, not everything. There's enough that I could bear a child."

He didn't know what to say for a moment, then Marc Antony and Cleopatra lost patience and reentwined. This time, however, Marc Antony kissed his beloved's face, her mouth, eyes, nose, cheeks, and each ear. Then, before continuing his campaign down the length of her body, he whispered into her right ear, "Fortunately for you, *cara mia,* you have here the soul of a great lover in the body of a qualified diver."

Gabriella awoke to the call of a full bladder. She felt a little sore, oddly contented, and extremely disoriented. She opened her eyes and rolled cautiously onto one elbow. Except for the extreme edge of about a quarter of the bed where she lay, the rest was occupied by Mike, who sprawled on his back with a smile on his face and the thin sheet tented above his midsection.

Cleopatra seemed to be sleeping, too. Since Gabriella's side of the bed was pushed against a wall, she scooted to the end and slid off to get to the bathroom. Her bag sat by the stool, where she did not recall leaving it. She checked her watch. It said 7:00, which she took to mean 7:00 P.M.

Feeling a need to connect with her ordinary life after so many extraordinary events, she pulled her cell phone and charger out of the bag and plugged them in. She smelled like low tide, so she decided to shower next. She realized suddenly that she hadn't bathed for almost three days and was retroactively embarrassed to have had her first sexual encounter when she wasn't even clean, much less as glamorous as the women in the movies. Though that hadn't seemed to matter to Mike any more than it had mattered to Cleopatra and Marc Antony.

Her cell phone rang while she was drying her hair.

"Dr. Faruk? Dr. Mazar would like a word with you if you'll stay on the line please." *Merde.* Someone had probably reported her for greeting Mike too enthusiastically in the café.

"Gabriella? Glad I caught you. The BA called after you left the other day and said your voice mailbox is full. Apparently there is an international film crew that needs your help. Dr. Hubbard is with them. I have taken the liberty of acquiring their contact number for you."

"Thank you, Akim. I'll get in touch with them at once."

"And Gabriella?"

"Yes?" she said calmly, thinking, Oh no, here it comes.

The line was quiet for a moment, then he said, "Never mind. But good for you and that man, whoever he is. I for one think it instructive to be reminded that not everyone around here is dead."

"Thanks, Akim," she said. He had a reputation as something of a lecher, so perhaps that was why he didn't mind. But she was glad of his tolerance anyway, and it made her feel warmer toward him than she had before.

She stepped back into the bedroom for a moment. She didn't need to look to know that Mike was still sleeping, as he lay on his back, snoring. She hoped he didn't do that when he was off doing something dangerous and sneaky. His enemies would hear the snore and think a lion was lying in wait for them. She wanted to go back and snuggle up next to him again, to feel his warmth and touch his skin, which seemed like an extension of her own now, and most of all to have him touch her again with his large, blunt-fingered hands. She sighed. One more call and she would.

But before she could tap the keys again the phone burped in her hand. She silenced it with a whispered, "Yes?"

"Dr. Faruk?"

"Yes."

"This is Iris Morgan of Edge TV. I got your number from Dr. Hubbard, who is with us. We badly need your help with this project, both because of your position and because you are the cofinder of Cleopatra's tomb. We need to interview you for our program and wanted your input at this stage of the production. Where are you now?"

"Cairo. Look, I can't talk right now. Give me your number, and I'll ring you back in a couple of hours."

"In a couple of hours we'll be in Luxor. Right now we're in Cairo, too, not far. I'll send a car for you."

"No!" Cleopatra cried from within her.

"Yes," Gabriella said into the phone. She dressed quickly. Mike was still asleep, so she scribbled a note, restrained herself from kissing him and starting something she could not finish, and hurried downstairs, where the driver waited for her.

It wasn't until she was inside the car and the door closed behind her that she remembered she hadn't told Iris Morgan where in Cairo she was.

CHAPTER 19

As soon as Gabriella left the room, Mike opened his eyes. He listened for her footsteps specifically as they retreated down the hall amid the roar of vacuum cleaners, the occasional slam of a door, and the chattering of maids. Their room overlooked the street, and he stood at the window and watched as she climbed into a cab.

Marc Antony wasn't going to be happy about this when he made his presence known, but Mike Angeles needed a little thinking time. While part of him wanted to drag Gabriella back into bed, another part of him was really worried if she'd respect him in the morning, so to speak. She seemed to have had a pretty good time, but it was hard to tell if that was her or Cleopatra.

"Yeah, but does she love me for myself?" he asked aloud in a melodramatic voice, the back of his wrist to his forehead in a matching gesture.

"Of course, she doesn't," Antony answered. *"She loves you for myself."*

"Bite me," Mike replied. *"I'm talking about Gabriella."*

"*I know that, naturally. She loves me, too. I always enjoyed threesomes. You are nothing but a vehicle for my amorous talents, son, face it.*"

"Yeah yeah yeah. *They hadn't even invented some of my moves back in the ancient times, old man. Even Cleopatra was pleasantly surprised by some of it. And she wasn't bad herself.*"

"*So why did you let her go?*"

"*Because I was actually wondering how we were going to lose her anyway. We have treasure to find, remember?*"

"*I rather thought she could finance it, as she did in ancient times.*"

"*She doesn't have the wealth of Egypt behind her now, old boy. In fact, she needs us to find the treasure to grubstake the political future she wants. Providing we're going to go along with that. Personally, it sounds to me like as good a way as any to avoid the high cost of nursing homes. But we're going to need someone with deeper pockets than Cleo and Doc, whatever we decide.*"

"*But who else . . . ? Ah, the* other *Cleopatra. Is she wealthy?*"

"*No, but she has influence with someone who is.*"

"*Yes, but she loves him, not us. Why would she or they help?*"

"*The usual reason. We'd cut them in.*"

"*She left a note,*" Antony said, as Mike's eyes returned briefly to the bed. "*You didn't read it, did you? Read it. Where did she go?*"

Mike skimmed it and grinned. "*She's gone to help the TV crew. Great minds, General. Great minds. Let's go.*"

After the pyramids of Giza and the sphinx, Leda's sec-ond spirit was disappointed. "*They look smaller somehow, and duller. There used to be more, too,*" Cleo had said mournfully.

"*Well, they are,*" Leda replied, "*and you can see the others when we get back to Cairo. They used the stones from the pyramids to build the city.*"

She was wringing wet with sweat, no new thing in Egypt,

very tired from her interrupted sleep, worried about how she would present Cleo, or Cleo present herself, during the programming conferences, and she itched from bug bites, in spite of the repellent, which also usually raised a rash on her skin. The crew and cast members had wandered about in ones and twos making frames with their hands or expounding at length on technical points understood only by each other.

Andrew had kept close to her, and when he suggested that they slip away to preview the boat before the rest of their party arrived, she was relieved.

Just stepping onto the gangway leading from pier to boat she felt the temperature drop a couple of degrees, even though the boats were bow to stern all along the dock, which buzzed with noise both mechanical and conversational. Andrew had bragged about the boat's air-conditioning, one of his modern touches, but the engine room and all of the other technical hovercrafty things he showed her weren't in that part. Still, in spite of everything, she was amused and touched at his enthusiasm and tried to make very practical, sailorlike comments and suggestions. She refrained from mentioning that her particular specialty at sea had been submarines or asking how deep the boat could dive.

Then suddenly a wave hit her that had nothing to do with water and everything to do with overwhelming lust.

Andrew had just taken her up the ladder to the passenger decks and opened a door into a less-than-spacious but still fairly deluxe cabin. "This is one of the first-class staterooms. As you can see, we've had to refit the heads but . . ."

"They're just perfect," she purred.

"*Now,*" Cleopatra fairly whined.

"Oh, Andy, please can we close the door for a moment."

"What is it?" he asked. He looked startled when he saw her expression, but simply asked, "Oh?"

"Oh, yeah."

"I suppose I'd better lock it then, huh?" He asked, fumbling for the lock as she peeled off his shirt and began unbuckling his belt.

"Good idea. There's four of us already. Any spectators would be a real crowd."

"Leda? Your Majesty?" he asked.

"What?"

"Since you seem to be in this mood, I was wondering if we might try something."

"*Any*thing," Cleopatra promised.

"Well then, and I promise I'll buy you a new one but, may I, just for the sake of research, mind you, rip your bodice?"

"Oh, Andrew, you beast, you *nas*ty animal, you, how could you make such a lewd suggestion to little old me?" Leda asked, wiggling her quite substantial prow under his nose in a suggestive manner that made it rather difficult, just for a moment, for him to find the target. She was wearing a T-shirt at the time, and it was quite a challenge to rip the material; but after she, squealing protestations of offended innocence the whole time, pierced the material with her nail scissors to give it a head start, he managed quite masterfully and to the satisfaction of all concerned, as was the rest of the encounter.

Leda awoke to the ringing of her cell phone and the drum of feet on the deck outside the stateroom. Andrew no longer lay beside her. She sighed, rolled over, and reached for the phone.

"Hello?"

"Dr. Hubbard?"

"Yes."

"You spoke to our director earlier today about wishing to contact Dr. Faruk?"

"Yes. Is she there?"

"I'm afraid not. She was here earlier, but left before you phoned. I called to tell you that she just telephoned us and was given your message, but said she was already on her way to some emergency at a dig near Karnak and wanted you to know that she would be out of contact for a couple of days, but would try to meet you in Luxor."

"Does she realize how important this is?" Leda asked, piqued.

"I couldn't say, madame. I was asked to give you this message, and that is all that I know."

"If she phones you again, tell her I want her to call me. Here's my cell number. I've left it before, but since I haven't heard from her, I can only assume she didn't get the message."

"Yes, madame. I will pass it on," the secretary—Leda presumed the woman was a secretary—said in a stiff and, Leda thought at the time, defensive tone.

After a quick wash in the teensy head to wipe most of the pleasantly sexy stink off the humid tender bits of herself, she dressed and ventured back out on deck to find Andrew and break the news.

He and the others were less concerned than she'd feared.

"We're just picking up local color between here and Karnak anyway," Ro said. "Besides, if there's anything relevant, she can tell us on the way back up. There's nothing we actually need permission for at this point. We'll just be doing the touristy, 'what Cleopatra might have seen on her journeys with Ceasar and Antony' sort of thing for this part of the trip."

The reassurance didn't ease Leda's mind as much as she would have thought. She still felt a vague anxiety, left over, no doubt, from a troublesome dream just before she woke up. Too bad she couldn't quite recall it.

"Well then," Iris Morgan said briskly. She was attired in

a Hollywood version of a kaftan, silken glittery fabric trimmed with gold and cut almost to her waist in the front, and wore coin earrings that brushed her shoulders. "I suppose since everyone else is aboard now, we may as well go. There's still time to get away from the city and see the sun set on the Nile this evening, isn't there?"

Andrew exchanged a brief glance with Leda, who shrugged, then gave the order to cast off.

The taxi from Heliopolis stopped at the bustling dock. Mike jumped out. Fancy luxury cruise boats in various stages of coming, going, and staying put churned up the waters, in spite of their relatively slow speeds.

A glistening wedding cake of white, teak, and brass with an incongruous little skirt around the bottom was pulling out into midstream. The skirt did not belong on that kind of a boat, in Mike's experience, but it didn't look too bad. It reminded him of an old-fashioned lady with her long skirts extending below her bustled stern to hide her feet. An officious-looking Egyptian woman was writing something on a clipboard. She wore a head scarf and sunglasses, like a movie star, except that the rest of her was much more covered up.

"Excuse me, ma'am," he said. "I was supposed to meet the rest of my TV crew here, but my train was delayed. Do you know which boat belongs to Mr. McCallum? Andrew McCallum?"

She pointed to the white one disappearing beyond a larger and more modern blue job.

Mike groaned but thanked her.

The cab driver was yelling at him about paying. Mike suppressed an urge to tell him to "follow that boat."

He shoved the money at the man and asked him in Turkish Arabic where he could hire a boat. Boats boats everywhere, but would any of them take him where he wanted to go?

Too bad he hadn't thought to have Gabriella prepay for the hotel room, but it had seemed unimportant at the time, in the heat of the moment as it were. His funds were dwindling rapidly, and he expected the hire of the felucca he needed to catch up with the cruise boat would take a lot of what he had left.

The cabbie waved vaguely farther down the shore and drove off. Beyond the big pleasure boats, Mike finally found a makeshift fleet of the small traditional sailboats, the like of which had been plying the Nile since ancient times.

One of the captains waved him over. He was a large white-haired, white-bearded fellow with a blue baseball cap and a turquoise shirt, unusual among the sailors there, who mostly wore the white djellabas for the sake of the tourist trade, though some who were working on their boats were bare chested.

"You wish a river trip, *effendi?*"

"Yes. Do you see that boat way down the river there?"

"I can see that boat very well, *effendi*. My boat is not like that boat."

"I know. But can your boat catch up with that one? I want to board it. I have some business with the people on it."

The man whose white teeth bore a striking gold accent when he smiled ingratiatingly, said, "One can but try, *effendi.*"

"How much?"

"It depends upon the length of the trip, *effendi*. Get in. If we are to reach your friends, we must start now."

Mike was a little surprised the man didn't insist on being paid in advance but did as he was told.

There was a good breeze on the river, and the sails caught it readily. The white-haired guy was a good sailor, but, try as they might, the felucca never quite caught up with the cruise boat. The sun set. The boatman stopped tacking, as he had been doing all afternoon, and made for the west bank.

"Why are we stopping?" Mike asked. "There's a full moon. We could catch up to them when they dock for the night."

"There is no need for such haste, *effendi*. They will sleep very late in the morning, and we will catch up to them then. It is forbidden to sail after sunset. But as you see, we have sleeping bags and very delicious foods with us. Soon the other passengers will join us, and we will have camping out just like your Boy Scouts. That will be a good thing and very much fun for everyone, yes?"

Mike reached for his wallet to offer baksheesh then realized that he probably didn't have enough to make up the standard fee, much less extra, unless he could borrow from Gabriella once he reached the cruiser. He didn't much care for the idea of doing that, but when he found the treasure, they would share it, so he could pay her back that way. He thought they might be sharing quite a few things in days to come. Most of all they'd be sharing their inner extra selves with each other, but it went further than that, though he didn't wish to reflect on it too deeply for the time being.

"Cheer up, son, this will be like it was when I was campaigning. Just us and the stars, the stench of death, and the eyes of the jackals in the darkness beyond the campfire."

"You really are a romantic, aren't you, General?"

The boatman tied the little boat to a small homemade dock, a short wooden extension beyond the stone-walled riverbank. Once ashore, the men built a fire with some of the suspicious-looking fuel the boatman had on hand and arranged sleeping bags beside it. Other than the dock, the place was less inhabited than any he had seen that day. The other boats had disappeared, apparently each tied up elsewhere. They were probably lucky to have this spot to themselves. But it seemed funny that nobody at all was there, not even the flocks of ragged kids who would normally swamp any tourist with sacks full of trinkets, clothing, "really authentic artifact from tomb of King Tut, mister," and other such goods.

Maybe a couple of miles away was the outline of a small village, lamps glowing like lightning bugs in the night. Since the dams were built, more of the villages now had electricity. That was probably where the kids were. Home watching satellite TV or doing their homework on computers.

No sooner had the boatman begun boiling water, however, than company at last came calling. The twilight was long, and Mike could make out that everyone coming toward them seemed to be walking on two legs except for one, a dog, which barked impatiently and was the first to reach the fire. The shapes looked strange in the dying light, the heads seeming larger than they needed to be, the shadows thrown across the ground by the moon grotesquely elongated and more active than they should have been, since the people who cast them seemed to walk sedately enough.

"Ah, the other passengers arrive," the boatman said.

"What other passengers?"

"The other passengers who also wish to board the fine boat you seek, *effendi.*"

"You mean you were going there all along? For these other people?"

"That is what I mean, yes. But something delayed me, and now it seems I awaited your arrival before departing to meet these passengers."

"How did you know to pick them up here?"

"Why, they hired me before they left Cairo, *effendi,* and told me that they wished to see a place that is near here. And so I brought them here, but they wished to stay for a time before I took them to the fine boat. So I returned to Cairo seeking other fares."

"What are they, archaeologists?"

"People interested in Egypt's great past, yes, *effendi*. That is who they are."

His gold tooth gleamed in the firelight. The dog charged toward them from the shadows, but a sharp call made it return the way it came.

A man with a patch over one eye walked into the fire circle, his hands both holding the dog by the collar. "You must excuse him," the man said. "He is an excitable beast."

Except for the eye patch, the man looked like any other upper-crust tourist, as did the two women and six other men behind him. They all looked to be between thirty-five and fifty, though perhaps the light was kind to some of them. One of the women and one of the men had an Asian cast to their features, at least two of the people were definitely Middle Eastern or Semitic anyway, and since this was Egypt, they probably weren't Jewish. The other five all appeared to be Westerners, European, Australian, American, maybe South African. One of the women even sported a pith helmet with a veil. Otherwise, they were dressed in a collection of sports gear, T-shirts with animals on the front, and camouflage, khaki, or olive drab pants with a touch of the paramilitary about them, though he saw no firearms among them.

Then the last man arrived, much quieter than the outfit he wore. He sported a knit golf shirt, the kind with the gator on the left breast, but this one was printed with big tropical flowers, the colors sepiaed by the low glow from the fire. It was a variation on a kind of shirt that was the stereotypical badge of male American tourists and was universally tacky except in Hawaii or at a retro fifties party for gay men. Over it he wore a loose, striped vest of the kind some Egyptian men wore over traditional white tunics.

It was overdone, an effect not improved by the hand-tooled and painted cowboy boots with the dancing skeletons on them. Mike recognized those boots first, then he recognized the man. The hair was graying but still red, buzz-cut instead of windblown, the always rather sunburned face clean-shaven, and he now wore spectacles, but it was Jaime. Jaime, *El Jefe*'s lieutenant. No last name that Mike had ever heard, and, of course, if there'd been one, it probably wouldn't have been his real one. He was called *El Rojo* because of his perpetual sunburn. Mike didn't think he was Mexican, but you couldn't always tell. Some Spaniards were red-haired and freckled. Jaime spoke flawless Spanish and heavily accented English. Now he sat next to Mike, the glasses magnifying his eyes, and said in another accent, a Texan one this time, "Hey, when's supper?"

Mike's gun was on his right side, farthest from the fire, and he eased his hand toward it slowly. He didn't really think Jaime would avenge their former boss in front of all these people, but then, Mike didn't know who all these people were. They could have been a consortium of Central American drug lords for all he knew, here to witness his execution. Nah, now that was where paranoia left off and delusions of grandeur began. Mike just wasn't that important.

"I wouldn't do anything stupid, Miguelito. Not in front of all of these nice people."

"Wouldn't you? I'm glad to hear that. I won't if you won't. When *are* you planning to kill me exactly? Just so I can say my prayers and make out my will and that kind of thing."

"Kill you? Why would I want to kill you, *amigo?*"

"Didn't the syndicates send you to take me out to avenge *El Jefe?*"

Jaime chuckled, "That would be really funny if they did that."

"Yeah, I'd die laughing."

"Because I know for a fact that you didn't kill *El Jefe*."

"How do you know that?"

Jaime nodded. "Because I did, as soon as you began to look more interesting."

The conversation was carried on in very low tones that would sound genial to anyone else.

"*You* did?"

"Yeah. Why, were you getting attached to him?"

"Oh yeah. Drug lord who trafficked not only in narcotics but also in highly overpriced and watered-down prescription drugs. He was a doll. I miss him terribly. But what do you mean I looked interesting? Was it your week for boys or something?"

Jaime looked pained and rolled his eyes, the whites glistening and reflecting the fire, giving him a demonic aspect that was not totally out of character. "Oh, yeah. You bet. I've missed you, you big handsome brute."

"*He's a bit old for us,*" Marc Antony observed. "*A youth once in a while for variety is one thing . . .*"

"*Don't worry about it. He's not gay, and neither am I. Doing a youth once in a while nowadays will get you thrown in prison if you get caught. Of course, if you're inclined that way, which I didn't think you were, being the great lover of Cleopatra's you're supposed to have been, prison can be full of romantic opportunities. But not in* my *body you don't.*"

"So you killed *El Jefe* for my sake and followed me to Egypt out of sheer devotion? How'd you find me?"

"How do you think? You're bugged, of course."

"How?"

"That would be telling. Don't get all upset. It was for your own good, to protect you from falling in with more evil companions like *El Jefe* and getting stuck serving some insignificant evildoer instead of fulfilling your destiny."

"Fulfilling my *what?* And speaking of evil companions,

you missed one, buddy. And he was trying to kill me, which would have really screwed up both our plans."

Jaime shrugged. "Oh well, you wouldn't be any good to us if you couldn't get yourself out of a little trouble once in a while. Once you were here but your main contact, Dr. Hubbard, wasn't, the plot against the Biblioteca put you right where we wanted you, always providing you managed to, you know, escape getting killed."

"Your faith in me is touching. Don't try to tell me you knew I'd come here though. And how did you know about Leda?" Mike tried to keep his eyes on Jaime, but the tourists were distracting. One of the women seemed to be doing a little dance, and somewhere behind her he saw another pair of eyes, iridescent gold-green at about the height of a cat or a coon, sometimes glinting red with reflected flames. *"She's very tempting, but you'd better pay attention, son. This man is trying to tell you why he hasn't killed you so far. You don't want to miss anything."*

"Jaime always liked to hear himself talk. Funny that he never said any of this before. Some people can say all kinds of stuff, and none of it is the important stuff you really ought to know about them."

"I probably know more about Dr. Hubbard than you do. She's been on my list for quite a while. Imagine my joyous surprise when I saw how you reacted when your old girl-friend was on CNN for finding Cleopatra's tomb. You showed an enthusiasm over that I never much noticed in you while we were working for *El Jefe.*"

"That's right. We were cooling our heels watching TV in *El Jefe's* living room, doing sentry duty while he got it on with that FDA officer's wife in the bedroom. I guess I got all focused on what Leda was doing and forgot you were there. But meanwhile you considerately offed *El Jefe* to keep me from having to give notice so I could expand my career horizons?"

"Not entirely. I also offed him so I could avoid being killed myself for quitting to expand my career horizons. And here I am."

"Doing what? Seeing the sights?"

"Security. Same thing as before except these people are a lot more influential than a thug like *El Jefe*. They pay better, too."

"Damn. You must have found a better class of meeting than I did." Oddly enough, Jaime had been his sponsor at the first meeting he attended in Mexico, and was the one who suggested he apply to *El Jefe* for employment.

"I've been cultivating my own contacts for quite a while," Jaime said. "In fact, I was just moonlighting, working for *El Jefe*."

"Well, it just goes to prove what my granny always said. You never do really know people, do you? So you're CIA, right?"

"Not exactly, though they report to us."

"Really? That sounds pretty powerful. What is it then? Don't tell me. Oh, no, I should be able to get this one. I've heard enough conspiracy theories by now. So—is it the Knights Templar? The Rothschilds? No? Rockefellers maybe? How about the Illuminati? Okay, the Masons, then? Elks? Rotary Club?"

Jaime looked like he was nobly rising above the impulse to shoot Mike, but merely said, with exaggerated patience, "If you'll stop with the questions for a minute, I'll explain."

"Please."

"You're not too far off in some ways, actually. I guess you've heard about the New World Order."

"Yeah, sure."

"Well, the people I work with are dedicated to trying to keep the world *in* order. In spite of what we hear in the States about how it's all up to our government or the UN to police the world, it just doesn't work that way. You need

a larger network of dedicated operatives with loyalties beyond borders, people who are interested in seeing that whatever is going down doesn't rock the world's boat too much."

"Who decides what's too much?"

"That's a little more complicated. But basically it's these
people around us and others like them."

The other people didn't seem to be paying much attention to Jaime's recruiting spiel if that's what it was. They
murmured among themselves and stared into the fire, accepting cups given to them by the boatman and sipping
from them almost ceremoniously.

Jaime picked up a stick and wrote letters in the dirt.

"WWVI?" Mike read them aloud. "World War Six?"

Jaime gave his head a slight shake. "World Wide Vested
Interests. These are the real owners of multinational corporations, the powers behind thrones, the people who pretty
much keep the earth spinning on its axis."

"Sounds heavy."

Jaime gave him a rueful smile. "It is. But we're not without our sense of whimsy. You've no doubt heard of the men
in black? They report to us, too. We're known as the men in
vests." Then he nodded toward the two women on the opposite side of the fire. "Or maybe I should say people in
vests. It would be a real waste of talent if we were all men."

Mike studied the other people more closely. Sure enough,
each and every one of them wore a vest of some sort. Even
the woman in the pith helmet wore one of the vests with
lots of little pockets.

Marc Antony stirred. *"Some things never change. Power over
power over power and men like us, fighting men, seldom get to be
more than pawns."*

"No shit."

"Well. So. If these vests are the good guys, why were you
working for *El Jefe?*"

"Keeping an eye on him mostly. And the world is a funny old place, Miguelito. People and power structures and good guys and bad guys—it's kind of what you might call an ecostructure on its own. Even the vermin serve a purpose, as long as they don't overrun the place."

Mike nodded. He'd have to think that one over, but it made a weird kind of sense. "Okay. But why would all these high-and-mighty vests be interested in little old me?"

"At first they weren't. We were all more interested in your connection with Dr. Hubbard."

"It's not like she isn't closely connected with other people, too."

"Closely, perhaps, but nothing like a romantic involvement. So much more possibility for intrigue there."

"So you thought I might make a male Mata Hari—in a vest?"

Jaime shrugged. "It's a big pond, Miguelito. I'm just a small frog. A scout in some ways. Various scenarios occurred to me. If, once I removed *El Jefe* from the scene, you went somewhere else and didn't pursue your involvement with Hubbard, we might have found a way to give you a little push or found some other way to approach the matter. However, you did what I thought you might."

"I'll try not to be so predictable next time."

"Then when you met up with Kronos, just prior to his removal . . ."

"So his death was no accident?"

"Don't be naïve. Of course not. Cesare Rasmussen's minions, the ones who were with him at Nucor when he tried to get himself transferred into one of them, and the ones who were with him on the yacht when he 'hosted' Doctors Hubbard, Faruk, and Chimera among what seemed like a cast of thousands, those people were loose cannons."

"And I'm not?"

"Let's say the jury's still out. Anyway, we liked the way you handled that situation, and when you turned the tables on Abdul Mohammed and got cozy with Dr. Faruk as a result, that was so much better that we made sure nobody interfered with you two kids getting to know each other better."

"*You* took out the sniper?"

"I thought you needed a little privacy with the damsel in distress. And if one of you got plugged the first time you left the compound, it would have been a bummer after everything had lined up so nice to get you two kids together with only a little nudge or two from us. I was disappointed at first when you disappeared, but then when I realized you were going to Kefalos and taking her bait and Kronos's free ticket to an extra life, well, you made me proud."

"Anything to oblige. But let's get something straight. Neither Leda nor Gabriella had anything to do with me going to Kefalos. I went because I was curious about something Galen said to me before he died."

"No, of course they didn't. Dr. Hubbard wasn't there. We know that. She was attending her father's memorial service in Oregon. And it was Cleopatra, not Gabriella Faruk, who tricked you into keeping the DNA of her dead lover and going to Kefalos to blend with him, supposedly to find some obscure treasure or the other. She knew very well what would tempt you."

"*It is a good thing that engaging in Cleopatra's other temptations required us to remove our shoes,*" Marc Antony observed.

"*I'll say. Four of us was plenty without a cast of thousands underfoot listening to our pillow talk.*"

Mike changed the subject. "I don't think I understand exactly why you wanted to get rid of Galen. This Rasmussen sounds to me like maybe someone who would be in your organization."

"Naah. He thought he was but believe it or not, keeping the global gyroscope spinning smoothly is not a job that calls for megalomaniacal egos. However, Cesar's interest in the Nucor installation on Kefalos and his subsequent association with Faruk and Hubbard did bring their activities to our attention. It also brought into focus what had been mostly rumors about the so-called blending process invented by Dr. Tsering Jetsun, now known as Chimera. Our inquiries revealed that some of our members had been approached about having this blending process, but dismissed it as a crackpot idea that would probably cost Nucor a great deal in liability when people found out it couldn't possibly work."

"Didn't any of them think about getting blended?" Mike wanted to know.

"If they did, they haven't seen fit to mention it. As you can imagine, we have a big, multifaceted job. Our senior members keep track of each other, but they don't know everything about one another. The blending thing is a new wrinkle. And a potentially catastrophic one."

"How so?"

"Well, for instance, Cleopatra was the most controversial and dangerous woman of her time and thanks to your girlfriends there's now two of her—a hedonistic pagan woman who wants to take back the country she used to rule, now under the control of fundamentalist Muslim men who own a lot of the world's oil. That's bound to make trouble."

"And upset the world order. I get that. How do you know she wants to take anything back, though?"

"We find these things out."

"So you have mind readers, huh?"

"Something like that, although we hope to do better in the future. So what's it going to be, Miguelito? You know enough to make a decision now."

"About whether I join you or you kill me?"

"Essentially."

"You haven't answered my most important question. What's in it for me?"

"Sorry. What was I thinking? A grave oversight on my part. Let me explain."

CHAPTER 20

The woman waiting for Gabriella inside the cab was not Iris Morgan nor anyone so Western. This woman was fully covered by the burkha or abaya, head-to-toe black robes and veil. With the sun lighting the sheer lace panel covering her eyes, her reddened lids showed that she'd been crying.

Gabriella recognized the robes. They were much richer than average and had an edging of brocade trimming the distinctive lace faceplate.

"You!" Gabriella said to the Saudi princess who had been the source of so much trouble. "What are you doing here?"

"Atoning for my bad judgment," she was told.

"Not to me, you're not. You betrayed me, my aunt, and all of the others who tried to help you. I won't risk anyone else to try to help you again."

"No, you won't. You will not have the opportunity." And with that, the princess raised her hand to point at Gabriella. There was a hiss, then Gabriella's face and eyes caught fire.

Fortunately, the pain did not last for long. The woman swooped down upon Gabriella as she pawed at her burning

face, and smothered it with a cloth that smelled even stronger than the other chemical. But after the first whiff, Gabriella plunged into darkness.

Cleopatra's narrative:

Feeling the real world fall away from us as the cloth touched our nostrils, I instinctively cried out for my "elder" sister. Although Gabriella's mind was befuddled with the drug, Leda Hubbard's was not. My *ba* within her flew to my aid, quite as birdlike in that way as our priests had once depicted it. Thereupon, we joined forces and thus I maintained an inner clarity, perceiving all around me while my hostess's own *ba* flew elsewhere, driven out by the drugs.

Rough hands hauled our hapless body from the cab and carried her with her arms over two sets of shoulders, as friends might carry someone who had imbibed too freely of wine. Our toes bumped painfully upon steps as we were dragged up them until at last we were deposited on the heavily carpeted floor of a chamber cooled with fans. The treacherous Saudi woman sat beside us, twitching with nerves or possibly fear. Two men sat in thronelike chairs woven of reeds, and both sneered down at us. The larger and more portly wore flowing robes and a headcloth, whereas the other, thinner, with receding hair on top compensated by a triangular beard upon his chin, wore a costume similar to those assumed by males in Leda's country.

Otherwise, their types were all too familiar to me. The robed man was a spoiled prince who had never had to fight for his position as I had, but had inherited virtually uncontested wealth and power. He was perhaps somewhat shrewd and no doubt well educated, but his erudition had never penetrated his spirit. Perhaps he was greedy for something he had been taught was fine to own, perhaps he simply took such things for granted as his due. Other than a high birth, the two of us had nothing in common except a belief that certain relatives were too much trouble to be allowed to live; for instance, the princess niece who had betrayed us twice.

The other one was no aristocrat but nevertheless well educated, perhaps relatively wealthy. He had achieved a high income if not a high station by his own efforts and talents. I have seen that face on executioners, punitive priests, and military officers skilled in interrogation. His spirit was closely akin, in fact, to Octavian's. He liked to know things, control things, and hurt things most profoundly. Especially precious things.

Seduction was out of the question, even if not for Gabriella's maimed body from which only the tenderest of lovers could coax pleasure. (Ah, beloved! If I live not another day at least we have been reunited one more time. Such bliss is worth dying for all over again, but not if I can help it.)

In any case, the kind of desire these men held for women attained its ultimate expression if the woman in question was served with a good wine and some well-prepared side dishes. Afterward, they would prefer to continue enjoying her by having her stuffed and mounted, probably in some degrading position. Leda's vocabulary has supplied an appropriate expression. They gave me "the creeps." These were the very sort of men who dreamed up the horror that was visited on Gabriella's girlish body.

The fat one unseated himself long enough to reach down and squeeze our breasts, as if testing melons, except hard enough to leave bruises.

"No wonder she tries to subvert other women. She has less chest than I do!" he said, quite accurately, as far as I could tell. His robes concealed a multitude of flaws, but I have seen similar shapes wearing nothing but a pleated linen kilt. "No matter. She's too thin for my taste, but the miners of the Sudan are not so particular about their whores. I doubt she'll bring much money, but at least she will acquire a thorough understanding of her role in life and will no longer be able to lure other foolish women away from their families. I did not have that option with her accomplices, who were Muslim women, but she is an infidel, so it does not matter."

"It is certainly a fitting end for her, Your Highness, but unfortunately, for her to endure it, it must be private. Her shame will not be public to cause grief to her family and friends or joy to her enemies. One such enemy provided us with the lure that brought her here, and I feel it would be a good thing to permit him to gloat over her downfall."

"Well, he cannot have her here. My own women are here, and I will not permit that any but this guilty one"—and he indicated the traitorous niece with a flick of a finger—"be aware of such dealings. For her enlightenment, we travel with you as far as Abu Simbel, where her new master will take possession."

"There is another way."

"We tried your other way, and it failed."

"But I had only a mummy then, not the woman herself. This is not, as you have noticed, a natural woman. She has no husband, no children, no mother or father, only a collection of secondary relatives. Admittedly, selling her into whoredom will bring her down to the level where such creatures as she belong, but she would be more damaged, even beyond death, her family more humiliated, perhaps even driven permanently from their home by the government, if she is found to betray the trust and responsibility so recklessly given into her unworthy hands."

"I don't know. I like to think of her as a miner's whore."

"Yes, yes, and that would be a terrible fate for anyone, it is true. But she is a woman with pride of her mind and her high position, and not especially of her body. Who knows? Although we were told she was with a lover before we lured her from the hotel, my sources say she has been for the time they've known her an arid old maid. Perhaps she would actually relish a life with many men to service her? Some of these women who fill themselves with loose Western ideas might see the life that way instead of the other way around."

The uncle spoke to the niece. "Is that so, ungrateful girl?"

The girl said nothing, for which there might have been consequences, except that the thinner man forged ahead with his argument. "My plan would shame her publicly, nationally, and her name would become as hated as it is now respected. And, of course, she would be dead and no bother to you any longer."

The amir said, "But before . . ."

"And it is a fate your niece could share with no dishonor to you, since you are not Egyptian and she was known to have run away from your protection."

"Ah, now that is a very good point."

He would think so. Killing two women was a better plan for such a man even than sexual slavery for one. I felt certain that the skinny man's argument that we might enjoy ourselves did almost as much to convince the princeling as including his niece in another punishment.

I cannot help but feel Octavian and his advisers may have had such a discussion about my ultimate fate. "What would give Cleopatra the most pain?"

The answer, of course, was to kill my children and take me in chains to display me as conquered and a slave in the city where I should have reigned as empress if its government, in its treachery, had not murdered my Caesar and later sent Octavian to cause the death of Antony. Like

Gabriella, I had been alone, without relatives (well, that was largely my own doing in my case, out of necessity) or friends save only my handmaidens and my priest, Anoubus, who ultimately cheated my enemies of the joy of burning my body and destroying my chance for an afterlife—this afterlife, as it happens.

The uncle said to his niece, "Call your maids and have them drag this harridan into a corner of the women's quarters. You may tend to her physical requirements yourself."

"Uncle, have mercy!" she cried. "I helped you, and you said if I did, I would be forgiven!"

"And you for your part have promised many times to be a good and obedient girl but you have never been." He turned to the maids, who had just arrived. "See that she is given a thorough beating."

The thin one put in quickly, "Should your niece attempt escape, Your Highness, it is not beyond the scope of my plan that we should execute her and plant her body beside the other. However, any marks on the body would badly undermine the impression we wish to give."

"So—no beating? I could do it so that it would not show."

"No, Highness. This woman's associates are skilled in the forensic sciences and could tell from your niece's remains if she had been abused beforehand. Take solace in the fact that she will be contemplating her end all the way up the Nile. Does she swim?"

"Of course not!"

"That is well. Confinement, restraint when necessary, but no beatings. I promise their deaths shall be painful and as prolonged as possible, so they are given time to contemplate their sins."

"Well, I suppose that's something."

* * *

Mike slept better than he expected. He even dreamed a little about Gabriella, her fingers making little clutching movements against his chest, her nails sharp and penetrating, licking his hands with just the tip of her tongue, her hair brushing his cheek, purring. Purring? He woke up abruptly. As he sat up, so did the rest of the company. He caught a glimpse of a tail disappearing behind the two women.

The dog didn't seem to notice, however.

He revised his opinion of the company slightly. They were all fit and lean, obviously athletes and probably hikers from the looks of their shoes and other attire. He saw several Earth logos on equipment and a few "save this, save that" stickers. Even Jaime had stripped out of the loud shirt down to a black T-shirt with a green gator—no, croc, on it, with the words SAVE SOBEK beneath its snout. Cute. Sobek, if he remembered correctly, was the name of the Egyptian crocodile-headed god.

They climbed into the boat, none of them needing much help except an extra hand to finish hauling them safely on deck. When the last person (and the dog) was seated and the boatman was about to cast off, all of a sudden from behind a scrub bush a cat ran straight for the boat and jumped in. Nobody seemed surprised, or claimed it. It hopped over two other passengers and the boatman to reach Mike, and sat with its butt on his left knee, tail curling around his leg, looking at him expectantly.

It was crystal clear to him what the cat was trying to tell him. "Hey, I guess we kind of skipped breakfast, didn't we?"

"No matter," the boatman said, flashing a gold-toothed grin, "the fine boat is very near, and surely they will have many good things to eat."

Mike wasn't sure how he knew that, but the boatman was correct. Just around the next bend in the river, he saw the cruiser's stern.

* * *

Leda, the Wolfes, and Chimera were standing together watching the village of Beni Suef disappear in the distance when Leda had another of her "spells." All of a sudden her friends, the boat, and the Nile disappeared, and Leda literally hit the deck.

Gretchen knelt beside her, checking her carotid pulse and examining her head for any injuries from the fall.

"What's the matter, kid?" Gretchen asked with Duke's inflection. Then, anxiously, "You're not pregnant, are you?"

Leda opened one eye. "Dad, I had a hysterectomy, remember?"

"Oh, is that what that operation was? So, not pregnant. What is it then, your problem?" Toward the end of the speech, Duke receded, and Dr. Gretchen Wolfe came to the fore again.

"It's Cleo." She turned her head to look at Chimera and pulled the scientist down to her. "She left me, Chimera. Just like that. Something about being called by her sister *ba* or something like that, but it's not like we talked it over or anything. I didn't get a chance to tell her to be back by midnight or pick up a jar of peanut butter on the way home or anything. She just left. She can't do that, can she?"

"Apparently she can," the scientist said. "It is not part of the process, of course, but it may be part of Cleopatra, who was schooled in magical arts as well as others."

"You mean she may just be having an out-of-*my*-body experience?" Leda was rising to her feet now with the help of the Wolfes. "I don't suppose you could install a time clock for her, could you, Chimera?"

"Leda! Someone told me you'd fallen. Are you hurt?" Andrew McCallum, trailed by some of the other guests, hurried over to them.

"Just my feelings. Cleo took off and left me."

"Where did she go?"

"I don't know. It was very quick. Something about Gabriella's Cleo. Could we call the police, please? I think Gabriella might be in real trouble."

"You bet. Uh, what shall I tell them to look for?"

"Good question. I don't know."

"She's supposed to be somewhere near Luxor now, isn't she?" he asked.

"Yes. I guess that kind of distance doesn't mean much to . . ." She stopped. Wolfe and Chimera were both staring at someone behind Andrew. "What?"

"Nothing," Wolfe said, smiling. To Chimera, he said, "You saw it, too, didn't you? The hippo crossing the river just there?"

"We—oh yes, we did."

"I'll ask the Luxor authorities to check with the museum and see where Gabriella went, then make sure she's okay," Andrew told Leda. "I won't be a moment."

The people who had wandered over with him left the same way, like a school of fish all swimming together, little bubbles of conversation drifting back toward Leda and the others.

Chimera stared after them with an expression that was both bemused and wary.

"What is the trouble?" Gretchen asked him. "You, too, are unwell?"

"No," Chimera said. "But we seem to have met two of our host's guests before. Except they were then in the habits of Tibetan monks."

"But now they've lost the habit?" Leda asked, almost automatically. "Sorry, I couldn't help myself."

Chimera was in for another surprise later that evening when the Padma Lama also appeared at the captain's table. "Rimpoche!" Chimera said. "But—we had heard you were still in Colorado, despite being told by other people that you had gone to Dharmsala."

"I am on my way there now, but decided to accept Sir Andrew's invitation to join you since the Nile is much closer to my destination than Aspen. I regret that we did not have time to meet and converse as we discussed, but it is my hope that we can remedy that situation on this trip."

Chimera bowed over steepled hands, and the Rimpoche did the same. Chimera asked, "Do Brother Jones and Brother Lhamo-Dhondrub always travel in secular clothing when accompanying you on these journeys? For security purposes perhaps?"

"Who?" the Rimpoche asked.

"Those gentlemen at the purser's table," Chimera said, nodding across the ballroom. "When we met them they said they had come from you to tell me that the monastery had been destroyed in an avalanche and that you were in Dharmsala."

The Rimpoche smiled. "No and as you see, I am here. Perhaps they were monks in another life, and you are seeing them with old eyes?"

Chimera considered the Rimpoche's explanation and found it inadequate. The Rimpoche was a holy man, wise and respected. He did not trouble himself, apparently, with such trivial worldly matters as people who impersonated monks.

As if reading the scientist's mind, the lama leaned across the table, and said, "In old Tibet, before the Chinese liberated our people from everything they valued, much of our population became monks or nuns, at least for a time. Since our liberation, those who have chosen to remain monks or nuns do so at a high cost. We do not usually concern ourselves with fears of identity theft."

Leda, as de facto hostess, sat between Chimera and Gretchen Wolfe, at the opposite end of the table from Andrew. The captain was not present. Andrew, as the boat's owner, presided over the table and the dinner entirely. He seemed to be in his element. This, she realized, was his Sir Walter Scott side. The Andrew McCallum side, he had confided in her, was more used to eating soup from a hot plate while he worked around the clock.

The boat had been restored to its art deco look from the Agatha Christie film. While it was not on the scale of the *Titanic,* there was a small dance floor, a chandelier, dark-paneled bar, and lots of white linen and gleaming silver, sparkling china and wonderfully chilly air-conditioning from which to view the Nile vistas by moonlight.

But she felt very much like a right hand that didn't know what its sinister counterpart was doing.

She had grown used to having Cleo's voice in her mind, she realized, and felt disoriented without it. Even more disorienting was that she did actually have an awareness that Cleo, like the truth, was out there somewhere, still tethered to her own body, if incommunicado at present.

She retired early to her assigned stateroom and pretended not to hear the quiet knock on her door and Andrew's tentative, "Leda?" Remembering Cleo's opinion that Andrew was too good to be true, she thought about all of these unexplained guests and began to wonder. Just because he wasn't the same kind of bastard her daddy had been—before getting killed and ending up in Gretchen Wolfe's body—didn't mean he wasn't another kind of bastard. And even for physical anthropologists and ex-Navy chief petty officers, the Cinderella myth was hard to overcome. "Someday my sugar daddy, if not prince, will come." She had had some other feelings for him, but she could be mistaken about who he was. He did seem too good and too innocent and kind to have all that money and success and to wield the power that he did. Well. Shit. She did fall asleep, and that, of course, was when Cleo returned.

* * *

Cleopatra's narrative:

When they had deposited us among the women belonging to the fat foreign princeling and first the curtain to the women's quarters, then the outer door closed behind two sets of retreating footsteps, I at last dared to open our eyes.

Beside me, the woman who was the instrument of so much trouble wept as bitterly as if she and not Gabriella had been betrayed. Another woman now held and rocked her. Even from where I lay, in a deeply shadowed corner of the room, I discerned the darker shades of bruises on the comforter's face. The younger woman confided to the other that she was to be slain along with me by the devil in her uncle's service.

I struggled for something to do or say that would convince the women to help us. Gabriella and Leda Hubbard believe that deep down, all women are sisters and allies whose problems are often, if not always, caused by men. We, who were forced to have two of our own sisters killed before they did the same to us, naturally do not entirely share this perception. While men may have caused some of our problems, they proved to be a solution to others.

However, in this instance, I prayed to Isis that my hostesses were correct about some women and this lot was among them.

From my corner I searched their faces, trying to find an ally. The niece obviously was not. Who then? The battered crone consoling her? Unlikely, considering her sympathies.

"Forgive her." Leda's voice came to the part of me that ordinarily resided with her.

"But why?"

"It'll drive her nuts, for one thing. Trust me. I was raised by the Queen of Guilt. And Isis only knows guilt is appropriate in her case."

"*Very true. She is indeed guilty. So why should I forgive her? She deserves to be executed.*"

"*Because, if she has any sort of a conscience, and we must hope that she does, it will make her feel really really bad. And in case you haven't noticed, we don't have the power to execute her. See, your understanding of guilt is a queen thing and although royal, is a bit on the simplistic side and pardon me, because I know Alexandria in your day was the height of cosmopolitan sophistication— but your approach is also a bit savage. In my family we have learned far more refined methods of excruciating torture. So trust me. Forgive her.*"

I moved slightly to draw attention to myself and cleared Gabriella's poor throat, a bit parched from the drug. "I forgive you," I said in a throaty croak that could have been mistaken for deep emotion.

"She spoke!" someone pointed out, tapping the culprit on the shoulder, and with a swirl of a fingertip directing her to face me.

So I would have to do it all again, much against my better judgment.

"*Go on,*" Leda's voice urged. "*Once more with feeling. Like a martyr. Oh, you guys weren't really all that into martyrs, were you? Okay, like you'd say to Marc or Julie when they went back to Rome to hang out with their wives, then came back and brought you a really really nice present to apologize. Be—magnanimous.*"

"*Oh, why did you not say so?*" I asked, although I felt it only fair to point out that the Saudi woman had brought me no gift nor anything else except deceit, mistreatment, and captivity.

"*So she's a little attached to family values,*" Leda said. "*Rise above it. Go on.*"

I raised Gabriella's chin high and caused her voice to throb with pity and sorrow, the latter not entirely feigned, as I said once more, "I forgive you."

I had everyone's complete attention and, having never been short on a feeling for the dramatic occasion, continued, improvising, "I know you sought only to escape that man's wrath, and having brought it upon yourself and your family—is that your mother? What a loyal and devoted daughter you have, if you don't mind my saying so. He is truly the master of you all, and you are powerless to oppose his will—as, thanks to you, now I am as well. But nevertheless I forgive you. We have in the past delivered many women in situations like yours to lives of freedom and joy, and can now no longer do so, but I do understand that such freedom is beyond your grasp—and now, alas, mine. But no matter. I'm sure you meant well."

Then, in an inspired gesture, I gasped in pain and clasped my side as if a recent injury had given me a sudden pang.

It was the miscreant's turn to stifle a sob. I twisted the knife once more, feeling Leda's silent approval. "I only hope he does not torture any of you too severely to force me to give up the names of more brave women who have risked their lives and homes to save you and others in your situation. I cannot bear to see others suffer."

At this the mother and daughter uttered loud wails and collapsed into tearful lamentations each upon the breast of the other. An older woman clucked her tongue and left the room for a moment, returning to offer me a cup of water and two pills. I feared it to be another drug and it was. The word ASPIRIN was written across it.

At that point the men returned, saying we were to embark upon our journey. How different this trip would be from the ones I had taken aboard my barge inspecting my temples and granaries, I could not help reflecting, as I was loaded aboard like a sacrificial animal, and dumped without ceremony onto the floor of another room. I heard a wail and felt someone fall against me and guessed our betrayer was now imprisoned with me.

Hours seem to pass while I listen to the gulps, sobs, and hiccups of my unworthy companion, yet I do not despair. The river is long, and we are not to be killed until some spot near Luxor, it seems, so perhaps we will find an opportunity to escape before then.

CHAPTER 21

"Kid? You awake?" Duke Hubbard asked in a stage whisper that held just a hint of Gretchen's feminine German accent.

This time Leda arose, more confused than ever, and went to the door of her stateroom and opened it. Not only Gretchen but Wilhelm Wolfe and Chimera as well stood there looking over their shoulders like rather exotic adult versions of the Hardy Boys and Nancy Drew. She ushered them in.

"What's on your minds?" she asked, her voice still husky from a sleep in which she had spent a lot of time arguing with Cleopatra. "Because I can tell you, with Cleo's latest news there's quite a lot on mine."

Closing the door behind them, Gretchen leaned against it. "Tell them, Wilhelm."

"Chimera says that two of Andrew McCallum's associates were monks who drugged him and stole secrets pertaining to the process. I also have seen one of the men before. He sat two chairs down from McCallum on the left, and I believe was introduced as the head of a special effects company," he told Leda. "He caused me to have special effects when I saw him last. My memory only now returns. He is one of those who kidnapped me at the conference and drugged me. No doubt also to obtain secrets, as Gretchen has had my blood tested and finds traces of truth serum."

"That does it," Leda said, standing. "I'm going to go find Andrew and ask him what kind of an outfit he's running here anyway."

Chimera gave a little cough. "That may not be the best approach, Leda."

"Maybe not, but we do have to know what's going on here, don't we? What are kidnappers doing with the TV crew? Maybe they're planning to kidnap Andrew. Did you think about that?"

"Perhaps," Chimera said. "But they do not seem surprised or alarmed to see us here or worried that we will remember them and warn Mr. McCallum. In fact, if we are not mistaken, the spurious Brother Jones winked at us earlier, from which we gathered he was not contrite for his part in stealing our data."

"Andrew wouldn't have had anything to do with that. He's a major stockholder."

"As was Rasmussen," Gretchen reminded her.

"You got me there. But I still think he owes us an explanation. Personally, I think we should turn this thing around and go back to Cairo and see what the authorities are doing about Gabriella. Nobody has done anything very television productionish that I can see since we've been on the boat. I'd say it was more of a pleasure cruise for them except they don't seem to be having a particularly good time either. I asked Andrew what the authorities had said about Gabriella when we were at dinner, and he got distracted all of a sudden." Which was funny when they'd been sharing every reaction and thought—well, mostly hers, come to think of it—for the last week or so. Suddenly he was too distracted to tell her what he'd found out about something so important?

"We'll go with you," Wolfe said. He still looked peaked and wobbly but determined. He was not the kind of guy who was used to being helpless, and he hadn't cared for it.

"Yes," Gretchen said. "If any of us are to vanish, we will vanish all together and so will not really vanish at all as we will each know where are the others, *ja?* You betcha." The final two words were in her Duke voice.

And so they opened the cabin door to see the sun peeking over the eastern shore of the Nile.

On their first day they had traveled from Alex to Cairo, then by car to Giza to view the pyramids, continuing by road to Abu Sir and Saqqara to view the Step Pyramid designed by the great Imhotep for King Djoser. *"Rosetau,"* Cleopatra had murmured. It once had been another name for the necropolis of Memphis at Saqqara, but had come to mean the entrance to the Other World at the boundaries of the sky, the place where Osiris's body was supposed to be buried. For a Greek and a well-educated woman, Leda thought, Cleopatra took Egyptian magic and religion quite seriously.

Leda had allowed Cleopatra some rein to play tour guide to the crew, but to her surprise most of them seemed more interested in wandering off alone or in couples or small groups to contemplate the various mysteries without her guidance. And truthfully, except that the monuments had been newer in Cleopatra's time, the queen had little insight into their history or origins. More research had been done since then than was done before, and the pyramids were ancient long before Cleo's time.

As the sun rose over the stern of the boat, so did something else—the heads of a group of people Leda had not seen before. They looked like well-heeled tourists for the most part, with one very notable exception.

"Leda!" Mike Angeles greeted her.

"Hey, Mike. We can't go on meeting like this," she said, taking three giant steps backward thinking of the magnetism that had drawn them together at the beginning of their last encounter.

The medium-sized, dark-haired, and still fairly hunky man grinned back at her. "No problem. Actually, I wanted to talk to your boyfriend. And to Gabriella." He looked around her and then, in a different voice said, "Where is she? What have you done with her?"

"Who?"

"My love," he said, looking as if he'd cut her down if she didn't produce Cleopatra instantly. "She is no longer with you."

It was safe to draw closer then, she realized, and she stepped away from her three friends until she was within whispering range. "Nice to see you, too, Antony. I haven't done anything with her. She's off on a self-appointed mission. We need to talk. Out of earshot from the Sierra Club types you brought along."

He cocked an eyebrow at her, inquiring.

"But I have to talk to Andrew first. Meet me on the top deck in a half hour?"

He nodded and headed for the teak-and-brass staircase leading topside.

The new tourists glanced at her at first blandly, then with a bit more interest. *Assessment.* That was the word. They assessed her. And as she saw that, she saw that they were an unlikely group of casual tourists. Each and every tanned and thirty-to-fiftyish, T-shirted man and woman among them had the eye of a commanding officer who expected unquestioning deference, if not obedience. Until the blending with Cleopatra, Leda had never been that sort of person. True, she knew what was due her in terms of respect for authority—but hers had always been borrowed authority, and mostly she relied on reason and fairness to gain the cooperation of her so-called inferiors. These were the sort of people from whom her authority had been borrowed.

Andrew appeared, his hand outstretched to shake the hands of these new guests. He fit right in, something she would not have guessed from their recent association. Though she should have. Cleopatra was right about that.

Gathering all of the queenly bearing she could, she turned to him and said, "We need a word with you, Andrew."

"Of course, Dr. Hubbard," he said, using her title for the benefit of his guests, who reacted to it with slight shifts in their facial expressions. "In a moment. I'd like you to meet our guests. These people represent one of our sponsors, the Save the Nile Foundation, a subsidiary of the Maat Society for the preservation of Egyptian culture. They are responsible for reintroducing the traditional wildlife to the river in an attempt to heal its ecosystem of the damage done by the dams."

She put on a big bright smile worthy of Duke at his most charming—or Cleopatra at hers. The queen's *ba* might be elsewhere, but her memories and attributes remained, though without Cleo's advice on how to deploy them to best advantage.

"Admirable," she said, shaking hands all around. "Pleasure to meet you folks. I understand what the T-shirts are all about now. HELP HAPI, the baboon, SAVE SOBEK, the crocodile, HONOR HORUS, the hawk, ASSIST ATEP, the hippo, REESTABLISH THOTH, the ibis, and my personal favorite, BRING BACK THE BLUE LOTUS."

"You're being facetious in your interpretation of the animal emblems, Leda," Andrew said, "But you're closer to the truth than you know. Each of these people is personally responsible for repopulating the Nile with an animal or plant species in an effort to rebalance and maintain the harmony of the environment."

the dark woods with a velvety sheen and making the brass sparkle almost beyond bearing, the crystal glisten like stars. The place smelled of sandalwood and lemon, probably Pledge, Leda thought. Andrew leaned against the long bar, its face carved with pyramids, palms, and hieroglyphics that matched the etched pattern on the mirror behind it.

His face seemed as open and concerned as ever. "What is this all about?" he asked, sounding genuinely worried.

"Oh, we are thinking you know," Gretchen said, giving him a sly smile and a wag of her forefinger.

"Know what?"

"*You* know. About Interpol. Or perhaps you did not, and this is all an accident?"

"I'm afraid you've lost me," he said.

Leda explained, "Chimera and Wolfe have spotted some suspicious characters among your handpicked crew, Andrew."

"Really?"

"Yes," Wolfe said. "I recall seeing the face of the assistant director just before I was shoved into a van and drugged. At that time, the assistant director seemed to be directing the people abducting me."

Andrew shook his head slowly, regretfully, "I know after all you've been through it's hard to trust people, but I don't see how it could be the same guy, Wilhelm. Mario Conti was handpicked by Ro, who says he is very well known as an up-and-coming director of short films. He's a member of the union and everything."

"And your videographers?" Chimera asked softly. "They seem to have renounced their religious vocation since they escorted us part of the way to Dharmsala. Perhaps they became disillusioned by the information they found in field notes and on the plans for the upgrade of our transfer device they stole from us while we slept," Chimera said. "Perhaps it came as a shock to them that one could have a reincarnation

Now when did he become such a bloody expert on Egypt, sl wondered. It must have been because these people wei sponsors. He had made it his business to know about ther because they represented money. Funny he hadn't men tioned it before, though.

"As I said, admirable. Nice to meet you folks."

Andrew turned, smiling at the Wolfes and Chimera, and introduced them, too, without specifying who they were. The SNF members assessed them, too. Then Wolfe cleared his throat, and said softly into their host's ear, "Andrew, that word? It is quite urgent, I assure you."

"Certainly, certainly. Excuse me, ladies and gentlemen. The steward will show you to your rooms." As he turned back toward them, the crew on the deck below cast off the lines and the cruiser's wheel began once more to churn up a wake of white froth in the blue waters of the once green Nile.

As they turned away from the tourists to join Andrew in the lounge, Leda felt Gretchen hesitate. She turned her head slightly and caught *Frau Doktor* Wolfe—or was it her father?—winking conspiratorially at the red-faced man in the crocodile T-shirt.

"What was that all about?" she asked Gretchen in a low voice.

"That was about I think maybe we do not have so much to worry for after all, *Kinder*. The fellow wearing the crocodile?"

"Yes, I saw. What about him?"

"He is with Interpol. He is the one who took us to Wilhelm. So possibly Andrew McCallum is aware of what we will tell him but is helping with the investigations, *ja?*"

"I hope so," Leda said.

Andrew seemed himself again when the small delegation confronted him in the lounge. The sun poured in through the panoramic windows that formed most of one wall, enriching the dark woods with a velvety sheen and making the brass sparkle almost beyond bearing, the crystal glisten like stars. The place smelled of sandalwood and lemon, probably Pledge, Leda thought. Andrew leaned against the long bar, its face carved with pyramids, palms, and hieroglyphics that matched the etched pattern on the mirror behind it.

His face seemed as open and concerned as ever. "What is this all about?" he asked, sounding genuinely worried.

"Oh, we are thinking you know," Gretchen said, giving him a sly smile and a wag of her forefinger.

"Know what?"

"*You* know. About Interpol. Or perhaps you did not, and this is all an accident?"

"I'm afraid you've lost me," he said.

Leda explained, "Chimera and Wolfe have spotted some suspicious characters among your handpicked crew, Andrew."

"Really?"

"Yes," Wolfe said. "I recall seeing the face of the assistant director just before I was shoved into a van and drugged. At that time, the assistant director seemed to be directing the people abducting me."

Andrew shook his head slowly, regretfully, "I know after all you've been through it's hard to trust people, but I don't see how it could be the same guy, Wilhelm. Mario Conti was handpicked by Ro, who says he is very well known as an up-and-coming director of short films. He's a member of the union and everything."

"And your videographers?" Chimera asked softly. "They seem to have renounced their religious vocation since they escorted us part of the way to Dharmsala. Perhaps they became disillusioned by the information they found in field notes and on the plans for the upgrade of our transfer device they stole from us while we slept," Chimera said. "Perhaps it came as a shock to them that one could have a reincarnation

Now when did he become such a bloody expert on Egypt, she wondered. It must have been because these people were sponsors. He had made it his business to know about them because they represented money. Funny he hadn't mentioned it before, though.

"As I said, admirable. Nice to meet you folks."

Andrew turned, smiling at the Wolfes and Chimera, and introduced them, too, without specifying who they were. The SNF members assessed them, too. Then Wolfe cleared his throat, and said softly into their host's ear, "Andrew, that word? It is quite urgent, I assure you."

"Certainly, certainly. Excuse me, ladies and gentlemen. The steward will show you to your rooms." As he turned back toward them, the crew on the deck below cast off the lines and the cruiser's wheel began once more to churn up a wake of white froth in the blue waters of the once green Nile.

As they turned away from the tourists to join Andrew in the lounge, Leda felt Gretchen hesitate. She turned her head slightly and caught *Frau Doktor* Wolfe—or was it her father?—winking conspiratorially at the red-faced man in the crocodile T-shirt.

"What was that all about?" she asked Gretchen in a low voice.

"That was about I think maybe we do not have so much to worry for after all, *Kinder*. The fellow wearing the crocodile?"

"Yes, I saw. What about him?"

"He is with Interpol. He is the one who took us to Wilhelm. So possibly Andrew McCallum is aware of what we will tell him but is helping with the investigations, *ja?*"

"I hope so," Leda said.

Andrew seemed himself again when the small delegation confronted him in the lounge. The sun poured in through the panoramic windows that formed most of one wall, enriching within a mature living body already inhabited by another personality. It may have caused a crisis of faith."

"Dr. Chimera, are you being sarcastic with me?" Andrew asked, smiling, obviously amused by the idea that Chimera would exhibit a less-than-serene attitude, regardless of the provocation.

He was also sidestepping Chimera's question, Leda thought. Glancing at her, Andrew sighed, and said, "Look, folks, I don't know why you're seeing these people as you are. I've been assured that they are all top-notch professionals. I'd think perhaps you were experiencing some sort of meltdown in the blending process that was causing you each to have delusions, but in case it's slipped your minds, I am also blended, and I have experienced no such episodes of déjà vu with anyone. Also, of course, Mr. Wolfe and his wife are not themselves blends, so that explanation wouldn't suffice for them."

"Of course not," Gretchen said hurriedly. "But also there could be some other explanation, *ja?* These people have been brought aboard by you to assist Interpol in their investigation. Were that true, perhaps you would not tell us everything, eh?"

"Were that true," Andrew agreed equably. "Though I see no reason why I would keep anything of that sort a secret from you. You were the victims Interpol assisted after all."

"Perhaps the bad guys are then being herded here under some ruse of Interpol's to expose them all in a grand denouement as in Hercule Poirot?" Gretchen suggested.

"If they are, nobody let me in on it," Andrew said.

Leda said, "About Gabriella . . ."

"I haven't been able to learn anything new. The river police and the tourist police are both taxed beyond their capabilities by the regatta, and my calls haven't even been returned. I'm sorry."

"Then we need to turn around," she said, and began telling him what she knew from Cleo 7.1. "She's been kidnapped by the people who broke into her home twice. Some of them are the relatives of that Saudi woman she was trying to help. The head guy is an amir. And there are terrorists involved, too. They've taken her onto one of the yachts."

He shook his head, his expression troubled but cautious. "Yes, but which one? As you all know, I am extremely—er—comfortable financially, but there are a lot of people on the river right now who can buy and sell me. I don't have that much influence by comparison. The Egyptian police are very reluctant to inconvenience wealthy and influential people. I was told that, by the way, to reassure me. As for turning around—Leda, look out the window."

She did so and saw boats of all descriptions fore, aft, and port of them. The wall was on the starboard side, but she was pretty sure there were boats there, too. Feluccas and small motorboats maneuvered between the larger craft like motorcycles among eighteen-wheelers on a crowded highway.

"Then what are we going to do? They're going to kill her. You know my source is reliable, Andrew. Surely you can use some connection to get the police to listen to us?"

The door to the lounge flew open and the representatives of the Save the Nile Foundation flowed in. Andrew glared at the steward trailing helplessly behind them. The man shrugged.

"Please excuse us, but we are having a private conversation," Wolfe said in his own best command voice.

"Oh, don't let us interrupt you," said the well-toned dark-haired woman in the hippopotamus T-shirt. "Go right ahead and talk, but we are simply perishing from thirst. Is the *barista* off duty now?"

"It *is* only seven o'clock in the morning," Andrew pointed out reasonably.

"Orange juice or tomato juice or even coffee would be fine," she replied.

"I know my way around a bar pretty well, McCallum," the Interpol man said. "I'll take care of my friends. Don't worry about it."

"But while you're here, McCallum," another of the men said, "I have a few questions."

Andrew rolled his eyes at Leda and mouthed the word "sponsors," then turned back to face them.

Surely with the little she'd been able to say he would realize how important it was and think of something. Or— meanwhile Mike Angeles was waiting for her on the top deck, and he was probably better prepared to deal with it than Andrew was anyway.

Mike was deep in conversation with a grizzled stocky man sporting muttonchop whiskers and gargling at Mike in a broad Lowland Scots accent.

"Leda, this is Captain McGregor. McGregor, Dr. Hubbard. He's been telling me about the hovercraft technology."

"Andrew showed the system off to me earlier," she said.

"He's aye proud of it," McGregor said. "Has been a learnin' curve for us rivermen as works for the rich yacht owners, but now that it's more common, we pool information, if you tak' my meanin'."

She did, among the many rolling r's of his speech. "You mean Andrew's not the only one with a hovercraft?"

"Och, no, madam. No indeed. It's become quite the fad. Not all has it, mind you, but the very wealthy. I'd best get me back to the pilothouse now. This stretch of water's filled up a bit since we started, and navigation is gey tricky. A pleasure, sir, madam," he said, and strode toward the bow.

"So, about Gabriella?" Mike said, as if she needed reminding.

"According to Cleo, she's on one of these yachts."

"Which one? There are quite a few."

"Well, it belongs to the amir uncle of that damned woman they tried to help."

"Yeah, but what was her name?"

"I don't know. Gabriella didn't say. I suppose she and the contessa keep that sort of thing secret—wait a minute. I can call the contessa."

But of course she got no cell signal so far from Cairo.

"Never mind. How many Saudi Arabian river yachts can there be anyway?" Mike asked. "I'm going to take the dinghy and search among these. Nobody's got a lot of speed on at the moment, and it's pretty much gridlock from here back to Cairo. I ought to be able to narrow it down."

"Just a minute," Leda said, and clattered back down the gridded metal stairs, ducking back into the lounge, now full of the TV people as well as the Nile savers, who were deep in conversation with the Wolfes and Chimera. Stalking over to the videographers Chimera had identified as the phony monks, she scooped up one of the cameras on the table between them. "I need to borrow this for a minute, fellas," she said, and ran away as quickly as she could, before they had a chance to object.

As she pushed through the lounge door to the outer deck, she heard their rapid footsteps on her heels, but Mike met her at the steps and apparently they decided not to try to take him on. From the corner of her eye, through the long glass wall of the lounge, she saw them returning to their table, gesturing back toward her. She handed the camera to Mike. "Here you go. You're filming the event for US Satellite TV distribution, as a videographer for Edge TV."

"A cover! And on such short notice. Gee thanks, Chief."

"Do not let the general go storming aboard every ship demanding that they return his woman. It won't work, and it could get you killed."

"I risk getting killed for a living."

"Yeah, I know that. If it's just you, that's one thing. But Gabriella's involved here, too, obviously, so only very sneaky heroism is allowed." She handed him her cell phone. "When you find the right boat, call the river police and tell them to search it for explosives. Cleo said something about terrorists."

This bit she called over the side, as he had already grabbed the line mooring the Zodiak dinghy to the boat, descended the small ladder running down the hull of the stern, hopped into the boat, and was starting the Mercedes-Benz motor.

CHAPTER 22

"Leda, what's all this about you taking a camera to give to Mike?" Andrew asked mildly, approaching her as she turned back toward midship. He was trailed by most of the people who had been in the lounge.

"He needed it," she said flatly. "*He* is going to try to help Gabriella."

"So are we," Andrew said reasonably. "We've talked it over, and I'm on my way to discuss it with Captain McGregor. I wish you hadn't been so hasty. Even I can't act unilaterally in compromising the production, you know. There are our sponsors and investors to think of as well."

"I thought you said you were the moneyman?" Leda said.

"I am, but even backers need backers. My power is not absolute. These people are important to us all, trust me."

"I'll worry about them when they've been drugged and dumped in the hold of some sexist sultan's ship until he and a few friends can find a way to blow them up," Leda said.

"But, Dr. Hubbard," said the woman with the baboon T-shirt. She had an Asian face—Japanese? And an upper-class

British accent. "Once Andrew explained the situation to us, we were as concerned as you are. Heavens, we can't do what we're trying to do here without Dr. Faruk! She's crucial to this endeavor. I just hope your friend knows how to use the camera so he can get some good footage of her rescue."

"Leda, while I speak to Captain McGregor, I think you should return to the lounge and explain the situation *fully* to these ladies and gentlemen. Quite aside from their sponsorship of this production, these are extremely influential people. Dr. Chimera and Mr. Wolfe have already filled them in on the blending process and their own current relationships to Nucor." He headed topside.

They returned to the air-conditioned lounge. Wolfe, Gretchen, Chimera, the lama, and Iris were there. Everyone else seemed to have evaporated. As they settled into the comfortable sofas and armchairs, these upholstered in terracotta leather and a Nile green brocade with stylized tomb paintings in the design, stewards bearing chaise lounges appeared outside the window wall and began setting them up. Soon afterward many of the other crew members, including the ersatz monks, settled into them to sun and watch the boats go by, she supposed.

Then suddenly the boats were going by somewhat faster, falling astern of them like telephone poles along a highway as seen from a speeding car. Well, good. Andrew was moving. It was in the wrong direction—forward. But then, he couldn't go back, as he had pointed out. At least it was movement, and she'd settle for that for now.

"Okay, so how is it you know Dr. Faruk is in trouble, Dr. Hubbard?" the man in the Sobek T-shirt asked. He was red-faced, red-haired, and red-freckled and could have been a vacationing accountant except that there was something in the lines of his face and the shading of his eyes that reminded her of Mike when he wasn't trying to charm, or be funny, or thought no one was looking. His mouth and chin were set in a hard line, but his eyes opened too wide and too innocently for those of someone his age. It should have made him look softer, but it didn't. He had seen terrible things, done terrible things, but he hadn't intended them to be terrible, they just had to be done. He had maybe cried a little while he did them, as though he were whistling while he worked. Big crocodile tears. Sorry to hack, poison, drown, or torture you. Nothing personal, mind you. Just part of my job. I'm a very sensitive guy really.

Mike looked haunted. This guy looked like any haunting going on in his vicinity was done by him, in a very corporeal way.

"You might say we have a mutual friend," she told him.

"And that would be—Queen Cleopatra?" the baboon lady asked. Leda would have liked it better if she had been a little breathless and impressed, but it seemed to be a rhetorical question.

"Okay, who's been breaking our secret oath?" she asked the Wolfes and Chimera. "Turn in your decoder badge and shoe phone right now."

Gretchen winked at her, annoyingly, and though it was meant to reassure her, it did not. It was not Duke's wink. Duke probably thought, as Leda did, that the Sobek guy was as much an Interpol agent as the croc on his T-shirt. Gretchen, more of a believer in what she saw and heard herself than what anyone suspected, had met him as an Interpol agent and still thought he was one.

He gave her a big croc grin. "So, yes, we know about Cleopatra. That you are partly her and she is part of you but is also part of Dr. Faruk. Mr. McCallum plans to reveal that aspect of your research during this production, I understand. He says you are the first two people to be blended, I believe Dr. Chimera calls it, with the same DNA."

"Is that what he said?" she asked, looking to Chimera and the Wolfes. Chimera's head inclined slightly in assent.

"Of course," Sobek-guy said. "He said he'd discussed this part of the program with you, and you agreed."

"It was a private conversation at that point," she said pleasantly enough. But something inside her that was pure Hubbard was balking. Gretchen's eyes lit with the warmth of her father seeing the signs of the family mulishness surfacing in his baby girl. "And if what you say is true, there are at least two other people involved who are not here at the moment. Also, I have heard it said that there are extremely stiff legal penalties for anyone claiming to have done what you say I have done even if they do so privately— never mind publicly. If I ever tried to claim anything like that, I'd want written permission from Nucor Helix. With all due respect to Dr. Chimera and Mr. Wolfe, they are not in the drivers' seats any longer, and my pockets are damn shallow when it comes to lawsuits from people with lots of nasty lawyers. Mr. McCallum and I have been on excellent terms thus far, but he has not extended legal protection to me. Now, if we were to locate Gabriella, perhaps she would feel differently, in which case there might be some cause to have a discussion."

"You don't have to blackmail us, Dr. Hubbard. We have already said we wished to assist you in locating Dr. Faruk," said the Thoth-lady. "And between our members, Dr. Chimera, Dr. and Mr. Wolfe, and Mr. McCallum, we hold a controlling interest in Nucor Helix."

"Good," Leda said. "Then getting a contract giving me permission to disclose any knowledge I may have promised not to disclose shouldn't pose any problem. Along with guarantees of legal help and payment of any kind of penalties or lawsuits that might be waged against me—or Dr. Faruk—as a result of anything we should disclose at your request. Meanwhile . . ."

The cruiser gave a couple of toots of its whistle, and the large boat outside their window fell away behind them.

Then they picked up speed so quickly that, as Leda tried to stand to make her exit, she was thrown back down into her seat again.

For several minutes sand, cane fields, cotton fields, palms, workmen, and spectators out to see the regatta flashed past. The people in the lounge chairs cheered and waved at people waving from the bank. Then Andrew walked into the lounge, looking confident, smug even.

"McGregor is an excellent pilot. We'll be miles ahead of the others before long."

"Yes," Leda said, "but now the boat that has Gabriella is also miles behind us, as is Mike in the dinghy."

"Which gives us options that simply trying to catch up with them if they were ahead of us would not," he said. "We can pull over and tie up ahead of this pack and let them go by until the culprit in question comes abreast of us, then—"

"If we can find out by then who the culprit is," Leda said. "That's what Mike's trying to do now."

"*Is* he?" Sobek asked.

"Well, yeah. Some people don't just talk about helping. They actually do something," Leda said. "I'm thinking it might be a good idea for me to get off this vessel when we dock and catch a train back to Cairo to try to convince the police to take us seriously."

But Gretchen shook her head. "That would not be helpful, I think. The city police are very busy and not likely to wish to conduct a search of the yachts of wealthy people already under way. The river police are few and very limited from what we saw in port. And your friends would be out here on the water while you would be ashore and behind everyone. This would not be good, *ja?*"

"Well, yeah, *ja,*" Leda agreed.

"Besides," Sobek said smoothly, "you've already been brought here at Mr. McCallum's expense to consult on this program. You were worried about lawsuits and contracts a moment ago, so I thought I'd mention that."

"Thanks," she said sweetly. "It's so good of you to consider my welfare."

McCallum groaned and buried his face in one hand.

Mike hadn't noticed the little cat jumping into the dinghy as he cast off, but there she was, sprawled gracefully across the seat closest to the bow, her bat ears slightly flattened as she lifted her black nose to the sun, eyes shut in catty bliss. Fortunately, she seemed to realize that kneading the inflatable dinghy with her claws would probably spoil her good mood, because her paws lay still, though her tail curled and uncurled in a happy sort of way. Mike just hoped she'd have sense enough to get out of the way if anything violent went down.

The most violent thing that seemed likely to happen for a long time, though, was maybe colliding with one of the other boats as he weaved in and out among them, scanning the names on the bow and the owner's name and country stenciled on the sterns to see which were likely candidates for Gabriella's captors.

Twice he stopped when he found craft with Saudi points of origin, but one was crewed by only two people, brothers, and didn't seem large enough to hold the women Leda had mentioned.

The other was larger, but didn't seem as well maintained as he would have expected an amir's vessel to be.

He passed Syrian boats and African ones from the Sudan and Kenya, Botswana, and Ethiopia, Zimbabwe, and other places even more unlikely. Lebanon, Jordan, Turkey, Iran, Iraq, and almost every other country in the Middle East was represented except Israel, of course. Likewise France, Italy, Greece, Holland, England, and several American states were flying their colors. He was beginning to doubt he'd ever find the right craft among all of these damn gilded tubs when he saw someone he recognized.

Abdul Mohammed stood on the bow of a yacht even fancier than the one owned by McCallum.

"Well, shit," Mike said to himself, *"I might have known he'd be involved, I guess. Especially with all that talk of blowing things up."*

Marc Antony filled himself in on Abdul Mohammed. *"But this man is a political criminal,"* he said. *"A terrorist, as you say. Why would he want to blow up our beloved? Does he know she is the Queen of Egypt?"*

"No. At least I don't think so. But this isn't his boat. He's Egyptian, not Saudi, and I didn't get the impression he was anywhere near wealthy enough to afford a craft like this one. But Doc has made herself other enemies with her female-smuggling sideline. Looks like her enemies and my enemy are in cahoots."

"I beg your pardon?"

"Codependents, Marco. Enabling each other to do bigger bad."

"Well, we must stop them! I've only just found her again. I'm not about to lose her so quickly."

"Calm down. I'm going to make like a law-abiding citizen and call the river cops."

Except he couldn't get through. First he had a hell of a time finding information to get the number, then he was answered by an endless loop of voice mail options. *"I guess we have to go haul the cavalry's asses back here ourselves. I really didn't want to do that."*

"Nor I. Who knows what harm may befall her while we seek these incompetents? This is no warship. We are armed. I say we board, dispatch our enemies while we have the element of surprise on our side, rescue our beloved, and commandeer the vessel for our own."

"Super idea, but it breaks several national and international laws, especially the last part."

"*Very well, then we won't commandeer the vessel. But we must do something, man.*"

"*Okay. I think I'll make another phone call.*" He looked in the memory files of Leda's phone and found several names and numbers, only one of which was familiar to him.

McCallum answered on the third ring. Mike gave him the name and registration of the boat. The *Mubarraz Falcon*, Saudi Arabia. He started to say more when he was hailed from above.

"You down there, move it!" someone called from one of the other boats. He was so focused on the *Mubarraz Falcon* he hadn't noticed that he was closely surrounded on all other sides by even larger craft—so surrounded now that there was nowhere for him to go.

"Move where?" he asked, gesticulating like an angry Alexandrian cabbie. "You think I can go straight up? Have a little courtesy! I am a television reporter filming this event." He held the borrowed camera in the air and shook it for emphasis. "Our viewers want to see your fine vessels and share in this momentous event, too. I'd like to film your re-action to what you've seen so far today."

"No comment," the person said grumpily, but others be-gan calling out in a friendlier manner—including a group of black-clad women, at least he supposed they were women, who gathered at the rail of the *Mubarraz Falcon* like a flock of crows seeing someone with bread crumbs.

"You should come up here!" one of them called down. "My son is very proud of his yacht. He is an important man. You should talk to him."

Abdul Mohammed was no longer in sight. The invita-tion did not necessarily need to be engraved for him to see an opportunity. He wasn't sure what he was going to do with it exactly, but he didn't see how he could help Gabriella otherwise at this point. He tied the dinghy up behind the *Falcon* and climbed aboard, brandishing the camera.

The sun was low in the sky by then, beginning to droop toward the western horizon. They were well beyond the heavily populated Cairo suburbs. Mike thought he recognized an area where Jaime's delegation had passed that morning in their boat, on the way to meet up with McCallum's.

The women fluttered up to him as he boarded, and surrounded him, herding him. He hadn't expected them to speak to him at any length, but he had expected more giggling and twittering. Their mood, once he was among them, was grimmer and their steps purposeful. He wondered for a moment if they had guns under those burkhas, but they didn't try to threaten him in any way. They led him along the deck and up a flight of stairs, then to an inner corridor. One of the women unlocked a door.

Inside Gabriella lay in a puddle of black, slumped against a wall. She wasn't tied, but at first she stared off into space and didn't seem to be aware of him. Then her head turned a fraction, and her eyes lit with recognition.

"I will save you, my queen!" he called to her, or rather Antony did, and fortunately he did it in his own antique Latin.

"Yes," said the woman who had spoken to him originally. "That is what I wished to show you. My son is very angry with that woman and with my granddaughter. Can you take them away with you?"

"Absolutely," he said. "But how?"

"Very simple," she said. Two other women stepped into the room and pulled up the headpiece to the black robe, placing the veil across Gabriella's face while she batted at their hands ineffectually, then seemed to realize they were trying to help her and adjusted the veil herself.

The women absorbed her and one of the others supporting her, herding them and Mike back to the stern.

Unfortunately, Abdul Mohammed was there as well, along with a large fat man in traditional Saudi robes and very dark sunglasses. Mike looked at them and grinned.

"Oh, man, what is this anyway? The Laurel and Hardy of international terrorism?"

The old woman said to the fat man. "Allah be praised, my son, you are here! We found this man leading the Egyptian woman away from her room. We could not force him to stay but tried to delay him. I fear we could have done so no longer except that you are here now, and it is in your hands, and Allah's."

CHAPTER 23

The hovercraft engines carried *Agatha* past Beni Mazar and two small islands, then to the bridge at Minia. Rose-gold sandstone cliffs climbed steadily higher into a gory-looking sunset as they traveled upstream. Leda knew they were near the rock tombs of Beni Hasan and shortly after-ward would pass Mallawi on the western bank, then to Tel el Armana. Here ruins marked the site of Akhetaten's great city, where he and Nefertiti had ruled rather briefly when their attempts to convert all of Egypt to fundamentalist Aten worship went against the grain of the people and the powerful priesthood who found more gods, if not merrier, at least more lucrative.

"He's found the boat," Andrew McCallum announced as he clicked off his cell phone.

"Did he call the river police?" Leda asked.

"He couldn't get through so he called us, which will do just as well."

"How do you figure that? We can't put a net across the river without catching a whole bunch of other yachts."

"No, but we can wait for them to catch up and make sure

we enter the locks with them at Karnak. It should be very easy to board them while we're inside the lock."

"Damn, and I forgot my cutlass!" Leda said, snapping her fingers. "Did you forget the part where I mentioned explosives? And terrorists. Which probably means, you know, guns and things?"

"We are not without resources," Andrew said stiffly. "Isn't that right, ladies and gentlemen?"

Murmurs of assent issued from the T-shirted Nile savers.

"Meanwhile, daylight is fading, and it's time to tie up for the night. My chef has prepared us a late supper."

They were far ahead of the other boats, so Captain McGregor could pick his spot. McCallum wanted him to pick a place where the boats had to pass through a narrow stretch of river, to make the *Mubarraz Falcon* easier to spot, and to fall in behind. McGregor did better than that. Their burst of speed in hovercraft mode had carried them far ahead of the others. Leda looked longingly toward Tel el Armana, but they sailed past it.

Captain McGregor kept the boat in hovercraft mode until they encountered the large islands in midstream just north of the bridge called the Assuit Barrage. There the river tightened its belt, buckling it with the islands. The eastern channel was somewhat narrower than the western and McGregor pulled up to moor to the southern tip of the smallest of the four islands, where they would have a clear view of the other boats passing. Here the larger craft would be able to travel no more than three abreast.

Standing on the upper deck, Andrew paced it, giving a good imitation of Captain Ahab, while McGregor directed the businesslike business of securing the craft for the night. They had traveled almost two hundred miles from their starting point at Beni Suef, thanks to the wonders of the hovercraft technology. Leda looked downstream, hoping that Mike would remember to get gas. He'd need it if he was to return the dinghy and, she hoped, Gabriella, to the *Agatha*.

Supper was late and rather formal. Leda wore a purple native kaftan belted low, with a matching embroidered and fringed scarf she'd acquired in the souk in Alex. With it she wore a beaded broadcollar and a scapular of a winged scarab, the central part of the scarab surrounded by the loop of an ankh. McGregor wore a dress uniform that was not quite British navy, but close. Andrew got himself up like Lawrence of Arabia in flowing white robes, though he skipped the headdress. The environmentalists had actually brought something besides T-shirts. The men wore tuxes that had cummerbunds and ties in prints featuring their chosen creature. One of the women wore a slinky purple evening gown with what looked like roses sequined and glittered into a pattern but turned out to be hippos. The other lady's wrist was adorned with a broad gold bracelet cast in the shape of a baboon.

After everyone was seated, Iris and Ro made their own grand entrance, Iris in a slim, pleated white gown topped with an unusual evening wrap of some silky material, the sleeves long and draping and painted in shades of blue, green, red, and trimmed with gold. She raised her arm in greeting, and Leda saw that the sleeve actually formed a feathered wing of the sort depicted on Isis figures in tomb paintings and funerary furnishings.

Ro's black silk turtleneck was "tied" with an ebony-and-gold figure of Anubis, and beside him trotted the dog who had boarded with the environmentalists, a black Lab maybe or some kind of hound? It looked not unlike the dog figure of Anubis.

The Padma Lama and Chimera arrived deep in conversation, and neither had changed from their customary attire. The Padma Lama wore his saffron-and-maroon robes and Chimera the stylish black pajamas the scientist always favored.

Leda was seated next to the lama and overheard the exchange between the two Tibetans. It wasn't exactly small talk.

"Have you considered that in bringing these beings back into this life, you may be depriving them of the subsequent incarnations that would eventually lead them to nirvana?" the lama asked.

"Not really," Chimera replied. "We believe the blends to be a tangible and scientific method of creating the tulku. Tulkus are sometimes known to be reborn into more than one person and to manifest the same spirit within different personalities."

"Yes, but they are customarily born into that personality," the lama said. "Not artificially inserted. And what about your—what is it you call them? Hosts? How do you suppose the insertion of the new personality will affect the rebirth of the person hosting it?"

"We don't know that," Chimera said. "It was one of the things we wished to discuss with you. How do you think it would affect them?"

The lama shrugged and did not look displeased. "I don't know that either."

The man with the hawk printed on his tie said, "If you split a personality off into different hosts, how many of one person would there be eventually? Enough to take over the world? There are certainly enough DNA samples in one body alone that if that were done, the original donor would constitute at least one large country."

"We would never do that," Chimera said simply. "And also, the donor is not necessarily always going to be the portion of the blend that will dominate. That depends on the personality of the host."

"So," said the lama, "if your late wife were blended with someone else, then the result would be very different from herself?"

"Oh yes. Even if the host was very much like Tsering in temperament and background, they would not have the history with Chime, the years of growing close, that we had. Although initially we wished to share our own happy experience as a blend, we quickly realized that our case is unique."

Chimera answered with seeming ease.

"How about if your blended DNA was blended with a third party?"

One of the videographers, the ersatz monks, seated at an adjoining table, intruded on the conversation. His expression was very hard and unmonklike, in Leda's opinion. "That person would have all of your knowledge of blending as well as the shared history, wouldn't he? I would think he would be able to do anything that you can do and would even know how you would behave in any situation."

"Perhaps," Chimera said. "It would depend, of course, on the personality of the host and how receptive he or she was to the blend."

"What do you mean? You'd be part of them, wouldn't you?"

"Yes, but how many people really pay attention to all aspects of themselves? How many actually know their own minds, much less a—spirit perhaps is a better term than mind—superimposed on theirs?"

"They could be trained to be alert for that sort of thing," the video-monk said.

Gretchen leaned over to the other table and tapped the ersatz monk on the back of the hand with a long red fingernail. "This is not good dinner conversation I think. We talk of something else, *ja?* Has anyone noticed that there is lightning in the western sky?"

Much as the man would have preferred to ignore her, a huge thunderclap and a fork much closer than a distant horizon commanded everyone's attention. That was when the lights went out.

Andrew excused himself and went to see to the restarting of the boat's generator, while a steward lit the candles in the candelabras on either end of the table and another steward discreetly placed a flashlight at the elbow of each guest.

As if she, too, had been kindled into being, Cleopatra's consciousness popped back into Leda's, and asked, *"Did you miss me? Or perhaps I should ask, did I miss much?"*

"How's Gabriella? Did Mike find her? Are they on their way?"

"In reverse order the answers to your questions are yes, yes, and well—he found her, but he, too, has been taken prisoner. They are imprisoned together with the niece of the amir. He and that scrawny terrorist still intend to kill them all farther down the river. Otherwise, nothing is happening with my co-ba. Marc Antony and Mike protect her and Gabriella. She will call out again if she needs further help, but for now we felt you were in more immediate danger."

"How's that? I'm surrounded by friends and politically correct hippo-huggers."

Cleopatra looked around the room through Leda's eyes. This time Leda still saw Wolfe, Gretchen, and Chimera as she always had. But Iris, the Padma Lama, and each of the environmentalists wore masks that flickered off and on with the candle glow and lightning. Dimmer, clearer, brighter, darker, higher, lower, eight masks, each an aspect of one of the Ennead, the council of nine gods that presided over the judgment of the dead.

Iris, though her arms were at her sides, seemed to have spread her Isis wings, although her face bore the blunted features, horns, and cow ears of Hathor. *"Her cosmetic surgeon wouldn't care for that,"* Leda observed, trying to hide even from

Cleopatra how shaken she was to see the group through the queen's eyes. Horus, the falcon, Anubis, the hound/jackal, Thoth, the baboon, Atep, the hippo, who was also an aspect of Isis, and of course, Sobek, who didn't look a lot different to Leda with the mask than he did without, his godhead persona was so well suited to his personality. The Padma Lama was Khepri the scarab, symbol of rebirth, and Ro was Duamutef, the dog-headed son of Horus.

"Where's the ninth?" Leda asked, though her heart hammered and her breaths came quick and shallow. She had studied the pantheon of ancient Egypt for so long that even though logic—after all, these people weren't even Egyptian—argued against visual perception, she found herself battling an unwelcome wash of religious awe. There was a small part of her that wanted to genuflect and beg. Very small, but it was there, however she fought it. *"Ennead means nine. Who are these people trying to kid? They're not Egyptian gods. They can't even count!"*

"Of course, they're gods," Cleopatra said. *"Can you not see that they are? But that is no reason to lose our dignity. We are—that is, I was—myself the embodiment of Isis, and I must say I was better at it than Iris, who is far too coarse to be convincing."*

"I see that Cleopatra is in now," said the Padma Lama, eyes twinkling in a fashion that still seemed humorous and kindly but in a beetleish way, as if you were a particularly amusing piece of dung he was about to roll uphill.

"They're just people," Leda tried to convince herself. *"Maybe not ordinary people, but people."*

"Of course they are. Didn't you realize that? The gods are merely the bureaucracy of Ra, the administrative cabinet of the sun, you might say, this one in charge of wisdom, that one in charge of good winds. Nevertheless, they still probably control our future, whether it be immediate or everlasting."

"So what do we do now?"

"What people have always done. Bargain, cajole, and, when necessary, lie."

"Lie? Aren't they omniscient?"

"Is your Secretary of Defense omniscient? Please! We tell them what they wish to hear. Usually people have priests to do it for them."

"Like lawyers?"

"Somewhat, yes. Fortunately for us, I was, in addition to being the embodiment of Isis, her high priestess."

"We are Cleopatra," the inner queen said in her most regal tones. "Queen of the Upper and Lower Nile and Isis incarnate. Who are you who seek audience with us?"

"We are the Ennead of Maat," proclaimed Iris/Isis, obviously irked at having competition for her own chosen role.

"The what?" Leda wondered. *"That's a new one on me."*

"It must be some new cult," Cleopatra said.

Sure enough, Ro continued, saying, "We are the ennead devoted to maintaining harmony and balance in this land of Egypt. We are here to ascertain your intentions and to judge whether or not they will promote that which we seek for the land that is the flesh of our flesh, the blood of our blood, the—"

"I get the picture," Leda interrupted, less awestricken with every word. "You are also, let me guess, the outfit that kidnapped Chimera and Wolfe and probably Gabriella and have the gall to bring your minions on board this vessel and flaunt them in our faces."

Andrew returned and she turned to him, "Andrew, these people—aren't . . . who . . . you . . . think . . . ?"

Cleopatra was seeing Andrew in a different guise than that he had worn with them in the past, so Leda saw it, too. This Andrew's robes weren't the flowing white of the romanticized desert dweller. His white garment was a funerary one—mummy wrappings with only his arms loose and where his silver-and-copper hair had been was a head wrapping like a skullcap. He carried a staff in his hand. "Ptah!" Cleopatra cried. "*Et tu,* Andrew?"

"Nothing to worry about," he said, resuming his fancy dress but nongodlike appearance when she blinked.

Leda realized now that Cleopatra's view of the ennead wasn't fostered by a miracle of any sort, or even special effects. It was the same sort of thing she did with the landscape sometimes, seeing it with her inner eye as it had been known in her time rather than through Leda's more up-to-the-minute retinas.

Mildly scolding, Andrew said to the others, "You might have waited until I returned to question her."

"We did not," Iris said. "*She* knew somehow."

The thunder drowned out the next few comments. The boat bounced and bobbed on the wind-driven waves, and Andrew had to fling himself inside and slide the door closed behind him, clinging to its frame to keep from falling.

Some of the others began to look a bit ill. They could get a new television movie out of this experience. *The Gods Must Be Seasick.*

To Andrew, Leda said, "I guess it was pretty funny hearing me moan and groan about my missing friends and all of those other missing blended people when you were one of the ones behind the kidnappings. I thought we were friends!"

"We were—we are, and more, on my part. But we became part of this before we met you. And we had nothing to do with the kidnappings of Chimera or Wolfe. That was the European branch of the organization."

"What are they? Roman gods? Greek? Norse?"

"Merely human beings taking on the responsibilities people once assigned to religion and gods, except our organization does it on a global as well as regional basis. We are among the movers and shakers of the world, you might say, except we try to guarantee that the moving and shaking being done is more often beneficial than harmful to the values and enterprises we hold dear. We need—mankind needs—some sort of checks and balances, guarantees that the change doesn't destroy us. So we take charge, managing as best we can, of guiding the process into constructive and useful channels, and for that it is often necessary to control those who implement the changes."

"So—let's see, as a result of some of the changes yourself, being a blend and all, you're controlled by being taken into the power structure, right?"

"I have been a part of the power structure long before my blend. You know that. The form that power takes in this organization is simply better defined than it has been in the past, and more hands-on, you might say. Wilhelm, Chimera, I apologize for what happened to you. I told my colleagues that you could be trusted, that taking the samples through trickery was unnecessary. I regret that my personal guarantee was not sufficient to save you the inconvenience and distress you experienced."

Horus, who, Leda realized now, she had seen on the cover of *Fortune,* spoke. "It was only a precaution. Dr. Chimera's and Mr. Wolfe's past actions are an eloquent testimony to their integrity. Gentlemen, as long as you maintain your standards and cooperate with a few additional requests occasionally, you will be able to forget we ever harvested your cells. Should you somehow become corrupted and threaten to upset the balance—we'll be able to take appropriate action."

"Corrupted as in the new administration at Nucor Helix?"

"To some extent. The new policies also serve our ends, however, in that more widely disseminated blending and the ability to blend others could prevent the power ownership of the process confers from being concentrated in the hands of a few. To that end, we detained you briefly to gain our own piece of the pie."

"With that accomplished, we have other business here," said the hippo lady, turning to Leda. "What are your plans, Dr. Hubbard, and Cleopatra's regarding the current socio-political and religious mores in Egypt?"

"I don't have any, except to be allowed to visit and maybe to get dig permits once in a while."

"And the queen?"

Cleo looked through Leda's eyes at Andrew and sighed, then gave a one-shouldered shrug. "I intend that we shall become very wealthy, as that seems the only way to rule these days. Perhaps we will seek membership in your organization someday." The last was uttered in a flatteringly wistful tone.

The hippo lady was unappeased and pressed onward. "You have no plans to challenge the leadership of Egypt? Does the other Cleopatra? The one in Dr. Faruk?"

"You'll have to take that up with her," Leda said. "And in order to do that, it looks like you'll have to wait until she's available again and not being held by murderous thugs. Who are, by the way, the ones you ought to be trying to control."

"We're willing to do what we can," Ro said soothingly. "We told you that already."

"But sometimes these things work out by themselves," the lama said gently.

"We'll stop them when they pass us," Andrew told her. "They can't get by without us spotting them, and when they do, we'll stop them."

But he was forgetting that even the most powerful people can't control everything. Four hours later, when dawn did not break because the sky was too full of roiling bilious clouds, the *Mubarraz Falcon,* revealing itself also to have hovercraft capacity, sped past them.

When Captain McGregor tried to give chase, the air cushion failed to engage, seven of the eight engines having filled with sand and silt.

CHAPTER 24

Cleopatra's narrative:

For the beat of a bird's wing, it seemed that all was not lost. The old woman, the amir's mother, had relented and led our beloved to our prison. Disguising Gabriella's body and that of the princess with the ugly black robes all women of their kind wear, they led us and our love back to the stern of the boat, where we would escape in his boat.

And then, disaster. The amir and his accomplice met us, weapons in hand, and forced us to return to the hot little room, this time throwing Antony inside with us.

Not only was our situation desperate, it was also mortifying. There was no toilet in that room nor water to wash with or even to drink. Our fragrance was pungent, our throat parched, and our morale very low.

"It'll be okay," Mike/Antony told us quietly. "I was able to phone a friend and give him the name of this boat. They'll be looking for us. Probably the cops know and are on their way now."

Mariam, the Saudi woman, was not comforted. "My uncle will buy them off. They will not find us," she said in English.

"If it was just us, I'd say you were right," he replied. "But Abdul Mohammed, his little buddy, is a terrorist who likes blowing up national monuments."

"We know," she said. "He intends to blow us up with one."

"Yeah, well, when the police hear about that, your uncle is going to have a little more explaining to do than he's used to," he said confidently.

Meanwhile, we made the best of our situation by continuing to get reacquainted, once more embracing and kissing, whispering endearments and mutual reassurances. But it had been a long day and I laid my head on his shoulder, despite the heat, to sleep. The last thing I was aware of before I slept was Mariam creeping over to claim his other shoulder. Neither of us had the heart to turn her away.

A noise awoke me. By Antony's wristwatch, I saw that hours had passed well into the night, yet the boat's motors continued, if anything more energetically than ever, speeding us forward as if the oars in the galley had been quadrupled.

Antony also stirred. "They're in hovercraft mode, now," he said after opening and closing his mouth and trying to wet his lips with his tongue. His voice was harsh and rasped with thirst. "With everyone else tied up, we'll be covering a lot of river very quickly. But don't worry. The boat Leda's on is a hovercraft, too."

I thought for a moment that the change in speed was what had awakened me, but, no, the door to our prison opened and the terrorist Antony knew as Abdul Mohammed stood framed in it, a bottle in his hand.

"You must be thirsty," he said in a voice dripping with false sympathy. "I've brought you a drink. Take care, ladies, to drink yours first. Once Michael has tasted this, he may forget all manners and refuse to share. How long has it been, Michael? Twenty years did you say? No need to deprive yourself any longer. You will have no time to reacquire the habit."

Mike growled something about Abdul Mohammed in a pharaonic relationship with his mother, but the coward, still holding us at gunpoint, set the bottle down near enough that we could smell the contents but not close enough for Mike to grab it to use as a weapon. Then the villain withdrew, closing the door behind him, although it seemed that the tail of his shadow slipped back inside the room before the light vanished again.

"He's right," Mike told us with some difficulty. "Ladies first."

We could not refuse, for we were far too thirsty. I fetched the bottle and drank a long draught of the sweet red wine within, then passed it to Mariam. She shook her head. "It is forbidden."

"Surely your gods will forgive you," I said. "You cannot survive with nothing to drink."

"Booze is actually dehydrating," Mike said in his American voice, then in the tones of my Antony. "But it's wet."

I giggled, the drink having an instant and strong effect on me. I had had no food or water for many hours and the liquor quickly infused my entire being. "How funny! You are arguing with yourself, my love."

Mariam changed her mind and grabbed the bottle from me, drinking, sputtering a little, and going back for a second drink.

"When we're found, they'll say we were too drunk to realize we weren't out of harm's way when the place—wherever it is—exploded," Mike continued. Mariam lowered the bottle, burped, and extended it toward him. He reached for it but suddenly it flew from her hand, clattering to the floor and spinning across the room, spraying the liquid left within it across our legs and feet.

I distinctly heard a noise as if something was lapping the spilled liquid, but it was overpowered by Antony's groan as he threw himself onto his belly and tried to lick the wine from my pant legs and shoes.

Mariam withdrew, perhaps in disgust, but I wished only that I had the power to change the wine to water and gather it back into the bottle for the benefit of us all, but especially so that my poor tormented lover could slake his thirst.

When he gave up trying to suck the liquid from the carpet, he returned to rest beside me again.

"Don't worry," I told him, still feeling gay and giddy from the drink. "Your friends are coming, remember?"

I felt rather than saw his head shake in negation. "Something's wrong. It's late. The cops . . . McCallum . . . Jaime . . . someone . . . should be . . . stopping this tub. Asking questions."

He held up his arm and I looked again at the luminous dial of his watch. I was drunk enough to have neglected to bother with it for almost two hours since Abdul Mohammed delivered the wine.

I feared he was right, but there was nothing I could think of to do, so I patted him on the shoulder and settled back to sleep again.

I did not feel surprised to see the boatman waiting for me again, and as I stepped into his boat, I was not surprised to be alone with him. I knew him now for who he was: Osiris, ferrying me through the underworld to judgment.

Long, long we traveled through the endless night, but my hunger and thirst were gone. My people would have said this was because enough offerings of food and drink had been left with my body when I was laid to rest, but I knew it was because my other self, now combined with me, had feasted recently. She it was who identified the gods as we passed them. Anubis of course was there; and Horus; Thoth; Atep/Isis and Isis/Hathor to whom I prayed copiously for their protection for myself; their faithful priestess, Khepri the scarab; Duamutef the dog-headed; Sobek, looking hungry; and

Ptah. They spoke, but my ears were yet closed, and I could not hear them. I only kept praying, "I have led a good life—two times and in three bodies—and I have hurt no one, murdered no one (political assassinations do not count). I have not stolen. I have not performed abominations. I have not dishonored my name or my gods." And so on and on I spoke of my virtues in the negative sense. If my heart was weighed against a feather, I did not know it. If my fate was decided, I did not know it. I only traveled on and ever onward, this last journey upon the river mother of my land.

When I awoke again and looked at the watch, I was not sure whether it was day or night, or how many twelve o'- clocks had passed since I was first imprisoned. It seemed to me that the boat had once more slowed its pace to a leisurely one. It also seemed that Mike had been correct about the wine, for my mouth was so dry my tongue was swollen.

Again, I had been awakened by a sound from without and again, the door opened. Food and drink were laid inside the door. More wine and couscous, as Gabriella identified it. Abdul Mohammed said, "If you are expecting help from Mr. Andrew McCallum, Michael, you will be disappointed. We passed the *Agatha* hours ago. It seemed to be having engine trouble. Alas, we could not stop to help."

"How did you know?" Mike croaked.

"Simple. We pressed the little button on your telephone to see which number you called last. It was easy to identify the party as a fellow yachtsman. Mr. McCallum will no doubt be shocked to learn he had received a telephone call from the terrorist who blew up the infidel temple of Abydos while dying himself in the same explosion."

"That is my temple!" I protested angrily the sacrilege he was about to commit.

"Yes, miss, and so all the more reason that you be blown up with it."

The couscous was damp enough to moisten our mouths. When Mariam and I had both had a swig of wine, Antony reached for the bottle, but before it touched his lips, Mike dropped it again. He wept without tears for the loss, his shoulders shaking, but he did not try to retrieve the fallen liquid again. Instead, he let the couscous linger in his mouth, although from my own taste of it I felt sure someone had befouled it.

When the food was gone, after perhaps an hour's time, the door opened again. We were dragged to our feet and all of us, Marc Antony/Mike included, smothered in the black robes worn by the amir's women. Thereafter, we were forced into the dinghy that had almost been our salvation, but this time it was piloted by two burly henchmen while Abdul Mohammed supervised.

The other passenger must have hidden under the hem of one of our robes, for it was not until later that she made her presence known.

By the time the *Agatha*'s engines were repaired, many of the other yachts had caught up and now sailed between the *Agatha* and the *Mubarraz Falcon*.

Andrew paced the upper deck, once more doing a good imitation of Captain Ahab minus the handicapped parking permit, Leda thought. In spite of everything, his agitation pleased her, letting her hope that he actually cared about what happened to Gabriella and Mike.

He was on the telephone constantly, but the authorities told him coldly that they had detained the *Mubarraz Falcon* and found no evidence of prisoners or explosives on the amir's yacht. Furthermore, the amir had been highly insulted and threatened diplomatic repercussions.

"Obviously," Andrew said aloud, "obviously they have already off-loaded Mike and Gabriella. If only we knew where."

Without thinking about it, or wondering, Leda said, "Abydos." Cleopatra 7.1 had returned!

"Are you sure?"

She shrugged. Cleopatra within her repeated firmly, "Abydos. The most holy temple to Osiris, where his head was buried."

Andrew immediately called the police again, but although they promised to have their officers at Abydos look into the matter, they wouldn't say when they were going to do so.

Andrew looked at the boats surrounding them and buried his head in his hands. "I don't see how we can possibly get there in time. We can't get through all of these, even if we were willing to damage ourselves and them doing it."

"Put me ashore," Leda said. "I can find her. I know I can. I'll hijack a train or a car and get there faster than we can in the boat."

"We'll both go," Andrew said.

"We are coming, too," Gretchen said in a husky voice that resembled Duke's growl as well as Gretchen's own guttural accent. Close on her heels came her husband and Chimera.

With some difficulty, Captain McGregor pulled *Agatha* up to the bridge at Sohag so they could disembark.

The town was one of the larger ones, with a fair amount of highway traffic generated by the regatta and the forthcoming new flood, scheduled to begin in two hours.

Leda didn't wait for the others but strode up the embankment and out onto the road and stuck out her thumb.

Close behind her came Andrew and Gretchen, followed by Wolfe and Chimera. On the river below, eight of the ennead stood like T-shirt-clad temple statues on the upper deck of the *Agatha,* simply watching.

A cab pulled over, and the driver opened the door.

For some reason, Leda was unsurprised to see that the cabbie was Gabriella's cousin Mohammed. "Abydos and step on it, Mo," she said, sliding in ahead of the others. "Our Gaby is about to be blown up."

"Yes," Mo said. "Mr. McCallum called a friend of mine, who called me. I was on my way to meet her in Luxor, ignorant of her predicament, when this news came to me. How do you know she is in Abydos?"

She sat in front with Mo while Andrew, the Wolfes, and Chimera climbed in back. Once they were in, Mo took off. "I didn't know you had a warp drive on this thing," she said, then answered his question. "Our mutual friend the queen has kept us in touch."

He nodded but did not make a verbal reply. His beard jutted out as his jaw clenched. His hands took a death grip on the wheel, and his eyes focused on the road like a hawk tracking prey as he weaved in and out of traffic. His taxi threatened car, truck, minivan, and donkey cart alike. Some of the other vehicles did the unheard of and actually pulled over to the side of the road to let him pass.

The traffic was almost entirely Egyptian, since tourists had been banned from traveling between rural towns along the lower Nile until very recently, because of a terrorist attack in 1997 in which tourists at the temple of Hatshepsut at Luxor were massacred.

The new government of Egypt had relaxed many restrictions already to promote further tourism. Because of the festivities surrounding the new Nile flood, things had relaxed even further, although Leda could tell that the security forces weren't equal to the task, since they weren't even answering their telephones half the time.

After about twenty minutes, no doubt to the relief of the other drivers, Mo turned off the main highway onto a secondary road. It was much rougher than the main road though not as full of traffic, and the minivan flew over and around potholes at an alarming rate. Mo would have aced a slalom course.

"*I don't suppose there's an Egyptian god in charge of making sure tires hold up, is there?*" Leda asked.

"This is no time to be amusing," Cleo replied.

As they arrived at the temple complex by the back road, two busloads of tourists joined the ones already milling about, reading inscriptions and admiring statuary. Usually the buses held European or Japanese tourists, but these buses seemed to have almost as many Egyptians and other Muslims as the usual sort. The river festival was getting everyone out to see the sights. Not a good thing in this case.

Almost everyone else came from the river, about six miles east of the complex, but Mo's route brought them in from the north, at an oblique angle to the complex, which was huge.

The Osiris temple enclosure was closest to them, hemmed in by the funerary palaces of past royalty. At what seemed a great distance away stood the temple of Ramses and, farther still, the Temple of Seti. Down a hill from that, the Osireion lay out of sight. A peculiar complex that was part temple, part cistern, it was believed to be the oldest and at one time, the most sacred structure in Egypt. Leda knew all of this from her previous trips and her reading. But Cleopatra said, *"I've never approached it from this angle, and, of course, I was always carried in from my barge in the Nile. Have some of these ruins been uncovered since my day? They don't look at all familiar."*

Andrew scrambled out of the cab and looked all around. The site covered a good five kilometers, including a number of small funerary palaces, two villages, a tent hotel and restaurant, and three temples in various states of disrepair. "Now what?" he asked.

Gretchen said something so like Duke it made Leda want to bawl. "If we find the target, we will find our friends, *ja?* And that target will be the most important structure here. So!" And she pointed to the Temple of Seti, the most complete of the structures.

"Good thinking, Da—" Leda began then finished,

"Damn good thinking, Gretchen. The Temple of Seti it is. Of course, this whole place was a site of pilgrimage for the ancient Egyptians, kind of like Mecca for the Muslims, but the Temple of Seti was supposedly built on or near the tomb of Osiris, so that's probably the target.

"Get in, *effendi,*" Mo said to Andrew. "I will drive us there," Mo said.

Outside the temple was a concession stand, which was doing a brisk business. Leda suddenly felt bone dry, and said, almost muttering to herself, "Man, I could really use a Coke right now. Or six."

"I will get them for you, Lady," Mo said. "For all of you."

She nodded, and said, "Someone had better let the security police know what's going on, too, and warn them about the terrorist threat."

Chimera said, "We'll do that. I see them over there now."

The rest of them ascended the long double flight of steps, once an inner staircase, now the main approach to the temple. "There used to be a double row of sphinxes here and a huge tapered pylon, but they've been destroyed," she told the others.

They crossed the two ruined forecourts, roughly the size of a football field, to enter the hypostyle hall, its massive columns still more awesome than the average government building in the States, and with better artwork, larger-than-life-size reliefs depicting the kings and gods of the time, not only Osiris, but Isis, Horus, and Seti, who had himself grafted onto the divine family tree.

"*Let me see,*" Leda said, finding her way through the second hypostyle hall back toward the chapels and closed rooms, where presumably the captives and/or a bomb could be hidden. "*Right about here's where that helicopter hieroglyph they show on the Internet all the time ought to be!*"

"*Never mind that!*" Cleopatra said. "*She's dying here. I can feel her presence, but I can't get to her. We must find her quickly.*"

"We're working on it." Leda sighed.

"You should go back, *liebchen,*" Wolfe said to Gretchen. "We do not know when the explosion may occur, but if it will be in the temple, your skills will be needed. You must not be injured, too."

Gretchen looked at her wristwatch. "In five minutes time the first flood will be released. Then it is I think that the explosion will be set to occur. It will draw attention away from the good that the flood may do and focus it on the terrorists, and the explosion may be mistaken for the roar of the waters as they pour into the Nile. So. We have no time for back turning. We go!"

"No," Leda said. "No, you're both right, I think. We have maybe five minutes, but after that, people will be needing a doctor with all her parts together. Meanwhile, someone had better clear this temple. Andrew, Wolfe, you're used to giving orders. Get everyone the hell out of here. I know what's here, and I'll do better if I'm by myself, so the Cleos can get through to each other without interference if possible."

Wolfe began accosting people while Gretchen, using the direct approach, snagged a woman by the arm and began dragging her back toward the entrance.

"You're not doing this alone, Leda," Andrew, who hadn't moved, said sternly. "If nothing else, when you find them or the bomb, you may need help. I stay with you."

"Fine. Then come on." They found themselves before the seven chapels to the gods, with the locked Osiris rooms in the back. "You start at this end, I'll start at that one. Pound, yell, and for Christ's sake listen for any noise they might make."

He didn't answer because he was sprinting off toward the first of the chapels.

Mike tried to look at the good side. At least they weren't quite so damn dry anymore. Of course, that was the bad side, too. That and that there was water, water every-where, but if he tried to drink it, should he survive the ex-plosion by some chance, he'd die of something really nasty and slow almost as soon.

"You see?" Antony chided, *"Water is not for drinking. It's far too dirty. You should never have turned down that perfectly good wine."*

"If it was perfectly good, what the hell is wrong with the girls?" Mike asked. Gabriella and Mariam, the Saudi princess—well, by now probably ex-princess—were un-conscious. After their captors sealed them in, Mike had hauled the women up out of the stagnant, insect-infested water. Not even the mosquitoes had caused the women to stir.

"A sleeping draught surely," Antony said. *"It must be a sleep-ing draught. She cannot have gone before me. I was fooled once be-fore and fell on my sword, but not again. See her breast rise and fall? She lives. We will die together again. Though I had hoped not so quickly."*

Mike sloshed some of the stinking water over his face and got to his feet, feeling shaky. At least the water had cooled him off a little, so he was only dying of thirst, not baking to death. Their prison was the side room of a tomb, he expected. The man had said they were at Abydos, and Mike knew that had something to do with tombs, though he wasn't sure what. He didn't think tombs were usually this wet. He wished he hadn't been so sick and dizzy when they were first taken from the dinghy and put into a van and driven here—still dressed like the harem ladies on an out-ing. Somehow or other, Abdul Mohammed and his burly employees had dragged or carried the three of them past guards and tourists and into this place where apparently neither one came, at least not real often. And once the bomb went off—well. Abdul Mohammed remarked that if the explosion didn't kill them, they'd probably drown when the Nile reestablished its connection with the temple through this very tomb. Several colorful Spanish expletives occurred to Mike, but his tongue was still swollen, and he didn't want to waste the breath when Gabriella was not awake to hear him.

His ears pricked up at every noise. He thought he could hear the ticking of the timing device, then it seemed like the scratching of claws on stone, someone's footsteps. He hoped to God they'd get the hell out of there. It wouldn't be long now. The flood was set for noon. It was two minutes till.

CHAPTER 25

"Who will speak for the Osiris Cleopatra?" the judges asked in the Hall of Judgment.

Cleopatra wanted to protest that her new body was not yet dead, that she herself was once vindicated, and had returned to join this new person in a new life, and that this was not fair. But though Gabriella lay in filthy stinking clothes in a filthy stinking pool beside her love and their betrayer, Cleopatra stood before the gods clad in pure white, the kohl around her eyes, the rouge on her lips, her hair combed and shining and her jewels and badges of office adorning her. And yet she could not speak. Had her mouth not been opened? No, it would not have been, for she was not yet dead.

Hers was a living death, and she could not defend herself further.

"I speak for the Osiris Cleopatra," a low and rather nasal voice began, "I am Bast, the goddess of joy, the goddess of wind, and a protector of women, and this one was also a protector of women. I shall protect her against her enemies. I shall keep her from the flood and shield her from hailing stone. I proclaim her the vindicated Osiris Cleopatra."

The others followed, Nephthys, Isis, Horus. It was good to be vindicated, good to be protected, but she wanted to go back to Gabriella, back to Marc Antony and Mike Angeles, back to life. She had only just come from death, and it wasn't fair, it wasn't time.

At 11:58 Andrew found the bomb in the Hall of Sacri-fices. Leda didn't realize it until she saw it in his hands, an old-fashioned train case, a squat rectangle with a handle on the top. It was ticking. "God, Andrew, put it down!" she said. "Let the police handle it. Chimera will be back with them soon."

"There'll be no demolition squad way out here, Leda," he said. "The temple has a back door, does it not?"

"Yes, theoretically, but I don't know if it opens. I—what are you doing?"

"There's no time, lass," he said, Sir Walter firmly in control. "I have to carry it out of this building and away from everyone. Show me the door."

The rear of the temple was a maze of pillars and walls and small rooms, but she remembered the location of the door well enough from diagrams she'd seen and led him to it. To her relief, it stood wide open. Andrew strode briskly past her onto the path leading down to the Osireion, the false tomb of Seti I believed at one time to be the tomb of Osiris himself.

"I'll just carry it past here and out to the desert," he called back over his shoulder.

Before she could protest, they heard a familiar voice crying, "Mitzi, mitzi, mitzi, come *Katze,* do not go in there."

A small short-haired red, gray, and cream-colored striped cat whose bat ears Leda could make out even from where she stood pounced onto the walkway, and shortly after her came

Gretchen Wolfe, rubbing her fingers together to make a cat-calling noise and continuing her entreaties, which seemed to be falling on deaf feline ears.

Andrew picked up his pace, stepped off the path, and, avoiding ruins and boulders, kept walking as quickly as possible, as far away from them and any other structure as he could go.

The cat passed him at a run, joyfully eluding Gretchen, Leda believed, but then suddenly it stopped atop one of the overhanging stones topping the galleries along the sides of the Osireion. The cat looked down and lowered itself to scratch energetically upon the rock, as if trying to dig a hole. Then it looked up and mewed.

"*Katze*! Little mitzi, come back here!" Gretchen called. "I have for you fishes," she lied.

The cat, evidently knowing a fishy story when she heard it, stayed where she was, meowing.

"Gretchen, get out of here," Leda yelled. "Andrew found the b—the device. It'll go off in"—she looked at her watch—"a minute and a half. That is if our watches are syn-chronized. Go on, run!"

"Help!" a hoarse voice called, issuing from somewhere under the cat. It was so faint it blended with the cat's meow, and she wasn't sure she really heard it until it called again.

"Mike?" Leda scrambled the rest of the way down the path.

"Leda!" Chimera called from the open back door of the temple. "We have brought the police."

"And I—at last I have brought the soft drinks!" Mo cried triumphantly from behind him.

Leda looked up from the bottom of the slope leading to the entrance of the Osireion. The open complex that seemed to be part tomb and part baths had baffled archaeologists for some time but now the fact that it was largely roofless was helpful. She stepped onto the top of a wall, climbed down to a less-complete section, and ended standing in a couple of inches of scummy water. She saw a snake swim by, but they ignored each other.

"Here, we're here," Mike's voice rasped. "We're—okay—but I think Gab—and—you know, her—poisoned."

Gretchen was already climbing down beside her.

"Get away from there, ladies," the policeman ordered. "This is a restricted area."

Only the little cat obeyed, jumping straight up and hightailing it for the parking area, where tourists with treats might be persuaded to share.

"I'll leave if you help them leave, too," Leda said, pointing at the apparently seamless stone wall from which Mike's voice issued, albeit very faintly. "We have people trapped in here and a bomb about to go off."

She turned to see Andrew still retreating farther down the hill, past the edge of the village and down a long ditch that would have been called an arroyo in the deserts of the Southwest back home. "Andrew, lose that damn thing now!" she cried, but she wasn't sure he could hear her at that distance.

Gretchen pointed her finger at the policemen in the doorway and ordered, in a combination of her doctor voice and Duke's cop one, "You two, come down and help us get these people out. Chimera, Mo, you help . . ."

Her last words were drowned out by a thunderous blast that knocked them all off their feet and sent rock and dirt sliding. The cops and Chimera came rolling down the pathway, but Mo stayed seated, his arms still full of aluminum pop cans.

Leda found she was screaming and she swung around to see the flame bloom up from the desert, then a pall of smoke that covered everything except a low fence of fire where it had caught on some ground cover. Fortunately, there was little in the ditch to catch fire. But the rumbling from the blast seemed to go on and on.

She did not see Andrew, and, without thinking about it, she sprinted down the pathway toward the smoky billows, Gretchen hot on her heels.

She nearly tripped over Andrew when he stood up, several hundred yards west of the explosion. "Andrew!" Cleopatra cried, and flung her arms around him before Leda could pull herself off. She settled for asking, "You okay?"

"I am. I threw it when I realized I couldn't run far enough in the time remaining."

"I must check you," Gretchen said, and circled behind him. "Turn around," she said. When he did, Leda saw that his clothing had bloody holes ripped in it and the flesh of his back was black with rock and debris. "We must clean you up. Have you pain?"

"Ooh, ow, now that you mention it . . ." he said, and he started shaking all over, his knees buckling.

The women helped him up the hill.

"You were worried about me? Really?" he asked Leda. "In spite of—"

"Hey, for a fake Egyptian god, you're a real mensch. But don't push it," she said.

Inside her Cleopatra scolded, *"Have you not an ounce of love in your soul? He would have died for us!"*

"Yeah, and then what good would he have been to us? You have to learn not to let them get away with that kind of shit, Queenie. It's not good for their character development."

The first policeman had found the key to unlock the security gate securing the stone door to the cell, probably another chapel of some sort, containing Mike, Gabriella, and the Saudi woman.

Gretchen entered the cell and plucked Gabriella's hand

from the murky water, feeling her pulse at the wrist, then at the base of her jaw. She did the same thing to the Saudi woman.

Mo appeared and Mike attacked him, tearing a soft drink from his hands so that Gabriella's cousin had to juggle very quickly to keep from dropping the others. Mike popped the top and drank the drink in one gulp, then threw up in the scummy water, improving it not at all.

Gretchen checked the women's eyes, lifting their lids, felt their limbs and torsos, and finally said, "We move them now."

"Is it poison, Doc?" Mike asked. "Or a sedative or what?"

"I do not know. Is there a hospital or clinic near? I will be needing a stomach pump."

"A small clinic in the village, Doctor," one policeman said.

"I will drive them there," Mo said, handing out cans of pop to Gretchen, Chimera, Leda, and another to Mike, who took a swig to rinse his mouth out, then small sips.

The rumbling sound that began with the explosion was now so loud they had to raise their voices to be heard over it.

"The flood is coming," Andrew said. "Imagine, seven miles from the river, and still we hear it so loudly."

Mike tried to lift Gabriella but was too weakened to do so alone, but Mo helped him, and the two of them began carrying her down the slope toward the entrance to the parking area.

"Not that way!" Cleopatra within Leda said suddenly. "Through the temple! Quickly."

It was much harder, of course, being uphill, but the policemen lifted the other woman and began to carry her the same way. Mike and Mo had Gabriella to the temple door and the second policeman had just climbed up to join his comrade and lift the sick woman's feet again when the wall of water came roaring down the ditch where Andrew had thrown the bomb. Gretchen, Chimera, and Leda were already on the path above the soggy floor of the Osireion when the water hit, flooding the interior in successive waves.

"It has been said that there was once a path for the Nile to nourish the temple," one of the policemen said. "It seems the river has found it once more."

CHAPTER 26

The *Mubarraz Falcon* made it halfway to Luxor. Once more it was in hovercraft mode. The amir strolled along the top deck, enjoying a fine view of the red-gold cliffs. He was wearing wireless earphones and listening to classical European music, a secret vice. This in part he did so he did not have to hear the keening and lamentations from his faithless women, locked into the salon on the deck below. He would not prevent their grieving. After all, one of the bereaved was his own mother and the grandmother of his whorish niece. If they wanted to spend this beautiful trip crying over such an unworthy creature, he would not stop them, but he did not intend to let their sentimental nonsense interfere with his own pleasure.

He had one bad moment only when McCallum's boat, the *Agatha,* which he knew because he had ordered his captain to look up the registration, sailed between the *Falcon* and the cliffs. Nine people stood on the upper deck, staring across at him with expressions worthy of Egyptian statuary. For one moment, as they emerged into sunlight from the cliff's shadow and just before another shadow overcame them, they seemed to actually *be* statues and not people at all—animal-headed beings, rather, with human bodies and the heads of a jackal, a crocodile, a hippopotamus, a baboon, a dog, a cow, a falcon, and a lioness. Such optical illusions were no doubt half the reason for the Egyptian pantheon of animal-headed monsters, he thought. Something caused by the interaction of the river, the heat, and the cliffs. Like a mirage, perhaps.

A short time later, the waters were released. He was at least forty-five miles from Abydos and did not expect to hear or see the explosion, but the distant roar of the oncoming flood reminded him that only now would the temple be destroyed and the two wicked women and the Egyptian slut's lover with it. Abdul Mohammed was making sure this time. If he expected any further support from the amir for his operations, he would succeed.

The waters were not yet upon him when he saw the hippopotomi surfacing beside his boat, nostrils, ears, and piggy eyes showing above the water. An engine cut out, and a blossom of red appeared on the starboard side at the same moment a hippo roared. The *Falcon* lurched, and he lost his balance. From the other side of the boat, another hippo roared, a deep-throated grunting sort of roar, like an enormous dirty pig.

"My rifle!" he commanded the servant who was bringing a tray with a soft drink and a glass of crystalline ice cubes.

The rifle was in the same room where the women had congregated to mourn, and he had no wish to go there himself.

Before the servant returned, the other engines died, and the hippos banged against the boat's hull. No one would be able to repair the boat with all that going on.

He picked up the rifle and took aim at the nearest animal, a cow with a calf swimming beside her. *Bolero* pounded in his ears as he raised the rifle. From the corner of his eye, he thought he saw a flash of black, as black as the Egyptian statuary of Anubis or Bast, the cat goddess.

The boat lurched again—or was it only he who lurched? He lost his footing on the slippery deck and tumbled over the railing. He fell to the river, toward the stumpy but large teeth in the wide-open mouth—no doubt she was surprised—of the hippo.

He thought perhaps it would be a good time to learn to swim, but first the hippo caught him, then the rolling wave of floodwaters struck hippos, *Falcon,* amir, and all. The boat, as it was intended to do, rode out the storm. The hippos were carried to new feeding and breeding grounds. But all that was found of the amir were a few pieces that washed up along the banks where the waters sluiced into the new ditches and dikes prepared for them.

The royal women, including the amir's honored mother and his senior wife, who jointly inherited the bulk of his holdings, as he had no sons, said that they had been crying for fear of the wild river when it happened. They had seen nothing, heard nothing, knew nothing until the boat finally stopped its wild ride, crashing into the cliffs somewhere near the river's bend at Quena, near Hathor's Temple at Dendara, the one with the reliefs of Cleopatra on the walls.

They would sadly miss their son and husband, their protector, their benefactor, of course, but these things happened, and at least he had died doing something he enjoyed.

Only the servant who brought the rifle experienced a moment of relief that the women claimed that they had been unable to even try to save the amir because the door to their salon had been locked. The servant could not remember locking it behind her.

Once the prisoners had been entombed and the bomb planted, Abdul Mohammed and his henchmen watched

from a safe distance at the edge of one of the villages. When
the blast shook the entire Abydos area, the terrorists drove
back toward Cairo. There was no need for them to continue
on the amir's boat. In fact, it was too risky. The henchmen
returned to their homes and Abdul Mohammed retained the
van to return to an employee who worked for the car rental
company in Cairo.

The flood, what he could see of it, was most impressive,
filling up the new ditches and challenging the new dikes,
while washing into the areas where it was supposed to leave
its deposits. By about two o clock in the afternoon, almost
all of the boats had been washed back toward Cairo by the
floods, and though there had been some collisions, by and
large everyone seemed in high spirits and thought the river
surfing good sport, according to his car radio. Nothing was
mentioned of the destruction of the temple at Abydos, but
perhaps no one from the news had been available to report
it, with everything else going on. Abdul Mohammed
frowned. Of course, the goal had been accomplished anyway, but he hated to have his operations upstaged by a mere
publicity stunt on the part of those infidel environmentalists and green party people from Europe.

The other annoying thing about this changing of the
Nile's path was that it sometimes flooded the road, too,
causing delays and detours. So inconvenient and time-
consuming did these become that darkness had fallen by the
time Abdul Mohammed drove into Beni Suef.

He was very tired, and his eyes blurred as he drove on the
darkened highway. It had been a long day. Fortunately, the
road had cleared of most of the other traffic, and Cairo was
not so far now.

Then, just in front of him, a man stepped into the road
and put up a detour sign. Abdul Mohammed yelled at him,
but the fellow yelled back that the road ahead had washed
out completely and he would have to follow the pilot car up

to Faiyum and take the desert road the rest of the way to Cairo.

Another minivan, the same sort that was used for taxicabs, with a large yellow revolving lamp on its roof, pulled out in front of him.

He followed it for endless weary miles. No other cars came behind them, just he and the pilot car.

At Faiyum he thought the pilot car would turn right toward Cairo, but it continued to go straight, and he saw that there was another detour sign, so he followed the yellow lamp down the darkened and very rough road.

It was so rough that first one headlight, then the other, blinked out. The damned pilot car had chinked rocks up into the lights! He stopped the car and got out, surveying the damage. Now how would he make it to Cairo? He would have to stop for the night. He could not proceed after dark. The truth was, he no longer saw as well in the dark as he once had.

The yellow light had vanished, but it looked as if there was another small village up there—he seemed to recall that some vendors of tourist goods lived up near the old temple in this area. One of them would take him in. The laws of hospitality demanded it.

So he made his way to the lights, creeping slowly.

There was only a sliver of moon, but by this and the starlight, he saw a glimmer of water between himself and the shelter. Maybe he would sleep in his car after all. Where had the pilot car gone anyway? He dare not pull over since he could not see where he was going.

He sighed and folded down the backseat and lay upon it.

Without the engine going, he could hear the slap of the water against the tires. No matter. He could do nothing until daylight.

He fell asleep entertaining revenge fantasies against the

company that had created the detour and the idiots who had dreamed up the new Nile flood.

When he awoke, the moonlight no longer shone. He looked out the window and saw nothing. He needed to relieve himself, however, so he swung his feet to the floor of the car. Instantly, he was up to his shins in water and he felt the car shift beneath him. He would drown here! The water was rising!

He could swim a little, and how much water could it be, here in the desert? He would make it to dry land and find someone to take him in for the night after all.

He slid the side door open and instantly that side of the van began filling as the vehicle lurched sideways. He lay down and swam out.

He thrashed around for a few moments, trying to get his bearings. As his eyes adjusted to the darkness, he saw that the road led through a ruin of some sort, perhaps an archaeological dig. His feet could not touch bottom. Somehow, the car had floated off the road and into a deep pit or trench already there. But if nothing else, he could swim to one of those crumbling pillars and stay dry there—or at least see dry land from there.

As he was making for it, a yellow revolving lamp came to life a few yards ahead of him.

The pilot car! The idiot who had led him into this mess! He would swim, walk, or fly if he had to up to that pilot car, jerk the driver out of the van, and shove the revolving yellow light up his rectum.

As he swam toward the car, however, he felt the water move to counter him, as if something was sliding *into* it, quite near him. He stroked on toward the van and peered into the window. A dead man's face grinned back at him, and the pilot car gunned away. Shaken, he braced his hands in the mud to pull himself out onto dry ground. Then it was that the creature that had slid into the water slithered out and dragged him screaming back into it.

The next day, no one could imagine how the rental van had come to be in the bath pit at the recently excavated ruined temple of Krokodilopolis. There it was that the sacred sons and daughters of Sobek would play and breed and receive ritual sacrifices. Like the one whose ripped clothing, some of it still containing shreds of that unfortunate person, had accidentally become. How was it that the sacred crocodiles knew to return to this place? Instinct, species memory perhaps. Anyway, if one could avoid ending up like the poor fellow from the minivan, one could make an extra pound or two by showing tourists a crocodile temple that once more contained actual crocodiles.

Gretchen, Chimera, and the clinic staff worked all night on the two women. The Saudi princess died at three o'clock in the morning, but Gabriella Faruk for some reason survived. Once her system was purged of the poison, her vital signs improved, and she began to get stronger.

The staff tried to insist that Dr. Wolfe send away Dr. Hubbard, who after all could do nothing for her, but Gretchen flatly refused. Although Leda Hubbard had taken no poison herself, she lay sleeping beside her friend, holding her hand, and everyone wondered if there wasn't something a little funny about their relationship.

But no, the wealthy Mr. McCallum stood close by, as did Dr. Wolfe's husband, and by morning Dr. Faruk was able to sit up and take a little nourishment.

The police had taken the rather astonishing statements of all parties concerned, and, of course, there was no doubting men of such standing as Mr. McCallum and Dr. Wolfe. They agreed that no one else should know for the time being, and no representatives of the press should be sent for.

Though the police had their doubts about Mike Angeles,

who was known to be something of a shady character, they finally acquiesced when he and Dr. Faruk's cousin joined some other companions from the *Agatha,* later in the afternoon, after Dr. Wolfe was fairly certain Gabriella Faruk would live. Angeles and Mohammed apparently had some urgent errand in Cairo but, true to their word, they returned to Abydos by morning. It was very touching, the embrace between Mike Angeles and Gabriella Faruk. Indecent of course, but such passion! Like an American movie.

Cleopatra's narrative:

I confess I was thrilled when I learned what Antony and his associates had done for our sake, though I admit to some concern for the health and well-being of the sacred animals of Sobek after ingesting such filth.

He did not wish to tell me, had promised his accomplices, one of whom was Gabriella's dear cousin Mohammed, to keep the truth of the matter silent. But of course, the first time we made love I persuaded him to tell me. And that was without the benefit of the wine. Antony now sees the tactical validity of Mike Angeles' beliefs about liquor—and I must say abstention has improved even his former stellar performance in other areas.

Once I knew, of course, my sister *ba* knew as well, particularly as I learned the truth when we were in close proximity to each other, finishing our Nile cruise aboard the *Agatha*. And, of course, the circumstances of Antony's confession were rather stimulating, something that always strengthens our bond.

It strengthened another bond, too.

Sir Andrew needed all of Sir Walter's literary eloquence to convince Leda to finish out the Nile cruise and give him a chance to regain her trust.

She was very difficult to convince. "You mean to tell me that just because you're one of the evil would-be overlords of the universe that doesn't mean you don't need love, too?" she asked. "Puh-leeze!"

"We are not evil—at least, not intentionally, though of course one's intentions may not always produce the desired result. And I certainly am not evil. If I were, do you think I would have decided to try the caber toss with a train case of Semtex? In this sort of thing, one cannot always speak for everyone else involved, of course, but personally I have no desire to rule the universe, the earth, or any particular country. I have enough control over my companies and my books to keep me in migraine headaches, thank you. I wish only to preserve the things—and people—I value in this world against those who are truly power-mad."

At this point, as I understand it, my sister *ba* was overcome with my own sensations as Antony/Mike and Gabriella/I began ministering to each other's wounds.

Of course it was necessary for Leda to look very closely into Andrew's eyes to judge the truth of his protestations. No doubt due to her own exertions on behalf of ourselves and the temple, she became short of breath once more as she drew near to him. "You mean, not so much like the Illuminati and more like the X-Men?"

"Yes, but without the super powers," he said. And then, thanks to us, they were irresistibly drawn into each other's arms, for which my *ba* thanks the gods and Chimera, since otherwise Leda's stubbornness might have kept them apart as neither of them wished to be.

"None at all?" she asked, pulling him down with her.

"Well, a couple perhaps," he said.

Later she asked, "Did your—friends—have anything to do with the amir's death, Andrew? Because that was a shame."

"You think so? You may put your mind at rest, however. Other than supplying the hippopotomi to shake the boat up a bit, they had no part in his actual demise."

"I wish I could believe that."

"Hmm, well, it's true. But I don't know why you're so concerned about it. He was a perfectly vile man, persecuting your friend and his own family members. And he actually was very close to *being* one of the real evil overlords who trouble you so much. A thoroughly unpleasant fellow, and he would never have received justice in his own land."

"I know. But actually, Cleo 7.2 would like to do a bit of overlording herself—or overladying, I suppose, and with Gabriella, she certainly wouldn't be evil."

"A very good reason to be rid of men like the amir."

"Yes, but wouldn't it be better to get them to come around to her way of thinking? It seems to me we have a ready-made tool to instill a little empathy for womankind in general and Cleo's cause in particular in the arrogant SOBs. After all, we do have a terrific source of Cleo's DNA in her mummy in the storeroom at the museum . . ."